HOLIDAY ROMANCE

Maggie felt his arms go around her, lifting her. "The door, Sterling," she managed to say as he rained kisses down the side of her throat.

"Taken care of," he whispered into her ear before nipping at her earlobe, lightly licking the sensitive skin behind her ear.

She buried her face against his shoulder as he carried her down the hall, toward the bedroom. "You did plan this, didn't you? I wasn't wrong. You planned to seduce me tonight, didn't you?"

They were inside her bedroom now and Alex set her down on her feet, his arms loosely looped around her waist. "Among other things, yes. I will admit I had hopes."

"Other things? What other things?"

He'd moved his hands now, hadn't he? Not a sudden move, but a very smooth and practiced one that ended with his palms lightly brushing the outsides of her breasts. Nothing too overt. Just a gentlemanly hint of what could be, if she were willing. "Do you really want to know, sweetings? *Now?*"

"Oh, hell no," Maggie admitted truthfully, unable, as she would say of one of her Regency heroines in this situation, to summon a lie. And that was pretty much the last even remotely coherent thought she had for quite some time . . .

Books by Kasey Michaels

Published by Kensington Publishing Corporation

HIGH HEELS AND HOLIDAYS

KASEY MICHAELS

KENSINGTON BOOKS
KENSINGTON PUBLISHING CORP.
http://www.kensingtonbooks.com

KENSINGTON BOOKS are published by

Kensington Publishing Corp.
850 Third Avenue
New York, NY 10022

All Kensington titles, imprints and distributed lines are available at special quantity discounts for bulk purchases for sales promotion, premiums, fund-raising, educational or institutional use.

Special book excerpts or customized printings can also be created to fit specific needs. For details, write or phone the office of the Kensington Special Sales Manager: Kensington Publishing Corp., 850 Third Avenue, New York, NY 10022. Attn. Special Sales Department. Phone: 1-800-221-2647.

If you purchased this book without a cover you should be aware that this book is stolen property. It was reported as "unsold and destroyed" to the Publisher and neither the Author nor the Publisher has received any payment for this "stripped book."

ISBN-13: 978-0-7582-0883-5
ISBN-10: 0-7582-0883-9

First Trade Paperback Printing: November 2006
First Mass Market Paperback Printing: October 2007
10 9 8 7 6 5 4 3 2

Printed in the United States of America

For Kay Ghram,
definitely a woman of excellent taste.
Thanks!

*For great wrongdoing there are great punishments
from the gods.*
—Herodotus

*It's not that I'm afraid of death, I just don't want to
be there when it happens.*
—Woody Allen

Prologue

Dear Fred,

First off, Fred, you're probably wondering why I'm calling you Fred. It's a valid question, especially since I don't know anybody named Fred.

You see, I found Sterling's journal about our lives the other day and, although it's delightful and pretty close to the truth—Sterling is delightful, as well as dedicatedly honest, unfortunately—I began worrying what people might think if in four hundred years somebody found his journal still in one piece in some old box or something and read it, read about me, and figured I probably should set the record straight. Straighter. Something like that.

Okay, truth time, huh? Here's the deal, Fred. For some strange reason, I'm worried about future generations thinking I'm a few bricks shy of a full load. So just bear with me because you, Fred, have just been named the star witness for the defense (of me and my mind, that is).

Not that Sterling's sweetly naive account of what's happening in our lives wouldn't take the archeologist's mind off wondering about the societal implications of stuff like the concept of speed dating or the sex life of SpongeBob SquarePants.

But back to you, Fred, if just for a moment. Sterling addresses his musings to Dear Journal, and I didn't want to copy him. That confusion thing again, you know? And Dear Diary? I don't think so! I outgrew Dear Diary a lot of years ago. Right after my mother found mine and read my poem at the dinner table ("Alone, I am alone. We live and die alone." Something like that anyway—it would seem I've finally successfully blocked most of it). You want to see a grown woman rotate her head like Linda Blair in *The Exorcist*? Write something like that when you're twelve and then lose the key to your Barbie diary.

Anyway. I know a lot of other writers keep journals, or diaries, or Internet blogs, but I'm not one of them. I don't write unless there's a reasonably good chance I'm going to get paid for it, which I think makes me practical and Alex says proves I'm cheap—but he's only kidding. I'm simply frugal. So this is a departure for me, but I think a necessary one, Fred, or I wouldn't be doing it, especially since Bernie told me my last manuscript was pretty much crap (she was right, but I had a good reason, and his name is Alex), and I've got a deadline coming at me pretty soon.

Okay, enough stalling, Fred, here we go. And anybody reading this—if anyone still reads anything written on paper in four hundred years—please just skip over that first part. I was just easing my way in, you know? I'll get better at this as I go.

My name is Margaret Kelly and I am a writer (stop laughing, I said I'd get better as I go along!). I always was a writer, even at twelve, although I'm glad I gave up poetry, because who wants to get paid in copies? Also, I don't look good in berets.

Writer. Right. One with a marvelously organized brain, obviously (that's a joke, Fred).

I was born and raised in New Jersey and then got out of there as fast as I could. Not that I don't like Jersey. Jersey's great—sand, surf, casinos, what's not to love? In fact, there's only one problem with the place—my family lives there. They wouldn't have minded if I wrote poetry and starved in a garret. But popular fiction? With S-E-X in it? Enough said.

So I came to New York City, naturally, and damn near starved in a fifth-floor walk-up while I wrote historical romance novels under the name Alicia Tate Evans. If I was lucky, my publisher printed three copies (none bought by my family). I mean, I bombed! The market was glutted with romance novels, and if you didn't hit the *Times* by your fourth or fifth time out of the gate, you were history. Within a few years, I was history. But I had Bernie, bless her. Bernice Toland-James, my editor, who snuck me back in the door at Toland Books once her ex-husband had cut me.

Now I'm Cleo Dooley (What can I say? I think *O*'s look impressive on a book cover), and I write a historical mystery series set in Regency England (that's between 1811 and 1820, Fred), starring Alexandre Blake, the Viscount Saint Just, and his comic-relief sidekick, Sterling Balder. Yes, that Sterling. Fictional Sterling—who's currently writing a journal in New York City. I've got your interest now, Fred, don't I? Thought so.

A little background on Saint Just is probably a good idea, Fred, just to get you in the picture. Saint Just is, you see, perfect. I created him to be perfect. The perfect Regency hero, that is. Drop-dead gorgeous, as I made him up out of the best parts of some of my favorite movie stars (can we say Val "I'm your huckleberry" Kilmer's mouth, just for starters? That reminds me, I need a new DVD of *Tombstone*, having worn the other one out).

Saint Just, my creation, is also rich. Intelligent. Witty. Sophisticated. Deliciously arrogant. The world's greatest lover. He can dance, fence, box, swim, shoot, etc., etc., etc. You getting this, Fred? I pulled out all the stops, created this perfect, to-die-for hero, and plopped him down in the perfect romantic era. Throw in a crime he solves while expertly bedding various gorgeous and extremely grateful young things, and, wow, I had a winner. Every woman's fantasy. Definitely mine.

I hit the *NYT* with the second Saint Just mystery, and now I not only hit the list, I stay in the top five for a good six weeks. In other words, I'm not starving anymore. Mom is *so* not proud.

Life was good. Dull. Boring. But good, you know? And then one day a couple of months ago I turned around in my condo and there stood Alexandre Blake, dressed in all his well-tailored Regency finery. Next to him was cute, pudgy, friendly Sterling, munching on the KFC chicken leg I was saving for my lunch.

I recognized them both immediately. Hell, I'd made them, remember? It was a shock. But I reacted well. I fainted.

Alex explained what happened—I call him Alex Blakely now and pass him off as a distant cousin from England I'd patterned Saint Just after, although Sterling is still Sterling because he'd get too confused with an alias, and he still calls Alex Saint Just. According to Alex, I'd made him very real. Sterling, too. Made them so real that they came to life inside my head, kicked around there for a couple of years getting to know the place, then decided I was a mess who needed their help, and *poofed* themselves into my apartment, into my life.

I know this is tough to swallow, but I mean it, Fred.

That's exactly what happened. *Poof*! And it's still happening!

Do you know what it's like to have the perfect hero making himself at home in your condo apartment? Huh? The gorgeous, yummy, to-die-for man you created out of all your personal hopes, dreams? Okay, and desires and even fantasies. I admit it. There's that stuff, too.

Well, Fred, I'll tell you what it's like. It's not all good. I mean, you cannot know the depth of my sympathy for Dr. Frankenstein! I read that Mary Shelley was high on opium when she wrote that book, but I don't even have that excuse.

So what's my problem, you ask, Fred? For one thing, arrogant Regency heroes can be a pain in the rump. I am not a helpless female, but try telling that to Alex, who thinks his purpose in life is to protect me. Granted, I've needed a bit of protection now and then these past months, as I seem to have developed this way of . . . well, of tripping over murders. I think it's Alex's fault, frankly, because I never even saw a dead body until My Hero showed up.

He's really complicated my life. You try writing a love scene with the object of that love scene living in the condo across the hall and waltzing in and out of your condo all the time without warning, looking luscious in person just as you have him . . . well, have just written him into the middle of an insert tab A into slot B situation. Creepy, I tell you. Especially since I'm writing those love scenes from memory, considering the nonexistence of my own personal love life these days.

Now for the part I want to clear up for posterity, okay, Fred? You see, Sterling seems to think that Alex and I are meant for each other. You know . . . *that* way? Hey, I'm here to tell you and anyone who finds this, not that way, not *no* way! Think about it. Alex is here, no getting around that. But for how long, Fred, huh? He poofed in—he could poof out again. And where does that leave me?

Okay, so we know where that leaves me. Lusting after my perfect hero, that's where, and knowing I'd have to be a total idiot to start something we might not be able to finish.

Steve Wendell—he's a cop, Fred—now this is a guy I should be going nuts over, you know? Cute, rumpled, fallible, and incredibly sweet. But every time I look at him, I think about Perfect Alex. The man has ruined me for other men. I always thought that was a dumb saying, and way too melodramatic, but that about says it.

So, Fred, if you've been keeping score here, everything is Alex's fault. Everything. I'm the innocent party here, and none of this imaginary hero come to life stuff was my idea.

I just wanted to make that clear, Fred, okay—for you, and for posterity.

Maggie Kelly

P.S. You know, I feel a lot better now, Fred. Maybe I should keep writing to you once in a while, huh? You're sure cheaper than my weekly sessions with Dr. Bob. That's a joke, too, Fred. Sort of.

Chapter One

Saint Just stood just inside the small wire cage at the very back of the basement of the Manhattan condo building, a scented handkerchief to his nostrils as he looked at the tightly tied green plastic garbage bag lying on the cement floor.

"Grateful as I am, Socks, that you are cognizant of the strictures as laid down by all of the many crime-scene investigation programs on television, I do believe you might have safely disposed of the body. Unless, of course," he added facetiously, turning to his friend Argyle Jackson, doorman of said condo building, "it was your thought that I might wish to perform an autopsy?"

Socks held his hands cupped over his nose and mouth as he shuffled in place, clearly wishing himself anywhere but where he was at the moment. "Hey, Alex, when I called you in England you told me to not touch anything. I'd already opened the box, so I just tossed everything in that bag and brought it down here until you got home. You never said to throw away the body."

"Were there identifying marks with which we could

trace the thing, Socks? Scars? Distinctive tattoos? A wooden leg, perhaps?"

Socks shook his head. "Okay, okay, I get the point, Alex. It was a rat. Just like every other rat in Manhattan, except that this one was dead."

"Then you could have safely disposed of the thing, and I apologize most profusely for not being more explicit. Now, before we open it, could you tell me what else is in the bag? And remind me, please, of the particulars of the delivery of the package. I was rather involved with other matters when last we spoke."

"You really want to do this now?" Socks asked, taking another step backward. "You just got home from the airport a couple of minutes ago. Some trip, too, from what Sterling told me before he headed upstairs to see Henry. Isn't that something, Alex? Give one of them a white fur coat and he's a pet, like Henry. Make another one ugly and he's just another damn rat. Would that be discrimination, you think? Sterling said you solved more murders while you were in England, huh? You sure have all the luck."

"We will discuss all of that later, Socks, if you don't mind, as I'm anxious to begin my investigation. According to you, there has been a threat on Maggie's life. I don't believe there is anything to be gained by delay, do you? Besides, Maggie is busy upstairs, undoubtedly cudgeling her brain for reasons to put off unpacking for at least a week, and won't notice that I'm gone."

"Okay, but do I have to be here?"

"To tell me what I've just asked you to tell me, yes, you do," Saint Just said, manfully lowering the handkerchief, because he'd just remembered reading that allowing your olfactory senses to be inundated by the sickening smell of decomposing flesh was the best way to shut down those senses, render himself at least temporarily immune to the stench. Of course, the shutting down part took several minutes, and he only hoped the rather pitiful chicken salad sandwich he'd had on the plane had already been fully digested.

"All right," Socks said, still speaking through his cupped hands, "but I'm going to have to take my uniform to the cleaners again, and I just paid twenty bucks for the first time, when I opened the package. Mrs. Loomis said I smelled like a three-week-old gefilte fish, and threatened to report me to management."

"Remind me to give you forty dollars when we get back upstairs," Saint Just said, breathing as slowly as possible through his nose. Socks might be happy with a newly cleaned uniform, but Saint Just had already mentally consigned every stitch he wore to the dustbin. Which was a pity, for the black cashmere sweater was one of his favorites. Ah, the sacrifices he made for his Maggie.

Socks appeared slightly mollified by the offer to pay for cleaning his uniform. "Okay, Alex, thanks. So the mail came, and there was this package for Maggie, see? Came right through the mail, an overnight delivery package, so you tell me how careful Homeland Security is, huh? Run that sucker through an X-ray machine and, bam, little rat skeleton. Little rat head, little rat teeth. I'm asking you, who could miss that?"

Saint Just continued to eye the garbage bag. "Another topic for some other time, fascinating though it is, Socks. Continue, please."

"I put the package under my desk, like I always do with packages, but when I got to work the next day I noticed the smell. I wasn't sure where it was coming from at first—I always have five or six packages under there—but then Maggie's package started to leak, you know? That's when I opened it, and then I called you."

"So it was a standard overnight packaging?"

"Oh, yeah. Damn. Either one- or two-day delivery—

I forget which. Sorry, Alex. But you'll see it—one of those red, white, and blue boxes with an eagle on it, you know? I do remember that it was postmarked here, in Manhattan. Anyway, I opened it and out came two more things—a clear plastic bag and another package. I think the bag had been filled with dry ice—to keep the rat cold, you know?—but that was pretty much gone. And the other bag was *really* leaking. And really reeking. I brought everything down here before I opened it, and out came the rat." He moved his hands from his mouth and nose, to hold them on either side of his face and make up-and-down motions with his fingers. "Whiskers. Those long, pointy front teeth. Definitely a rat. And then the note."

"Ah, yes, and now it becomes interesting. But you didn't keep the note separate, did you?" Saint Just asked, pulling on a pair of thin latex gloves he'd purchased at a drugstore some weeks earlier, when his own interest in television shows showcasing crime-scene investigation had been piqued. Preparedness was half the battle in crime solving, he believed. Brilliance was the other half, exemplary powers of deduction. His forte.

"It was already all wet, Alex," Socks protested, his hands over his nose and mouth once again. "You're just lucky I didn't just call the cops, or at least Steve Wendell. But then I figured you'd kill me if I did that, so I used my master key to get into Mr. O'Hara's storage locker and used his grabber to pick up everything— you ever see one of those, Alex? They're really cool. Old people use them to reach things on high shelves. When Mr. O'Hara broke his hip and couldn't reach stuff he had me go buy one for him, so I knew where it was, since Mr. O'Hara's been just fine this past year or more. Married again and everything, and by the looks of Mrs. O'Hara, if he didn't know how to use his hips she'd find someone else who could, you know what I mean?"

While Socks was giving his informational talk on grabbers and . . . well, grabbers, Saint Just had been undoing the twist tie on the bag. Once opened, the smell, which had been unpleasant, became nearly unbearable. Still, Saint Just persevered, using a small flashlight to peer inside at the contents.

If there had been a return address on the box, the decomposing rat had made reading it impossible, and any address would most probably be bogus at any rate. Saint Just was luckier, however, with the note, as it had landed on top of the box and was relatively undamaged. Calling upon what he believed had to be awesome untouched powers he hadn't known he possessed, Saint Just reached into the bag and snared the note, then quickly replaced the twist tie and retreated with more haste than decorum from the storage cage.

"You're not going to throw that away?" Socks asked, or perhaps pleaded. "What am I supposed to do with it?"

"As having the rat bronzed or stuffed and mounted is probably out of the question, I suggest the Dumpster in the alley," Saint Just said, holding onto the note by the edges as he stood beneath one of the bare light-bulbs that hung from the ceiling. "Computer generated, I would say, which narrows down the suspects to all but about three people in the entire country. I imagine that, even in its present sorry state, there exists some way to extract fingerprints if there are any, but we'll leave that for now, shall we? More important, and more ominous, is the note itself."

Socks had commandeered Mr. O'Hara's grabber yet again and was busy inserting the foul-smelling green garbage bag inside a second, larger green garbage bag. "So you can still read it?"

"Yes, indeed. *Roses are red, violets are blue. This rat is dead, and you could be yourself.* How very charming. I believe we can rule out Will Shakespeare, Socks."

"Yeah, yeah, yeah. Are we done here? We can turn over all this stuff to Lieutenant Wendell now that you've seen it, right?"

"I think not, Socks," Saint Just said, slipping the note into a clear food storage bag he'd brought down to the cellar for just that purpose. Detecting had become more sophisticated since the Regency, but Saint Just considered himself nothing if not adaptable. "I'd rather Maggie not know about this, at least for the moment."

"She'll murder you," Socks said, shaking his head as the two of them headed back through the maze that was the basement of any building of any age in Manhattan, heading for the stairs.

"Yes. I'm shaking in my shoes at the prospect of her righteous anger, Socks. But let's think about this, shall we? A dead rat and some execrable poetry. All the makings of a one-off prank, don't you think? A disgruntled reader, most likely. As Maggie is wont to say, everyone's a critic. This particular critic simply had access to a dead rat. Now that he's vented his spleen, said what he had to say, that should be the end of it."

"And if it isn't?"

Saint Just stripped off the thin gloves and tossed them in a nearby empty bucket that didn't seem to have a purpose, so he gave it one: waste can. "If it isn't, we'll know soon enough. In any event, we will all—you, Sterling, and myself—stay very close to Maggie for the next three weeks, until she and Sterling and myself adjourn to New Jersey to celebrate Christmas with her family. If there are no more rats, and nothing untoward occurs, we can then probably safely conclude that this particular rat had no siblings."

"She's still going to murder you," Socks said, grinning. "Maggie doesn't like secrets. Hey, you didn't say—did you see how the guy signed the note?"

"No, I didn't." Saint Just stopped beneath yet another bare bulb and held up the note inside its plastic covering. "I don't see . . . oh, there it is. N . . . e . . . *Nevus*? What in bloody blazes is that supposed to mean? Nevus? A nevus is a—"

"A mole," Socks said brightly. "I looked it up. A bit of skin pigmentation or birthmark."

Saint Just tucked the plastic bag back into his pants pocket. "And you still think we should take any of this seriously, Socks?"

"No, I suppose not. Anyone who'd call himself a nevus has got to be a little crazy."

Saint Just stopped, turned around, looked at Socks. "Well, thank you, my friend. Now, for the first time, I do believe I'm a trifle worried. Yes, we'll all stay very close to Maggie, won't we?"

"And you'll talk to the lieutenant? You know, like without telling Maggie?"

"Possibly. Although I doubt there would be much of anything he could do unless the threat becomes more specific. I'll think on it, Socks."

"I saw him the other night," Socks offered carefully as they continued their way through the rabbit warren, Saint Just pausing only to pick up his sword cane, which he'd retrieved from his condo and brought downstairs with him. He felt naked without his sword cane, which was Maggie's fault, because that's how she'd made him.

"You saw the *left*-tenant? And why does that sound so ominous, Socks?"

"Well, he wasn't alone."

One corner of Saint Just's mouth curved upward. "Really, Mr. Jackson. Feel free to expand on that most intriguing statement, if you please?"

Socks looked to his left and right, as if expecting

Maggie to be hiding behind one of the stacks of boxes. "I'm not one to gossip. . . ."

"No. Definitely not, Socks. You are the soul of discretion and I commend you for that. Indeed, I am in awe of your powers of circumspection. And now that we have that out of the way—please go on."

The doorman grinned. "A blonde, and hanging on his arm like she couldn't navigate without him, you know? They were coming up out of the subway just as my friend and I were going down. We looked at each other, and then pretended we didn't see each other— you know how it is. But, man, did he look guilty. Do you think Maggie will be upset?"

"Only if she believes it wasn't her idea that she and the *left*-tenant stop seeing each other as anything but friends."

"You want to run that one by me one more time, Dr. Phil?"

Saint Just smiled. "Please, don't attempt to compare me with a rank amateur. It's simple enough, Socks. If Maggie stopped seeing Wendell as a beau, which I do believe she has already decided to do, that would be fine with her, as she's already realized that she thinks of him as a good friend, but no more. But for him to stop seeking her attention in favor of some other female before she can make that clear to him, let him down gently, as I believe it's called? No, then she'll decide she's just managed to allow what could have been the man of her maidenly dreams slip through her fingers. It's all in the timing, my friend, so we will not mention that you saw Wendell with another woman."

Socks shook his head. "Women. It's times like these that make me so glad I'm gay."

Saint Just chuckled, then frowned as he lifted a finger to his mouth, warning Socks to silence. "Someone's approaching."

A few moments later Maggie popped her head around the corner of a pillar, holding a shovel in what some might consider a threatening manner. She sighed, and put down the shovel, the look in her green eyes daring him to mention the makeshift weapon against Things That Go Bump in the Cellars. "Alex? I thought I heard someone talking. What are you doing down here?"

"Maggie, my dear," Saint Just said smoothly, inclining his head in acknowledgement of her presence. "One could reasonably ask the same of you. I was assisting Socks here with something he had to carry downstairs for Mr. O'Hara. You?"

"You carried something down here? Performed manual labor? Why can't I get a mental picture of that?" Maggie said, turning back the way she'd come, Saint Just and Socks exchanging "whew!" glances before they followed her. "But I'm glad you're here. I was upstairs, just sort of looking for something to do."

"Something such as unpacking your suitcases?"

"Yeah, right. My favorite thing," Maggie said, stopping in front of one of the many wire storage cages that lined the walls. "Anyway, I was looking around, and I suddenly realized that it's December, and we're not going to be here for Christmas unless we have a blizzard and they close the New Jersey Turnpike—which has never happened, even though I've prayed for it every year. I usually put up my Christmas decorations over the Thanksgiving weekend, so I can enjoy them longer, but we went straight to England from Jersey this year and now the condo looks naked, you know? So . . . who's going to help me get all of these boxes upstairs?"

Saint Just peered through the wire of the cage, at the stack of boxes that seemed to be three deep and reach to the rafters. "Your holiday decorations are in those boxes? *All* of those boxes?"

"Yes, most of them anyway. And you love manual labor, right, Alex?"

Socks shrugged. "I'll go get the dolly, and we can use the freight elevator."

"Thank you, Socks," Maggie said as she slipped a key into the lock that hung on the door, then stepped inside the storage area. "My mother hates Christmas, you know. The Grouch Who Stole Christmas, every damn year," she told Saint Just, who was still mentally counting boxes.

"So, naturally, you adore the holiday to the top of your bent, correct?"

Maggie's grin was deliciously wicked. "You know me so well. Oh, Alex, you're going to love New York during the holidays. The tree at Rockefeller Center, the office party drunks ice skating nearby, the department store windows. Barneys is always so *out there*. Oh, that reminds me. I've got to get to Bloomie's for a cinnamon broom. I get one there every year—it's a tradition. I *love* the smell of cinnamon. And cookies. We're going to make *lots* of cookies."

She lifted up two fairly flat cardboard boxes and handed them to Saint Just. "You see, I've just decided something. Bernie's already got next year's hardcover in-house, so I'm just not going to worry about writing again until after the new year. You've been here for months now, Alex, you and Sterling, and I've never really shown you New York. So that's what we're going to do." She added a third cardboard box to the two Saint Just was holding. "Right after we decorate the living crap out of my condo. Come on, Alex, *smile*. It's Christmas!"

Chapter Two

Maggie stood in the middle of her living room, wondering why she'd thought it was such a good idea to start this when she was probably still suffering from jet lag. It looked as if Christmas had just burped all over the room.

"What's this?" Sterling Balder asked, sitting cross-legged in the middle of a multitude of open boxes, and holding up yet another, to him, unfamiliar ornament. He looked so cute and cuddly, with a string of golden garland around his neck, and a Santa Claus hat on his nearly bald head.

Sterling was the child Maggie had always tried to believe she could be, the adult she would have grown up to be if her childhood had been different. Sweet. Kind. Loving. Trusting. When she'd conjured him up, she'd thought it had been, as they said during the Regency Era, "out of whole cloth," that he was a total figment of her imagination. But that hadn't been true, as she'd discovered to her amazement and slight embarrassment once Sterling had shown up in the flesh. Sterling was her good self. Which, of course, left Saint Just to be her not so good self, although she tried not to think about that too much.

"Plastic mistletoe, Sterling," she said, taking it from him. "And it goes in the garbage because it's really ugly. I wanted to buy real mistletoe, but the berries or the leaves are poisonous, someone said, and I couldn't take the chance that Napoleon or Wellington wouldn't take a bite."

As if on cue, Napoleon, one of the pair of Persian cats Maggie had figured writers should have, appeared out of nowhere to launch itself at the ball of plastic leaves and white berries. Maggie raised it out of the cat's reach, and Napoleon landed in the middle of a string of fairy lights that became instantly tangled—after Maggie had spent the last half hour untangling them.

"Napper, knock it off," she ordered, and the cat gave her a look that probably should not be translated from Cat to Human if said cat still wants a nightly pinch of catnip from said human, and walked off in a huff, dignity intact except for the loop of lights caught on its tail.

The tree was already assembled and decorated, thanks to Sterling's assistance, but there was still so much . . . so much *stuff* to be spread out through the condo. The bad part was that Maggie was rapidly running out of enthusiasm, and gas, considering the fact that less than twenty-four hours ago she had been bimbo diving in a rain-swollen lake for a murder suspect. "Sterling? You want some of this for your place?"

"Oh, could I? We have nothing, you understand, and I'm afraid everything will look quite naked after this. Well, not precisely *naked*. I shouldn't have said that. Do you suppose Saint Just will allow a tree?"

"Allow, Sterling? It's your condo, too, you know."

Sterling's smile was indulgent. "Now, Maggie, we

both know that's not true. Saint Just labors long and hard posing for Fragrances By Pierre to earn the funds required in order to keep us in such marvelous style, and all of that. I am only in residence thanks to his generous spirit."

Maggie snorted. "Yeah, right. Alex would be lost without you, Sterling. And you know what? He wouldn't want to hear you say you're there on sufferance. You're his best friend."

Sterling shook his head. "No, Maggie. *You* are his best friend. I am in the way of a boon companion. Indeed, there are times when I believe Saint Just sees me as a somewhat dim child he must protect, and all of that. But I am as you made me, Maggie, and I'm perfectly happy with that. Although I do sometimes wish you hadn't chosen to make me so sadly lacking in hair. Especially now, as it is sometimes so very cold outside."

"I'm sorry, Sterling, sweetie," Maggie said, unwrapping one of the three Wise Men and placing him in the nativity arrangement that she always set up on the credenza beside the front door. "But, as Rogaine wasn't invented back in the eighteen-hundreds, I'm afraid you're stuck with wearing a hat. We'll get you a nice knit cap when we're out shopping, okay? Maybe one that comes with earflaps? You'd look terrific in earflaps. Oh, damn, there goes the phone. No, don't get it, Sterling. We'll let the machine pick up."

As if in suspended animation, Sterling sat and Maggie stood, both of them unmoving, staring at the phone as it rang five times before the click of the answering machine could be heard.

"Margaret? Margaret, are you there?"

Maggie went down on her haunches, wincing, as if physically hiding herself from her mother's voice.

"Margaret, I just saw the newspaper, and read about

your latest embarrassment. I can scarcely believe it! It wasn't enough to make a spectacle of yourself in New York? Now you have to go international with your ridiculousness? And with that sweet little girl who is the spokesperson for Boffo Transmissions? Why, there must be at least a dozen outlets in our area of New Jersey alone. What? Oh, wait, your father is bellowing something from the kitchen. *What now, Evan?*"

Maggie and Sterling exchanged glances, Maggie rolling her eyes almost in apology.

"Margaret? Your father says there are fifteen Boffo Transmissions in southern New Jersey alone—as if the man had nothing better to do than count them, which he doesn't. But that's not the point. You have no consideration for us, do you? You write those filthy books, and now you're on the news every other time I turn around, consorting with lowlifes and murderers. I have to go to the supermarket at five o'clock, when no one else is there, I'm so embarrassed."

"Yeah, yeah, yeah, nothing new there. Shame, shame on Margaret. Get to the point," Maggie grumbled, wondering how many sessions with Dr. Bob it would take before she could do more than hide and grumble.

"But to get to the point of this call . . ."

Maggie's eyes popped open wide. "Wow. That's almost spooky," she said as Sterling giggled.

"I know I said you and your strange friends could stay here at Christmas, but that was before your brother decided to bring some of his friends with him. I'm sure if you call now you'll be able to get rooms somewhere in town. The prices will be outrageous, but you're such a big-shot *author* now, I'm sure that's no problem for you. And your brother did buy us this house—I thank God every day for Tate, I swear it. You can see why he has to come first."

"Yeah. Why should this year be any different," Maggie told Sterling, who was looking at her in that sad, sympathetic way, as if she was a puppy who had just showed up on his doorstep, hungry, and wet to the bone from a cold rain. "Shouldn't the computer chip have filled up by now? I've got to get a cheaper machine."

Alicia Kelly's voice dropped to a near whisper. "I'm in the other room now, away from him. One more thing, Margaret. I wouldn't discuss this with Tate, of course—he's much too sensitive for such news. Erin is never available, and Maureen is already sneaking way too many of those little pink pills she thinks I don't see her taking. Girl goes around grinning like a loon most days, over nothing. But at least you aren't sensitive. You're like a duck—water rolls right off your back. You get that from your father's side. So I'm telling you, mostly because I have to tell someone, and because things may be more than a bit strained while you're here and I need someone to shield Tate from any unpleasantness. Margaret, your father is having an affair. There, I've said it. Now, since you're the only one he seems to tolerate, I also expect you to have a firm talking-to with him when you get here. Her name is Carol and she works at the best jewelry shop here in town. He's been seen with her twice in the last week, right out in the open, and I will—"

The answering machine clicked off, its memory full.

"Maggie?" Sterling reached over to touch her arm. "Maggie—your mouth is open, Maggie. Are you all right? You're not going to swoon or anything, are you, as I don't think we have any feathers we can burn under your nose."

Maggie blinked several times, and then shook her head as if that might help clear it. "My father. My father is having an affair? That's impossible. Mom'd kill him." She looked at Sterling without really seeing him. "She sounded upset though, didn't she? Almost *cowed*, and Mom's never cowed. And she wants *me* to talk to him? *A firm talking-to* with him? What the hell am I supposed to say to him? *Attaboy* probably won't really do it, huh? Man. My father. Having an affair. I didn't think he had it in him. What was the woman's name?"

"Um, Carol. Do you want me to fetch Saint Just, Maggie?"

"No, why would I want that?" Maggie asked, wishing she didn't want Sterling to do just that. "I'm fine. Honestly. My father is having an affair, that's all." She bent her head and pressed her hands to her ears. "Ohhhh, *why* did she have to tell me? How am I going to look at him? Look at either of them? And she can tell me because I'm not *sensitive*? How can somebody give birth to somebody and then not understand that somebody at all?"

"I'll just go get Saint Just," Sterling said nervously, getting to his feet and escaping from the condo to his own, directly across the hall.

Maggie was placing the Baby Jesus in the manger with exaggerated care just as Alex entered the condo without knocking, one eyebrow raised slightly as he looked at her from the doorway. "Are you all right? Sterling seems to think you might be on the verge of a small come apart, or at least that's how he phrased the thing."

"I'm fine, Alex," she told him tightly. "I told Sterling I was fine, and I am. My father's having an affair. Good for him, huh? And I'm fine with it. I've been wondering for years why the two of them never got a divorce. I mean, it would take a saint to live with my mother, and Daddy just proved he's no saint, not if he's having an affair. Maybe it's not the first affair? Maybe he's just been pretending to be a milquetoast all these years, all ground down under Mom's heel, but he's had this secret life nobody knew about, and he's had a *string* of Carols. *Dozens* of them. Little chippies, my mom would call them. But I'm fine with it. Really. Just fine with it. What's not to be fine, anyway? Their kids are all grown and gone. It wouldn't be as if they were breaking up some happy family—we've never been the Cleavers in the first place. So—so what? No skin off my nose, right? Oh, *damn it*!" she ended just before the third Wise Man hit the far wall with a bang and fell to the floor in three pieces.

"Yes, you're obviously fine," Alex said, pulling her into his arms.

She slid her own arms around his waist and buried her head in his shoulder, giving in to the need to hold on, to be held. But she didn't cry. There was no point in it, was there? Did that make her insensitive, or just practical?

"My father goes bowling three nights a week, Alex," she whined into his shirtfront. "He doesn't slink around to sleazy motel rooms with little chippies. Oh, how am I going to go there for Christmas and act as if nothing's wrong? You know—hi, Dad, *anyone* new? I can't do that."

Alex kissed the top of her head. "Then it's settled. We won't go."

Maggie pushed herself slightly away from him, realizing that she was getting entirely too comfortable in his arms. "We have to go, Alex. It's Christmas. It wouldn't be the holidays if I didn't have to lug a bunch of wrapped presents to Ocean City and then have everyone ask me for the receipts so they can take it all back because it doesn't fit or it's the wrong color or they already have one. Last year I bought Tate a star. A star, Alex—you know, up in space? And he said he already had one. Christmas is my yearly dose of crap so that I don't have to see any of them the rest of the year—I mean, it's the only time they're all in one place, especially after Erin didn't show up for Thanksgiving. If I don't see them now, I'll have to show up a bunch of times, to see all of them. Mom keeps score."

"You Americans are the strangest people," Alex said, lightly stroking her back. "Very well. As long as I'm there to protect you."

Maggie winced. "You do not *protect* me, Alex. I'm a big girl, I protect myself. But I do want you there, I won't say I don't. Even if it's just to keep me away from sharp objects. I told Tate off over Thanksgiving, but you know that isn't going to last. He'll be his same condescending neocon self when I see him. Oh, and we have to stay at a hotel. That's the only good news I got today."

"Maggie, you do know that you are your own person, that your family is just that, your family, and not your responsibility?"

She nodded, tears finally beginning to sting behind her eyes. "I know. It's not their fault I'm the square peg in the round hole, and it's not mine, either. So I'm okay. You can let me go now. Alex? I said, you can let me go now."

"Ah, my dear Maggie, what if I don't want to?" he asked, and her stomach did that funny little thing it did whenever Alex talked to her like that, in that particular tone. God, he was good.

And she was feeling all too vulnerable. "Alex, how many times do we have to have this conversation? You're not real."

"I don't feel real?" he asked against her neck. Breathed against her neck. "I'm not really holding you?"

Maggie swallowed down hard, dipping her head to avoid the intense look in Alex's Paul Newman blue eyes. She'd likewise ignore the young Sean Connery as James Bond voice, the thick black windswept hair á la that great pen and ink drawing of Beau Brummell, the sexy slashes in his cheeks and the equally sexy crinkles around the eyes that were so Clint Eastwood in those ancient spaghetti westerns. The long, lean, hard young Clint body . . . Peter O'Toole's perfect aristocratic nose. The sensuous pout of Val Kilmer's mouth. *I'm your huckleberry.* Dangerous and seductive at the same time. Everything had come together in one damn delicious whole. Freaking amazing, that's what it was, what Alex was. Man, she did good work. . . .

"You know what I mean, Alex. I . . . I just can't af-ford to go where you seem to think we might be going. You weren't here four months ago. How do I know where you'll be four months from now? And don't give me that *evolving* thing again, okay? I know you're adapting well . . . very well, to being here."

"Making myself more real, just as I said, and thus more permanent," Alex said, trailing the side of his finger down her cheek, using its tip to raise her chin so that she had no choice but to look at him.

"Oh yeah, that works," Maggie breathed, swallowing yet again. "But—"

"Maggie," he interrupted almost kindly. "Let's consider this, all right? If I, as you say with depressing regularity, were to *poof* back out of your life—"

"How I hate that word," she said, watching his mouth.

"And I agree. But if I *were* to poof, would you rather be left with memories—or regrets?"

She shifted her gaze to his eyes. "You're such an arrogant bastard."

"Yes, I know. The perfect Regency Era hero."

"Living in the twenty-first century on the Upper West Side of Manhattan," Maggie pointed out over the buzzing in her ears. "Alex, I don't know if I can take that chance."

"But you want to," he said, his smile gone now. "You want to be daring. You want to not think, but to make that last great leap of faith into the unknown. You long to know, just as I do, if our two halves make a whole. If what we need to be complete, both of us, is at this very moment literally within our grasp."

"The . . . the thought has occurred," Maggie admitted, sliding her hands up the front of his sweater. Cashmere. He liked the feel of cashmere. He liked the feel of fine things. He was a sensual man. Would he like the feel of her?

"Saint Just? Is Maggie all—oh, a thousand pardons, Saint Just. I didn't realize you were romantizing," Sterling said from the door.

"Some people's kids," Maggie mumbled in an attempt at humor as she stepped completely away from Alex. From temptation. "I'm much better now," she told Sterling. "But you know what? I'm also starving. What do you say we leave this mess and go out for something to eat? Alex?"

"Certainly, my dear," he said smoothly, just as if they both didn't know what had been about to happen if Sterling hadn't showed up. "I must admit that I, too, am famished."

Maggie shot him a quick look, trying to decide if what he'd said had some sort of double entendre in there somewhere, then decided she was overreacting. "Famished, huh?"

"Exactly," Alex said, leaning down to whisper in her ear. "I believe I could happily nibble on you all night."

"Oh, okay, so I wasn't wrong, and shame on at least one of us. And that's a lousy line, by the way."

"I know. It was the best I could conjure up at the moment, however, as I admit to being under some considerable stress. You will forgive me, and allow me to try again some time?"

"Bite me," Maggie said, just before she winced. She

was so used to saying that when she ran out of come-
backs, but this time? This time it was a very bad choice.
"Pretend I didn't say that."

"Never," Alex said, then, gentleman that he was, he
went off to retrieve her coat.

Chapter Three

"Hide me," Bernice Toland-James pleaded plaintively as she swept past Maggie and into the condo at ten the next morning, then stopped dead five feet inside the living room. "Christ. Who does your decorating, Maggie? Salvador Dalí in his melting clocks period?" She pushed a heap of gold garland onto the floor and collapsed her long, slim, liposuctioned and nipped-and-tucked frame into one of the flowered couches in a cloud of scent.

Maggie was all-American Girl, with a heavy dose of Irish coloring and cleverly streaked honey-colored hair that was her one vanity. She rarely wore makeup and seldom thought about clothing beyond whether or not it was comfortable. In fact, her usual at-home uniform was pajamas that only sometimes matched. Bernie, on the other hand, was Victoria's Secret runway, and as long as her plastic surgeon kept his magic touch, visually stunning.

"I'm not done yet," Maggie said defensively. "But the tree is up and decorated—see? My pride and joy."

"Very nice," Bernie said, peering at the tall, pre-lit

tree now covered in a lovingly collected assortment of individual gold, crystal, and burgundy ornaments, as well as enough carefully placed multicolored silk poinsettias to make Martha Stewart proud. "If she shows up, I can stick a poinsettia between my teeth and hide in it."

"So much for my hard work." Maggie picked up the garland and tossed it in the general direction of one of the opened boxes. "And there you go again. Hide? Why? And she who?" She wrinkled her nose. "Whom?"

"Felicity," Bernie told her, reaching into her overlarge Fendi purse and pulling out a full-size box of tissues. She snatched two tissues and lustily blew her nose, for all the publisher of Toland Books had gotten out of her trip across the pond was a rotten English cold. "She's on a rampage."

"Faith?" Maggie said, as she refused to call her one-time friend Felicity. The one, happily the only, Felicity Boothe Simmons.

Not that Maggie had anything against pseudonyms. But she hadn't demanded that her supposed closest friends stop calling her Maggie and begin calling her Cleo, even in private, just because she'd hit the *NYT*. Momma pin a rose on me! Jeez. "So why's our Ms. Boob-Job on a rampage this time?"

Bernie scrunched up the used tissues, pulled a plastic bag from the Fendi, and the tissues joined a bunch of their similarly abused mates. "I read that this is supposed to be more hygienic—and this purse cost the earth so I don't want to get it soggy. There is that, too," she explained as she zippered the bag shut. "I love it when you call her that, by the way. Someday she's going to knock someone out with one of those things. She asked my advice, I told her a C, like me, so naturally she went for the double-D. Woman has no sense of proportion. And she fell off the *Times*, that's why. And

I mean *all* the way off, even the extended list. Only three weeks. Then again, considering the boobs, maybe she *bounced* off the list. Oh, God, that was lame—blame it on the head cold."

"Not even the extended list? Really?" Maggie said in some glee, then frowned and repeated more sympathetically, "Really? Ah, that's too bad. Only three weeks, huh? Bummer. Poor Faith, she must be absolutely devastated."

"Oh, please, you'll be drooling in another minute. Naturally, it's entirely my fault. I didn't print enough copies. I didn't do enough promo, certainly not enough radio. I should have sent her to more cities on her tour, found a way to get her on the *Today* show—like that was going to happen, but ever since you were on last year, she's had a bug up her backside about it. Hell, I would have sent her to the moon if I could have—I mean, you've never been there, she could beat you to it. Think how proud she'd be, up there in orbit. And how blessedly quiet it would be down here."

"Wow, you're in a good mood."

"I have a headache. That book is a headache. *Destiny of Desire* was a stinker out of the gate. I knew it, she knew it. The title doesn't even fucking make sense."

Maggie nodded, still attempting to feign sympathy for Faith. "Well, it happens after eight books in the same series. *Moment of Desire. Night of Desire. Season of Desire.* On and on. Sooner or later, you run out of good words. And plausible plots," she added under her breath.

Maggie and Faith went, as the saying goes, way back. Back to when they were both struggling authors fighting the often losing battle of the mid-list. Then, just as Maggie's first alter ego, Alicia Tate Evans, had bit the big one, Faith had rocketed to the big time as Felicity Boothe Simmons, newly crowned queen of the historical romance novel, and the friendship had gone from equals to that of the Big Star only occasionally deigning to smile in the peon's direction.

But when Maggie had hit as Cleo Dooley? Hit much larger, higher, and harder than Felicity Boothe Simmons? That's when Faith had turned flat-out mean. As a matter of fact, if Maggie hadn't recently saved Faith's life in what she still considered a moment of insanity, the two women would meet only when it was impossible for them to keep their distance. Like at conferences, and the annual Toland Books Christmas party.

"Oh, I just had a thought. Are you going to continue Kirk's Christmas bashes, Bernie?" she asked, thinking unfondly of Bernie's recently deceased ex-husband. Hell, he'd come within a hair of becoming deceased in her own apartment . . . a fact Maggie tried not to dwell on.

"No, no more parties. We're still in negotiations over the sexual harassment suit last year's Santa brought against us," Bernie said, pushing her hands through her wild, flaming mop of expensively cut and colored hair.

"Against you, you mean," Maggie pointed out, grinning.

"Hey, a stripping Santa should be prepared for the occasional grope. We're sending out hams to everybody. Legal suggested it. Damn!"

Bernie reached into her bag yet again, this time coming out with her cell phone, which she held at arm's length so that she could read the caller ID, because she might still look mid-thirties, but the illusion had yet to notify her eyes of that fact. "Felicity. Sure, like I have a death wish," she said, dropping the phone back into the purse. "You know, now that I think of it, she'll probably call here next, if she hasn't already. I had to tell the office where I was going, just in case my battery died. We're in the middle of a three-day auction for some nonfiction about global warming, or maybe it's that shrinking rain forest business? Some hot-button topic. Anyway, Felicity might call here."

"Here? Oh, thanks, Bernie. Remind me that you're getting coal in your stocking this year," Maggie said as, sure enough, her phone began to ring, at just about the same moment Maggie changed her mind, thinking it might be fun to talk to poor de-*Times*'d Faith.

"Let the machine pick up."

"Oh, I don't think so. I've been waiting for an opportunity like this for a long time. Besides, she's being nice to me lately. That's gotta stop—she's so fake and sugary she makes my teeth hurt. Ready?" She waggled her eyebrows at Bernie, and then snatched up the phone, smiling as she looked at the caller ID. "Hel-l-l-o-o-o?" She grinned at Bernie. "Oh, hi, Faith, how are you? Really? Oh, my gosh, Faith, homicidal is never good. You want to know if Bernie's here?"

Bernie reached for the table lamp beside her and lifted it threateningly. With most anyone, that would be a threatening gesture, but that's all it would be. Bernie was another matter, and Maggie really did like that lamp.

"No, Bernie's not here. We just got back from England yesterday morning on the red-eye, you know. She's probably at home, catching up on her sleep. Did you try her there? Oh, okay. Gee, Faith, you sound a little . . . agitated. Is something wrong? Can I help? I mean, anything I can do, you know that."

"You've got a mean streak, Maggie Kelly," Bernie whispered, replacing the lamp. "I love it—now quit while you're ahead."

Maggie put her finger to her lips, and then held the receiver with both hands as Faith spilled her tale of woe. "Oh, man, Faith, that sucks," she said at last, dancing in place. "Only three weeks? Wow." It was time to plant a seed in the fertile soil of Faith's insecurities.

"So, hey—you're afraid Bernie's maybe going to drop you?"

Bernie groaned and buried her head in her hands.

"Know something? Me? No, of course I don't know anything, Faith. Don't be ridiculous. My goodness, you're a major talent. Some people would say you've had a good run, and you should maybe just be happy about that, but that's just silly. I mean, maybe I've heard a *rumor* or two about some new up-and-comer Bernie's nuts about—but who listens to rumors, right?"

Maggie replaced the receiver and rubbed her hands together as she returned to plop herself down on the couch facing Bernie, resisting the urge to stick a finger in her ear to make sure it wasn't bleeding, that Faith hadn't ruptured an eardrum when she'd slammed down her own phone. "I think that went well. And now I don't have to worry about her showing up here with a Christmas present, as I'm pretty sure she's probably gotten past that saving her life business. Man, I didn't know Faith even *knew* that word."

"If I had children I'd want them all to be just like you," Bernie said as her cell phone began to ring again and both women ignored it. "Hey, not to put a pin in your Christmas spirit, but did you hear about Francis Oakes?"

Maggie had a vague recollection of a long ago Toland Books Christmas party and a small, rather timid man with suede patches on his worn tweed blazer and a terminal case of menthol breath. "Francis? Sure. What about him?"

"He's dead, that's what's about him," Bernie said, getting to her feet. "You have anything nonalcoholic around here? I'm taking some kind of sinus pill that's dried up all my saliva and my mouth feels like a suburb of the Sahara. You know, if I could treat this cold the way I usually do. . . ."

"You'd be back in rehab," Maggie said, following Bernie to the kitchen. "So, how did Francis die? He wasn't that old, was he?"

"In his mid-forties, I'd say. Thanks, kiddo," she said, accepting a cold can of soda and popping the top. "Poor guy just never quite got it together, you know? Kirk took an interest for a while, but we all remember how fickle Kirk was—oh, let me count the ways. Anyway, Francis sort of faded away at Toland Books a couple of years ago. According to the obituary, he lived near CUNY, in one of those student-clogged apartment buildings—making ends meet by writing term papers for undergrads, I'll bet. Anyway, it must have all gotten to be too much for him, and he committed suicide last week. My secretary clipped the obit and left it on my desk. Not that I could do anything about it. By the time I saw the clipping this morning Francis was already flying freight on his way back to Minnetonka or somewhere."

"You're such a caring person, Bernie," Maggie said as they sat at the kitchen table, Bernie dying for a drink, Maggie wishing she had a cigarette. "Suicide, huh? I wouldn't have thought Francis Oakes had the guts to remove a splinter, yet alone kill himself. What else was in the obituary?"

"That's it. Mourners pay by the inch now, you know, like they're fucking buying ads—sorry, I can hear my friend Johnnie Walker Red calling me a lot today."

"Tell me about it," Maggie said, reaching into her jeans pocket and pulling out her nicotine inhaler, the plastic tube whose end was beginning to look as chewed as her pencil erasers had when she'd been in the third grade, trying to master long division. "Mr. Butts keeps singing love songs to me, too. Ever notice that nobody ever gets addicted to broccoli? But broccoli could be bad for you, right? We could stop selling it in public places, tax it, write editorials on the dangers of second-hand broccoli breath—"

"Oh no, you don't. No riffs on the antismoking Nazis today, Maggie. I'm walking a fine line here. Now, you asked me a question. No, there wasn't anything in the obit but the basics. Poor, forgettable Francis. But, hey, that's the way it goes. Unhappy people are even more unhappy around holidays. Everyone knows that. Francis just decided he couldn't face one more lonely Christmas, I suppose."

"I guess so," Maggie said, sighing. "I should call Steve, tell him I'm home, and maybe he'll come over tonight. I'll ask him if he can get us some more information."

"To what end, Maggie? Writers sometimes commit suicide. They drink, they smoke, they kill themselves. It comes with the job. I could probably name at least a dozen who pulled the plug on themselves, right off the top of my head." Bernie leaned over the table. "You're feeling happy, right? No problems, nothing worrying you?"

"Funny," Maggie said, immediately thinking about her father and his little chippie. "My mother called yesterday. There was something in the newspaper about our little adventure in England. She was *not* amused."

"Tough on her," Bernie said, hefting the soda can as if toasting Maggie. "Sales of your Saint Just novels have been going through the roof ever since you've been getting into the tabloids. Another month, another murder. The reading public is eating it up, Mags. Hey, do you suppose we could work good old Francis in there somehow?"

"You're a ghoul, Bernie." Maggie leaned her forearms on the table, the better to look around the corner of the kitchen and down the hall leading to the living room. "I've got to start locking my door again. Hello? Who's there?"

"It's only us, Maggie," Sterling called out moments before appearing in the kitchen, dressed for a noonday stroll in beautiful downtown Siberia. He had a heavy brown corduroy coat buttoned up to his neck and topped by a thick knitted yellow scarf, red mittens, and a red knit cap on his head—complete with a huge yarn pom-pom on top. They'd stopped at a small store after their dinner last night, and Sterling had instantly fallen in love with the hat. "Some of the boys have invited me to go to the park with them. Isn't that nice?"

"The boys?"

Alex leaned one burgundy cashmere–clad shoulder against the doorjamb. "Sterling has become quite the bon vivant, my dears. He's taken up an association with several lads from the neighborhood during his scooter rides. Haven't you, Sterling?"

Sterling blushed beneath his bright red cap. "We're going to build a snow fort. I think it sounds a jolly idea."

"And it is, Sterling," Maggie told him. "I think it's wonderful that you've been making friends. I'm only ashamed to say that I didn't realize it snowed last night."

"Maggie the hermit. Shame she doesn't have any windows, isn't it, boys?" Bernie said, lifting her soda can in yet another toast.

"Hey. Snow is sneaky. No lightning, no thunder, no raindrops piddling against the windows. You just wake up, and there it is. Poof!"

"Poof indeed. She has such a way with description, doesn't she, Bernie," Alex said as he retrieved a can of soda from the refrigerator, pouring its contents into a glass he'd loaded with ice cubes, of course, as the Viscount Saint Just didn't drink from *cans*. "You toddle off, Sterling, but please take care to return before three."

"What happens at three?" Maggie asked, waving goodbye to Sterling. "What am I missing?"

"Nothing too terrible. I've invited Mary Louise, George, and Vernon to stop by so that I can properly thank them for their help in my last case."

"Your last case," Maggie said flatly. "You're something else, Alex. What happened in England wasn't your *case*. And, if memory serves, you weren't in it alone. I was there, too, remember?"

"Now, now, children. Mommy's already got a headache," Bernie said as Alex sat down at the table. "You were both marvelous, even if my cold and I slept through most of it. But what did your motley crew do, Alex?"

"In point of fact, Bernice, they were the source of some important information."

"Yeah, Bernie, remember? Mary Louise and company are the ones who filled us in on Nikki Campion's *connections* here in New York. Okay, so they helped. What are you planning for them, Alex? I should contribute, too."

He had the devil in his eyes as he said, "I had thought new automobiles would be welcome."

Maggie knew Alex was trying to get a rise out of her, just so he could point out how frugal she was, and she decided to play along. "*Cars*? Are you nuts? Do you have any idea what that would cost?"

Alex smiled at Bernie. "I thought that would rattle her cage, as you Americans say. But relax, Maggie, I only wanted to see how committed you are to the project."

"I'd have to *be* committed before I'd agree to three new cars. But, now that I've made you happy by playing your straight man, what you're really saying is that you haven't a single idea what to get them and you need my help, right? Without coming right out and asking for it, of course."

"I am as a pane of glass to you, my dear, aren't I? But I've already stepped out and purchased a rather lovely necklace for Mary Louise—a single small diamond teardrop on a silver chain. As befits a young woman. Understated elegance, which is what I've been attempting to impress on Mary Louise, and I'm happy to say that she only wears two earrings in each ear these days, which I see as a major accomplishment on her part. But suitable gifts for George and Vernon? I fear I must admit defeat there. I'm much more used to buying baubles for the ladies."

Maggie took a sip of soda, and then reluctantly nodded her agreement. The Viscount Saint Just was always dropping diamonds or rubies in the laps of the women he then replaced with other women, the cad. And yet the readers loved him. If her fictional creation ever fell in love and got married, the series would tank in a heartbeat. "Okay, I see the problem. What do you buy for a Snake and a Killer?"

"They've left those unfortunate appellations behind them, Maggie, as well you know, just as they have abandoned their, shall we say, innocently nefarious ways. They answer strictly to Vernon and George now, and strive daily to raise themselves above their more unfortunate beginnings."

Mary Louise and Snake and Killer had been the very first people Alex had encountered in New York, and Mary Louise had, for a price, supplied Alex and Sterling with counterfeited identification—just one of the many things Maggie knew but kept trying to erase from her memory. Now Mary Louise was posing with Alex for Fragrances By Pierre while attending college, and Snake and Killer had gone straight, or maybe just weren't as crooked as they used to be. Only in America. . . .

"And now they're your business partners in the Street Corner Orators and Players, doling out sage advice and heartfelt sermons on the sad state of the world. Right. Like I could forget. I know—why not put both of them up for the Nobel Peace Prize?"

Bernie sat with her chin in her hand. "You two fascinate me. I've never met two people more suited to either becoming lovers or killing each other," she said, and then sniffed. "I passed one of your street corner orators on the way over here, Alex. He had quite a crowd around him, too. I only caught a few words. What's today's message? Crass commercialism in Christmas?"

Alex smiled. "Why go with the obvious, Bernice? No, today's message is a rather lovely description of Manhattan in June. The park, the flowers, the street performers, the children frolicking, trips to the ballparks to see the Mets or the Yankees, et cetera. Nostalgia on a cold, snowy day. I'm confident our revenues will reflect the correctness of my choice."

Bernie shrugged. "Looked to me like a few pockets were opening. You know, I still want to publish a collection of your speeches one of these days."

"Oh, please, Bernie, don't encourage him. He's already got about fifty employees and thinks he's the Donald Trump of street corners." Maggie had thought Alex's idea to create a flow of income without actually having to work—as Regency gentlemen collect income from their estates, or invest in the exchange, they do not *work*—would be a bust, a failure. She should have known better. Between his orators and his modeling contract with Fragrances By Pierre, the man's income had skyrocketed in the few short months he'd been in New York. Hell, the man had an accountant. He wasn't real, but he had an accountant. Sometimes she got a little dizzy, just thinking about that one.

"I'm not encouraging him, Maggie. I think the book would be a hit, in a weird sort of way. You know, how an Englishman looks at America, that sort of thing? Now, back to gifts for the boys."

Maggie looked at her friend in some confusion. "Why? You don't care about that."

"No, of course not," Bernie said in her usual honesty. "But I do want to talk about Francis, now that you put the idea in my head, and who better to talk to than Alex, our resident supersleuth?"

Alex looked to each woman in turn. "I'm missing something here, aren't I? Who is Frances? Do I know her?"

"Francis Oakes, Alex, and he's a he. Well, was a he, used to be a he."

Alex waved a hand in front of himself. "Would this be anything like Socks's friend Jay-Jayne?"

"I think I've got your headache now, Bernie," Maggie said, getting to her feet and tossing the empty soda can in the recycling bin. "No, Alex. Jay is a cross-dresser. Francis Oakes is just dead."

"Really. How unfortunate for the man," Alex said, following after Maggie and Bernie as they returned to the living room, where Bernie's Fendi bag could be heard playing the first few bars of the *William Tell Overture*. "Bernice, isn't that your phone?"

"I'm ignoring it," Bernie said, stuffing a cushion over her purse as she sat down, drawing her long legs up on the couch. "Oh, and you could get your business partners subscriptions to the *Wall Street Journal*. If they can read?"

"*Et tu, Brute?*" Alex said, seating himself in Maggie's swivel desk chair.

"Yeah, Bernie, insulting remarks are my job," Maggie complained as Wellington jumped up on the couch beside her, a gilded miniature pinecone in his mouth. "Give," she commanded, holding out her hand, which Wellington ignored, so that within moments a tug-of-war ensued, with Wellington growling and Maggie pleading.

"Oh, for God's sake, Mags, let him have it," Bernie said, piling another pillow on top of her purse, because the ringer must have been on Excruciatingly Loud. "If that's the office, by the way, they'll ring you next, so I'm not missing anything."

"Let him have it? Sure, so he can barf it up on my bedspread at midnight. Damn cat thinks he's a dog. Wellington *give!*"

"You could turn off the ringer, you know," Alex suggested as he walked behind the couch, snapped his fingers, and then held out his upturned palm to the cat, which promptly gifted him with the pinecone.

"I hate you," Maggie said without heat as Alex then dropped the pinecone in her lap, complete with cat drool. "But he's right, Bernie. Please turn off that damn ringer. Every time I hear that ring my mind starts repeating *the cereal that's popped from guns* over and over in my head. My dad used to sing it every morning as he poured his puffed rice into the bowl."

"Oh, all right," Bernie said, flinging the pillows to the floor and then reaching into her bag and pulling out her cell phone. "Wow, nine missed calls, and all from our tragedy queen. Persistent, isn't she? I may have to go to the Hamptons for the weekend and leave my cell phone at home."

"Again, I'm missing something, aren't I? But, being a gentleman, I won't pry," Alex said, returning to the desk chair. He hit the *return* button on Maggie's computer keyboard so that the computer woke up, and then opened her search engine, typing in *Francis Oaks*. "*Oaks* as in grand old oak tree, or with an *E*?"

"With an *E*. And he's off! You had to tell him, didn't you?" Maggie complained to Bernie through clenched teeth.

Bernie shrugged. "Really, Mags. How long do you think a sophisticated New Yorker like myself could be fascinated with choosing gifts for snakes and killers? Especially sober. Besides, knowing Alex, he'll get us more information on Francis than Steve will give us."

"True. I hate to admit it, but true. Alex? Find anything?"

"I'm looking at Amazon.com at the moment, Maggie, which is where Google led me. You didn't tell me Oakes was a writer," Alex said, his back to the women as he punched keys. "Four books, all of them out of print. And all of them published by Toland Books, the most recent one six years ago. This is an intriguing title, *The Axeman Cometh*. Ah, here's one of those reader reviews you abhor, Maggie. *Couldn't finish it.* Well, that's pithy. The mind boggles at the audacity, however, that Bookluver—that's l-u-v-e-r—from Phoenix believes his or her opinion to be definitive."

"Why shouldn't Bookluver think that? Everybody's reviewing books these days," Maggie said, wrapping the soggy pinecone in the tissue Bernie had handed her. "And the supposed pros aren't much better. Bernie? Remember that one review on my last book? *Dooley writes with a sort of accidental panache*? Now I ask you, what the hell is *accidental panache*? I can't do panache unless it's by accident? How does the guy know it was an accident? Maybe I *planned* that accident. Maybe it was *on purpose* panache. Does the guy even know what he's saying, or is he just pulling words out of his—head," she said after a slight hesitation during which she remembered Alex was still in the room, "thinking he's impressing people? You know, in my next book, I think I'm going to have to do a riff on critics. Maybe something lousy one of them said about Jane Austen, or something. I'll say the critic believes she employed accidental panache."

"Careful, Maggie," Bernie warned. "You know what they say—never piss off a critic."

"Wrong, Bernie. Never piss off a writer. More people read us. I mean, come on, Bernie. Accidental panache?"

"There's a second definition of *panache*, you know, Maggie," Bernie said, winking at Alex. "The first is, of course, dash, verve. But the second is a bunch of feathers or a plume, especially on a helmet. So maybe the reviewer believes you got a bunch of feathers in your hair without intending to do it?"

"You're such a help," Maggie grumbled, and then looked at Alex. "Anything else? Or am I going to spend the next hour wondering if I can stick some accidental plumes into my next book?"

"Ummm," Alex said, heading back to Google. "I took a moment to read that *accidental panache* quote on Amazon, and discovered a new reader review. It would appear that Barb-Four-Books believes, and I quote, 'Saint Just can park his high-topped Hessian boots under my bed any time.'" He swiveled around on the chair and grinned at her. "Imagine that."

"Thanks," she said, deadpan. "You're always such a big help." She tried to look past him. "A new page just came up on the screen. What are you after now?"

"I've discovered the obituary," Alex told them, turning back to the computer, then scrolling down the page he'd found. "Author . . . forty-eight years old . . . discovered by a student . . . suspected suicide." He swiveled the chair to look at Maggie and Bernie. "You didn't mention that. Only suspected? It's not definite?"

"I guess the coroner hadn't ruled on it yet when that was published," Maggie said, wishing she could keep her mouth shut. But what was the point? Once Alex knew anything, he needed to know everything. "I'm kind of shocked, to tell you the truth. Francis was such a milquetoast." *Just like your father*, Maggie's inner self reminded her, *yet look at the old boy now!* "But I really didn't know him very well."

"Perhaps not, but you're having difficulty accepting his death as a suicide, is that correct?"

"Oh, here we go," Maggie said, rolling her eyes. "No, I am not second-guessing anything. It was suicide, Alex. That's what's in the papers, that's what it was."

"Suspected suicide," Alex pointed out, much too seriously for Maggie's peace of mind. "I'm sure the good *left*-tenant will be able to supply us with more information. Details of the cause of death, manner of death."

"And now he's dazzling us with technical terms. Secret Squirrel is on the case, Bernie. Are you happy now?"

Bernie shrugged. "I don't mind, Mags. If he discovers anything interesting, maybe Toland Books can reissue Francis's old books. Suicide is good, if he was inventive about it, but murder would be even better. Or did you forget that Francis wrote murder mysteries?"

"You know, if anyone *sane* ever eavesdropped on any of our conversations, we'd all be locked up," Maggie said, then they all turned as the door opened and Sterling clomped his way into the living room.

"Hello, all," he said, brushing snow from his pompom. He was snow from head to foot, actually, a living snowman, his clothing crusted with the stuff. His nose and cheeks were a cherry red, his grin one of pure delight. "We had a snowball battle. I won."

"You don't look like the winner, Sterling, sweetheart," Maggie said, guiding him back to the small rug in front of the door, when he made a move toward one of the couches, Wellington weaving between her legs so he could sniff at some of the frozen snow that had already hit the floor.

"Oh, but I am. Whoever gets hit the most with snowballs is the winner," Sterling informed them, then frowned slightly. "I would have thought it would be the other way around, but the boys said they were certain of the rules."

Maggie laughed, and gave Sterling a smacking kiss on his ice-cold cheek. "I love you, Sterling."

"Thank you, Maggie," he returned solemnly. "The boys were happy, so that's all right, isn't it? Sometimes we can choose to pretend not to know what we know, if it does no harm and serves to make someone else happy, and all of that."

Sweet, dear Sterling and his often startling insights on life. Once again, Maggie thought about her father. He was happy, or at least she supposed so. So should she pretend not to know what she knew, what her mother had told her? Was life ever that uncomplicated, that easy? No, not with her mother around, goosing her every chance she got, ordering her to talk some sense into her wandering father's head. *Why me? Why is it always me?*

"Maggie?"

"Hmm?" she asked, blinking at Alex.

"Will Wendell be stopping by any time soon, or should I call him?"

"Steve? About what?" Her mind was fully occupied with her own personal pity party, and she'd lost the trail of the conversation.

"About your friend Francis Oakes? You are interested, aren't you?"

"I couldn't really say he was my friend because I barely remember him, and I'm not going to lose any sleep over his death, no. He committed suicide. It's sad, but that's all it is. But okay. Yeah, sure, if you and Bernie want to play detective, go ahead, you can ask Steve. Why ask me? I'm not in charge of him, you know. Why would you think I'm in charge of him? I'm not in charge of anybody. And I am, too, sensitive!"

"Jet lag," Bernie said around the tissue she held to her nose as Maggie ran out of the room. "Oh, damn, there goes my phone again. . . ."

Chapter Four

"How kind of you to meet with me on such short notice, Wendell," Saint Just said as he slipped into the opposite side of the booth at an establishment known for its greasy food and its disinterested clientele. Saint Just had ordered a cup of coffee on his way back to the booth, and managed to hide his distaste when he saw the half-eaten hamburger on the lieutenant's plate. "Crass of me to point it out, *left*-tenant, I know, but there's a small dribble of mustard on your chin."

"Oops, sorry," Steve said, grabbing a fistful of thin paper napkins from a chrome-sided container and rubbing at his mouth. "You want one? Best hamburgers on the island, no question."

Saint Just adjusted the long, thin knitted scarf at his neck, all the extra protection from the weather he'd needed other than his navy cashmere sports jacket. He'd walked to the restaurant, occasionally swinging his gold-topped ebony sword stick, happy to enjoy the sunny, blustery day if not the sadly abused gray slush on the sidewalks. "Yes, I'm convinced you're correct. And how wonderfully convenient that we're so close to Lenox Hill Hospital. I've often wondered. Can you actually *feel* your arteries clogging, *left*-tenant?"

Steve grinned around another bite of hamburger. "Maggie says you're always watching that health channel, whatever it is. You know, Alex, one hamburger isn't going to kill you."

"Ah, true, and I have reason not to worry about my own health, as I swear, I don't believe I've aged a day since I arrived here," Saint Just said, enjoying his private joke. "But still so much better to employ my George Foreman grill, you know. A truly mind-boggling invention. America is crammed rather full with amazing inventions, you know. I'm fond of my computer, of course, and my plasma television machine but, by and large, I'd have to say I am most fond of my George Foreman grill. I've penned a letter to Mr. Foreman, as a matter of fact, apprising him of my admiration, as I am a firm believer that excellence should be rewarded."

"You are so freaking weird," Steve said, popping the last huge bite of hamburger into his mouth. "How's Maggie? You guys sure had a crazy time of it in jolly old England from what I've heard."

"We're seldom bored, Maggie and I," Saint Just agreed, smiling up at the waitress who carefully placed his coffee cup on the tabletop, then asked if there was anything else she could get him. Like her phone number.

"You're too kind, dear lady," Saint Just told her, and she walked away, backfield in motion, to yell to another customer to keep his freaking pants on, she'd been serving the *gentleman*.

"I've always wondered. How do you do that?" Steve asked, leaning his elbows on the table, the left one squarely into a blob of ketchup. "I mean, seriously, Alex. Women fall all over you everywhere you go. Except Maggie, of course. I mean, being your distant cousin and all." He narrowed his eyelids. "Exactly how distant is that, again?"

"So distant the connection is very nearly nonexistent," Saint Just said, pulling three napkins from the dispenser and holding them out to Steve. "You've had a slight accident with your sleeve."

Steve lifted his elbow and took a look. "Oh, would you look at that. This is my best shirt, and I have a—yeah, thanks, Alex."

Saint Just took a sip of his coffee and then carefully replaced the cup in the saucer. Steve had a rather crude earthenware mug of coffee in front of him, but the waitress had discovered a cup and saucer somewhere for Saint Just. He must remember to be more than his usual generous self when leaving the dear woman a gratuity for her services. One never knew when one would have occasion to revisit such a place as this.

"You were about to say something, Steve? An admission you would rather keep to yourself? But, please, allow me to hazard a guess. You have what you Americans call a date? Why, you do, don't you? You cad."

"No! I'm not—that is, it's not exactly a—ah, hell. How do you do that?"

"I'm merely observant," Saint Just told him. "Your hair is combed, which is a departure. It's seven o'clock in the evening and you're still wearing your tie—I would suggest you remove it, but, then, I've never been partial to claret and yellow stripes. You look freshly shaved and I can smell your cologne. You applied mustard and ketchup with your usual gusto, but refrained from adding a slice of raw onion. And, of course, the dead giveaway, as I believe you'd term it—you blushed quite thoroughly when you realized you were about to say something you'd rather I, of all people, did not know."

He did not add the damning information that Socks had already given the game away, because there was no need for such unnecessary honesty. He would much prefer Wendell be awed by his impressive powers of observation.

"No, I don't want you to know. Because you're Maggie's cousin," Steve said, pushing his fingers through his shaggy sandy hair. "And a royal pain in my ass. Yeah. I have a date. But you can't tell Maggie."

"Believe me, my friend, as I say in all honesty, nothing could be further from my mind. But you will tell her, won't you?"

Steve waved his hands in a wonderfully discombobulated gesture. "I don't know. It's not like Maggie and I are really . . . you know, *getting anywhere*? I like her, I really do, but things always seem to get sort of *weird* around her, you know?"

"No, not at all," Saint Just said with a carefully straight face. "Oh, wait. You're referring to the murders, aren't you? Surely you can't blame Maggie for a few unfortunate incidences? Even if you did suspect her of murdering her publisher, didn't you? That was unfortunate."

Steve gave his stained shirtsleeve one more swipe, and then glared at Saint Just. "I didn't think that for more than a couple of minutes, not once I got to know her."

"Of course. You might even say that's why you're still aboveground. Now, tell me about your new friend."

Steve grabbed the last potato chip and then pushed his empty plate away from him. "There's not a lot to tell. I met her in the subway when some jerk tried to grab her purse. The thing is, Alex, Christine's *normal*. I mean, she works as a secretary to an orthopedic surgeon over on Park Avenue. She likes to cook, she loves going to the movies, she still lives with her mom. . . ."

"And she doesn't land in the briars on a fairly regular basis," Saint Just finished for him. "In other words, she's boring."

"No! Not boring. *Normal*. I like Maggie, Alex. I

mean, she's beautiful, she's smart, she's a lot of fun. But she's . . . all of you, actually . . . you're just a little, I don't know. Out there?"

"Out there," Saint Just repeated, calling on every bit of control he had in order to keep from laughing out loud at this poor, confused specimen.

"Yeah. Out there. I spend my days with wack jobs, Alex—and that's just the guys I work with at the Homicide table, even before I get to the perps. I want to be . . . I want to be able to relax when I'm off duty and with a woman, you know? Maggie's life is just too full of . . . craziness. Are you getting this?"

"Some of it, yes, although I think I lost you for a few moments at *wack job*. I'm not certain, but I believe you mean she's slightly crazy?"

"No, that's not it. Wacky, you know? Her life is wacky. Offbeat—and that's being kind, Alex. She's just always in the middle of something, and it's never normal somethings, like she lost her wallet or forgot to pay her electric bill. When Maggie says she has a problem, it usually means something fairly bizarro is going on and I'm either going to have to bail her out or rescue her from some lowlife."

"Maggie is fairly good at rescuing herself, and she always has me, you understand. So, if she isn't crazy, are you saying Maggie is still a . . . wack job?"

"Yeah, all right. A wack job. A cute wack job, but a wack job."

"I see. And the rest of us? Sterling, for one."

Wendell considered this for a moment. "He calls you Saint Just because Maggie made up her Saint Just guy by describing you. And it's not like he's trying to be funny—he seems to mean it. You're calling that normal?"

"For Sterling, yes. But this is interesting, really. Do you include Tabitha, Maggie's agent, in this mix?"

"Scarf lady? Nah, she's just blond."

One corner of Saint Just's mouth began to twitch in amusement. "Oh, dear. I can see you've given this all some considerable thought, *left*-tenant. Who else? Ah, I know. Socks. And Bernice, of course. Your opinion, please?"

Wendell shrugged. "Socks is okay. As for Bernie? You're kidding, right? You really need an answer to that one?"

"No, I suppose not. And that leaves me. Am I a . . . wack job?"

Wendell shook his head. "No. You're freaking scary, that's what you are. And I think Maggie likes you, even if she won't admit it to herself. I've never come in first, you know?"

"Indeed," Saint Just said, taking another sip of coffee. "So you're bowing out of the competition? I'd like us to be clear on that, my friend."

Pulling a fat brown wallet from his back pocket, Wendell said, "Hell, Alex, I was never in it. Not really. I think I knew that from the beginning. The only thing is, how's Maggie going to feel about . . . well, about Christine?"

Saint Just pondered this for a moment, but only for effect. "She'll be surprised, certainly. I should let her down slowly, were I you."

"How would I do that?"

"Be her friend, *left*-tenant, as you've always been. Just nothing more. For instance, Maggie is concerned at the moment about a recently deceased gentleman. A fellow author, who purportedly put a period to his own existence five days ago, I believe it was. Now, if you were to assist her in gaining any additional information about this man, about his death, you understand, that would be the act of a friend. You do wish to continue the friendship, do you not?"

"Well, yeah, of course. I like Maggie. So I keep it friendly. I just don't ask her out to dinner anymore, or to the movies, right? Just platonic. I can do that."

"Splendid, Steve," Saint Just drawled, reaching into his sports coat pocket and extracting a neatly folded computer printout of Francis Oakes's obituary. "We are told it was a suspected suicide, as I said—"

"You did? When?"

"I said he put a period to his own existence, *left*-tenant. As one would put a period at the end of a sentence—to *end* it? Consider it a euphemism, one meant to spare the listener's sensibilities, instead of coming right out and baldly saying he'd killed himself."

Wendell grinned. "You were worried about my sensibilities?"

"Not particularly, no," Saint Just told him, returning the smile. "But to continue? We are told it is most probable the gentleman *offed himself*—"

"Better."

"Thank you. I am nothing if not amenable. But I could find nothing more definitive on my own about the unfortunate Mr. Oakes. However, with your connections . . . ?"

"Sure, sure, give it over and I'll check it out. It's the least I can do for Maggie," Wendell said, the hook neatly slipping into his mouth. "Suicide. No problem. How bad could she screw this up, right?"

"How badly indeed," Saint Just said, reaching for the check the waitress had just deposited on the table. "Please, allow me. And do enjoy yourself this evening, *left*-tenant. Oh, wait, I've just had a thought. Perhaps you should give the information about poor Mr. Oakes directly to me, say, tomorrow at two, at Mario's? Not as much contact with Maggie, you understand . . . thinking platonically."

Wendell shrugged. "Sure, okay. Hey, thanks for picking up the check. I gotta go, I'm meeting Christine in a half hour."

"May you both have a wonderful evening," Saint Just said as Wendell walked away, and then added under his breath as he brought the coffee cup back up to his lips, "Sometimes it's almost too easy. . . ."

A few drops of cooling coffee splashed onto Saint Just's shirtfront as the good lieutenant leaned down to whisper in his ear. "You're up to something again, aren't you? Be ready to tell me all about it, or my information on Oakes stays in my pocket."

"How remiss of me to forget that you delight in playing the fool, *left*-tenant. Shame on me. But I agree. Tomorrow we will share information."

"Because there's something going on? What? Cripes, Alex, you guys are only home for a couple of days. What the hell could have gone wrong that fast?"

"Possibly nothing. Hopefully nothing. Then again, if the information you bring me turns out to be what I sincerely hope it is not, possibly quite a lot."

"Why? Because your Spidey sense is tingling?" Wendell said in a fairly good attempt at sarcasm.

"Yes, I suppose that's it, although I was thinking more of a mammal than an arachnid. Until tomorrow at two, Steve?"

Chapter Five

"Gin," Maggie said, discarding a six as she laid down the rest of her cards with a flourish. "That's twelve million dollars you owe me, Sterling. You don't want to play anymore, do you?"

"No, I suppose not. But we could do something else, couldn't we?"

What was going on here? *Something* was going on here, that was for sure. She decided to see if she was right. "I could grab my jacket and we could go to the park, see if your friends are there. You could stay with them, let them pelt you with snowballs, and I could go do some shopping. I don't have a single gift bought yet, you know. How does that sound?"

Sterling's complexion turned white, then rosy red. And the guy wondered why he couldn't win at cards? "Oh. Oh, no, Maggie. I shouldn't think you'd want to go shopping *alone*. We could go together, I suppose? Although it's fairly cold outside, and it's so nice and warm in here. We should stay here. Yes, I think we should stay here. It's better here. Alex would want to know where we are, don't you think?"

"Where did you say Alex is, Sterling?" Maggie asked as she stood up, stretched, then walked over to admire her tree, hoping she sounded only politely interested, and not like she wished Sterling would go find Alex, and then the two of them could go somewhere. Like to the moon. Right after one of them told her what the hell was going on.

Alex had "joined" her for breakfast, which meant that he'd come strolling in with the morning newspaper and a suggestion that she consider bacon and scrambled eggs as a fine start to another lovely crisp, sunny December day.

The pans were still soaking in the sink, damn him, and she'd given in to the urge to try the homemade plum jam Socks's mother had sent over a month ago and she'd been pretending hadn't been sitting in the cabinet. Stop smoking, gain ten pounds, lose two, eat plum jam, and gain back three. It was just the way the world worked. . . .

She'd kicked Alex out at noon, after a morning spent discussing the debacle that had been their trip to England, and within moments Sterling was at the door, volunteering to help her with the rest of her Christmas decorations. Not one to turn down a volunteer, they'd spent the next hour setting out Maggie's favorite pieces, winding fairy lights around two of her fake potted plants, and then dragging all of the empty boxes to the freight elevator and back down to the basement storage area. After that, Sterling pulled a deck of cards from his pocket and sat down at the game table in one corner of the room, as if digging in for the duration—whatever the duration was.

When Sterling didn't answer her question, Maggie finished adjusting one of the crystal bells on the Christmas tree and turned to look at him. He was wearing the Santa hat again, and admiring his reflection in the mirror. "You look very nice, very festive. Getting in the spirit, are you?"

Sterling frowned, pulling off the hat. "I don't think so, no," he told her, dropping back onto one of the couches. His sigh was deep, and heartfelt. "It's all this crass commercialism, you understand."

Biting back a grin, Maggie decided it was time to pull up a couch of her own and try to take a peek inside Sterling's mind. "Crass commercialism? Where did you hear that, Sterling?"

He spread his hands. "Everywhere. It's all about gifts, and decorations, and more gifts and . . . well, and more gifts. It's all very depressing. Almost enough to put a person into a sad decline."

"Yes, I can see that," Maggie said, rubbing her chin. "What would you like Christmas to be about, Sterling?"

He shrugged, looking at her over his gold-rimmed glasses. "I'm not sure. I . . . well, I just don't think your Santa Claus helpers should be selling watches and purses and such on street corners, do you?"

"You mean they should be giving them away instead?"

Sterling's expression went unnaturally stern. "No, I don't think I mean that at all, Maggie. But should Santa Claus be *selling* things?"

"I'm sorry, sweetheart," she said, reaching for her nicotine inhaler. She was pretty sure she'd been a nicer person when she smoked. "There are other Santas, you know, Sterling. Santas who collect money for, uh, for those less fortunate."

"Tell me," Sterling said, leaning forward on the couch, and Maggie found herself giving him a thumbnail sketch of holiday charities and holiday Santas, all of which served to return a smile to Sterling's unusually sad face.

"Okay," she then said, clapping her hands together

as she got to her feet. "Now what do you say we give the tree one last inspection, and then I think I'll go take a shower?"

Sterling got to his feet and walked over to stand beside Maggie as the two of them looked the tree up and down.

Maggie reached out after a few moments and bent one of the smaller branches on the artificial tree so that the tassel on one of the ornaments could hang straight. "That's better."

"It all looks very nice, even if it isn't real," Sterling agreed. "You really do like Christmas, don't you, Maggie? And all the fol-da-ral."

"Fol-da-ral? Wow, Sterling, that's a good one. But, yes, I do like it. I adore Christmas."

"Even when you get it wrong," Sterling said, and then quickly clapped his hands to his mouth.

"Excuse me?" Maggie rather glowered at Sterling as he backed away from her. "And why does that sound like you opened your mouth, Sterling, but Alex's voice came out?"

"Oh, no. No, certainly not. Surely not."

Maggie made come-to-me-speak-to-me gestures with her hands, and Sterling backed up another step. "What did he say? He had to have said something. God knows he's always got to say something."

"Well," Sterling said, forced to stand still now that he'd inadvertently cornered himself between Maggie and the back of the nearest couch, "you just made a simple mistake, that's all. Nothing important, really. Oh, you know what, Maggie? I think I forgot to feed Henry. Poor thing, running on that wheel of his all day. He must be famished. I really must be going now, and surely Saint Just will be back at any time. It's already past three, isn't it? So that's all right."

"Right, it's past three. And we'll get to that next,

Sterling—why it's all right, whatever *it* is, because Alex will be home soon. But for the moment, let's get back to me getting it wrong. Getting what wrong, Sterling? Where? How?"

"It's . . . um . . . not that it wasn't an honest mistake . . . and you were much less experienced at the time and . . . why, anyone could make the mistake . . ."

Maggie reached into her pocket, took out a fresh nicotine cartridge, and held both it and the nicotine inhaler up in front of Sterling. She opened the empty inhaler and dangled the cartridge over it, just as if she was going to drop a bullet into a gun. "I've been good. I've been sucking air, Sterling, for three days. Don't make me use this."

"You had a Christmas tree in a book years before Christmas trees ever came to England," Sterling told her quickly, then took a quick breath. "There, I've said it. Now put that away, Maggie."

Maggie slipped the two plastic pieces and the cartridge back into her jeans pockets. "I what? No, that's impossible. I research everything. Sure, I make a few mistakes, who doesn't? But Christmas trees? Everybody has Christmas trees."

"We didn't," Sterling told her, obviously feeling more confident now that Maggie had holstered her nicotine inhaler. "Yule logs. Holly berries. Crape myrtle. But not trees. Yet you mention one, in some detail, actually, in one of your Alicia Tate Evans books. Saint Just pointed it out to me."

"I did? Oh, wait. Yeah, I remember now," Maggie said, nodding. "Alex read my Alicia Tate Evans books?"

"No, I don't believe so. At least not for several years."

Several years? Maggie felt a shiver ice-skate down her spine as she fumbled in her pocket for all the pieces of her addiction. Alex hadn't even been here several years ago. As of about seven years ago, he hadn't even been invented, the Saint Just mysteries hadn't been invented. "Run that one by me again, please, Sterling."

Sterling looked as comfortable as a balloon in a room full of pin cushions. There was nowhere to go where he wouldn't end up in trouble. "Um, he hasn't read them at all?"

"Not at all," Maggie repeated, fitting the cylinder into the holder. "But he knows about them."

"Yes. Precisely. Not me, of course. I came later. The finishing touch, as it were, that made the rest of it possible. Well, I should go feed Henry."

"Oh, stay a while, please," Maggie told him quietly, and Sterling, who had been eyeing the door, slouched against the back of the couch. "I want to hear all of it. Now."

"But there's really nothing to say, Maggie. You know Saint Just lived inside your head until he decided to come out."

"No, I don't know that, Sterling. It's what I've been told, but I don't *know* it. As a matter of fact, I try very hard not to think about it."

"You really shouldn't, if it makes your head hurt, or any of that. I hadn't lived there quite so long—in your head, that is—and Saint Just was already firmly in residence when I got there. I once asked him how long he'd been with you, and he said he'd been there since the beginning."

Now here was something she hadn't heard before. "From the first day I began writing? Is that what you mean? What he means? That he's been the glimmer of an idea in my head for as long as I've been writing?"

"No, from the beginning, Maggie. I think, now that I consider the thing, he mentioned the word . . . um . . . puberty."

"Oh, God," Maggie said, staggering over to her desk chair and collapsing into it. He'd been with her that long? She'd been measuring men against him ever since she'd first looked at Jimmy Gilchrist and decided maybe boys weren't all dopes? Except they'd all turned out to be dopes, hadn't they? Dopes, or duds. All these years, she'd never found one, not a single one, who could measure up to, live up to . . . to the imaginary man living in her head? Maggie blinked, trying not to faint. "He's been with me that long?"

Sterling was on firmer ground here, it seemed. "Oh, yes. Evolving, you understand. And then, at last, you named him, which he appreciated very much by the way, for it's just the name he would have chosen for himself."

"*Just* the name, huh? The Viscount Saint Just," Maggie heard herself say over the ringing in her ears. "All along? All these years? I'd been . . . *building* him?"

"Your perfect hero, yes. I am just delighted that you chose to make me believable as well, or else I shouldn't be here, should I, and where would Henry be without me?"

"Hungry," Maggie muttered, waving Sterling toward the door. She needed to be alone. She needed to think about this. "Wait! There was something else, wasn't there? Oh, right, I remember. Alex was here this morning, you showed up the moment he left, and now you're concerned as to when he'll be back, because you want to be gone. I'm being babysat, Sterling, aren't I?"

"I'm afraid I don't understand the term," Sterling said, now backpedaling toward the door. "Truly, I don't."

"Oh, yes, truly you do," Maggie said, already calling up her search engine on the computer. "But never mind. I'll figure out the why of it on my own."

Sterling escaped, and Maggie typed a few words into the search engine, and then clicked on one of the articles that appeared. Christmas trees were introduced to England from Germany around 1841. Maggie's books, those written as Alicia Tate Evans and those written as Cleo Dooley, all dealt with the Regency, 1811–1820. She'd written about a Christmas tree in one of her Alicia Tate Evans books, and nobody had caught it. Not her, not the copy editor. None of her half dozen fans of those older books. Nobody.

"Well, now, that's embarrassing," Maggie said, cupping her chin in her hand as she called up her Solitaire program. There was no sense getting involved in anything else, not with Alex bound to show up for babysitting duty any moment.

Where could she take them? Some place that had the potential to drive him crazy would be nice, some place that would bore him out of his mind up until the moment she melted into a crowd and watched as he went nuts looking for her . . . which would serve him right for growing in her mind.

"Since puberty? Jeez . . ."

Chapter Six

Saint Just's meeting with Steve Wendell had been, at the very least, interesting. At the very most, it had been unsettling, not that he had been about to inform the good lieutenant of that particular reaction to hearing the NYPD's conclusion as to the details of the passing of one Francis Oakes.

Even hearing what he'd heard, Saint Just had been reluctant to share his own knowledge with the man, as it would seem to serve no clear-cut point. What Steve had given him was another small piece of a puzzle that, unfortunately, now had only two or three pieces, not even enough to make all four corners, let alone a reasonable border he could then fill in as his investigation proceeded.

Which, to Saint Just, along with the firmly held conviction that he was more than capable of both protecting Maggie and solving any case with which he might be presented, was enough to tuck away any thought of mentioning the package that had been delivered in Maggie's absence.

After all, if he, the Viscount Saint Just, could not as

yet prove whether or not there had been a crime committed, what hope did the New York City Police Department have? Less than none, Saint Just had decided.

So he'd thanked Steve for the information and then asked him about his evening with the unknown Christine, and then gently chided the man when he'd told him they'd had a "great" night. They'd gone to Brooklyn. On the subway. To go bowling.

There'd never been any hope for the man if Steve had been serious in his pursuit of Maggie Kelly. None. Saint Just knew he could picture Maggie in Brooklyn. He could even picture her bowling. He could not, however, picture Maggie Kelly voluntarily on a subway at night, traveling to Brooklyn to bowl, even if her date did carry a pistol.

"Christine has her own ball and shoes," Steve had told Saint Just, obviously pleased to impart what had to be a part of the woman's attraction.

"As do you, I'm sure," Saint Just had responded smoothly. "A match fashioned in heaven, Wendell, you lucky devil." He'd then reminded Steve that Maggie was not to see him or even hear from him for at least another few days—part of that "letting her down slowly" idea he'd planted in the man's head—and the two men had parted ways.

Whether Steve Wendell had believed everything Saint Just told him, swallowed it all whole, or whether he was playing the simpleton again remained to be seen. It was difficult to know with the lieutenant.

Then again, the man had used the never to be repeated opportunity of a first date and first impression to take the woman of his choice—egad—bowling.

"I have an idea," Maggie said now, interrupting Saint Just's reverie as he sat at her computer, catching up on a few of the news blogs he enjoyed. "Let's go bowling."

He swiveled slowly on the chair and lifted his quizzing

glass to his eye as he looked at her. "Surely you jest," he said, seeing the unholy gleam in her eyes. "Ah, heaven be praised, you do." He let the quizzing glass drop to the end of its black grosgrain ribbon. "I must say, for a moment there, Maggie, you had me worried about you. Wearing shoes worn by hundreds before you? I think not. Perhaps if we were to equip ourselves with all of the necessary paraphernalia, but surely not until then. Whatever possessed you that you even mentioned such an unpalatable idea?"

Maggie shrugged. "I don't know. I'm not sure I even like bowling, to tell you the truth. I think Steve mentioned it when he called a while ago. He went bowling last night with some of his buddies from the station."

Saint Just dangled the quizzing glass between his fingers for a few moments before sliding the thing into the breast pocket of his sports jacket. Once again, he thought, he'd underestimated the good lieutenant. Or overestimated him. "Indeed. I had been wondering about the man's absence. Silly me, I'd assumed he was fully occupied pursuing dangerous criminals, and too busy to visit us."

"Visit *me*," Maggie corrected, "and he is busy. We barely had time to talk when he finally returned my call."

"Ah," Saint Just said, getting to his feet. "You phoned him." *And he lied to you*, he added silently. *How wonderful. The man is digging his own grave, and all I did was to innocently hand him the shovel.*

Maggie rolled her eyes. "Yeah, I *phoned* him. What of it? And why are you back here anyway? Because if you think I'm feeding you again, you're crazy."

"On the contrary, my dear, it is my intention that Sterling and I should feed you. May I suggest Bellini's?"

"You can, but I don't want to go there," she told him, doing a quite good imitation of Mary, Mary, quite contrary. "I want to go to the *Fêtes de Noël*. But you don't have to go, I can go alone."

"No, no, quite the contrary, my dear. I'm sure Sterling and I would be delighted to join you. Precisely what do the citizens of this fair city consider a *Fêtes de Noël*?"

"It's a . . . it's a fête. They set it up in Bryant Park— that's on Forty-second Street, behind the library. It's really nifty. Shops. Lots of them. Terrific striped tents everywhere, and a huge Christmas tree. All sorts of good stuff. I can wander in those shops for hours. *Hours*, Alex. I'm sure we can grab something to eat somewhere on the way to the park. Hot dogs? Yeah, hot dogs would be great. I love hot dogs in the cold, don't you? Oh, right, I forgot—you don't. And, hey, one of those fat pretzels for Sterling? I like the smell of roasting chestnuts, but I don't eat them. The custom is English, I believe—even during Regency times, unlike Christmas trees, which weren't introduced to England until about 1841. Then we'll shop till we drop and you can help me carry it all home. Yeah, it'll be so great to have you guys to carry my packages for me. I'll go tell Sterling. It'll be a hoot."

"A hoot, of course. Sterling would enjoy a hoot, I'm sure. And your enthusiasm seems even to have caught me up in the notion of just such an adventure. Indeed, I can scarcely contain myself."

"Okay, okay, so it isn't Covent Garden at the height of the social season. You're still going, darn it."

"Ready when you are, my dear." Saint Just politely got to his feet, and then watched her as she fairly stomped from the room, leaving the door open to the hallway as she knocked on the door across the hall. He heard her call Sterling's name—cheerful little dickens that she was—and then disappear inside the other condo.

At which time Saint Just lifted the quizzing glass out of his pocket once more and began swinging it back and forth as he cudgeled his brain for a reason behind Maggie's too-chipper-by-half demeanor. She'd certainly gotten the bit between her teeth once she'd begun talking about this fête, hadn't she? Talking nineteen to the dozen, just as if he might interrupt her to suggest some alternate entertainment. *Nifty? A hoot?* And that business about the history of Christmas trees?

Oh, yes, either she had slipped a gear and begun babbling—which he sincerely doubted—or the woman most definitely was up to something.

Or knew something.

Steve Wendell could have spilled the soup. That certainly had to be one consideration.

Except that Maggie didn't know about the rat she'd received, or the note. Having Wendell tell her about the circumstances surrounding Francis Oakes's demise may have upset her, but there was no way she could possibly connect Oakes's death with herself.

Besides, if she did know that he had asked Wendell for information she would not be smiling at him, be acting in the least cheerful, or even coy. She would have greeted him at the door with her Irish up and accusations that would have been, at the bottom of it, rather well justified.

But she hadn't. She'd been determinedly smiling ever since he'd come back from his quick meeting with Wendell, never once asking him why he'd planted himself in her condo, with what had to appear to be no intention of ever vacating it again.

Ergo, Saint Just decided, the woman knew nothing. Well, almost nothing. She knew that he and Sterling were suddenly sticking to her like a mustard plaster. Sterling, bless him, was not known for his powers of discretion or his ability to hold tight to a secret, even if all Sterling knew was that Saint Just wanted Maggie watched.

Which meant, Saint Just concluded, that Maggie was about to punish him and then, being Maggie, find some way to slip from his grasp while they were at this Bryant Park she'd mentioned. Mentioned? No. Thought about. Considered. Decided upon as the best place for both her punishment and her revenge.

The woman was a menace.

How he adored her!

"We're back, and we've got company. She was just coming off the elevator," Maggie said, skipping back into the living room, too cheerful by half. "Did I forget to tell you that Bernie said she'd love to go with us?"

"Wrong, twinkle-toes," Bernice Toland-James corrected, brushing at the sleeve of her full-length sable coat (the one she had two years previously protected from a splash of red paint by pulling out her stun gun and doing a little *proactive protesting* of her own). "I said that if I have no other alternative, I might as well go, satisfy the inner masochist in me or something. And since the alternative was to have dinner with an overzealous agent *and* pick up the tab—and do both while sober—I suppose a visit to Bryant Park is doable." She pulled her stun gun from a pocket of the sable. "At least I'm dressed for it."

"Bernie, there are people, very serious people, who object to other people wearing fur," Maggie said. She was one of them, but at the same time she objected to fur, she also objected to destroying private property in order to make one's point.

"I know that, Mags," Bernie said, sliding the stun gun back into her pocket. "But as I tell everyone, it was already dead when I found it."

"Right. Fifth Avenue roadkill sable. Happens all the time."

Sterling appeared in the doorway, already buttoned

up to his chin in his brown corduroy jacket, his beanie hat on his head. "Saint Just, your cane," he said, handing over the gold-topped sword cane and accepting his friend's thanks.

"You'll need a topcoat, Alex," Bernie told him. "It's cold as hell out there."

"But, Bernie," Sterling questioned, frowning. "Hell would be hot, correct? Oh, wait, that's one of those things you people say, but don't mean the way you say them, isn't it?"

"He's very literal, Bernie, remember? Don't confuse him," Maggie whispered as she stepped past her friend, slipping her arms into a navy peacoat she'd had for five years and still loved dearly. "Damn," she said, looking down at the front of the jacket as she began to button it. "Napoleon slept on it again. Look at this—it's covered in hair, and I don't have a single damn idea what I did with my lint brush. Wellington probably ate it."

"Too bad," Bernie told her. "That much white fur could get you your own can of red paint."

"Funny," Maggie groused, pulling off the coat. "Now I have to find something else. I'll be right back."

"That will take a while," Bernie told Saint Just, who was just slipping into the black cashmere topcoat Sterling had fetched for him, along with a pair of black leather gloves and an approximately eight-foot-long, thin white silk scarf Saint Just wrapped twice around his throat. "She only owns one winter coat. I know how much money she makes. I sign the checks. She still thinks it's all going to disappear one day and she'll be back to tomato soup and peanut butter sandwiches. Plus, that old coat is warm and comfortable, or so she tells me—not to mention that she has all the fashion sense of a twelve-year-old. Make the woman buy a new coat, Alex. A *grown-up* coat. Please!"

"But not fur," Saint Just said, pulling on his gloves. "I'll see to it. Bernice? Have you heard anything else about the sad demise of that Oakes fellow?"

"Me? No, nothing. What did you learn? Is there a story there, one I can put out as I reissue his books?"

"I'm afraid I really know very little," Saint Just told her. "Although I have been giving the matter considerable thought. He committed suicide, surely, or else we would have read more about the death in the newspapers, correct? But what prompted the man to take his own life? It's an intriguing question, don't you think?"

"No, not really, at least not enough to warrant reissuing his books. I'm sorry for him, but he's dead. Maybe he just found out he had some terrible disease. Maybe he was being evicted. Maybe he got a depressing fan letter," she said, shrugging. "Hell, who am I kidding? The man hadn't written a word in years, and what he did write was a long time ago. Who'd be sending him fan mail, good or bad?"

"Okay, I'm ready."

Saint Just had been about to ask Bernice a question concerning fan letters, but it went completely out of his head when he turned to see Maggie reenter the living room.

"My, aren't we . . . original," he drawled as Maggie stomped her feet into a pair of high brown leather boots.

And the boots were fine. So were the dark brown slacks she'd tucked inside those boots.

It was from there on up that things became a tad . . . dicey.

"What?" Maggie said, spreading her arms as wide as the several layers of clothing she wore would allow. "It's a sweatshirt."

"It's several sweatshirts," Bernie corrected, circling her friend. "Which one has the hoodie? I can't tell. But you might want to reconsider wearing the white one on top. You look like a Michelin tire commercial."

"It's the biggest sweatshirt I have, so it has to go on top," Maggie argued, struggling to pull up the hood of one of the other sweatshirts—the red one. "We're not going to a fashion show."

"And aren't we fortunate for that small mercy," Saint Just said, thinking Maggie looked fairly adorable. Round, but adorable.

Maggie finally looked at him. "Oh, great. Mr. *GQ*. How does it always end up this way? You looking so put together, me looking so . . . so—"

"Thrown together?" Saint Just suggested. "Ah, well, there's always a consolation, isn't there? It will be decidedly difficult to lose you in the crowd."

Maggie's eyes narrowed dangerously. "I'll find the damn lint brush," she said, stomping back the way she'd come.

"How'd you do that?" Bernice asked curiously. "I would have ragged at her and she still would have gone out like that. You say two words, and she goes off to change."

"It's all in knowing which few words to say, Bernice. Maggie and I . . . we understand each other. Even when we wish we didn't."

Chapter Seven

"We could have walked," Maggie said as she stepped into the warm, plush confines of Bernice's limousine, one of the few possessions of her ex-husband she'd refused to part with, even before she'd discovered that dead husbands often resulted in hefty inheritances. "It's mostly short blocks."

"Except for the long ones," Bernie pointed out, folding her sable tightly around here. "Besides, I'm not exactly dressed for walking."

"You mean your heels."

"No, I mean the sable. You own a coat like this one, Maggie, and there are responsibilities that come along with it. One of them is this limousine. Alex, are you comfortable?"

"Extremely, my dear, thank you," Alex said, completely in his element as the black Mercedes sliced through the theater traffic and beyond.

"Sure," Maggie groused, slipping down onto her spine and plopping her booted feet on the facing seat, directly between Alex and Sterling. "He was born for this, weren't you *just*, Alex?"

"You know, Maggie, anyone would think this small sojourn wasn't your idea," he said, smiling at her through the dark interior.

"Bite me," she said, but quietly, because what had once been an insult now seemed to be more of an invitation he was willing to accept. "Look at that, we're here already. And no hot dogs, in case nobody's noticed. I'm starving."

"Would you relax? There's bound to be something to eat," Bernie said as the limousine slid to a halt in the middle of traffic. "Come on, kiddies, pile out before that nice policeman over there decides to give us a ticket. I'm pretty sure I've already hit my quota for the month."

"We're barely into December, Bernie," Maggie said, following her out, and pretending not to notice Alex's hand graze her backside, the louse. "And since when is there a monthly quota?"

"I have no idea. But it got you moving, didn't it? Now, where to first?"

Maggie looked around at the sea of people and the many green and white–striped tents and, damn, the ice rink. "I forgot about the ice rink," she said, sure Alex would have hated it—those rented skates, like rented bowling shoes. They'd be an insult to his sensibilities.

The thing was, she had her own skates, and was probably just as queasy about wearing rentals.

"Oh, look at them," Sterling said, standing beside her, his expression rapt as he watched the skaters glide by. "It's like being on my scooter—without the scooter. I should dearly love to try that, Maggie. I think I should be quite good at it."

"Then we'll purchase skates tomorrow, Sterling," Alex assured him as Maggie spied a hot dog cart and took off without waiting for anyone else, sure that Alex, at least, would follow. She'd give him the slip sooner or later, but for now, the aroma of hot dogs seemed more important.

"This reminds me very much of Green Park in the winter," Alex said as they strolled the area after consuming their dinner, Bernie trailing behind, still trying to wipe a blob of mustard from her sable. "I hope it's ruined," a red-nosed man shivering in a thin jacket told her when he saw her, upon which Bernie, without missing a beat, suggested the man perform a feat not especially easy for anyone who was not double-jointed.

"I love New York," Maggie said with a grin, waiting for Bernie to catch up. "Everyone's so friendly."

"Yeah, yeah, yeah," Bernie said, tucking a wad of used paper napkins into her pocket. "Are we done having fun yet, or do we have to do something else before I can call José and have him drive us somewhere warm? Not that I can have a hot buttered rum, can I? I love hot buttered rum. Mostly the rum. Hey, Maggie, did I tell you about this idea I've had? A drinking book."

Maggie smiled in sympathy for her recently dried-out friend. "Who would read a book about drinking, Bernie?" she asked as they entered the first tent after Alex, who was already inspecting a shelf filled with handblown glass.

"I don't know. I would. The history, the lore, all that good stuff—you know, a highly illustrated coffee-table book. Or, in this case, a bar book. I've been rounding up quotes that could be scattered through the book. Observations on drinking, you know? Let me run one by you, from Jackie Gleason. Remember him? Anyway, he said, 'Drink removes warts and pimples. Not from me. But from those I look at.' Isn't that fabulous—and so true."

"I don't know. It's also sort of insulting. Do I have warts and pimples now?"

"Not until tonight, no. Here, I'll give you another

one. 'The trouble with the world is that it's always one drink behind.' That was Humphrey Bogart."

"Yes, I thought I recognized the imitation. I think I'd rather buy the furniture line someone's pushing in his name. What else have you got?"

Bernie picked up a handblown decanter, and then put it down again. "No use for that, unless I fill it with pretty Kool-Aid. Okay, Bette Midler. 'I try not to drink too much because when I'm drunk, I bite.'"

Maggie looked over at Alex, who was in the process of purchasing a tall glass sculpture that might have been a dolphin. Or a semicolon. "I don't like that one. No mention of biting, okay?"

"John Wayne. 'I never trust a man that doesn't drink.'"

"Gosh, I don't know. Half your readers might not even remember John Wayne, and the ones who do wouldn't like reading that he said that. Honestly, Bernie, I think you should give it up."

"One last one. And remember, they wouldn't be all that's in the book, but just sort of sprinkled through it. Elizabeth Taylor. 'I had a hollow leg. I could drink everyone under the table and not get drunk. My capacity was terrifying.'"

Maggie turned to look at Bernie. "Okay, now that one's interesting. Elizabeth Taylor really said that?"

"I found the quote."

"Did you *learn* anything from it, hon? From any of them? I mean, I'm mentally substituting smoking here, for drinking, and it's making me uncomfortable. But, hey, you're the publisher."

"Hey, good for you, you finally got the point," Bernie said, pulling her sable more snugly around herself. "It would be an exorcism, Maggie. Get that drink out of my life by writing about it."

"Whoa. *You'd* do the writing?"

"Why not? I'd consider it a part of my rehabilitation.

Plus, if I'm right—and I usually am—there's every reason to believe it would sell well. Not great, but at least fifteen thousand copies in hardback. A perfect conversation piece for the suburban whoopee room, or whatever the soccer mom and dad crowd call their home bars these days."

"Whoopee room? Bernie, how old are you, anyway?" Maggie laughed and shook her head. "Whoopee room. That's just pitiful. But I'm betting you can pull it off, if anyone can. So I say go for it."

"Oh, goody, I have your permission," Bernie gushed theatrically. "I was so worried."

"Oops," Maggie said, wincing. "I'm being a pain in the neck, aren't I? I think I need to do some serious shopping or something. Exercise the old charge card. Christmas shopping always puts me in a good mood."

"That sounds good to me. But not glass, not if you're looking for something for your beloved editor's stocking. Let's see what's in the next tent."

Alex came back to them, carrying his purchase in a clear plastic shopping bag. "What a delightful place. I'm so glad you suggested this, Maggie. Shall we move on?"

"Sure, why not," she said, wondering how she could have misread him this way. She was sure he'd hate it here. The cold, the crowds, all of it. "Oh, hey, look. Over there. Isn't that J.P. Boxer?"

"No, it can't be," Bernie said, stepping behind Alex as she dropped back into her fractured Humphrey Bogart impersonation. "Of all the gin joints in all the world—hide me, big boy."

"What's the matter, Bernie?" Maggie asked, watching as J.P. Boxer spied them, waved, and began walking toward them. The lawyer who had represented Bernie that fall, when she'd been suspected of murder—a fairly reasonable assumption, as Bernie had awakened after an alcoholic blackout to find a very dead man in her bed—was an imposing figure. Very tall, rather large, she was dressed in one of her trademark running suits. This one was berry red, and her high-top sneakers matched perfectly.

"She wants me to publish her book instead of taking any payment for her services, that's what's wrong. I've been ducking her for weeks."

"Have you read the book?"

"God, no," Bernie said with a toss of her head. "Why would I do that? I already know it's horrible. Lawyers can't write."

"Yeah. Not Grisham, not Scottoline, not—"

"*This* lawyer can't write. It would be different if she'd told me she'd written a legal thriller. Then I might be interested. But it's science fiction. Science fiction, Mags. And if I read it, and reject it, she'll want to know why and I don't want to deal with it, okay? I hate to say it, but the woman terrifies me." Bernie stepped out from behind Alex's back and smiled her professional smile. "Hey, J.P., gosh, it's good to see you. What are you doing here?"

The large woman said hello to everyone, including Maggie, who she insisted upon calling Little Mary Sunshine—which wasn't a compliment. "Same thing you're doing, Reds, I suppose. Soaking up Christmas spirit. Did you read the manuscript yet?"

"Well, um, *actually*, I've been really busy. You know, still cleaning up loose ends, taking the reins. . . ."

Maggie decided to rescue her friend before she dug a hole none of them would get out of without an extension ladder. This was so unlike Bernie, who could probably stare down a charging rhino. But she turned to marshmallow when it came to J.P. Boxer. "She gave it to me to read, J.P., because she's so busy. It's my fault I haven't gotten to it yet. I've been out of the country," she ended, thinking, wow, that sounds impressive. *Out of the country*.

"*You're* reading it, girlfriend?" J.P. repeated, verbally promoting Maggie from naive little girl to girlfriend. "I suppose that's okay. I've picked up a couple of your Saint Just novels, you know, gave them the once-over. Not too shabby, actually."

"Gee, thanks, I can die happy now," Maggie muttered quietly through a rather painful smile. What had she gotten herself into? And all because she'd been snarky with Bernie about her booze book and figured she owed her a favor. "Well, we've got lots to see, so we'll be on our way. Have a great holiday, J.P., and a marvelous New—"

"I'll be over tomorrow," the lawyer interrupted with all the delicacy of a charging rhino. "To hear how you liked the manuscript. Say around three?"

Oh, great. Maggie looked around for help. Now who was going to save *her*? "I . . . um, that is . . . I—"

"What Maggie's trying to say," Alex broke in smoothly, "is that we'd be delighted to see you, J.P., but we'll be out of town for the weekend. Most unfortunate. Tuesday, however, would be fine. Wouldn't it, Maggie?"

"You picked a hell of a time to open your mouth, after standing there like a statue for five minutes. And I was looking at you so you'd rescue me, not set up a playdate with J.P. Cripes. You couldn't have said after Christmas? After the New Year?" Maggie told Alex after J.P. had checked her date book and decided she'd deign to visit them at one o'clock on Tuesday and then walked away before Maggie could untangle her tongue to disagree. "How am I supposed to read her manuscript before Tuesday? I don't even have the darn thing, for crying out loud."

"I'll have it messengered over first thing tomorrow morning," Bernie said helpfully, hanging on Alex's arm as they continued their stroll and Maggie continued her stomp. "You're such a good friend, Maggie. I owe you one. Oh, and let her down easy, all right? I don't want to have her mad, and overcharging me."

"I hope she sends you a bill for a million dollars," Maggie said in all sincerity. "How does this happen? We go out for a nice evening. A hot dog, some shopping—and *bam*. Let's all sock it to Maggie."

"Now, now, my dear. As I recall, you did volunteer," Alex soothed, not bothering to hide his smile. "And one never knows when one will require the services of an attorney, does one? With that in mind, as Bernice suggested—be kind."

"She's a criminal attorney, Alex. Why would I need her, if that's what you're saying?"

"Yes, exactly. One never knows, does one?"

"One never knows, does one," Maggie singsonged, making a face at him. "I'm . . . I have to find a ladies room."

And she was off before anyone could follow her. It wasn't a subtle exit, but she really needed to put some space between herself and her friends. Between herself and Alex.

He made her so *mad*. And he did it deliberately, she was sure of it. She knew what he was doing. He was paying her back for bringing him here, for planning to desert him here, for—wait a minute. How would he know that?

He'd hinted, back at the condo. Saying that business about not being able to lose her in the crowd. But that had only been something he'd said to goad her into changing, that's all. He couldn't *know*, could he?

"Of course he does," she told herself as she scooted past a couple pushing a stroller and ducked behind one of the striped tents and into the dark. "I know he's sticking to me, and he knows I know and want to get away from him because I know—ah, hell, I don't know *any-thing*."

"Got a dollar, lady? Betcha got more'an a dollar, huh?"

"Ah, cripes, this just keeps getting better and better," Maggie said on a groan, turning around to see a fairly tall, cadaverous man who'd come up directly behind her. "No—no, this isn't going to happen. You're not going to try to rob me, Alex is not going to come out of nowhere to rescue me, flourishing that damn sword cane of his and playing the hero. Not this time. I'm sick and tired of playing Penelope Tied to the Railroad Tracks, you hear me, buster? Now get the hell out of here before I do something you're going to regret."

The bum looked at her purse, which she'd raised over her head as if ready to bash it into his skull, and backed up two steps. "Jeez, lady, I just wanted a dollar. Don't go all premenstrual on me."

"And you're two seconds from being pre-concussed. *Move it!*"

"Wait a moment, sir, please. Don't rush off," she heard Alex say from behind her, and she whirled about in a fury, just to have him neatly remove the purse from her grip. "I do believe the lady could be overreacting." He tucked his package under his arm, and then fished in his pocket and came out with a twenty-dollar bill. "Here you go, my good man. Have a nice holiday."

"You did that on purpose, damn it," she told him as she grabbed back her purse and they both watched the bum shuffle off. "I was handling it. Now all of a sudden I'm Scrooge and you're Santa Claus. Why does stuff like this always happen to me? Why does—oh, hell." She stepped closer and allowed her forehead to drop against his strong chest. "I'm such a mess. Nothing ever goes right for me. I need a cigarette. I need to lose ten pounds. Eight, I mean eight. I've got a *kick me* sign on me, Alex, and I'm the only one who can't see it. My clothes are too tight, J.P. is going to sit on me on Tuesday, you can just bet on that one. You keep kissing me, my dad has a chippie. I don't want to go home for Christmas, even in my dreams. And the worst, the very worst. I can't believe that you . . . that you've . . . oh, God, I'm falling apart. I nearly attacked that man! And my mother says I'm not sensitive? I should probably be on some kind of medication, huh?"

"*Shhh*, sweetings, it's all right," Alex said, stroking her back. "Sterling told me what he said to you this afternoon while I was gone. I understand why you're a trifle out of sorts. It must have come as something of a shock."

"Puberty," Maggie muttered into his coat, at last giving in to what had been upsetting her ever since she'd heard the word. "You've been around since puberty. I didn't know, you didn't tell me." She looked up into his face. His handsome face. The face she'd made. The man she'd made. The perfect hero she'd somehow conjured, the vision she'd nurtured, fed, molded and remolded until he'd been just that—perfect for her. Her perfect hero. And here he was with her, the imperfect heroine. "Why didn't you tell me?"

"Would you have believed me?"

"You're standing here, aren't you? I believe that. It hasn't been easy, but I believe it. Oh, Alex, what am I going to do with you?"

His smile nearly undid her. "You could enjoy me, I suppose."

She touched a gloved hand to his cheek. "I suppose. But you're not perfect, you know. I thought you were, but you're not. You're terrific as a Regency hero, but you're arrogant, and sometimes sarcastic, and a bit of a snob—and people keep getting murdered around you. You have noticed that, haven't you?"

"I solve crimes, Maggie. I save the heroine. I right wrongs. It's what heroes do."

"Yeah, sure," she said, pulling away from him before she could do something dumb, like let him kiss her. Like kissing him back. "I just didn't know I was fantasizing about Superman with a quizzing glass and sword cane. That's pretty embarrassing."

"Got more where that come from, mister? We bet you do."

Maggie felt Alex's arm tighten around her for an instant, and then she was semi-flying through the air, saved from a tumble into the snow only by falling into a low, snow-covered evergreen, which wasn't much better, actually.

By the time she'd caught her breath and was able to lever herself upright enough to see what was going on, two dark shapes were sprawled in the snow and a third was upright, but not looking too good as Alex pressed the tip of his unsheathed sword cane to the man's Adam's apple. "Alex, don't!"

"I wouldn't think of it, my dear. Unless the gentleman moves, that is. You aren't going to sneeze, are you, my good fellow? That would probably be most unfortunate for you. Now, if you promise to remain very, very still, I will lower my weapon. Agreed?"

The "gentleman" made some rather strangled sounds that must have indicated his agreement, for Alex lowered the sword cane, using it to indicate the two groaning shapes on the snow. "So very obedient. What an intelligent felon you are. However, if I might suggest that you assist your cronies to their feet and then take yourselves off before I lose this most astonishingly and laudable grip on my usual good humor?"

Maggie recognized the fairly snazzy, sophisticated but sarcastic line, of course. She'd written it for the Viscount Saint Just about three books ago. The trio of hapless muggers took off at a run and Alex neatly slid the thin sword back inside the cane before assisting her to her feet. "Oh, Alex. You just can't help yourself, can you?"

"I suppose not," he said, and then bent to retrieve his package. Naturally, the vase was still intact, as he'd aimed it at a pile of still soft, untouched snow—which was very different from where he'd aimed *her*. She was just about to point that out to him when she heard a noise behind her and tensed, only to relax when she heard Sterling's voice.

"Saint Just, there you are! Oh, and Maggie, too. I was so worried we might have lost her and you wouldn't have liked that above half would you." Sterling shut his mouth, grimacing, then looked imploringly at Saint Just. "I'm sorry. Spilled the broth there, didn't I?"

Maggie's sympathy for her creation—along with a variety of rather intriguing feelings she would examine later—disappeared with Sterling's words. "Yeah, Alex, you wouldn't have liked that above half, would you? Gotta keep her in sight at all times, right? *Why*, Alex? Hmmm?"

Alex tucked the vase under his arm once more, leaving both hands free to adjust Maggie's collar. "The woman is nearly assaulted by low-life felons, and she dares ask such a question?"

"I wasn't in danger of being assaulted by low-life felons in my apartment all day," she pointed out as the three of them picked their way back to the path, lights, and the crush of people stepping around Bernie, who stood blocking the middle of the path, a large something-or-other wrapped in brown paper propped against her, nearly toppling her. "But I'll get back to you on that. What the hell is Bernie holding up? It's bigger than she is."

"A portrait of her ancestors, actually," Sterling told

her, taking charge of the package that must be four feet wide and six feet high. "Isn't it exciting that she found them? Right back there, in that tent."

"Yeah, exciting," Maggie said as José ran up to them, clearly summoned by cell phone, and assisted Sterling in carrying the portrait to the limousine, Alex parting the way for them, Bernie and Maggie following in their wake. "You were adopted, right, Bernie?"

"Yes, sweetie. And now I've adopted ancestors. They'll look great over the fireplace, don't you think? Well, you haven't seen them yet, but believe me, they'll be perfect. I think there's even a dog. I'm going to name them all. Even the dog. Especially the dog."

"Bernie, honey, you have to stop this," Maggie said, broaching a subject she had been hoping to avoid. "You're trading one addiction for another."

"I am not. What do you mean?"

"I mean, you've become a buyaholic."

"Shopaholic, Maggie. There's no such thing as a buyaholic."

"There is now. Some people shop. You buy. *Everything*. I've been watching, ever since you got back from the . . . from where you went. Shoes, clothes, jewelry—Cuisinarts, for crying out loud, and you don't cook. You're substituting, Bernie, the way I've been substituting food for nicotine, and we both have to stop. But this?" she said, gesturing toward the large wrapped portrait. "I didn't even know they sold stuff like this here."

"They don't. The portrait was part of a display, to showcase some gallery. But I had to have it immediately, Maggie, I just did. Those people spoke to me, I swear it. So I whipped out my American Express, and now they're mine."

"This gallery doesn't deliver?"

"Of course it does, but I had to have it now. I can't explain it."

"I can. It's because you're a buyaholic," Maggie said, nailing home her point.

"Warts and pimples, Maggie. I'm seeing warts and pimples. Now, come on, I can't buy myself a Christmas present?"

"Ancestors. You're buying ancestors for yourself for Christmas." When Bernie made a face, Maggie threw up her hands, giving in. "Okay, okay. Just think about what I said."

"Don't I always? You won't mind waiting with me until the van José ordered shows up? It's either that or trying to find a cab in this mess, and good luck with that. While we wait, you can tell me why you're covered in snow."

Maggie was beginning to feel nostalgic for jolly old England and being marooned with a murderer. "I fell," she said dully, then looked at Alex, who dared to wink at her, sending her heart rate into overdrive. It was only a matter of time now, and they both knew it. Yes, she'd fallen, and she was still falling, and she might as well just give up and let it happen. Maggie down the rabbit hole . . .

Chapter Eight

Tagging along with Bernie to the Hamptons for the weekend had proved an excellent way to keep tabs on Maggie, keep her within his sight at all times, but did little to improve her mood, as she had barely spoken to Saint Just, obstinately staying in her room to read J.P. Boxer's manuscript (which she adamantly refused to talk about), and to do some research on the Web about what she'd informed him had become known as the War of 1812 between England and America.

She'd been thinking, or so she'd said, of having Saint Just become involved in exposing some sort of scandal and murder having to do with the Crown's dealings with American Indians, and promises made and broken, and—well, she'd been rather vague, but Saint Just was sure she'd abandon the idea by the time they returned to Manhattan, so he didn't press her. Only if she came up with a title would he begin to pay attention, for then he would know she was serious.

There simply were times when a gentleman does not push, and this, definitely, was one of them. Besides, she hadn't been hounding him for the reason he'd been keeping her so close, and since he didn't have an answer for her—at least one he wished to give her—Saint Just was content to spend his own weekend reading books by Michael Connelly, and in deep admiration of the man's clever creation, Harry Bosch. Rough around the edges, Harry was, but definitely intriguing. Although the man seemed to have little luck in his love life, which may, Saint Just was loathe to think, have given the two fictional men something in common, if only that both their creators sometimes delighted in making their creations suffer.

They returned to the city Monday at noon, traipsing into the lobby of the condo building while Socks went off to park Maggie's car in the garage a block away. Paul, who usually worked the night shift on the door, was behind the desk in the lobby, having stopped by to ask Socks to cover for him on Saturday night so he might attend a Christmas party with his girlfriend.

Saint Just and the others knew this because Paul told them so, even though no one had asked why he was there and could not have cared less, if truth be told. Paul was not Socks, not by a long chalk, and had definitely been hiding behind the door when the good Lord had been handing out common sense. In fact, he'd just three weeks previously opened the door to Mrs. Tannenbaum's condo for a "delivery man," and then assisted the miscreant in carrying out the woman's television set and stereo equipment.

Yes, Paul was a treasure.

"Got a package here for you, Ms. Kelly," he said as an afterthought, just as the elevator doors opened.

"Oh, thanks, Paul, I—"

"I'll take that," Saint Just said, neatly relieving the doorman of the package just as Maggie was about to grab it.

"Hey," Maggie said, lunging for the package, "give me that. It's mine. Does it have your name on it? No-o-o. It's got my name on it—I can see my name from here. And Paul said so. *Give*."

"I am not Wellington, Maggie," Saint Just said, taking the package over to one of the couches in the foyer and placing it on the table in front of him, already pulling the tab on the large brown postal bag.

"True. Him I can lock in my bedroom if he doesn't—never mind, I don't want to go there. And cut it out. Don't open that, Alex. I know what it is and—oh, cute. Really cute. Happy now?"

Saint Just returned the clear plastic bag containing something pink and lacy into the padded envelope and handed both to Maggie, feeling somewhat silly, but not about to let her know that. "So sorry. I ordered something in your name, as you already had an account, but this clearly isn't personalized stationery, is it?"

"No, it clearly isn't," Maggie told him, grabbing the package. "It's my free buy-two-get-one-free bra, damn you. And who said you could use my Internet accounts, huh? God. I'm going upstairs. Do yourself a favor and don't follow me!"

"That was unfortunate, wasn't it?" Sterling commented, speaking to Henry, who was happily running on the small wheel in the travel cage Sterling held up at eye level. "But we'll forget we witnessed anything, Henry, as a favor to Saint Just, who must be horribly embarrassed."

Saint Just looked at his friend. "I overreacted, I agree," he admitted. "This can't go on, Sterling, even if the esteemed NYPD is satisfied with a pronouncement of suicide. I'm going to have to tell Maggie about the dead rats."

Sterling quickly lowered Henry's cage to his side. "Please, not in front of the children and all of that. But

I agree, Saint Just. As you still harbor some reservations after speaking with the good lieutenant again, Maggie definitely must be told of your concerns, and of the R-A-T. I must say, I was rather disappointed in your decision to keep everything so very close to your own breast."

"I made a mistake, Sterling, and I freely admit to that mistake. Not with Wendell, but with Maggie," Saint Just said, amazed to hear himself so humble. "At the same time, I cannot rule out the possibility that I am overreacting, seeing bogeymen where there are none. She and I are . . . we're at the moment tussling with something rather disconcerting for both of us, and I didn't want to complicate matters, at least not until I'd done some digging, come up with some clues. Harry Bosch often labors under similar circumstances, you know, and he has always managed to persevere. So shall I."

"But you haven't, have you? Come up with clues, that is."

"No, Sterling, I can truthfully say I have not, especially after delaying my investigation by haring off to the Hamptons in the mistaken notion that I was doing the right thing. Tell you what I'll do, my friend. I'll give myself one more day to arrive at some answers on my own, and then I will tell Maggie everything I have learned."

"She'll forgive you," Sterling told him rather kindly.

Saint Just raised one well-defined eyebrow. Pity? From Sterling? Pity? From *anyone*? He, the intrepid, indomitable, unflappable Viscount Saint Just was being looked upon as an object of *pity*? Well, that tore it, didn't it? Perhaps Maggie was right to keep his fictional self flitting from flower to flower, rather than having him tumble into love. Love seemed to take the edge off a man, make him vulnerable, make him . . . fallible.

"Sterling?" Saint Just asked after a moment. "Would

you mind terribly carrying up my bag as well as yours? I do believe I would like to take a walk."

Sterling was still looking at him as if he might offer his shoulder, friend to friend. "Of course, Saint Just. Go, walk, clear away the cobwebs and all of that. Henry and I will watch over Maggie for you."

How very sweet, how very lowering. "Thank you, Sterling, you're a good friend," Saint Just said, inclining his head in a slight bow, then heading out onto the street, already knowing his destination. He walked confidently, his armor that of his well-tailored clothes, his black cashmere sports coat ample covering on such a crisp, sunny day, his red sweater vest and the whimsical sprig of holly he'd tucked into his buttonhole his tributes to the Christmas season. He also carried with him the gold-tipped sword cane he tucked under his arm, his outfit completed by the jaunty tilt of the wide-brimmed, low-crowned black hat Maggie teased him about but nevertheless admitted looked exactly right on his head.

Yes, he knew precisely where he was headed, and he'd probably put off the meeting much too long as it was.

He was off to see Dr. Robert Lewis Chalfont, known to Maggie and others by the unfortunate appellation of Dr. *Bob*. Maggie had been seeing the psychiatrist for approximately five years, at first to help rid her of her nicotine addiction—the man long had been a sad failure at that—and then to help her work through her unfortunate problem with her family, which Saint Just could have told him was a lost cause, as the problem did not lie with Maggie, but with that family.

Still, Dr. Chalfont had encouraged Maggie to realize there were things she could not change so it was better to learn what he called coping skills. As Maggie's coping skill with her brother, during their recent Thanksgiving visit to New Jersey, had consisted of telling Tate

Kelly "where to get off," Saint Just was fairly sure all Maggie needed was confidence in her own strengths.

She had no idea how very wonderful she was, how very talented, or how very competent. Hadn't that been the reason he'd given Sterling for their appearance on this plane: to help Maggie reach her full potential?

It had only taken one good look at her, one touch of her hand on his, to realize that he'd been lying to Sterling, and to himself. He simply wanted to be in Maggie's life. A part of that life. . . .

Saint Just tipped his hat to a pair of middle-aged ladies who seemed to appreciate his kindness. Yes, he was a kind man. When he wanted to be. Kind enough to wish to thank Maggie for creating him.

Or, as he'd heard someone say with typical American forthrightness, he'd wanted to *jump her bones*.

But laudable or not, he was here now, and evolving, as he persisted in telling Maggie, and he'd progressed far beyond the rather crude notion of simply seducing her. Far beyond.

Saint Just stepped inside the large office building, removed his hat, and made his way to the fourth floor. Once there, he entered a small, unimaginatively decorated anteroom empty of other inhabitants, and used the head of his cane to knock on a door marked *Private*.

He had no worries that Dr. Chalfont would not be there, and immediately available to him. He was, after all, a fictional hero, and fictional heroes rarely had to come back a second time, try again. Now Maggie? She would have been disappointed if she'd hoped to see Chalfont at this precise time, which was rather all right, as Maggie had necessarily grown accustomed if not resigned to frustration, as most people do. Heroes, however, were entirely another matter; their lives ran much more smoothly.

The rather fleshy man who opened the door a few seconds later wore an air of distraction and a woefully unfortunate choice of brown tweed jacket and blue slacks. "Yes? I'm sorry, but I'm afraid I don't take walk-in patients."

"I am Saint Just," Saint Just said, giving his name its French inflection—*Saint Juste*—then brushing past the man and into the good doctor's elaborate inner sanctum, which was decorated, in his opinion, in *conséquence fausse*.

Dr. Chalfont closed the door. "Are you now?" he asked in an annoyingly professional tone, walking across the deep burgundy carpet and lowering his bulk into a large leather chair. "Margaret's Saint Just?" he asked, using the American inflection. "Indeed."

"Yes. *Indeed*," Saint Just drawled, leisurely strolling about the office, employing the tip of his cane to align the top magazine with the others in a rather tall stack on one of the tables. "I thought it was time we two met." He turned, struck a pose of the sort he would hold himself to when gracing his hostess's Regency drawing room, and rather looked down his nose at the psychiatrist. "Met, sir, and had ourselves a small chat. To be perfectly honest, if descending into amazingly applicable cant, I've come to pick your brain if I might."

"Indeed?" Chalfont repeated. "Cant? Is that the same as slang, Saint Just? English for slang? That is, you're actually Alexander Blakely, Margaret's distant English cousin, correct? Not *really* Saint Just."

"Is that what you think?" Saint Just countered silkily, his smile deliberately nonthreatening. He had been aware of Dr. Chalfont during the time he'd resided solely in Maggie's head, but he hadn't actually been out in the world until he'd poofed, as Maggie called it, out of her head and into that world. Curiosity had prompted

him to read rather extensively on this thing called psycho-
analysis, and answering a question with a question had
been a part of what he'd learned. And how nice to turn
the tables on the good doctor. "Please, tell me about that,
how you came to that conclusion, that is. Take your time."

"You're an amusing man." Dr. Chalfont adjusted his
glasses on his nose. "I think, Mr. Blakely, that you may
possibly have allowed yourself to rather, well, *merge*
your personality with that of Maggie's famous Viscount
Saint Just, yes? Interesting. Really. And not as uncom-
mon as you might think." He swiveled to face his desk
and began paging through his appointment book. "I
happen to have an opening as of this morning—a full
hour free every Thursday afternoon. That should work
nicely for us, Mr. Saint Just. Let me just pencil you in?"

"I don't believe it will be necessary for us to meet
again, thank you," Saint Just said, seating himself in
the chair beside the large desk and placing his cane
against the corner. "I am here on a hypothetical."

Dr. Chalfont smiled knowingly, and then quickly
covered his mouth as he faked a cough. "I see. You're
here for a *friend*?"

"If that makes you more comfortable, certainly—
I'm here on behalf of a friend," Saint Just said, finger-
ing a brass paperweight in the shape of a fat goldfish.
"This hypothetical, if you please? Would you consider,
for instance, a person who sends a vaguely threatening
letter to be a real danger to, as you say, my *friend*?"

Dr. Chalfont punched at the bridge of his glasses
once more. "What sort of threatening letter? You'll have
to elaborate."

"Certainly. A badly composed poem containing a
vague threat, tucked up with the badly decomposing
body of a rat. Would you consider that to be a warning
of worse to come, or the onetime communication from,

shall we say, a disgruntled admirer, so that this friend should not overreact to the incident, as some might unfortunately do? In your educated opinion."

"Margaret? Someone's sent something like that to Margaret?"

"Tut-tut. Doctor, please, we're dealing in a hypothetical, remember?"

The good doctor leaned back in his chair and steepled his fingers beneath his chin. "If you insist. Very well, Alex—may I call you Alex, or do you insist on Saint Just?"

"I am amenable either way. Now, please, come, come—should my hypothetical be concerned, or be comforted with the notion that barking dogs rarely bite?"

"That's difficult to say. Nearly impossible, I'm afraid. Think of recent history. John Lennon, for example. There, it was the silent dog that barked, wasn't it? But there are other stalkers, other aberrations, most obviously the sort that targets an estranged spouse or girlfriend—for the sake of argument, we'll assume this person is male. Then we can see escalating violence, increased threats or avowals of undying love and, finally, the intent to actually kill. But that's not limited to spurned admirers, or to those who might feel betrayed or angered by the person they're stalking. There are many variations of what is basically the same theme— you did me wrong, and now you're going to pay for it. If I could—is it perhaps possible for you to show me a copy of this poem?"

"There's no need, as I have committed it to memory." Saint Just recited the few lines, then inclined his head to the doctor, indicating that it was once again his turn to speak, hopefully constructively.

Dr. Chalfont scribbled the lines on a yellow tablet. "You're right, that is fairly terrible. Perhaps to call special attention to the veiled threat at the end? And the rat? Perhaps a sort of . . . visual aid? Something disgusting enough to bring the point home, that point being that Mar—that is, that your hypothetical is on a par with a rat. Hmmm, rat. There are so many connotations, you know."

"Yes, I've delved into that myself," Saint Just said. "To rat one out—to inform on someone, betray someone's trust, or desert someone. Rats carry disease, there's that, and the association with plague, destruction, death. There is something else. The note was signed, but I can't make head nor tails of the why of calling oneself Nevus."

"A mole? This person calls himself a mole?"

"A congenital pigmented area of the skin, yes. A birthmark. It is puzzling. But the primary question remains—how real is the potential for danger, for an escalation of, shall we say—violence?"

"Truthfully? I'd be concerned," Dr. Chalfont told him, folding his hands on top of the yellow pad. "Mostly, I'd be concerned that a gentleman who has been known to be rather flamboyant—several recent incidents come to mind, all of them recorded for television news, as I recall—might think to take it upon himself to handle something like this on his own, without calling in the authorities. I'd be concerned that a man who seems to associate himself rather closely with a fictional hero might begin to believe himself a hero. That wouldn't be the case, would it? For Margaret's sake, I sincerely hope not."

Saint Just smiled and got to his feet. "Doctor, it has been a pleasure, and I thank you. But now I must be going, as I have another visit to make yet this afternoon. Good day."

"Wait!" The doctor got quickly to his feet. "Does she know?"

Saint Just picked up his cane, tucked it under his arm. "She will, I can promise you that. I was already fairly confident of my own conclusions, but do appreciate your professional input. Again, sir, good day."

"And Thursday?"

"Completely unnecessary. I know who I am, Doctor. That's never been the problem. It is who or what we may become that often is outside our control. The trick, I believe, is to know that, and even to embrace that uncertainty."

"Yes, but—"

Saint Just closed the door behind him and headed for the street once more, using his cane to hail a cab, as he was anxious to move on to his second stop, the apartment of one recently deceased Francis Oakes.

It was a long cab ride to Oakes's place of residence on West 133rd Street, a depressingly brown building that housed the man's attic-level apartment. The total lack of a doorman or any sort of security, however, made it a simple matter for Saint Just to climb the several flights and employ a credit card to pop the flimsy lock, and within moments he was inside the apartment.

He checked the door once he was inside, and saw that Francis Oakes had not one but four different security locks on the inside of the door. Once inside, with the bolts turned, the man would have been totally secure, right up until the moment he was convinced to open the door to the person who might, possibly, have been his killer.

At least Saint Just's search wouldn't take too long, as the apartment consisted of one reasonably sized room, with a most pitiful excuse for a bathroom tucked in under the eaves. Either Oakes had not been a very tall man, or he had showered on his knees.

There wasn't much in the way of furniture, but there were many, many books; stacked on the floor, piled up on the windowsill, shelved in makeshift bookcases. With his latex gloves in place and using the tip of his cane as he poked and probed, Saint Just was careful to protect himself from the fingerprint dust that seemed to be on every surface. At least someone had thought to make some sort of an investigation of the man's demise—and that might prove helpful at some point.

He found Oakes's four titles, all in paperbacks with particularly lurid covers, sitting by themselves on one shelf: *An Axman Cometh, Killing All The Way, Twice Upon A Crime,* and *King Konked.* Saint Just was not impressed. He did, however, remove the books from the shelf, planning to take them with him, for what reason he did not yet know.

It was only after he'd finished with the rest of the room that Saint Just stood at the scarred oak table in the very center of it and looked up at the open beamed, peaked ceiling. And there it was, what was left of the thick rope Oakes had used to hang himself; the medical examiner must have simply sliced through the rope to cut down the body, then left the remainder knotted to the thick beam.

Saint Just mentally reviewed Oakes's actions. Scrape marks on the bare wood floor, and a small rug caught and out of place as it fairly hugged one of the four legs, told him that Oakes had moved the table from its usual place in front of the window in order to use it to climb up and secure the rope.

After that, it would be a simple matter of fastening the noose about his neck and then stepping off the edge of the desk. Crude, but effective.

And all because someone had sent the man a dead rat and some bad poetry?

At least that's what Wendell had told him had been the conclusion of the investigators sent to survey the scene.

The reaction had seemed overly dramatic to something so distasteful but basically no more than malicious. However, now, looking at the man's life as it was represented by this apartment, perhaps the nudge had been all that had been needed to send the man over the edge . . . literally.

In any case, Oakes's death would not in itself ring any alarm bells in the heads of the detectives of the NYPD, of that Saint Just was certain. There was nothing Saint Just could see that would make even him suspect murder rather than suicide.

It was the coincidence of it, that Maggie had also received a dead rat in the mail, which still worried him.

"Who are you? What are you doing here?"

Saint Just turned about to see an unprepossessing young man who looked in need of both a good meal and a good night's sleep—and most definitely a good tailor—standing just inside the room, his hand still on the doorknob. "My goodness, people actually say things like that? You sound very much like some poor soul straight out of an inferior script, my friend. But, to answer your questions, I am a totally harmless fellow, here only to satisfy my curiosity. And you?"

"Jeremy Bickel. Your curiosity about what? Did you know Francis, Mr.—?"

Once again, Saint Just danced around giving the young man his name. "Alas, Jeremy, I'm sorry to say that I was denied that pleasure. I am, however, a friend of one of his acquaintances, a fellow author."

"So?"

Saint Just smiled. "This friend was upset to hear of Mr. Oakes's untimely demise, leaving me with the sad chore of clarifying a few things, a few questions this friend had about the man." He employed a flourish of his cane to indicate his surroundings. "Mr. Oakes was not having an easy time of it, was he?"

Jeremy shook his head. "Francis . . . Francis was unhappy, yes. He wanted so badly to be a success."

"Discouraged, was he?"

"You could say that. He wasn't a lot of laughs, you know?"

Saint Just returned to his inspection of the heavy oak table. "Was he a physically imposing gentleman? This is a heavy table."

"Francis? No. He was . . . well, maybe this will help. Two years ago some airhead coed from CUNY came up to him on the street, asking for his autograph. Francis was so excited, figuring she'd read his books, you know? But when he handed back the paper she'd asked him to sign, she threw it on the ground, saying he was nobody. You see, she'd thought he was Woody Allen."

"Yes, I do see, thank you. You've given me a good picture of both the man and his circumstances," Saint Just said, conjuring a mental picture of the slightly-built director. Moving this large table would have presented a challenge for a man built like Francis Oakes, but not to a determined man. "That had to have been discouraging."

"You could say it was the straw that broke the poor guy's back. He never left this apartment after that. Two years. And then I . . . well, it's no secret, I told the cops. I . . . broke up with him three weeks ago. I still brought him food, did his errands when he needed me to, but I told him, I couldn't go on the way he wanted anymore—never going out anywhere, never doing anything. . . ."

"Giving the man motive to end his existence, yes," Saint Just said, noting a clearer area of the table, where the crime investigation team must have dusted for prints around something the approximate shape of a shoe box. "The delivery of the dead rat and the threatening poem? That must have been the topper for him, yes? Or at least what the police would have concluded?"

Jeremy nodded, wiping at a tear on his cheek. "I killed him. Well, I didn't kill him, but you know what I mean. I'm sick about it. I'm just here to pack up his stuff, you know, maybe sell it to help pay expenses? Not that there's much."

Saint Just wasn't giving Jeremy his full attention, as something the young man had said earlier was insistently nudging at his brain. "You said Francis had not left the apartment in two years?"

"About that long, yeah. Agoraphobia. He had it bad."

"And you did all of his shopping for him, is that correct?"

"Yeah. Why?"

Saint Just aimed his cane at the high ceiling. "That rope is new. Am I to conclude that you purchased it for him?"

Jeremy looked up at the rope, blinking rapidly. "No. Why would I buy him a rope? What would Francis do with a—oh, God." He looked at Saint Just, his thin face going pale. "He didn't go out. Not Francis. I knew him, and he wouldn't go out on the street. And he'd *never* go into a store. No, not Francis. It . . . it was like he was paralyzed, you know, somewhere inside his mind? He got as far as the landing once or twice, but then he'd start to shake, feel sick, and I'd have to bring him back in here and have him breathe in a paper bag, poor guy. No, sir, he didn't go out, he didn't buy that rope. He didn't have a credit card, he didn't order anything online—nothing. I did it all. I didn't buy him a rope. And I never saw a rope here before. *Never.*"

It was time for Saint Just to deflect the young man away from what, to him, was the most logical conclusion. "Perhaps he had someone else purchase it for him?"

But, alas, young Jeremy didn't bite, as he was already much too busy chewing on quite another theory. "Who? He didn't know anybody. Well, he knew people, students he wrote papers for—but that's it. They said he killed himself, sir. Because of the rat, you know, and the threat. I broke it off with him, the rat showed up, and Francis just couldn't take it anymore, you know? He lost it, you know? That's what they told me. But he didn't kill himself, did he?"

"Now, now, Jeremy, we mustn't leap to conclusions."

"The hell we can't! And don't tell me he had another boyfriend, because that's not true. Somebody killed Francis. He didn't kill himself because of me, or that package somebody sent him. It was *murder*. We could . . . we could have a serial killer, right here at CUNY. Christ! I gotta go."

"Jeremy, wait—" Saint Just shook his head, then picked up the paperbacks and headed for the door. "The good *left*-tenant is not going to be best pleased with me, I believe," he said to the room at large. He had not introduced himself to young Jeremy by name, but even a cursory description of a tall, well-dressed Englishman carrying a cane would not overtax Steve Wendell's powers of deduction.

Saint Just reached into his pocket and pulled out his gold watch. Five o'clock. It takes time for rumors to find their way about town, more time for them to come to the attention of the constabulary or, as is inevitable, the media. Still, at best, he had less than twenty-four hours before Maggie would know everything.

Not a man afraid of females, Saint Just had to admit

to himself that he only began to feel slightly better once he'd decided to stop and pick up some New York strip steaks for his Foreman grill (the new, improved, Next Grilleration G-5, in candy apple red). He'd treat her to steaks, salad, crusty Italian bread, one of his most choice wines from his growing collection—and then a small confession.

It seemed a workable plan. . . .

Chapter Nine

"And so I took him there and he volunteered, they signed him up on the spot, and they've already put him to work," Maggie told Alex as she followed him out of the kitchen, carrying both their wineglasses. "So, you think that's fine? I think that's fine. I think it's terrific." *I think I should shut up, stop babbling. I've been babbling since I figured out we're alone here. Completely alone here.* "Alex?"

"I concur. I believe Sterling has found within him the true meaning of Christmas. Indeed, I find myself feeling quite humbled by his pure heart," he told her, holding out her chair for her. "And what is the name of this organization again, please?"

"Santas for Silver," she told him, looking down at her plate, at the perfectly prepared steak on her plate. "I never heard of it, to tell you the truth, but Socks had said he'd seen a storefront a couple of blocks away, so that's where we went. They don't ask for *paper* money, you understand. Just *silver*. Although, of course, there hasn't been any silver in our coins in a long time. It's just catchy—you know, Santas for Silver?"

Alex merely blinked at her, then offered her the basket containing thick slices of warm Italian bread.

Look at him, sitting there so calmly, looking so absolutely fabulous in the candlelight. Damn him, he had her needing to babble again. Did she look that good? Candlelight was flattering; she'd read that somewhere. Still, a little mascara and lipstick probably would have helped. "I've told you he's been issued a Santa suit, Alex? Well, he was. Red suit, white beard, big black patent leather belt, the whole nine yards. That's what he really wanted, although he calls himself Father Christmas instead of Santa Claus, which is really sweet, and everything he collects goes to charity. He's got the corner of Sixty-sixth and Central Park West—prime territory, I'd say, right across from Tavern on the Green." She shut her mouth with a snap and then opened it again to say, "I should eat, huh?"

Alex smiled. Looked so confident. So self-assured. So relaxed in his own skin. So *we both know what's really happening here, don't we?* He definitely was beginning to get on her nerves.

He'd shown up a while ago with the steaks, a prepared salad from Mario's, a long loaf of fresh Italian bread and two bottles of wine, deposited all of that in her kitchen, then went back to grab his ridiculous George Foreman grill. How does a woman turn down an invitation like that? Damn him.

He was fresh from his shower, his black hair still damp against the snow-white collar of the fine lawn shirt he wore open at the neck, the French cuffs of the full sleeves sans cuff links and unfolded so that they fell gracefully onto the backs of his tanned hands. The Regency Gentleman At His Leisure. It wasn't lace at collar and cuffs, of course, the way he'd relax at home in Regency England, but it was close, and he looked yummy. *Edible.* His black slacks had no pleats and rode slightly low on his narrow hips while they concealed most of the short black calfskin Eno Bruno dress boots he favored. He smelled faintly of Brut, which he insisted upon wearing even though Pierre of Fragrances By Pierre had given him a bushel basket full of sinfully expensive scents. She'd always liked the smell of Brut, even if you could buy it at Wal-Mart.

Maggie was also fresh from her shower, but she was wearing her faded blue Road Runner ("beep-beep!") nightshirt over a pair of shorts. She smelled of Johnson and Johnson Baby Oil, also available everywhere. She always coated her wet body with it before toweling off because it was an easy and quick moisturizer and it smelled good. Okay, and it was cheap; a leftover from her penny-pinching days. Her feet were bare.

Damn him.

As the grill heated, Alex had generously complimented her on her completed decorations, and then gone about the living room turning on the tree lights, the fairy lights. He'd lit several candles and turned off all the other lights, leaving the room glowing rather romantically. Damn him.

He'd opened one of the wine bottles, let the wine breathe, and then poured them each a glass, asking her about her afternoon as he inserted the steaks into the grill and turned to lean back against the counter and sip his wine as he looked at her over the rim.

Which had pretty much marked the moment when she'd begun to babble like a nervous virgin. *Damn him.*

"Ummm, perfect," she said now, around her first bite of medium-rare steak. "You really get some good ideas, Alex. So, what did you do this afternoon? Sterling told me you had something important to do."

Alex set down his wineglass. "Not really important. A bit of holiday shopping, my dear."

"Oh, goodie. What did you get me?"

"You'd have much better luck trying to pry that sort of information out of Sterling, which is why I plan to accomplish my shopping unaccompanied. Tell me more about this Santas for Silver, if you please. You did, of course, complete a Web search before allowing Sterling to join them?"

Maggie's fork clinked against the plate as she put it down with some force. So much for the romantic ambiance. "No, I didn't do a Web search. For crying out loud, Alex. They're Santas. They're collecting money on street corners. There are Santas all over Manhattan this time of year. You can't walk ten feet in any direction without bumping into a guy with a red suit and a bell. What's to search?"

"One of my Street Corner Orators and Players is stationed across from Tavern on the Green, if you'll recall. We have cultivated an extremely commendable reputation, and I wouldn't want it sullied by a supposed association with anything that is not entirely aboveboard."

"Oh. Right. Aboveboard. Like sweet little Mary Louise and her merry band of supposedly reformed felons. No, we certainly couldn't have that, could we?" She put her napkin on the table and got up, stomped over to her computer. "By all means, let's run a check on Santa."

Alex got to her before she could sit down at the desk. He took hold of her shoulders and turned her around so that they were just inches apart. "I'm sorry, sweetings. I was struggling for conversation, wasn't I, and succeeded only in putting my foot in it? We've been together for so long. It seems ridiculous to be nervous around each other, and yet I am feeling far from my usually confident self this evening."

"Yeah, join the club," Maggie mumbled, her hands having somehow found their way onto his chest, her palms flat against the soft material of his shirt, the firm muscle beneath. He was standing with his back to the Christmas tree, and the white lights seemed to make a halo around him. He was real, yet almost unreal. And warm to the touch. "That is, me, too." *Wow, that was articulate. I are a writer, obviously.*

"Something changed for us, between us, while we were in England, didn't it?"

"I don't know . . . maybe." She looked up into his remarkable blue eyes beneath his fantastically sculpted brows, expecting to see his usual confidence and finding just a hint of uncertainty in their depths. Wow. He wasn't supposed to be uncertain, that was *her* job. He was supposed to be her hero, the man who knew everything, could be counted on for everything; brave, even fearless. "Alex . . ."

"Yes, sweetings?"

"Don't do that," Maggie said, shutting her eyes. "Don't call me sweetings in that voice of yours—you know what voice I mean. That sexy *drawl*. And don't look at me like that. Don't try to seduce me." Her eyes shot open as a sudden thought hit her. "You *are* trying to seduce me, aren't you?"

His smile had her stomach doing a small flip.

"To descend somewhat into the vernacular, I believe I like the way you think, my dear."

Swallowing was becoming a problem. "Well, um, I'd rather you didn't. I think. But you do agree with me? Oh, God, did I just ask that? What a lousy love scene. Bernie would be blue-marking it all over the place."

Alex moved closer, gently insinuated his right thigh between her legs as he rested his hands on her hips. "Perhaps if we borrowed from an expert? 'For God's sake hold your tongue, and let me love.'"

"That's . . . that's John Donne, isn't it? I had you quote

him in *The Case of the*—okay, never mind," Maggie said.

"*Shhh*, sweetings . . . and let me love . . ."

Maggie watched, mesmerized, as Alex lowered his head to hers, her eyes closing when he captured her mouth with his own. *I'm your huckleberry . . .*

She tried to protest. Really, she did. Even as she opened her mouth and Alex took sweet advantage of her new vulnerability to deepen their kiss. Even as her hands somehow found their way up and over his shoulders, to hold his head still as she broke the kiss, took a quick, deep breath as she looked deeply into his eyes, and then raised herself up on tiptoe to kiss him back.

Maggie felt his arms go around her, lifting her. "The door. Sterling," she managed to say as he rained kisses down the side of her throat.

"Taken care of," he whispered into her ear before nipping at her earlobe, lightly licking the sensitive skin behind her ear.

She buried her face against his shoulder as he carried her down the hall, toward her bedroom. "You did plan this, didn't you? I wasn't wrong. You planned to seduce me tonight, didn't you?"

They were inside her bedroom now, and Alex set her down on her feet, his arms loosely looped around her waist. "Among other things, yes. I will admit I had hopes."

"Other things? What other things?" *Why couldn't she shut up?*

He'd moved his hands now, hadn't he? Not a sudden move, but a very smooth and practiced one that ended with his palms lightly brushing the outsides of her breasts. Nothing too overt. Just a gentlemanly hint of what could be, if she were willing. "Do you really want to know, sweetings? *Now*?"

"Oh, hell, no," Maggie admitted truthfully, unable, as she would say of one of her Regency heroines in this situation, to summon a lie. And that was pretty much the last even remotely coherent thought she had for quite some time. . . .

Chapter Ten

Maggie awoke slowly, wondering why she was smiling in the darkness.

Oh. Right. Now she remembered.

Still smiling, she turned onto her side and stretched her hand out and over the sheets, expecting to encounter Alex's sleep-warm body. Maybe kind of sort of walk her fingers over his bare hip and . . .

. . . nothing.

She scooted more to the middle of the king-size bed, stretched out her hand again, ran it up and down the surface of the mattress.

Still nothing.

Panic, the kind that freezes the blood in your veins and prickles the hairs on your arms, sliced through her.

He was gone? How could he be gone? Sure, she'd wondered about it, wondered if . . . if doing what they'd done would change something somehow. Maybe make him poof back out of her life just as unexpectedly as he'd poofed into it.

But that was ridiculous. He'd been here for months. He wouldn't leave now.

He couldn't leave *now*.

Oh, God, what had she done?

She'd made love with a figment of her imagination, *that's* what she'd done!

And now that she had, maybe that would be the end of it; fantasy fulfilled. He'd leave, go away, go back into her head or wherever he'd come from, and she'd never see him again.

Because there had to be rules to this sort of stuff, right? Look, don't touch? Some sort of line they shouldn't have crossed? Like, hey, people can fall in love with imaginary heroes, sure. But they don't actually *make* love with imaginary heroes.

It was like that old joke about talking to God. When you talk to God, that's called praying. But when you start to think you hear God talking back to you, it's time for a psychiatrist.

Was it time for a psychiatrist?

Hell, she had one of those.

Sure. Like she could tell Dr. Bob any of this. Yeah, that would happen. . . .

"Oh, jeez, calm down, will you?" she ordered herself, turning onto her back, blinking as her eyes became accustomed to the near darkness. Then she saw the time as it was digitally projected onto her ceiling thanks to the nifty new clock she'd treated herself to last month. After all, if the hero could have a Foreman grill, the heroine—that would be her—could have a nifty gadget of her own.

Seven o'clock.

Well, that wasn't so bad, was it? It was morning, or at least it was on the other side of her room-darkening shades. Alex wouldn't have wanted to upset Sterling, so he was probably just back in his own condo across the hall. He hadn't *poofed*. He wouldn't *dare* poof. Would he? He could control that stuff. He'd poofed *in*, right?

"Right, that's settled then," Maggie told herself sternly as she stumbled toward the shower, dragging fresh clothing with her as she went. "Shower, dress, wait for him to show up again. No panic, no reason for panic, no— ah, hell. How do I even *look* at him again after last night?"

She got her answer sooner than she'd expected, once she was showered and dressed more carefully than was her custom—which meant she'd actually put on mascara and lipstick. When she walked out into her large living room, it was to see that the dishes and glasses on the table were gone, so that she retreated down the hallway, past her bedroom door and into the kitchen, to see Alex at the sink with his back to her, rinsing a wineglass.

Okay. This was good. This was great. He hadn't poofed. He was still there, and looking good in the clothing she'd come fairly close to ripping off him last night.

Very good. Except for one thing.

What was she going to say to him? What happens now? Where do you go after you've been to bed with each other? Because there's no going back.

"Good morning, Maggie," Alex said without turning around. "I attempted to be quiet until I heard your shower running, but the mess is fairly well cleaned up now. Are you hungry?" he asked, finally turning around to face her, the hint of morning beard on his face kicking off a series of butterfly flutters in her stomach.

"Ah. Yeah. Famished."

"Good. I'll just go attend to my morning ablutions and the three of us will adjourn to Styles Café for a hearty breakfast, all right? You look wonderful, by the way," he ended, dropping a kiss on her cheek as he breezed by her, on his way to his own condo.

That was it? Hi, let's have breakfast? A kiss on the cheek? No postmortem? No . . . God help her, no encore?

She held up a hand in a "wait a minute, we have to talk" gesture, and then gave it up because they might have to talk, but she'd be damned as to what either of them would say, so she just poured herself a glass of orange juice and retreated to her computer. She knew what she was doing at her computer, or at least she used to, before Alex showed up.

So what was he up to now? She'd made him, she ought to know.

Maggie opened her bottom desk drawer and pulled out the character description sheets she'd written before writing her first Saint Just mystery. She'd added to the description over the years as she'd learned more about her character, but could there be anything in those notes to tell her what to expect from him now?

Age: 35

Physical description . . . well, she already knew that one. One could say she now knew that intimately.

She knew about his youth, his relationship with his parents. She knew his hobbies, his likes and dislikes—from the color of his waistcoat to the flavor of jam he liked best on his morning toast—but there was really nothing to tell her how he'd react in a situation like this.

Had there ever been a situation like this?

Giving her investigation up as a dead-end pursuit, Maggie woke her computer and started her search engine, and then typed in *santasforsilver.org*, just hoping for an easy hit . . . and she found one.

The site certainly looked professional, or as professional as a site could look with a line of animated high-kicking Santas doing their Rockettes thing along the top of the page. The site was composed of several pages. One for locations of Santas for Silver both in Manhattan and on Long Island and Staten Island. Another page contained an application to become a Santa for Silver. Another page was loaded with hearty endorsements from people associated with soup kitchens, homeless shelters, youth clubs, all those good things, stating how Santas for Silver was always so generous, etc., etc.

"Nothing here to hurt anybody," she said and closed the page, deciding that a few games of Snood wouldn't turn her back into a Snood addict. She'd kicked nicotine, right? She certainly could play Snood without becoming hooked again. Besides, it was pretty hard to think of anything else when the Snoods were dropping, and she really didn't want to think about anything else. Anyone else . . .

"Good morning, Maggie."

Maggie looked up from the screen to see Sterling standing just inside the door, dressed in his Santas for Silver suit, a large brass bell in his gloved hand. He even had a small silver badge pinned to his chest. On it was a carved Santa head and *S-4-S*—Santas for Silver. Cute. "Oh, don't you look sweet," she said, getting to her feet and giving him a big hug. "Are you going to have time to go to breakfast with us?"

"No, I'm sorry to say, but I must be on duty in an hour, and I still must return to Santa headquarters to retrieve my chimney. Saint Just said you weren't feeling well last night, so he sat up with you until the wee hours, then fell asleep on the couch. He's a true friend, Saint Just is, isn't he? Are you feeling more the thing this morning, Maggie?"

"Sure, Sterling, thank you, it was . . . it was just a headache," Maggie said, one question answered. Alex wasn't going to borrow Sterling's bell and go around town ringing it and yelling, "I got some, I got some!" Thank heaven for small favors. . . .

"All set, Maggie?" Alex asked from behind Sterling who, although he had no hat to tip, graciously shook his huge red stocking cap, the one with the bell on the end, and then headed for the elevator. "Lord bless him, I'd hate to burst his happy bubble."

"You don't have to," Maggie said, grabbing her coat from the hook beside the door. "I looked up Santas for Silver, and they sure look legit. Legal, that is, if you don't know that term. Come on, I'm starving."

And she wasn't kidding. Until she took her first bite of scrambled eggs, she hadn't realized just how hungry she was, but once those eggs hit it was as if her body moaned "And it's about damn time, lady!" and it wasn't until she was munching on her second slice of bacon that it occurred to her that neither she nor Alex had said anything after giving their orders to the waitress.

"Um . . . thanks for covering for me," she told him, then quickly took another bite of bacon. "I mean, with Sterling. He . . . he might have gotten ideas, and we don't want to hurt him, get his hopes up or anything."

Alex merely nodded. "Have you spoken to your mother, Maggie?"

"Huh?" Talk about changing the subject, jeez. "No, and you know I haven't. I've been ducking her calls, just like the loyal, loving child I am. Why? Oh," she added a moment and one brain synapse later. "Oh, no. You're not going to—no, you wouldn't do that. Would you?"

"Travel to Ocean City with you for Christmas and apply to your father for your hand in marriage because I compromised you last night, you mean?"

Maggie could feel her cheeks going crimson. "Yeah. That. That honorable Regency gentleman happy horse hockey. You wouldn't do that, would you?"

Alex lifted his coffee cup and smiled at her over the rim. "No, I don't think so."

She collapsed against the red leather booth in relief and then just as quickly sat up very straight again. "Hey, wait a minute, buster. What do you mean, *I don't think so*? What? I'm not good enough for you?"

Alex took a sip of coffee, then returned the cup to the tabletop. "Very well, if you insist."

"No!" Maggie clapped a hand over her mouth and looked around the small café, hoping no one had overheard her. "No," she repeated quietly, "I don't want you to do that." Then she told the truth. "But you could have at least *pretended*, you know."

"I'm sorry. Should we go back and begin again?"

Maggie shook her head and then dropped her paper napkin on her half-eaten breakfast. "Nope. I'm done. We're done. What do you say we go check up on Santa Sterling."

"Father Christmas Sterling," Alex corrected. He smiled at the waitress who had been leaning on the counter, looking at him, and she flew to the table to ask if there was "anything else the gentleman needed."

"Boy, that torques me," Maggie told him after they'd paid the check—she'd paid the check, actually, just to let the waitress know she'd been sucking up to the wrong tipper—and they were out on the street once more. "I could have been a department store dummy you'd propped up across from you, for all the attention I get when I'm with you. But you eat it up, don't you? When you even notice. Not only that, you encourage them."

"I beg your pardon?" Alex asked as he tipped his hat at the female cop at the corner who waved back to him, called him by name. "I encourage what?"

"You know what. Women, fawning over you. You called that waitress by name—"

"Loretta, yes."

"Right. Loretta. She's been waiting on me for years. *Years*, Alex. I don't know her name."

"You're not a people person, Maggie," he explained. "You live in your work, your books. And, as a beneficiary of that myopia when it comes to the rest of the world, you have my gratitude. Ah, and there's our boy now. He looks so happy."

Maggie shifted her attention from glowering at Alex to grinning at Sterling, who was industriously ringing his bell and ho-ho-hoing each time someone stopped to give some silver to Santa.

"You know, that's kind of cute, in a cheesy, commercial sort of way," she said as she watched a child place a quarter inside what looked to be a large funnel inside the clear fiberglass chimney. The quarter began at the top, going round and round, descending by mere inches with each revolution, until it finally disappeared into the hole at the bottom of the funnel, at which time the chimney flashed red and green for a few moments and the child wailed to his mother, "More! I want to do it again!"

"And four quarters equal one dollar," Alex pointed out as the child dropped another coin and clapped as it did its descending rotations around the funnel. "American ingenuity at work. Quite impressive."

They watched Sterling for some minutes, then crossed the street to hear Vernon, aka Snake, his Byronic good looks and deep voice as enticing as the *Hamlet* soliloquy he was performing.

" '. . . a consummation devoutly to be wished. To die, to sleep—To sleep'—hiya, Alex—'perchance to dream.' "

"Handsome, even talented, but, unfortunately, dumb as a red brick," Alex said, sighing.

"Yup. Snort-snort and all that," Maggie said, grinning. "And, handsome and great voice and all to one side, he also has the bladder control of a poodle when he's upset, as I remember it, anyway. Do you remember the day we found that out? Oh, Alex, we've had us some fun, haven't —"

"Hey, shut up, lady. Can't you hear he's talking?"

"Hey, sorr-eee." Maggie rolled her eyes as the man who'd shushed her turned to listen to Vernon once more. "And you want me to get out more, Alex, interact and all that good stuff. Sure."

"If you can go out without causing a riot, yes. And speaking of riots," he said, taking her arm and steering her back the way they'd come, "I suggest we keep our faces averted and step lively."

"Why?" Maggie asked, trying to pull her arm free as she looked back over her shoulder. "What's the—oh, cripes. It's true—stand on a street corner in Manhattan long enough, and eventually you'll see everyone you know passing by. Man, I hate knowing that's true. Move it, Alex."

But it was too late.

"*You!*" Nikki Campion screeched in her unpleasantly high voice. "I thought it was you. Oh, this is terrific. You just wait right there while I get my Uncle Salvatore. Don't move, if you know what's good for you!"

Alex stopped at the curb, even though Maggie was pulling on his arm now. "Are you nuts? Don't listen to her. You *want* Salvatore Campiano to see us? After what we did to Nikki? Or are you anxious to see if you can tread water in the East River—with an anchor tied to your ankle? Alex? What are you doing? Don't just stand there."

"I'm remembering a quote about keeping your friends

close and your enemies closer," Alex told her as a large man in a camel colored wool topcoat with a real fur collar and wearing a fedora approached, two smaller men following behind him, in the way pilot fish follow a whale. "Ah, sir, a pleasure," he then said, extending his right hand to the man.

Salvatore Campiano looked at Alex's hand for a long moment, and then clasped it between both his huge paws. "I understand you put in a few good words with the coppers over in England. For my loopy niece here. *Stupido*. My arms are long, *capisca*, but not so long they reach all the way across the sea. What you want for your help, huh? I give you something. Fruit, yes. Much fruit I send you, fresh." He kissed the tips of his fingers. "*Molto buon*, grapefruit the size of the cantaloupe, I swear it. And," he ended in a near whisper, stepping closer to Alex, as he took his hand once more, "if you ever were to find a need for my services—you take my meaning here?—you call this number, *capisca*, and I take care of everything for you. Anything you need."

"Hardly necessary, Mr. Campiano, but I accept with gratitude," Alex said as Maggie half cowered and half peeked at the powerful mob boss, fascinated.

"Yes, yes, now thank the man, Nikki, and we'll be about our business."

Maggie's upper lip curled as Nikki Campion grinned at her, then sashayed—she really did; she sashayed—up to Alex and planted a big wet one square on his mouth. "Anything you need," she purred, repeating her uncle's words.

"I don't believe it. I don't freaking *believe* it—and I'm not talking about that kiss, because I know you didn't have any real choice there," Maggie grumbled a few minutes later as she and Alex made their way back to the condo building. "One, I don't believe you *put in a good word* for Nikki with the locals and got her off. And two, I can't believe you gave your address to that wiseguy. With a guy like that, that was as good as giving him a key. Oh, and three? Three is, why the heck didn't you ask for a lifetime of free transmission service, huh? Boffo *Transmissions*, remember? But you didn't think of me, huh, did you? Oh, God, listen to me! I'm angry because you didn't ask some scary mobster-type to check my transmission. What's happening to me? I need to seriously rethink my life, Alex. I really do."

"Maggie, you're overreacting," Alex said, slipping the mobster's business card into his pocket. "Mr. Campiano seems a very nice man, a gentleman."

"Uh-huh, sure. A gentleman. Right up until you wake up to a horse head in your bed, you betcha he's a gentleman. Socks," she called out as they neared the condo building just as the doorman was closing the door on a taxicab, "guess who Alex's new best friend is. Oh, come on, guess. No, never mind that, because you'd never guess. Salvatore Campiano. Can you *believe* it?"

Socks gave a low whistle as he held open the door to the building. "Way to go, Alex!" he said, following them into the building. "That's better than knowing the mayor. Oh, hey, Maggie, someone came by to see you a while ago, but I knew you were out. He didn't leave his name."

Maggie paused in the act of pushing the elevator button. "For me? I don't know any men. Well, I know some men," she added, rolling her eyes. "What did he look like?"

"Yes, Socks, what did he look like?" Alex asked.

"Down boy, you're not in charge, remember?" Maggie told him quietly. "We figured that out at breakfast."

Socks took off his billed cap and scratched his head. "What did he look like? Okay. Tall, black—blacker than me. I mean, the brother was *dark*. Seriously buffed. And good-looking, in a young James Earl Jones way, you know?"

Maggie shook her head. "Nope. I don't know him. Oh, wait, maybe it's . . . no, he wouldn't come here. Why would he come here?"

"Fascinating as it is, listening to you converse with yourself, *who* wouldn't visit you here?" Alex asked silkily.

"A writer I know. He lives about two blocks from here, actually. Bruce McCrae. He works with Bernie, too. Gee, I haven't seen him since last year's Toland Books Christmas party. Maybe he wants to know why there isn't a party this year? Oh, wait. Maybe it has something to do with Francis Oakes. You know, like maybe he wants to know about the funeral or something—he knows Bernie and I are friends." She shrugged. "Yeah well, he'll come back, if that was him. You coming, Alex?"

They were silent in the elevator, all the way to the ninth floor, Maggie suddenly feeling very *alone* with him again, so that she stepped out into the hall even as the doors were still opening.

"I'd like to speak to you, Maggie," Alex said as they walked down the hallway. "There's something we need to discuss."

Maggie stopped in front of her door, her keys already in her hand. He looked serious, and she wasn't ready for him to be serious. "No, Alex, we don't. Let's just play it by ear, okay? J.P. is coming at one, and I want to think a little more about what I'm going to say to her. That gives me what, two hours?"

"Shall I casually drop by a little after one, or are you able to handle her disappointment on your own?"

"She's a lawyer. A professional. She won't go ballistic on me, or anything. I mean—okay, stop over. *Casually*. Give me a half hour or so first."

"Until then," he said, stepping closer even as he put his hand under her chin, lifted her face for his kiss. "Ah, delightful," he then breathed against her lips before kissing her again.

By the time she'd recovered enough to ask him just what the hell he thought he was doing, he was gone, and she was standing alone in the hallway.

Chapter Eleven

Saint Just was angry with himself, on many levels. Most obvious was the feeling that he should be presented with a white feather for cowardice, as he had been more than happy to find all sorts of diversions rather than speak to Maggie about what was really important: their evening together, and Francis Oakes's murder.

He was not the sort who would ever wish to engage in a mutual retrospective on an evening spent in a woman's arms; the idea smacked too much of a critique, a plea for reassurance that the night had gone well. He was intelligent enough to know how the evening had gone, and it had gone very well. He would much rather move on to the next evening, and the next.

In the past, his past, that would have meant another evening, another woman. Maggie knew that; she had created him, guided him through more than a half-dozen years of amorous evenings with a wide assortment of comely creatures.

She knew this was different, what they'd shared was different.

Didn't she?

Well, perhaps he'd think about something else.

He'd only just sat down in front of his laptop computer, planning to recheck Maggie's conclusions on Santas for Silver, when there was a quick, loud rapping on his door.

"Alex, you in there?"

"*Left*-tenant Wendell," Saint Just muttered under his breath. "Perhaps I have left it all too late." He got to his feet, but by the time he'd opened the door, Wendell was knocking on Maggie's door. "Are we having a party, *Left*-tenant?"

Wendell turned around quickly and punched a finger in Saint Just's direction. "*You* we'll talk about later, okay? And don't tell me it wasn't you, because who else is a *handsome as sin Englishman*, huh? You've got an admirer, Blakely, and you know just who I mean, don't you?"

Saint Just smiled. "Ah, Jeremy, yes? You two have spoken?"

"No, Alex, me and Jeremy haven't *spoken*."

"Jeremy and *I* haven't—"

"Shut up. Jeremy and I haven't spoken—my *captain* and I have spoken. Not that I did much of the talking. You're famous, Alex, freaking famous. And if you get any more famous, you might just find yourself being charged with trespassing, impeding a police investigation, and anything else I can think of to stick on you, and we would have, except that the scene wasn't an official crime scene when you did your little B and E and you'll probably say the door was open when you got there and I don't have time for you anyway. What in hell were you doing at Oakes's apartment?"

"As you said, *Left*-tenant, we'll save that for later, shall we? Or are you here with more information for me?"

"For *you*? Yeah, that's happening. I'm here to figure out why you wanted to know about Oakes, okay? So just shut up and let me talk to Maggie."

"Of course," Saint Just said silkily. "And how is Miss Christine today?"

Wendell gave Saint Just a look that would have had a lesser man ducking for cover, but Saint Just only kept a politely interested expression on his face. "You're a piece of work, Blakely. All right, all right. I'll tell you this much. It definitely wasn't suicide. Oakes was— hey, hiya, Maggie."

Saint Just watched as Wendell attempted a kiss and Maggie turned her head just as the good lieutenant turned his, so that they ended up butting noses instead. Ah, the falling off of what had never been a great romantic bond in the first place. How delicious to watch. He cleared his throat politely, which earned him a searing glance from Maggie before she invited them both inside the condo.

"I'm glad you're back, Maggie. So, what's up? Anything new going on I should know about?"

Saint Just bit his bottom lip as he watched sheer panic leap into Maggie's eyes. Sterling, it would appear, wasn't the only one who could be very literal minded. She was flustered, obviously, and didn't quite know what to do with a question like that, or with her supposed boyfriend and her lover together in the same room, so Saint Just—gentleman that he was—came to her assistance by pulling out the desk chair and indicating that Wendell should seat himself while he—still playing the gentleman—searched the kitchen for liquid refreshments.

When he returned to the living room, three soda cans and three ice-filled glasses on a tray bearing the likeness of Crusader Rabbit, Maggie was telling Wendell about their recent trip to England.

"So I want to thank you again, Steve, for all your

help with background checks," she said, then looked to Saint Just. "Don't we, Alex?"

"Indeed, yes. The information about our fellow guests was invaluable. Soda?"

"Thanks," Wendell said, ignoring the glass in order to drink directly from the can. A good man, with a pure heart, but sadly lacking in the niceties at times, which was a pity. "Maggie, I'm sorry I couldn't get here sooner but, um, I'm working a new case. Two of them, actually— I just got handed a second one this morning. You know how it is."

"Oh, that's fine," Maggie said quickly, then too quickly added, "I mean, I was disappointed not to see you when I first got back but, um, well, you're here, right?" This time when she looked at Saint Just her expression bordered on pleading. Poor thing. She was so good with words on a page; the delightful turn of phrase, the quick comeback, the witty banter. But put her into a real-life situation where those same things are needed, and she quickly folded herself into a mass of insecurities.

How he adored her.

Saint Just sat down on the couch beside her, patting her hand as he told Wendell that the reason Sterling wasn't here to greet him was that he had become a Santa for Santas for Silver. "He's quite enthused about the thing. Have you by any chance heard of this organization, Wendell?"

"No, can't say I have. But they're a dime a dozen this time of year. Tell Sterling I said hi, okay?" Then he shifted slightly on the chair and looked to Maggie once more. "This case I've just been assigned to?" he began, sparing a moment to look at Saint Just as if to say *Yes, and it's all your fault, damn you.*

"A murder case?" Maggie asked, clearly happy to be

on ground that was not at all personal. If she only knew. . . .

"Yes, Maggie, and I'm wondering if maybe you knew the victim, since you're both writers."

"Oh, Steve," Maggie said, "this is New York, remember? You can't walk ten feet in any direction without tripping over somebody who tells you he or she is a writer. Just like all the waiters in this town are actors."

"But you might know this one, Maggie. He wrote for Toland Books."

"Francis Oakes?" she asked, leaning forward on the couch. "Really? Bernie told me he'd died, but the papers reported it as a suspected suicide. Is it Francis? No. Who'd want to kill him? The guy was about as threatening as—as Woody Allen."

Saint Just, who had been sipping from his glass, coughed and sputtered as politely as possible, earning himself a few slaps on the back from Maggie, who clearly believed his difficulty to be a distraction.

"Was it Francis, Steve?" she asked again.

"You all right, Blakely?" Wendell asked, and Saint Just could hear the amusement in the man's voice.

"Fine as ninepence, *Left*-tenant, thank you. But you fascinate us with this story, although you've said very little so far, haven't you? Please, do go on. I assure you, we're hanging on your every word."

"I'll just bet you are." Wendell got up and began pacing the carpet. "Here's the deal, Maggie. Yes, the vic is Francis Oakes. At first look the primary believed the guy hanged himself. You know, living in an attic, no money, no prospects—all that stuff. Oh, and his lover had just broken off with him a couple of weeks before he died. Top that off with the fact that we all know how many suicides there are around the holidays, and for a while Oakes looked like just one more unhappy schmuck who didn't want to face another new year."

"Poor guy, that's so sad. But it wasn't suicide? The first officers on the scene didn't get that? Francis would have left a note, if he'd committed suicide. He was a writer. He had to have left a note. That would be like an astronaut leaving earth without his spaceship. Well, something like that. Alex, didn't we say that about Sam Underwood? That he hadn't left a note, and writers would always leave a note? Hanging. Man, there's a lot of that going around, isn't there? Oh, sorry, Steve. I won't interrupt again, I promise."

"That's okay. But that was one of the things that stood out, Maggie, yeah. No note. Still, that isn't all that unusual. Some people decide something at the last minute, and then act on it before they can chicken out, you know? But there was something there, some kind of sicko poem from somebody who sent the guy a dead rat."

"A dead rat?" Maggie shivered. "That's just plain creepy."

Saint Just already knew this part, because Wendell had already told him about the poem, the rat. Yet, at that time, the police had still believed Oakes had committed suicide, that the poem and rat had been the proverbial straw that broke his writer's back. Wendell may consider what Saint Just had done as meddling, but it would appear that meddling had at least bumped the incompetent detective from the case and had him replaced with the much more competent lieutenant.

Which didn't mean Saint Just couldn't have a little fun at the man's expense. "This is all very interesting, Wendell. Could you tell us what prompted Oakes's COD to be readjusted to homicide?"

"Would you listen to him?" Wendell said to Maggie, shaking his head. "COD—cause of death. Everybody's into the lingo these days." He turned to Saint Just. "MOD, in case you're wondering—manner of death—is still asphyxiation by hanging. But we found a lot of pre-mortem bruises at post, indicating that maybe the guy may have had a little help taking that final leap. Can we get on with this now?"

"Yeah, sure," Maggie said, giving Saint Just a quick slap on the knee. "Stop interrupting, Alex. Tell us about the poem, Steve."

"I don't have a copy with me, Maggie. It was just four lines—maybe from a nursery rhyme? But the last two lines didn't rhyme, even though they easily could have, you know? The last lines referred to the dead rat, and hinted that Oakes could be just as dead."

Maggie hugged herself. "I'm trying to imagine opening a package and having a dead rat fall out on your lap. Poor Francis. A big, ugly, smelly rat. With those pointy teeth and that long skinny tail. *Blecch*!"

"Yes, thank you for that image, my dear. But let's try to concentrate on poor departed Francis, all right?"

"I know," Maggie told Saint Just. "But I was just thinking. We're afraid of rats because they're dirty, and ugly, right? But then there's the name—rat. That couldn't help, right? I shiver just at the word. I mean, what if they'd been called puppies? Would we still think they were ugly, with such a cute name, or would we think puppies was an ugly name? Think about it. How effective would it have been in that old movie, if James Cagney had said 'You puppy, you dirty puppy!' Nothing. It would have been a big nothing."

"Is this going anywhere, Maggie?" Wendell asked, earning himself a smile from Saint Just.

"No. But one more, okay? Shakespeare said a rose by any other name would smell as sweet. So he'd probably think a rat was ugly even if we started calling them puppies, right? Oh, and the other way around—puppies would be cute even if we called them rats, right? Have we talked about this before? It all seems so familiar. Maybe last month? No, I don't think so. Well, maybe.

Must have been another reference to Shakespeare. Jeez, a dead rat . . ."

Saint Just smiled in real amusement. "She goes on like this from time to time, Wendell. Endearing trait, don't you think?"

"Uh . . ."

Maggie's cheeks colored adorably. "I'm sorry, Steve. So the rat and the poem, right? They weren't connected with the murder, is that what you're saying? They were just a coincidence?"

"That's what we're not sure of," Wendell admitted, sitting down once more. "The threat—the poem was definitely a threat—might have been quickly followed by the murder. Except for one thing. If you got a dead rat in the mail, wouldn't you immediately get it the hell out of your apartment? So we started thinking maybe the killer brought it with him, although we can't think of any reason to do that."

"Are there fingerprints on the box, the wrappings?" Saint Just asked.

"No, it came back clean, which sent up another red flag. Damn shows on TV make people believe this stuff is checked in ten minutes, but it takes days. And who said the rat was in a box, Blakely?"

"Forgive me, *Left*-tenant," Saint Just said without missing a beat. "I am guilty of an assumption there, aren't I? I considered the logistics of the thing, if the rat had been delivered via the post. You did say it was *sent*, correct? I suppose it could just as well have been delivered via messenger. But consider the possibilities, if you please. A dead rat, in a bag, even a sturdy bag? The shape and feel alone might easily have alerted someone, not to mention the biological laws of decomposition that could have—"

"Okay, thanks Alex, we got it," Maggie broke in,

making a face. "Satisfied, Steve? Because he could go on if we let him. I'm not the only one who does that."

Wendell nodded, then said, "Where was I?"

"Mired in questions with, to this point, no answers," Saint Just supplied helpfully. "What a shame the trail of clues had been left to grow cold while the authorities labored under a misconception. You did say you were only very recently assigned to the case, didn't you, Wendell? I believe Bernice mentioned Mr. Oakes's sad demise had occurred last week. Heaven only knows how the scene may have been corrupted, isn't that right? Civilians tripping in and out of the deceased's apartment, disturbing valuable crime-scene evidence unless, of course, they were very careful, which the police, it would seem, were not. Yes, yes. A pity. Is it truth or fiction that any homicide that remains unsolved after forty-eight hours is often never solved at all?"

"Would you *stop* already?" Maggie whispered fiercely from between gritted teeth before she got to her feet and approached Wendell. "I'm so sorry, Steve. What can we, um, *I* do to help?"

"Probably nothing much," Wendell said, looking over her head to where Saint Just, being a gentleman, had also gotten to his feet and was now smiling most benevolently at the lieutenant. "We're looking for any background information on Oakes. His boyfriend wasn't a lot of help there, at least no farther back than the last two years. What do you remember about him?"

"Not a lot, actually. Toland Books is a small house, and the writers who live in the area do get to meet once in a while—at Christmas parties, dinners during semi-annual sales meetings, stuff like that. I sat next to Francis one time, at one of those dinners. He was already pretty much on his way out, I'm afraid. I was . . . I was sort of dating Kirk at the time, and he was Francis's editor, and he told me he'd turned down his last couple of proposals. So that was what—three years ago? Oh, wait, I do remember something, Steve. Francis had only moved to New York about two years or so before that, from somewhere in the Midwest. I think he was hoping for big things, but nothing ever really panned out. But that's it, that's all I've got, sorry. Maybe Bernie can help."

There was a beep on the intercom and Maggie walked over to press the button, to have Socks tell her that J.P. Boxer was on the way up.

"That's my cue to leave," Steve said, grabbing his coat that he had draped over the back of the desk chair. J.P. Boxer was a former cop turned defense attorney— meaning she'd gone over to the enemy. Wendell liked her, and J.P. considered him to be a good cop, but that didn't mean they exchanged Christmas cards. "Look, we're not making a lot of noise about this, not wanting to have the press start making up names for some CUNY serial killer or something. They break soon for the holidays anyway, and in the meantime there's a big police presence in the area, just not so you'd notice. They'll be on the lookout for anybody who doesn't look like he belongs in the neighborhood, stuff like that."

"We'll be as close as oysters, Wendell," Saint Just promised, taking the man's hint to not return to Oakes's apartment, because he would be seen.

"Yeah, right. Oysters. Who says stuff like that? A clam, Blakely—quiet as a clam. And I'll check with Bernie, Maggie. She was actually my next stop. Blakely? Can I see you outside for a moment?"

Saint Just prudently ignored Maggie's curious look and joined the lieutenant in the hallway.

"I'll make this fast, since J.P.'s on her way up—what don't I know? What aren't you telling me?"

"I don't understand, *Left*-tenant. It's just as I said. I

was inquiring about Oakes because of Maggie." Saint Just complimented himself quietly, as he had told Wendell the exact truth—in a way.

"And yet Maggie barely remembers the guy," Wendell pointed out. "If there's anything going on, Blakely, I want to know it right—"

"Ah, J.P.," Saint Just said as the elevator doors opened. "How wonderful to see you again. Say hello, *Left*-tenant."

"Hi, J.P.," Wendell said, already heading for the elevator, before the doors could close. "See ya."

"That was quick. What's he got up his—no, forget it. I just remembered who I'm talking to here," J.P. said as Saint Just opened the door to Maggie's condo and bowed to the attorney, inviting her to precede him inside.

"J.P., hi," Maggie said, standing behind one of the couches, rather like a person who hadn't had time to locate a better hidey-hole, but was still hoping she had managed to find some protection. "You're early. Let me take your coat. Oh, and you and Alex talk to each other a while, okay? I need to run down to Mario's to get some tuna salad for our lunch."

"I hate tuna salad, girlfriend," J.P. said, tossing Maggie her jacket, the green and white one with the white leather sleeves and the New York Jets logo on the back. "You can't spring for roast beef?"

"Uh, sure. Sure, I can. Alex?" Maggie asked, her eyes openly pleading.

"I'll be happy to entertain our mutual friend, my dear," he told her, sitting down across from her only after the attorney sprawled onto one of the couches. "You can tell me all about your book, J.P."

Maggie's pleading look turned hostile. "Not yet, Alex. Wait until I get back. Until we've had lunch."

J.P. spread her long arms out on either side of the

back of the couch. "No, I want to hear what you think now, Maggie. Just a quick thumbnail before we eat. It can't be that bad, can it?"

Maggie took two steps toward the couches, then stopped. "You do know I can't buy it, right, J.P.? And it's only one person's opinion."

J.P. looked at Saint Just, who raised his eyebrows back at her. "You get the feeling she didn't like it, handsome?"

"But it doesn't matter what I think. I can't—"

"You can't buy it. I got that. So? Is it crap? You can tell me. I'm a big girl, I can take it."

Maggie rolled her eyes. "Oh, sure, that's what they all say. But they don't *mean* it. You all want to be stroked, and told your book is the next *Da Vinci Code* or something, and if I tell the truth—which is just my opinion, remember—then suddenly I'm not only the bad guy, but you jump all over me. And you're not little, J.P., okay?"

J.P. looked at Saint Just again. "She thinks it stinks on ice."

"No! No, I didn't say that, J.P. I like the plot—a lot. Why did you tell Bernie it was science fiction? It's a legal thriller."

"I wanted to see if she'd really read it, or just hand it back with some baloney about science fiction not selling well, or something. And, no, I'm not paranoid. That's not half as bad as putting a hair between the pages halfway through the manuscript, just to be able to check if the editor really read that far—I picked up that hint online, among others, so you can see why I thought it was time to go to the professionals. But you read it, so now I want to hear what you think."

"Go on, Maggie," Saint Just prodded. "In for a penny, in for a pound."

"You're such a help, Alex," Maggie said, and then took a deep breath, let it out slowly. "The plot works.

Definitely. But your characters are sticks, and your dialogue is stilted, amateurish. How's that?" J.P. opened her mouth to say something, but Maggie wasn't finished. "For instance—I committed this one to memory—you have a character say, 'Your brother, Samuel, the blue-eyed blonde who graduated from Yale and now works for Hammer, Burns and Stone, is a suspect in the murder.'"

"Yeah? So? I was describing the guy. What of it?"

"What of it? Cripes, J.P., you were describing him to his *own brother*. In freaking *dialogue*. That stuff doesn't go into dialogue. Look, it's like I said—the plot works. It's really interesting. But everything else is . . . not so good. You need to read authors you like, see how they handle dialogue, point of view, all that stuff. And maybe read some how-to books, join a writers' group, get a critique partner . . . yeah, well, gotta go. Roast beef. Rare, right?"

"Hold it right there, sunshine. Did you take classes, read how-to books?"

"Me? No, I don't do that stuff."

Saint Just gave a slight cough of warning, but of course it was already too late, and both he and Maggie knew it.

"So you're telling me to do something you didn't do?"

Maggie smiled weakly, and shrugged. "I read authors I like—I still do—and try to learn from them."

"Uh-huh. So you're telling me to do something you didn't do, that you didn't have to do. And what else? A critique partner, you said? What's that? How about a mentor instead? We could do that. You know, you and me? What do you say, sunshine? You show me how to whip that puppy into shape and get it sold, and it's free legal advice for life."

"I think you may have just struck a chord, J.P.," Saint

Just drawled, thoroughly enjoying himself. "Somewhere around the word *free*, I would imagine. I am, of course, included in this arrangement."

"Bite me," Maggie said, and headed for the door, then hesitated with her hand on the doorknob. "Okay, it's a deal."

"Sweet girl, and a heart, as you Americans say, as big as all outdoors. There, with that said—I thought she'd never leave," Saint Just said, rising to go to the drinks table and hold up a decanter of wine, asking if the attorney cared for a glass, which she did. "And now that it's all settled between you, perhaps you'd be so very kind as to explain a legal term to me?"

"You're cashing in fast. Okay, handsome, what is it?"

"Impeding a criminal investigation. What does that entail, by way of penalties, I mean? Oh, and withholding evidence, that would be another one. If, for instance, you were to come upon what might be evidence, but did not know *was* evidence, at least not at that time, would it then, once you knew, become incumbent on you to immediately notify the authorities of the existence of that evidence?"

J.P. jammed her fists against her hips and grinned happily. "Well, shit, handsome, what did you stick your foot in now?"

Chapter Twelve

Maggie muttered to herself as she walked back from Mario's, head down, more than ready to say something nasty to the person who was clumsy enough to bump into her. But when she raised her head, her intended "Watch where you're going, buster" turned into, "Bruce? Bruce McCrae?"

"The famous Cleo Dooley. It is you, isn't it?" McCrae said, letting go of Maggie's arms once she was steady on her feet once more.

"Maggie. Nobody I know calls me Cleo, Bruce," she told him, looking up into his dark, handsome face. The guy was halfway to seven feet, and built like Terrell Owens, not an ounce of fat on him. "Are you still growing?"

McCrae showed her his fine white teeth. A lesser, more impressed female might even think the December sunlight winked off one of them. "You always had a mouth on you, didn't you, Maggie? I came by to see you earlier."

"So it was you," Maggie said, indicating that he should

fall into step beside her. "I thought you lived around here. What's up?"

His smile faded. "I don't know if you've heard, but the writing community has lost one of its own."

"Francis Oakes," Maggie said, nodding. "Yeah, I heard about that a couple of days ago. Look, you want to come upstairs? I've got some friends in, and I'm bringing them lunch. Join us."

They passed Socks, who was looking rather admiringly at McCrae, and headed upstairs, McCrae now carrying the bag that, Maggie noticed, had begun leaking potato salad. "I didn't want to say anything downstairs, Bruce, but you look a little . . . worried?"

"After we've had lunch," he said as Maggie opened the door to her condo and stepped inside.

"J.P., Alex—I've brought a guest," she said, trying not to laugh as J.P. all but flew to her feet, simultaneously pulling down the top of her purple running suit and smoothing her hair. "Bruce McCrae, fellow writer, please let me introduce you to my attorney and friend, J.P. Boxer, and my neighbor from across the hall, Alex Blakely. Say hi, everyone, okay, while I go get us some plates."

"Please let me help you, sunshine," J.P. said quickly, and actually pushed Maggie toward the kitchen. "I *love* working in the kitchen," she threw back over her shoulder as she went.

Maggie skidded to a halt in the kitchen. "Why, J.P. Boxer, shame on you. Big bad mama? Scourge of the courtroom? Look at you—you're giggling."

J.P. raised one eyebrow and tipped her head to the side. "Girl, you do have eyes in your head, don't you? That's Bruce McCrae out there. I buy him just for the photos on the back of the book. I didn't know you knew him. You could have said something you know, introduced us months ago. Girlfriends should think about this stuff. Gimme that," she said, grabbing the bag from Maggie. "Do you think he'd mind if I cut his sandwich into little bites . . . and fed them to him one at a time? Hey, do you have any grapes? I could peel them, lay him back over my arm, feed—"

"Down, girl, and that's half a sandwich," Maggie corrected, really not wanting that mental image burned into her mind. "I only bought enough for the three of us. But, since you're willing to feed him, you can give him half of yours. I'll pile them all on a plate and you remember to only take half, okay? Oh, and he is cute," Maggie said, lifting down plates from the cabinet.

"Cute? *Cute*? Sunshine, that's like saying the Grand Canyon at sunrise is *cute*. Is the Taj Mahal *cute*? No, cupcake—it's one of the freaking *wonders of the world*. And that man out there," she said, pointing one long arm in the general direction of the living room, "well, that man out there is the biggest, the blackest, the most *killer* man to ever draw breath. We clear now? You got that?"

Maggie giggled as she nodded her understanding, rather overjoyed to see someone else flustered besides her when it came to the men in or hoped to be in their lives. "I'd say I'd gotten it in spades, but I don't know if that's a funny play on words between friends or if it will get my nose broken."

J.P. seemed to consider this for a moment, and then said, "No, it's funny. Just don't say it again, sunshine. And then you can tell me why you never told me Bruce McCrae is a friend of yours. That was cruel."

"He isn't a friend, he's more of an acquaintance," Maggie told her, spooning potato salad into a large bowl. She didn't like potato salad, but people seemed to serve this stuff at lunches. Then again, she really didn't *do* lunches. At least not lunches where you needed more than a paper napkin to hold your slice of pizza. She really had to grow up, if she was going to start having luncheons. "He came to see me because he's upset about something, I think. I'm betting it's about poor Francis Oakes. Well, I'm not betting, because I already know it is. I just don't know exactly what he's upset about . . . about Francis, that is."

J.P. popped a potato chip into her mouth. "Poor who? That was clear as mud, sunshine."

Maggie explained as they loaded dishes and other paraphernalia onto a tray. "So that's it. According to Steve, it was meant to look like suicide, but it was murder. The police just don't know why."

"Well, maybe my soon-to-be honey out there has a few ideas on that one," J.P. suggested, picking up the tray and heading for the living room once more. "Here we go—who's hungry?"

Alex appeared next to Maggie's elbow and discreetly drew her over to the side of the room as J.P. and McCrae sat down at the table. "I couldn't get any farther with him than polite chitchat. But he's probably here about Francis Oakes. Remember, we're not to know anything."

"About the murder," Maggie said, and then winced. "Damn. I already told J.P. Oh, wait, she's my lawyer now, so that was privileged information, right? No, I suppose not. We'll just have to swear Bruce to secrecy, that's all."

"McCrae? Not J.P.?"

Maggie looked toward the table, where J.P. was fluttering her eyelashes at the writer. "It's probably too late for that one. She's about to tell him everything but her shoe size, and since I'm betting it's at least eleven, I don't blame her. Come on, we're being rude."

"I believe we're safe with J.P."

"Oh? What makes you say—you *told* her? While I

was gone, you talked to her about Francis? Man, she is good—in the kitchen, she never let on that she already knew. Why did you tell her?"

"Simply idle conversation, my dear. Don't fret. Mr. McCrae," Alex then said as he held out the third chair for Maggie, then sat down beside her, "Maggie here tells me you knew Francis Oakes, the writer who died recently, is that right?"

McCrae nodded around a mouthful of potato salad. "Suicide, or so they say. But I'm not so sure. It's the timing, see. So soon after I—well, I'm getting a bit ahead of myself, aren't I?"

J.P. laid her hand on his arm. "You just take your time, sugar."

Maggie and Alex exchanged quick glances.

"Thanks, Jemima."

Maggie and Alex exchanged quick glances again, and this time Maggie was grinning. The big bad lawyer's name was *Jemima*? All six feet of her? Maggie had wondered a time or two, but always decided that the *J* was for *jugular*, as in "go for the." What in hell did the *P* stand for?

"I hate to push," Alex said as J.P. and McCrae seemed to have gotten lost in each other's eyes, "but I believe you said something about timing, Mr. McCrae?"

"Oh. Oh, yes, I did, didn't I," McCrae said, looking at Alex, his smile sheepish. "I nearly forgot why I came, although I'm so very glad I did, or I wouldn't have met Jemima. Oh, and please, call me Bruce, Alex."

Maggie lost her appetite. It wasn't that she thought J.P. was unattractive or anything like that but, well, she wasn't any Beyoncé, either. Bruce, on the other hand, was an ebony Greek god. True, stranger things have happened. But have they happened so fast? Maggie didn't know what was going on . . . she just didn't want to see her friend hurt, and J.P. was a friend, damn it. You'd think the guy was lining up free legal service or something.

"You wanted to talk about Francis," Maggie prodded, giving J.P. a gentle kick under the table, then rolling her eyes at her in a "down, girl" look females usually understood.

J.P. spooned more potato salad onto McCrae's plate. Pitiful. Disillusioning. It was like she'd just learned that Martha Stewart ate frozen dinners over the sink.

"All right, it's like this. And Jemima, I'm sorry if this is upsetting—you too, Maggie—because this isn't exactly optimum lunchtime conversation. I, ah, I got this package in the mail the other day and . . ."

"Yes, please do go on." Now it was Alex nudging Maggie under the table, but she ignored him.

McCrae patted at his mouth with his napkin and pushed his chair away from the table, got to his feet. "It was some idiot reader with a supposed grudge and too much time on his hands, that's what I figured. But then Sylvia Piedmonte called me out of the blue—you know her, Maggie?"

"No, I don't. Who is she?"

"You don't know her? Sylvia *Piedmonte*," McCrae repeated in that annoying way people do when they darn well know they'd most certainly been heard the first time. "She wrote *Three Past Midnight* and a half dozen other unfortunately forgettable mysteries for Kirk a long time ago—I don't remember who she's writing for now. In any event, I think she was sort of feeling me out, until she finally told me she and a couple other authors had gotten similar packages in the mail. Sylvia, Buzz Noonan, and Sylvia's good friend, Freddie Brandyce. Pretty much the same thing I got, and around the same time last week. She was calling around to other local writers she knew. She wanted to know if I got one, too. I guess we can't help it—looking for conspiracies everywhere. It must come with a writer's imagination." He laid a hand on J.P.'s shoulder, gave it a squeeze. "Forgive me, but it's not every day a person gets a dead rat in the mail."

"O-*kay*," Maggie said, putting down her own napkin, as playtime was certainly over now. "Time to call Steve."

"Wait a moment, if you please," Alex told her, getting to his feet. "Please, allow me a question, if you don't mind. Are you saying that you, and other writers in this area—you did say *local*, correct?—that you *all* received packages containing dead rats?"

"Yeah, that's exactly what I said," McCrae told him. "And not just the rats. There were vaguely threatening notes, too, inside the same packages." He shook his head. "Poems. I took the rat and the poem—the package, all of it—to the police station the same day I got it, and the sergeant at the desk told me to get the expletive-deleted rat out of his precinct house and only come back again if I got a box with a human finger in it or something, unless I wanted him to lock me up for public littering." He smiled weakly at J.P. "You have to love New York, right?"

"So what did you do with it—the rat and everything, I mean? It's all potential evidence, you know, and should have been preserved," J.P. told him, at last acting like a lawyer and not some moonstruck teenage girl.

Bruce was no longer looking all that lover-like. "Do with it? I certainly wasn't going to take the damn thing home with me and have it bronzed."

Alex chuckled quietly at that and Maggie threw him a questioning look, but he seemed to be avoiding her eyes.

"So—what did you do with it?" Maggie asked, just to cut the sudden tension between Bruce and J.P. That had been a short-lived love affair.

"I threw it in the first trash can I passed and tried to forget about it. But then, when Sylvia called, I became more concerned. She'd already talked to Freddie, who, like Sylvia, had already tossed his rat in the garbage—just in case anyone was going to ask—and Buzz is in Africa, doing research. But his housekeeper told Sylvia that he had received a package that had an odor to it, so she'd thrown it out, unopened."

"So there's no evidence of any of these rats? That's too bad," J.P. said. "Are you going to eat the other half of that sandwich?"

Bruce sat down again and put his hand on J.P.'s and gave it a squeeze. "I'm sorry, Jemima, I was being abrupt. Please forgive me."

"That's all right, sweetie," J.P. purred, falling right back into goofy mode. "And, please, go on. I don't want to miss a word."

Maggie leaned over toward Alex and whispered, "Pull up the pants legs, it's too late to save the shoes."

Alex smiled at her. "You're such a romantic, my dear."

"Where was I? Oh, right. Buzz had to have gotten another rat, right? That made four rats, if anyone's counting. That was when I realized what Sylvia already knew, that there was a pattern here, and that was troubling. And all of us living here, in and around Manhattan. And then I read about Francis Oakes in the newspaper and . . . and I began to wonder. We're all Toland Books authors, or at least we all were. I mean, hell, the December royalties couldn't have been that bad, right? So I played our special writer's game of *what if.* What if Oakes had gotten a rat in the mail, like the rest of us? What if he'd killed himself over it? Worse, what if the rats are just warnings, and the next step is murder, with poor Francis being the first victim? Hell, Sylvia's already on a plane to California, to stay with her daughter, and Freddie took off for his cabin in Maine. Let me tell you, they're taking this seriously."

"Because you told them about Francis Oakes, and your theory?"

"Of course I told them, Maggie. Why wouldn't I? And, yes, because I also told them about how the cop wouldn't take *my* rat seriously. In the paper, it was *suspected* suicide, not *definitely* suicide, so it would only be a bunch of fiction writers—all of us mystery writers at that—up against the fact that nobody had been hurt. So now I'm trying to find out how many others got packages, and warn them. Was everyone at Toland Books getting rats for Christmas this year? I know Bernie's a bit of a flake, but cripes! No, it has to be some kind of vendetta. Against mystery writers in general, maybe, or just against Toland Books authors—but something sure as hell is going on."

"A writer's fertile imagination," Alex said. "Fascinating how you all think in scenarios, and worst-case scenarios at that. I think I could safely say that Maggie here would have come to the same conclusions."

J.P. looked at Maggie. "You get a package, sunshine?"

"Nope. It's hard to believe, but maybe I've finally lucked out on something," she told the attorney. "Still," she said, winking at Alex, "we'll play, right? Alex here loves looking for clues. Don't you, Alex? We'll call Steve, fill him in, and then ask to tag along."

"That's the second time you mentioned a Steve. Who's Steve?" McCrae asked, leaning his elbows on the table, which J.P. seemed to take as an invitation to rub his back. "Another writer?"

"No, he's a New York City police homicide lieutenant. We've worked together before, on other cases,"

Maggie told him, feeling some pride as she spoke, whether that pride was in Steve or in the fact that she "worked" with him, she was not anxious to consider at the moment. "Not only that, but he was just here a while ago, to ask if I knew Francis, because he's been assigned as primary on the case." With Alex's eyes on her, but pretending not to notice that, she confided, writer to writer, "You were right, Bruce. Francis *was* murdered."

McCrae sat back, and then slammed a fist on the tabletop, rattling the plates. "I knew it!"

"Not that he was supposed to know it," Alex said in an undertone as he dabbed at his mouth with his napkin. "I do believe now is the moment you're to swear him to secrecy, my dear."

Maggie shrugged. Alex was jealous, that's all. He liked to be the big guy, the guy in charge. The great Regency sleuth. Yeah, well, tough beans. "Bruce can help, Alex," she told him as he handed her a plate and motioned that she should follow him into the kitchen. "Think about it," she said as she loaded the plates into the dishwasher. "Bruce writes mysteries. I write mysteries. *Jemima* is an ex-cop turned top-notch defense attorney. You're a . . . well, you're nosy. Put us all together, and we make a pretty decent team. Steve could do worse than to have us on the case. And, hey, for once I'm not a part of the case. Thank God. I mean, think of the novelty of it, just for starters. I love being on the outside looking in—because I sure wouldn't want to think that I could be the target of some nutcase with a rat supply."

"Yes, about that," Alex said, taking hold of her shoulder as she started to return to the living room, as leaving those two lovebirds alone wasn't in her plans for the afternoon. "I think we should discuss that particular conclusion a bit more."

Maggie turned to him. Slowly. Looking up at him through her mascaraed lashes. "No. Oh, no. You're *not* going to tell me that—"

"Maggie? Alex? You'd better get in here!"

"She sounds upset," Alex said, motioning for Maggie to lead the way.

Maggie didn't move. "I got one, didn't I? I got my own personal rat—and you can take that one any way you want to." Her mind was ticking over in double time. "My bra. You grabbed that package out of my hands so fast I—that's why, right? You thought it was another rat? Or maybe something even worse? And that's why you've been sticking to me since—since we got *home*! You've *known* since then?"

"Maggie! It's Sterling. He doesn't look so good."

Alex was out of the kitchen before Maggie could fully digest J.P.'s last words, because her mind was too full with the humiliating idea that Alex had taken her to bed last night, stayed with her last night, because he was worried about her.

No! She wouldn't think that way. Too Stupid To Live heroines thought that way in bad romances, and the author then spent three hundred pages trying to get the hero and heroine to, for crying out loud, talk to each other. She was *not* a TSTL heroine, damn it. Alex had not taken her to bed. She'd walked there, on her own, knowing what she was doing, what they both were doing—succumbing to the inevitable.

But that didn't mean she wasn't going to kill him, first chance she got!

"Maggie! Bring water and towels!"

"Oh, shit—Sterling?" Maggie flew into action at Alex's command, grabbing a clean kitchen towel and running for the living room, only to stop when she saw

Sterling sitting on one of the couches, looking like he'd been run over by a truck. Several times.

His wig and beard were hanging askew, his bell-tipped Santa hat clutched in both his hands. There was black street dirt all over him, as if he'd been rolling around in a slushy gutter, and the right shoulder seam had been ripped open. He had the beginnings of a black eye and his bottom lip was split.

And he was smiling.

"Sterling? Honey, what happened to you?" Maggie asked, pressing the towel to his lip.

"Nothing too terrible, actually. I was accosted on my way home," he told her, taking the towel from her and dabbing at his own lip. "But I prevailed, and very little the worse for wear."

The door flew open and Socks skidded into the room, fairly breathless. "He all right? I've got his chimney safe downstairs, but I couldn't come up with him because Mr. Bolton in Six-B needed me to—wow, he's going to have a shiner, isn't he? Well, maybe not—but that eye isn't going to win him any beauty contests. Who'd mug Santa?"

"I lost my bell, Maggie," Sterling told her, slowly pulling off his wig and the connected beard. "But it did make a formidable weapon, I will say that. They didn't get any of my silver."

"You should have given it to them, Sterling," Maggie told him, looking at his rapidly bruising cheekbone. "They could have had weapons. Knives. Guns. Didn't anyone try to help you?"

"It's New York, Little Mary Sunshine, remember? A good mugging is like street theater to most people," J.P. said, gathering up her purse and jacket. "Bruce? You ready to go, sugar?"

Alex had been very quiet, Maggie realized. She knew

that particular silence—it was the one that did not bode well for whoever had attacked his friend if the Viscount Saint Just found him. "Alex? Shouldn't they stay?"

"I think we know all we need to know from them at the moment, my dear," he answered dismissingly as he continued to look at Sterling. "Bruce? I believe you'll be hearing from *Left*-tenant Wendell by this evening. Please tell him everything you've told us. And do take care, mind how you go."

J.P. slipped her arm though McCrae's. "Oh, don't worry about that, handsome. He won't be alone."

"I've got to have a talk with that woman about the concept of playing hard to get," Maggie said as Alex helped Sterling to his feet. "Do you hurt anywhere, Sterling? Do you want to go to the emergency room? Alex, don't you think we should take him to the emergency room, get him checked out?"

"Certainly," he agreed. "Are you in need of medical treatment, Sterling?"

"No, thank you very much, and all of that," Santa Sterling said, heading for the door. "I think a good soak will be enough. But what of my lovely uniform, Saint Just? It's fairly well ruined, isn't it?"

"That doesn't matter, Sterling," Maggie told him sternly, "because you're not going back out there again. It's too dangerous, if this could have happened in the middle of the day, with people all around."

"Oh, no, Maggie, I must do my duty," Sterling told her. "I gave my word, and the little children are depending on me."

"Ah, sweetheart, I know, but—"

"He'll be fine, Maggie," Alex told her, opening the door for his friend. "You just go strip out of that ruined suit, Sterling, and I'll be there directly to run you a tub."

"*You're* going to run his tub for him? The great Viscount Saint Just?" Maggie asked as the door closed behind Sterling. "To quote a line from some cartoon— *Fractured Fairy Tales*, I think—'Now there's something you don't see every day, Chauncey.' "

Alex smiled thinly. "I do ask, from time to time, that you develop Clarence's character more fully, in the hope he might one day join us here. The complete gentleman's gentleman. How I miss him."

"Yeah, yeah, yeah," Maggie said, waving away that old argument—as if she could *plan* having one of her characters poof into her life . . . their lives. "I mean it, Alex. Sterling isn't going back out there."

"He would be greatly disappointed if we were to deny him the pleasure," Alex pointed out. "But not to worry your head about such things. I already have an idea."

Maggie held out her hands in a classic "whoa" gesture. "No. I know what that means. You're planning to find whoever mugged Sterling and . . . and cane them, or something . . . make their guts into garters . . . whatever. And that's not happening. We've had this discussion, Alex, and you can't do that, remember? That's called taking the law into your own hands, and we frown on that here in the real world. I . . . I won't allow it."

Alex smiled in a very kind, maddeningly condescending sort of way. "Maggie. My dearest girl. It would be impossible for me to locate a few random thugs in this large metropolis. I would have absolutely no idea where to begin."

"You promise?"

"I promise. Now, if you'll please excuse me, I need to run Sterling's bath, and then make a few calls."

"Oh yeah?" Maggie said, walking after him. "Who to? To whom? Hell—who are you calling?"

"Why, Vernon and George, of course. It has occurred to me that they will make exemplary bodyguards. Is it street smarts? Yes, I believe that's the term. Vernon and George should have them in abundance, don't you think? Or, to put it another way—it takes one to know one? If there are suspicious characters wandering about, eyeing Sterling and intent on anything nefarious, those two exemplary young gentlemen will quickly send them about their business, don't you think?"

"You're kidding. You're going to have them guarding Sterling? They'd scare everyone away and Sterling wouldn't make a cent."

Alex stopped, seemed to ponder this for a moment. "Yes, I see your point. George would do well enough, but Vernon could prove a problem."

"People nicknamed Snake often do prove to be problems," Maggie pointed out, trying not to smile.

"Yes. I'll have to think on that. In the meantime, if you would please get in touch with the good *left*-tenant? I do believe it's time we all spoke again. In fact, I believe it would be easier, and very possibly better for us, if he meets Bruce McCrae here as well. For some time this evening—if the good *left*-tenant is free, that is. We probably should speak to him about your rat."

"You got that in one! And, just to put us both on the record here, you're lucky I'm speaking to *you* at all. Hiding the rat from me like that. The more I think about it, the madder I get. What were you thinking?"

Alex retraced his steps, cupping her chin in his hand. His gaze was hot, intense, mind-melting. She was beginning to feel some real pity for the imaginary ladies she threw in his path in their books. *Her* books. She really had to stop even mentally referring to them as *their* books. "Why, I'm thinking of you, of course. Of you, my dear. As always, only of you."

"Yeah, well, don't," she told him, backing away, figuring she'd get closer to sanity the farther she got from him. "I mean, not all the time. I mean, I can take care of . . . not that I'm not happy that you'd care enough to . . . that is—oh, go take care of Sterling."

Alex bowed, most elegantly. "Certainly, my dear. Your wish, as I believe it is said, is my command, and I remain, as always, your obedient servant."

"Yeah, right. As it is also *said*—and pigs fly."

Chapter Thirteen

Saint Just spent the better part of an hour on the phone, but by the time he'd finished he felt fairly well pleased with himself that Sterling would now be able to report for duty at nine the next morning and Saint Just would have no qualms about allowing the good-hearted man out and about with his chimney of silver.

Santas for Silver.

He didn't like the name, and he'd cared less for the entire idea when, at Sterling's request, he'd called the local headquarters to report Sterling's unfortunate incident. Not a single question was asked about how Sterling had fared in the attack, all the questions having to do with the costume, the chimney, the lost bell and, most definitely, the silver.

This seeming lack of compassion for one of their unpaid volunteers smacked to Saint Just of ingratitude, at the very least, and coldheartedness at the most. Quite an unusual thing in a charitable organization, one would think.

Saint Just did not consider himself to be naïve. In the course of *The Case of the Lingering Lightskirt*, he and Maggie had explored a considerable portion of the Regency London underworld, including more than a few unsavory denizens of Piccadilly, many of whom were experts in the way of manufactured infirmities, artfully applied running sores, and other such unpleasant artifices meant to goad the unwary to part with a few coppers.

Or a few pieces of silver.

During the course of his literary adventures, he'd learned that appearances very often were not the only criteria by which one should judge others, that much had been made clear as his character had found it necessary to wade through cruel pimps, depraved women selling their own children, clever liars, in order to get to the truth and solve the case.

In this particular case, it had been Maggie who had looked up Santas for Silver on the Internet and declared the organization to be aboveboard.

But, then, Maggie was so adorably innocent and trusting at times. Saint Just would much rather follow his own instincts when it came to ferreting out possible miscreants, and in this case, his instincts told him that Sterling's sacrifice of his body in order to protect a few pieces of silver meant for the underprivileged should have been met with more compassion by one Mr. Joshua Goodfellow.

Joshua Goodfellow? It was as if the man had been named especially so that he could elicit good*will*.

All of which took Saint Just back to his laptop computer and, within moments, to the Web site of Santas for Silver. Ignoring the heart-tugging photos and glowing testimonials, Saint Just concentrated on names, and was disappointed in the lack of them. Other than Joshua

Goodfellow himself, there were only three: Roberta Astley, Maryjane Rucker, and Marjorie McDermont. All women.

And, at times, women could be naïve . . . or as bad or worse than men.

Saint Just closed his laptop and retrieved his topcoat and scarf from the closet, his sword cane from the elephant foot umbrella stand. Lastly, he picked up the bag containing Sterling's ruined costume and told his friend he was on his way to return the thing and obtain another—yes, a size forty-two short, if one was available, and most definitely, a new bell. He had more than an hour before Lieutenant Wendell and the others were slated to convene in Maggie's condo. Just enough time to do a bit of sleuthing.

"Maggie?" he called out as he used his key to enter her condo.

She appeared a few moments later, her hair still wet from her shower, her slim body wrapped in a thick white terry cloth robe. She looked delicious, but he was a man on a mission. Truly, the sacrifices one must make for one's friends. . . .

"I'm glad you're here," Maggie told him, drawing the lapels of the robe more closely over her breasts—a move Saint Just could have pointed out did nothing but concentrate his mind on those same breasts as he had last seen them. "Let's talk about the rat, shall we? *My* rat?"

"Certainly, my dear, although I am on my way to procure a new costume for Sterling," he said, holding up the paper bag. "What is it you wish to know?"

"I don't know," she said, sitting down on one of the couches and drawing her knees up and under the bathrobe. "Let's start at the beginning. When did I get it? How did you know I got it? Was Socks in on it? I'll bet he was. Oh, and did it ever occur to you—to either of you—that you were tampering with the United States mail?"

Saint Just set the paper bag on the credenza beside the door and leaned on his sword cane. "Let's see, which question should I answer first?"

"Take them in any order you want, buster—just tell me what you know I want to know."

"Very well, and you look quite fetching, I feel it necessary for me to say. Soft and rosy from your bath, and with your skin gleaming, inviting. That scent—I so identify it with you, my dear."

"It's only baby oil," Maggie muttered, tugging the hem of the robe lower. "And don't change the subject."

"Yes, I sense that you won't be derailed," Saint Just said, smiling. "Very well, the truth. I received a phone call from Socks on my cell while we were in England, telling me of the package and its accompanying odor that had led him to open the thing, whereupon he discovered the rat. *Your* rat. Directing him to keep the evidence intact, I then personally inspected it the moment we returned—"

"In the basement. *That's* why you were in the basement," Maggie said, pointing an accusing finger at him. "I *knew* you'd never do physical work if you could find a way out of it. So the rat was there when I came downstairs? I was right there, wasn't I? And you *still* didn't show it to me?"

"Alas, the poor mammal wasn't quite fit for polite company by that time," Saint Just told her, "but I was able to rescue the poem that accompanied the thing."

"You did? Where is it? I want to see it. Steve needs to have it."

"And he will, I assure you, when he arrives. Now, if there is nothing else?"

"Oh, there's a lot else, Alex. For starters, you've got

to get it through your head that I'm a woman of the twenty-first century, and you are a man of the nineteenth. An arrogant man of the nineteenth. But you're here now, in the twenty-first century, and I'm not one of your innocent debutantes who need protection. I pull my own weight. You don't protect me. I want . . . I want to be seen as capable of taking care of myself."

"Certainly, my dear. By whom?"

"By whom? By *me*. I want . . . I want to believe in myself, okay?"

"At which point I will no longer be necessary?"

"No! Cripes, Alex, I didn't mean it that way. I love it that you . . . that you *care*. But don't hide things from me—not when they concern me. Are we clear now?"

"We are, most definitely. Please accept my most sincere apologies for not informing you that some demented creature, possibly with homicidal tendencies, sent you an odoriferous, decomposing rat that, clearly, I should have presented for your personal inspection the moment we returned from the airport rather than to dispose of the thing and then watch carefully over you to see if the rat was a genuine threat or just a malicious prank, and all in the mistaken notion that a man is placed on this earth to protect his woman."

"Hoo-boy. You're pissed," Maggie said, making a face. "I knew you'd be pissed. I mean, you can take the boy out of the Regency, but you can't take the Regency out of the boy—or something like that. Okay, Alex, I forgive you. Your heart was in the right place. But Steve may not be so charitable when we tell him what you did, you know? Have you thought about that?"

"I have. Indeed, J.P. has assured me that I could not have known how potentially serious the rat and poem were and, now that I'm more than willing to cooperate—now that I have more information—there's really nothing the good *left*-tenant can do about it. In other words, my lawyer does not think you will be forced to post bail for this sorry creature, as I believe is the term."

"You know, Alex, that was *my* free lifetime legal advice you were using. But I'm glad to hear it. J.P. is a good lawyer. Or she was, before Bruce McCrae showed up. Was that sickening, or what?"

"I have no fears for J.P. She was momentarily dazzled. Only time will tell if her emotions are truly involved. And now, as everyone is gathering here in less than an hour, I really should be on my way."

"So you're really going to let Sterling go back out on the streets?"

Saint Just opened his mouth to tell Maggie, well, to tell her not very much, actually, but he quickly reconsidered. "For the moment, yes, I am, although not without George and Vernon by his side."

"I still don't think that's going to work, Alex. Sure, George is gorgeous, but Snake—Vernon—has *criminal element* written all over him, poor thing. He'll chase away contributors. Especially the moms and kids."

"Yes, you mentioned that earlier, but I believe I've come up with a workable solution. George and Vernon are to be Santa's elves. Mary Louise has agreed to outfit them appropriately and have them here tomorrow morning, to escort Sterling to his assigned corner, where they will caper and cavort and in general behave as Santa's merry elves—all the while keeping a close eye out for potential trouble."

Halfway through his explanation, Maggie fell back against the couch, clutching her stomach as she laughed out loud. "Will they have feathers in their caps and . . . and pointy shoes with bells on them? Caper and cavort? Oh, God, Alex—that's hysterical!"

"Yes, well, I'll leave you to your unseemly mirth then, won't I. Oh, and I notified Mario that we'll need a reasonable meat tray, breads, and salads delivered by six o'clock, as well as a cake, preferably a flavor he knows Sterling to favor."

"Because I should at least offer to feed everybody, right. I would have thought of that," Maggie said, sobering. "Eventually. Thanks, Alex."

And with that he was gone, hastening his steps, but not so much as to seem to be rushing, like so many unfortunately harried-looking others on the pavement at five o'clock, as he made his way to the headquarters of Santas for Silver.

Once inside the small storefront, a bell above his head surely alerting anyone inside as to his presence, Saint Just was quickly confronted by a rather blowsy blond woman wearing clothing guaranteed to greatly constrict her breathing and possibly even the blood flow to her feet. "Good afternoon, madam," he said, bowing gracefully. "I am Alexander Blakely, here to exchange my friend's battered costume that has been damaged in a recent assault upon his person."

"Huh?" The woman shifted a large wad of gum from one cheek to the other. "Oh, right. You called, right? For that guy Sterling, right?"

"Right," Saint Just said, feeling facetious. "And you'd be—?"

"Oh, right. Marj McDermont. That is, I'm Ms. Marjorie McDermont. I'm Mr. Goodfellow's, um, personal assistant. I handle all sorts of things for Mr. Goodfellow. So you can just gimme that, okay?"

Saint Just handed over the bag and the woman opened it, poured out its contents on a remarkably clear desk, if one were to discount the bottle of nail polish, a nail file, and a copy of *Soap Opera Digest*.

"Wow, what a mess, right? You weren't kidding, were you?" She spread the bits of costume across the desk. "I don't see it. Where's the money?"

Straight to the heart of the matter, Saint Just thought, not feeling very in charity with Miss McDermont. "Safely tucked away until Sterling brings it to you tomorrow after his . . . shift, is it? Is Mr. Goodfellow available?"

Miss McDermont was shoving the costume back in the bag. "He's here, sure, but he's not—hey!"

Saint Just employed the tip of his cane to push back the small wooden gate in the low railing dividing the lobby from the few desks and opened the mottled-glass–topped door to what one could only assume—correctly, as it turned out—to be the office of one Joshua Goodfellow.

"Good afternoon, Mr. Goodfellow," he said loudly, so as to be heard over the noise of a fairly elaborate coin-sorting machine the tall, blond-haired man was operating. Saint Just had seen a similar machine in Atlantic City when he'd gone to one of the cashier windows to redeem chips he'd won at blackjack. A half dozen or more full burlap bags were already stacked in the corner, and the bags attached to the machine at the moment were fairly well bulging with newly sorted coins.

Joshua Goodfellow looked to be a man who enjoyed his work—but not interruptions.

"Damn pennies, they screw up the machine every time, Marj. Can't these losers remember not to—who are you?" he asked, turning off the machine. "Who let you in here? Marj! You in a coma out there, or what?"

Saint Just looked the man up and down, and then concentrated his gaze on Joshua Goodfellow's handsome face. "One of your volunteers, Sterling Balder by name, was accosted this afternoon and done bodily injury. Sir."

"Did he lose the money?"

Saint Just smiled. "Thank you, sir, for salving my conscience over any assumptions I might have made without first bothering to indulge my curiosity in any actual investigation. And, to answer your question, no, Mr. Balder did not relinquish the money. Indeed, he will be on duty at his assigned corner tomorrow morning, battered but unbowed. Loyal to a fault, Mr. Balder is, sir." He let the space of three seconds count out, and then added, his eyes squarely on the man, "As am I. Good day, sir."

"Wait!" Goodfellow came around the desk and put his hand on Saint Just's arm, then just as quickly removed it when Saint Just continued to look at him evenly. Coolly, even dispassionately. "I'm so sorry for your friend's trouble, and I'm guilty of giving completely the wrong impression, aren't I? It's just that . . . well, we've had so many incidents. Robberies. And we need every penny—well, every nickel, dime, and quarter, as we are Santas for Silver, aren't we, *ha-ha*. I'm . . . I'm *devastated* that your friend Sterling was injured in the cause. Is there anything I can do? He has our most heartfelt prayers, of course, but if there's anything else we can do, he has but to ask."

Saint Just allowed himself a smile, a softening of his features. "Why, thank you, sir. Your kind concern is more than enough, Mr. Goodfellow, I assure you, and I'll be certain to convey your best to my good friend for his rapid recovery. Tell me—as I do so worry about Sterling—have there been many robberies?"

"Well, one other, and we think the volunteer was lying, as we smelled liquor on his breath when he came to report the loss," Goodfellow said sheepishly. "But

Sterling makes two, doesn't he? It's just the idea of it, you know? We simply can't afford losses, not with so many mouths to feed."

"So you feed the poor?"

"Oh, oh yes, of course. Food, clothing. Anything we can do to help. Your friend Sterling is doing good works, sir, I assure you. Here, let me get you a pamphlet."

Goodfellow gave Saint Just two pamphlets, as a matter of fact, and within a few minutes he was back on the street, a new costume in the paper bag, leaving behind him the impression, he most sincerely hoped, that he thought Santas for Silver was a jolly good charity, one that had his full support, as well as the twenty-dollar bill he slipped into Goodfellow's hand, apologizing that it wasn't silver.

Which actually might have been true, were it not for the avaricious gleam in Joshua Goodfellow's unguarded eyes as he'd watched the coins swirl about on the tray of the machine, then drop into the bags. Or the way the man had, once he thought Saint Just was gone, slipped the twenty-dollar bill into his own pocket as he winked at his personal assistant.

As far as clues went, that twenty-dollar bill traveled straight to Saint Just's already suspicious mind, stopping briefly at his anger, but then coolly moving on.

Reaching in his pocket for his cell phone, Saint Just then took out his billfold to retrieve a business card with a cell phone number scribbled on the back in thick black ink. Stepping under the awning of an electronics store, he punched in the numbers, hit *send*, and a few moments later said, "Mr. Campiano? Alexander Blakely here. A question if you please. You did mean it when you said I could apply to you for a favor? Thank you, sir, I knew I recognized a gentleman of honor when we first so happily met. I would much rather not bother you, make my own inquiries, but I'm afraid I'm rather involved with another pressing matter at the moment, and feel certain you will find my needs a simple matter."

He listened for a few moments, then switched the phone to his other ear and smiled. "Yes, yes indeed. We most certainly are enjoying the fruit. . . ."

Chapter Fourteen

"Glasses, napkins, paper plates. Ice. Condiments. This isn't so hard," Maggie told herself as she inspected the informal buffet she'd assembled on the counter in the kitchen. She'd had parties before. Granted, they'd all been catered, soup to nuts. And this wasn't exactly a party, was it?

Definitely not to Steve, at any rate. She could feel him behind her, staring holes into her back.

"Look, Steve," she said, turning around, holding a Ritz cracker in front of her like a shield, "Alex thought he was doing the right thing."

"Yeah, I've heard that story a few times before, Maggie. He was withholding evidence."

"But he didn't *know* it was evidence when he withheld it. He only thought he was protecting me."

"And you're all right with that?"

Maggie hesitated, feeling defensive about Alex, and maybe about herself. "Yeah. Yeah, I'm at least sort of all right with that. He really can't help himself, Steve, it's just the way he's . . . the way he was made. Now come on, stop looking like the high executioner or something, the others will be here any minute."

Steve took the cracker from her, popped it into his own mouth, then followed her into the living room just as the intercom buzzed twice, Socks's signal that someone she knew was on the way up. "You know, Maggie, we probably should find some time to talk sometime soon," he said, looking—gosh, he looked sort of *guilty*, didn't he?

"Sure. About what?" *Not Alex, Steve*, she thought. *Please, tell me this talk is not going to be about Alex.*

"Uh . . . nothing much, it can wait. Somebody's already on the way up. I, um, I'm officially off duty, so I think I'll go grab a beer. You want anything?"

"No thanks," Maggie said, frowning as she watched him head for the kitchen once more. Were his ears red? Boy, he was nervous. What was he so nervous about? She was the one who should be nervous. She was the one who had—well, he didn't have to know *that*, now did he?

At the sharp knock on the door, Maggie trotted over to open it and admit Bernie, who had two fully stuffed briefcases hanging from leather straps over her shoulders.

"This had better work, Mags. I haven't lugged this much work out of the office since I was an assistant editor," she said, dropping the briefcases one after the other to the floor just inside the door. "Here," she said, pulling a jar of cherries out of her purse and handing it to Maggie. "Just ginger ale, four ice cubes, a cherry and some cherry juice in a highball glass, okay?"

"A Shirley Temple? I used to get those when we went out for dinner—when I was a *kid*. You want me to make you a Shirley Temple? *Shirley* you don't."

"Funny. No, sweetie, I want a Johnnie Walker on the

rocks, but I'll settle for Shirley. Just so it looks good. It's nobody's business that I don't drink anymore."

"It's not Bruce McCrae's business, you mean. Everybody else knows—and we're damn proud of you, Bernie."

"Oh, please. Next you'll be patting me on the head and saying good dog, good dog—like I didn't piddle on the rug, or something." She reached down and picked up the briefcases. "Where do you want these?"

"I don't know." Maggie pointed to the coffee table between the couches. "Over there? Wow, those are all fan letters?"

Bernie hoisted the briefcases, then plopped them down heavily on the coffee table. "Nope. Just the bad ones. We forward the nice ones to the authors, toss the slams, and keep the hate mail."

"Hate mail? We get actual hate mail? Not just unhappy mail—but honest-to-God *hate* mail?"

"Hate mail, wacko mail, die-you-bitch mail, you name it. Most of it isn't all that bad—amateur critics, *I'm-better-than-anything-this-gal-writes-I'll–bet-she-slept-her-way-to-the-top* idiots, way too many anal retentives who love to point out typos, and just plain unhappy people who need to get a life, I guess. We just don't let you authors see it, knowing how fragile your egos are."

"Well, hey, thanks, I guess, although I think whoever screens this stuff missed a couple of slams over the years and they made it to me. And I quote, 'You, Ms. Dooley, in your effete way, have only managed to contrive silly, flimsy, inconsequential murder mysteries that are little more than cheap paper stages on which to strut your creation's manifest superiority,' unquote. *Manifest superiority*—you gotta love that, if not the cheap paper stage. The guy must have used a thesaurus, and manifest means *to make real*, so hey, I was doing my job, right, since Saint Just *is* the focus of my books— so what the hell was he complaining about? And he went on, and on, and on like that."

"Not that you're the sort of writer who takes letters like this seriously," Bernie said, shaking her head.

"Yeah, right. I threw it away, if that counts."

"Barely. Not when I know you probably obsessed over the damn thing for a week first. Don't ever listen to people like that, Maggie, listen to me. I'm the professional, remember? And, for God's sake, never write back to them. You didn't write back to this guy, did you?"

"No, of course not," Maggie said as if the question was barely worthy of an answer, not mentioning that she'd actually wasted a full day writing three separate letters—one nice, one not so nice, one that should have been printed on asbestos paper—and only then threw all four letters into the garbage. Then again, there were still the nice ones that sometimes showed up and made her day. Like the e-mail she'd received via her Web site from Kay Ghram, a Kansas librarian, just about a week ago. God bless the woman, she'd written, "All your characters are so fleshed out and real, it's a wonder they aren't in your living room." *Oh, Kay, sweetie, if you only knew. . . .*

"I only write back to the nice ones, I promise," Maggie told Bernie, snapping out of her reverie. "But what if someone is actually dangerous? You can't just file those letters or ignore them."

"We send the worst ones to our lawyers, and they decide whether or not we need to contact the police. Oh, relax, Maggie, we haven't sent more than four or five to the cops since I've been at Toland Books. And three of them were from the same guy—he threatened all sorts of mayhem—and he was mad at Toland Books for turning down his opus, not one particular author. We have to take that kind of stuff seriously, you know."

"What happened to the guy?"

Bernie smiled, pushing back her riot of red curls. "That's the funny thing. He went to some nice place with padded walls for about five years, and then wrote about the experience. I understand it was on the short list for an Oprah book last year."

"You're making that up."

"Am I? Oh, hello, Steve."

"Bernie," Steve said, looking at the briefcases. "What's all this?"

"Not love letters," Maggie grumbled, and then opened the first briefcase. "Oh, jeez, this is going to take all night. How are they separated? They are separated, aren't they? By author would be great."

"And much too easy," Bernie said, gracefully collapsing on one of the couches. "They're divided by year, unfortunately. We keep seven years' worth, on the advice of counsel. I've got a folder in there for each year. After that, you're on your own."

The buzzer went again, and Maggie decided to just open the door, then returned to the coffee table. "This was Alex's idea, Steve, because of something Bernie said the other day, some mention she made of fan mail. These are all letters to authors at Toland Books—the nasty letters. We're figuring someone could have sent one to Francis." She eyed the open briefcases. "If we can find it in that mess."

"Great idea, I guess, but I don't think the budget is going to stretch to putting a whole team on the single murder theory, chasing down all these letters. We're already stretching it with more cops up at CUNY, and the damn UN meets for a special session next week, and then the president is going to show up at the end of the week for some fund-raiser, and we all know what that does to the budget," Steve said, sitting down on the facing couch and placing the can of beer on the table-top.

"That's okay. We volunteered, remember? All of us." Maggie opened the drawer of the table and pulled out a stack of coasters. She knew she'd forgotten something.

"Sorry, Maggie, I always forget," he said, grabbing one and sliding it under the sweating beer can.

Alex doesn't, Maggie thought. *For a guy used to servants, he's very neat. And what in hell am I doing—comparing men, measuring them by the way they treat my coffee table? That's just pitiful.*

"Knock-knock," J.P. said cheerfully from the doorway, Bruce McCrae standing close behind her. What, they were joined at the hip now? And J.P. was wearing actual clothes—a pale yellow angora sweater and well-cut dark brown tweed slacks, not one of her endless psychedelic running suits. Then again, Bruce was still in the same clothes he'd had on earlier. Did that mean anything? Oh, yeah, that meant something. J.P.'s triumphant grin meant even more. She didn't need to be a romance-cum-mystery writer to know there had been some definite boink-boinking going on.

Maggie blinked, trying to get rid of the mental image of J.P. and Bruce . . . okay, it was gone now, thank goodness. "Um . . . Steve? This is Bruce McCrae, the guy I was telling you about. The mystery writer, remember? Bruce, Lieutenant Steve Wendell."

The two men shook hands. "Wendell, huh? I think I've seen your name in the papers lately," McCrae said. "Weren't you the cop who—"

"Probably. You want a beer?"

"You know how modest Steve is," Maggie told J.P. nervously when the two men had disappeared into the kitchen. Then she turned around to glare at J.P. "And you, lady? You're *nuts*. You jumped into bed with him, didn't you? You left here, took him to your place, and . . . and—"

"Had my wicked way with him. Twice," J.P. supplied helpfully, holding up two fingers. "Hi, reds," she said as she sat down on the couch Steve had just vacated. "Little Mary Sunshine here is all bent out of shape, but you understand, don't you? Chances like that hunk in there don't come along every day at our age."

"Even every year," Bernie agreed. "You have to excuse Maggie, she's gone celibate on us."

"I have not!" Maggie protested a nanosecond before she realized she should have kept her mouth shut, because now both women were eyeing her curiously.

"Steve?" Bernie asked, and then shook her head. "No, can't be Steve." She turned more fully toward Maggie, all ten red-tipped fingers clutching the back of the couch. "You did it! You finally did it. Well, hot damn!"

"Finally did what?" J.P. asked. "Or is that finally did *who*?"

"I think you're both twisted. You're sick and twisted," Maggie said, feeling her cheeks grow hot. "And if you say anything, Bernie, if you so much as hint, I'll—Alex. I didn't hear you come in."

"Have I just missed something? Sterling won't be joining us, by the way," he said smoothly, handing her a bottle of wine. "He's still rather overset from his adventures earlier today. Ladies," he ended, bowing to J.P. and Bernie, and then inclined his head to Steve and McCrae. "As we're all here, shall we begin?"

"Yeah, Blakely, let's do that," Steve said, gesturing at Alex with his beer can. "Start with Maggie's rat, why don't you."

"You're off duty, *Left*-tenant?" Alex inquired, indicating the beer can with yet another slight inclination of his head. "Very well then, concerned friend to concerned friend. Yes, I was alerted to the fact that Maggie had received a package while we were still in England, the full gravity of which I did not comprehend, more's the pity, until we learned of Mr. Oakes's sad demise. Unfortunately, it would seem that others who received similar packages also did not preserve them intact. I did, however, manage to retrieve the enclosed note, which I most happily entrust to you now."

Steve took the clear plastic bag and held it up to the light. "You touch it?"

"*Left*-tenant, I vow, you wound me to the quick," Alex drawled, and Maggie had to bite back a laugh.

"Right, the junior G-man," Steve grumbled. "How could I forget that. Okay, I'll turn this over to the techs, but we already struck out on the fingerprints we found on the note in Oakes's apartment—nothing on file—and the paper is the kind you can buy anywhere in the city."

"True," Alex said, neatly opening the bottle he'd brought. "However, printers are rather individual, so if you were to locate a suspect, a comparison would go a long way in proving our case."

Maggie winced, knowing Alex was showing off, and that Steve was going to blow. Which he did.

"Look, Blakely, I've tried to be nice, but don't push, okay? One, I already know about printers. And two, this damn well isn't *our* case. It's *my* case, and I'm only here because I care about Maggie."

"A true friend," Alex agreed, "as we both are well aware, and honest to a fault. I must say, we all appreciate your candor."

Steve sort of . . . *deflated* right in front of Maggie, and she shot a quick questioning look at Alex, whose expression was one of wry amusement. What was going on here? *Something* was going on here. Man, she hated being left out of the joke—except she was pretty sure this joke wasn't funny. Why did she get the feeling—much as she hated the term, it sure was succinct—that there was some sort of private pissing contest going on here between the two men?

"Okay, that's settled then, isn't it?" she said to fill the awkward silence. "There's food in the kitchen—just go on and help yourselves, please—and Bernie's brought over all the hate mail from the past seven years, so we can each take a stack when we're ready and start looking for wack jobs."

"Wack jobs, yes," Alex said—seemed to purr, actually. "Wendell, do you agree to the plan? You are in charge of our little band of merry men and women."

"Just grab a pile and start reading," Steve told him gruffly as Maggie and Bernie exchanged looks, Bernie indicating with a few quick head shakes that she wanted to see Maggie in the kitchen.

They were halfway down the hall when Bernie pushed her into the spare bedroom, the one Alex and Sterling had inhabited until they moved across the hall and Alex had returned, to sleep in quite another bedroom, and Maggie wished her mind would just shut up, damn it, because if she didn't know better she'd think Steve knew that or had at least guessed and—"Oh, hell's bells."

"He knows," Bernie whispered in the dark. "Steve, that is. He knows. Who told him?"

"You're wrong. He doesn't *know*," Maggie said, trying to convince herself. "Does he?"

"You saw J.P., right? You saw her, and you *knew*."

"That's ridiculous, Bernie. With J.P., there were *clues*. Great big flag-waving clues."

"Exactly," Bernie said, her smile wicked. "If I hadn't already guessed, I would have known it the moment Alex got here. The way you look at him? The way he looks at you? For a minute there, I thought I heard violin music. Steve had to have noticed. He's a trained investigator, for crying out loud."

Maggie shook her head. "No, you're wrong. It's something else with Steve. He was acting funny even before Alex got here. Preoccupied. Maybe even guilty. Wow, do you think—do you think he's been cheating on me?"

Bernie gave Maggie a look best interpreted as her "duh" look. "You did hear yourself ask that last question, right?"

"Right, good point." Maggie dragged her fingers through her hair. "It was easier when I—"

"Wasn't getting any?" Bernie offered helpfully, grinning as widely as her latest BOTOX injection would allow. "Look, Mags, you just need to play it cool. We'll grab something to eat, you'll make me my Shirley Temple, and then we'll go back in there and read letters. Just let things take care of themselves for now. It's not all that bad, I promise. They're men, that's all. Only men."

Maggie folded her arms, rubbed at her bare upper arms. "Oh, Bernie, if you only knew . . ." she said, longing to give in to the temptation to tell Bernie everything about Alex. The only problem—besides the fact that Bernie could keep a secret about as long as Britney Spears could stay married—was that, while she'd been drinking, Bernie would have believed her, swallowed the whole crazy thing. Sober, she'd probably have her locked up somewhere, weaving baskets. Even the possibility of the terrific sales generated by a melodramatic Oprah book couldn't make her do that.

Five minutes later they were back in the living room, to see everyone else with a stack of letters in their laps, reading.

"You know, what gets to me is how the rat guy knew my address," McCrae said to no one in particular. "This stuff is all in care of Toland Books, right? I've got an unlisted number, so my address isn't public knowledge. So how'd he get it?"

J.P. swept the pile of letters off her lap and got to her feet. "Maggie, can I use your computer a minute?"

"Sure, go ahead. It's a Mac, so it might seem a little different to you," Maggie told her, watching as J.P. woke the computer. "Search through Safari, J.P. That compass icon over there, on the right. You are doing a people search, right?"

"Exactly," J.P. said, launching the search engine. "Come here, sugar."

McCrae came to heel like a puppy—pitiful, really—as J.P. typed into the search engine. "Hey, I have this same Mac. Love it, don't you, Maggie? I told you, J.P., I'm unlisted. I've looked on those people search sites, and I'm not there."

"Sugar, nobody's unlisted, not anymore, you've just been looking in the wrong places. I can get your address. I can even pay to get your cell phone records online, find out who you've been calling, who's been calling you. All I need is your cell phone number, and I've got that. Everybody's up for sale on the Internet, and will be until the government stops talking a citizen's right to privacy and starts believing in it. But let's stick to addresses. Maggie, I'll do yours first. Maggie Kelly. New York. Hit *search* and—bing-o!"

"I don't believe it," Maggie said, picking up her computer glasses and sticking them on her nose as she leaned closer to the screen. "There I am. Name, address—my unlisted phone number? I knew about the addresses part—and a lot of phone books are online now. But *unlisted* phone numbers? Why did I pay extra for an unlisted phone number? Who lets this happen? Type in Bruce's name."

J.P. did, and up popped Bruce's home address.

"Try mine," Bernie said, coming to stand behind

Maggie. When J.P. had done so, Bernie swore quietly. "Well, don't we all feel safe now? I'd been thinking about upgrading my security system. I guess this settles it. Or are they selling private security codes online now, too?"

"It's not that terrible. If someone wants to find you bad enough, Bernie, he'll find you," Steve said, shrugging.

"Really? But now somebody's giving out fucking directions."

"I can do that, too. Driving directions, zoom-in satellite photos, you name it, you can get it," J.P. said helpfully, and then seemingly changed her mind when Bernie glared down at her. "Hey, I'm sorry. But that's probably how it was done, sugar. Try typing in Hillary Clinton—and up pops Chappaqua. George Clooney, Jennifer Lopez, both the Bushies, you name it. Unless and until something's done about these sites at the federal level, we're all open books to the world—and any crackpot out there. I'm just glad I'm not with the police anymore. I couldn't stomach it, frankly. And you wonder why the big boys want to get rid of trial attorneys?"

"Okay, off the soapbox and back to work," Maggie said, clapping her hands together a single time. "Alex, give me a bunch of those letters."

They all worked quietly for a while, until McCrae asked another question. "Let me see if I've got this right. Get our rats in a row, as it were. Maggie, Steve said that you got a rat, too?"

"Yes, I did. I just didn't know that the first time you asked. You seem relieved to hear that."

"Not precisely relieved, no, but at least we can add to the pattern. And Francis? He got one."

"But that's not for public knowledge," Steve reminded him, unfolding yet another letter.

Bernie waved her sandwich in the air to get Wendell's attention. "Hey, down here, Steve. Why not release the information? Maybe if this *all* was public knowledge, we could get somewhere."

"Yeah, we'd get a bunch of crackpots crawling out of the woodwork, that's what we'd get," Steve said. "I'm already bending the rules here—again—just by sitting here with you guys. The rat mailings could be coincidence and have nothing to do with the murder. The rest of you are still alive and kicking, right? Plus, we've first got to rule out a killer working the CUNY campus area. That's priority, straight from the mayor's office. His favorite nephew goes to CUNY and lives in the same block where Oakes was killed, in case you're wondering. Again, since all of you are still alive, frankly, we have to consider that the rats were a one-off thing and just happened to happen now."

"Because barking dogs seldom bite, isn't that right, *left*-tenant? Unless, of course, they do. Granted, Mr. Oakes is our only fatality thus far, rat related or CUNY related. Or has there been another murder close by his place of residence we're not aware of as yet and that's why the mayor is so worried? You would share that with us, wouldn't you?"

"No, Blakely, no more murders. One B and E in the same block two days after Oakes was killed, but that was just a run-of-the-mill TV and stereo robbery. This could all end up being a one-off thing. All I'm saying is we have to have priorities here, we have limited manpower, and all you people have are dead rats and no more threats. So don't second-guess us—you, too, Mc-Crae, all right? We're doing our job."

Gee, this is fun, Maggie thought, picking up yet another letter. *I should give these little parties more often, except next time we should probably all play charades. It's quieter.* She removed the paper clip that held the envelope to the letter and began reading. "Oh, wait a minute, I remember this guy," she said after reading the first two paragraphs of the three-page, single-spaced letter. "George Gordon Bryon."

"Byron," Alex corrected punctiliously.

"He wishes," Maggie said, rolling her eyes. "He took me over the coals for something I wrote about the real Byron in one of my first books. The man slept with a loaded pistol under his pillow—that's known fact. But not to Bryon. I'd maligned his hero. But he never threatened me."

"So why is a letter from him in the file?" Steve asked.

"I don't know," Maggie said, quickly reading. "Oh, wait, this is probably why. 'To imply that Lord Byron had an incestuous affair with his half-sister is a blasphemy not to be countenanced!'" She smiled at everyone. "Another guy who writes with a thesaurus at his elbow. Anyway, he goes on, 'If you do not remove this offending offal from the shelves of every bookstore forthwith you may inform your author—let it be war upon you both!'" Maggie put down the letter, grinning now. "That last bit? That's straight out of *Phantom of the Opera*, maybe even word for word. I never touched that part of the Lord Byron story, because there are too many versions out there, some for incest, some against."

"There's somebody out there *for* incest?" J.P. asked, winking at McCrae. "And she says I need to clean up *my* dialogue? Oh, right. Maggie? I wanted to tell you— you're off the hook, sunshine. Bruce has volunteered to mentor me, haven't you, sugar?"

"Well, I'm crushed," Maggie mumbled, folding the letter and clipping it to the envelope once more.

"I'll take that, thank you," Alex said, snatching the letter from her hand. "There are two more from Mr. Bryon that I've located, and he was nice enough to include his return address, which is to Bryon's Book Nook.

The address is in Greenwich Village, I believe. I think it might be prudent to pay a small visit to the gentleman."

"But he never did anything," Bernie pointed out. "Hell, everyone in publishing knows about good old George G. Bryon. He's a flake, but he's harmless."

"This one doesn't sound so harmless," McCrae said, handing a letter to Bernie. "Valentino Gates. Does that name ring any bells?"

Bernie adjusted her rimless reading glasses and began to read, her lips moving even as her eyes widened. "Why in hell wasn't this one turned over to the lawyers?" She squinted at the envelope. "Postmark's here in Manhattan, late last year."

"What's in the letter, Bernie?" Maggie asked, walking over to lean down on the back of the couch.

"It's about Jonathan West," Bernie told everyone, "and it's directed to Kirk—you all remember Kirk, right?"

There was a general murmur of agreement, because they all remembered Kirk Toland, although some of them had only learned about him after his death. His murder, actually.

Maggie read the typed letter over Bernie's shoulder. " '*Greatest writer of our age . . . coldly, callously shunted aside . . . genius denied . . . a pinheaded idiot who wouldn't know talent if it jumped up and bit off his nose*'—yup, definitely directed toward Kirk," she ended, grinning at Alex.

"But no overt threat?"

"No, Steve, no overt threat," Bernie said. "Just creepy. There's just this underlying tone of malice. *Demand you acknowledge your mistake . . . Jonathan West will be avenged . . . you have six months*—damn it, that part is kind of overt, isn't it, if not specific? This should have gone to the lawyers."

"Valentino Gates," Steve read when Bernie handed him the letter. "You think that's an alias?"

Alex was already at the computer, as J.P. had left the search engine on the page where she'd demonstrated how easy it was to get anyone's home address. "He's real enough," he said a few moments later. "And here's a coincidence—his address also, I believe, is in Greenwich Village."

"Oh, wait a minute," Bernie said, holding up a hand. "Valentino Gates, I know that name. He's a writer— well, he *thinks* he's a writer. The truth is that if every published author in the known world suddenly was vaporized by a Martian death ray, Valentino Gates *still* couldn't get published. But what he's got to do with Jonathan West, I don't know. Just a dedicated fan, I guess. Very dedicated."

Maggie rubbed her hands together. "Okay, but now at least we're getting somewhere." Then she frowned. "Where are we getting?"

J.P. returned her pile of letters to the coffee table. "Maggie's right. This is nothing more than a fishing exhibition. So far, none of these letters are about Francis Oakes, and he's our stiff. You've got nothing, Steve, no grounds for warrants. Zilch. Speaking as a defense attorney, it's my opinion that—"

"Don't, J.P., please," Steve said, pulling the plastic bag from his jacket pocket. "Let's work on this a while. What's all over this, Blakely? Oh, wait, never mind, I think I know. And it's just another stupid poem, like the one we found in Oakes's apartment, and signed the same way. Nevus."

"Nevus? You didn't tell me that, Alex."

"A thousand apologies, my dear," Alex said, handing Maggie a glass of wine. "Our miscreant, it would seem, mails dead rats and thinks of himself as a mole."

"But that makes no sense, Alex," Maggie said, getting to her feet and going over to Steve, keeping her hands behind her back as she looked at the note. "And yet, there it is. Nevus. Maybe it's some sort of personal thing only the guy knows, you know? Maybe he's got a lot of moles?"

"Or one great big one on his nose, like the Wicked Witch of the West," Bernie offered, toasting Maggie with her Shirley Temple. "Try saying it backwards, Mags. I know you can say *supercalifragilisticexpealadocious* backwards."

"It's not backwards letter-for-letter the way Mary Poppins sang it. *Docious-ali-expe-istic-fragi-cali-rupus*. Just another of my enormous and completely useless talents," Maggie said absently, already mentally reversing the letters in nevus. "S-U-Suven? That makes no sense. How about Never Ever Violate US—no, sorry."

"Yes, well, not that this hasn't been fun," Steve said, checking his wristwatch as he got to his feet.

"Do you have an appointment, *left*-tenant?"

"No, Blakely, I've got a murder to solve. Here's the deal, folks. Terrific as this has been, we're not getting anywhere. Bernie, thanks for the letters. Mr. McCrae, I suggest you exercise vigilance but do not panic."

"We're good there, Steve," J.P. said, opening her huge purse and pulling out a gun that looked to be about a foot long.

Maggie ducked behind Steve, because he was closest.

J.P. waved the nasty-looking weapon in the air. "I've got him covered. Don't I, sugar? Any way you want to take that one."

"Jeez. You have a permit for that cannon, J.P.?"

"Everything I need to carry concealed, Steve, and I know how to use this baby, too."

"You were a cop, yeah, I know. But you worked in

the mayor's office, J.P. When was the last time you were at the range?"

"Details," J.P. grumbled as the weapon disappeared back into her purse.

Steve looked at Maggie. "Where the hell was I with you guys before I lost what's left of my mind? Oh, okay. There's still the very real possibility that the packages you and some other writers received were nothing more than a coincidence of timing, and that there's no killer loose at CUNY, and that Oakes's is an isolated crime. I already said that, I think. Right now we're taking a second look at the former boyfriend, although, personally, I'm pretty sure that's a waste, unless Oakes had a new boyfriend and we're dealing with the jealousy card."

"Is that how you're treating it, Wendell, even after reading these letters—as true love gone wrong?" Alex asked, walking Steve to the door.

"I'm not *treating* it any way at all, Blakely. We're considering all the angles and, statistically, the spurned-lover motive is usually pretty high on the list. No forced entry—Oakes knew his killer. I'm not saying you guys aren't close to being on to something, but I need another twenty-four hours to chase down these other leads. So just keep an eye on Maggie," he added quietly.

"It will be my pleasure, *left*-tenant," Alex said with a polite inclination of his head. "Do have a pleasant evening with your young lady."

"She's not—I gotta go."

"What was all that about, Alex?" Maggie asked, picking up Steve's empty beer can. Steve hadn't kissed her good-bye, had he? "He didn't even take the letters with him. This was a real bust, wasn't it?"

"Not entirely. We do have this fellow Bryon and Mr. Gates to drop in on, evaluate."

"Why? Neither of them threatened Francis, or any of us."

"True, but they both live here and the packages were postmarked here. When you have nothing, Maggie, you take whatever small crumbs you've been handed. That is the nature of detection."

"Maggie, Alex? Look at this," Bernie said, holding up several sheets of paper. "I've got two more letters from Valentino Gates and another from Lord Bryon— all about how we were so mean to Jonathan West, and all in the folder for last year. You think that's a coincidence? Oh, and something else I forgot to give to Steve. The lawyers sent over photocopies of the letters we forwarded to them. You know, the ones from the *real* nuts. I didn't look at them yet. Maggie—they're in my purse."

"Scott Imhoff," Maggie said as she handed the letters to Alex after quickly looking through them. "Remember him, Bernie? One of those celebrity stalkers. He was trailing after Faith for a while. Man, she really freaked out, didn't she? Not that I wouldn't have—this guy showing up outside her building, snapping her picture, giving her flowers. She finally got a restraining order, right?"

Bernie pulled the cherry stem out of her mouth. "She's not the only one. Imhoff was after Jonathan West, too." She blinked, looked at Alex. "Did I say Jonathan West? Aren't we *all* saying Jonathan West here?"

Alex took the letter from Maggie. "Mr. Imhoff, it would appear, also resides in Manhattan. Does anyone else have letters they'd like us all to look at?"

Bruce McCrae tossed two letters onto the coffee table. "So we're going on even without the lieutenant? Good. Those were a bit flaky, but one's from California, and I'm getting the idea we're trying to stay local. And the other one is six years old. So, no, sorry, I've got nothing. J.P.?"

"I've got one here from this Valentino Gates guy, about another author," J.P. said, sorting through the letters she'd been reading and pulling out one of them. "Told her she's no Jonathan West—so there's that name again. We're seeing a lot of him, aren't we?"

"He was one of our top-selling authors for a few years, so that's really no surprise," Bernie explained. "The bigger you get, the more you manage to bring out the weirdos. I'm surprised there aren't more, beginning when he started writing those stinkers, but I guess they weren't threatening, and we threw them out."

"But this one isn't just about West, remember? Who knows Sylvia Piedmonte?" J.P. asked, waving the letter. "Anybody?"

"Maggie," McCrae said, "Sylvia *Piedmonte*. Remember? She's the one who called me, told me about her rat, the rats that went to Buzz Noonan, to Freddie Brandyce?"

"Oh, right," Maggie said, nodding. "I'm sorry. I'm lousy with names."

"Names, faces, places," Bernie said as she returned from a quick trip to the kitchen, the open jar of cherries in her hand. "If Maggie had her way, the whole world would wear nametags. You know all of them, Maggie, because you met them all at one time or another at one of our dinners. But let me help you out—Buzz Noonan writes as Garth Ransom. Ringing any bells now, honey?"

"Maggie?" Alex prompted as Maggie stared into the middle distance, and then began counting on her fingers.

"That's it!" she said at last, grabbing Alex by the shoulders and kissing him square on the mouth . . . which was as good as screaming *eureka* any day of the week. "It's that stupid book I wrote!"

"I beg your pardon. My books are not stupid."

"*My* books, and I didn't really write it. Not all of it. Don't move, anybody, I'll be right back!"

Her hands trembling with excitement, Maggie ran into the spare bedroom and skidded to a halt in front of one of the many bookcases she had placed in every room of the condo. She kept stuff in this room that she really couldn't in good conscience throw away, but didn't want to look at every day.

What was the matter with her? She should have thought of this sooner, much sooner. It was Alex's fault, obviously. He'd distracted her, made her lose her focus. No wonder athletes didn't have sex before a big game. . . .

"Let it be here, let it be here, let it be—ah, it's here!"

Taking the book from the shelf, she ran back into the living room, holding it over her head. "This is it—I've found the connection!"

"My God," McCrae said, shaking his head. "Of course it is. It's so obvious. Why didn't I think of it?"

Maggie looked at him. Yeah. Why didn't he if it was so obvious? "I didn't, either, Bruce. It's no big deal."

"In all fairness to both of you, nothing hit me, either. But you're right, Maggie. That has to be it," Bernie said, chewing on another cherry. "Well, I'm glad that's settled. Anybody else want a cherry? Please say no, they're all I've got."

"Delighted as you all must be," Alex said, reaching for the book Maggie was still holding above her head like first prize in some contest, "may I?"

"Sure, here you go, Alex," Maggie said, realizing she was almost breathless with excitement. Giddy, even. She shoved the book into his hands. "See? *No Secret Anymore*. Absolutely the *worst* book in the history of the world. Look—see the names? Jonathan West—you can't miss his name, it's two inches high. Then Sylvia Piedmonte, Garth Ransom . . . and then the rest of us going down the cover like an inverted pyramid. The peons. Look hard, the print's that small."

Alex took his quizzing glass from his pocket and lifted it to his eye. "Why are the names so small?"

"Because we were all small potatoes, that's why," Maggie told him. "Book buyers weren't really supposed to see us, all hidden on the cover. Jonathan was the biggest draw and they were supposed to buy the book for him, and get us as a bonus they might not have wanted. So Jonathan got top billing, then Sylvia, then Garth—damn, I didn't know his real name was Buzz Noonan. I might have put the pieces together faster if I'd known that. But look, Alex—look at those names."

Alex read the names out loud. "Jonathan West, Sylvia Piedmonte, Garth Ransom, Kimberly Lowell D'Amico. And then, in smaller print, Lucius Santana, Frederick Brandyce, Bruce McCrae. And in even smaller print— it hardly seems possible—Francis Oakes, Felicity Boothe Simmons, Alicia Tate Evans. Ah, before my time, I see," he said with no small pleasure, handing the book back to Maggie, who made a face at him, then gave the book to J.P.

"One of Kirk's brainstorms," Bernie explained as Maggie grinned at her own brilliance. "Well, Jonathan West's brainstorm initially, but Kirk was all over it. He saw it as the perfect—and cheap—way to promote his mid-list authors. Buy the book for Jonathan, or maybe for Sylvia or Garth, and discover a new Toland author you might like and then buy. I'm sorry I didn't realize it sooner, which is probably because I've spent eight years trying to block the whole episode from my mind. We took a bath, critically and financially. Not because of you, Maggie, or even you, Bruce, but Jonathan got a very large chunk of change he never earned back."

"Right, the book bombed big-time, and the critics ripped Jonathan, also big-time. I don't think he ever recovered," Maggie broke in, because, hey, it was her idea, so it was her story to tell, right? Not that she was crowing or anything—but, boy, it sure felt good to be the one who came through with some answers, rather than Alex, always the great super sleuth Viscount Saint Just.

"Here's the deal. Bruce, Bernie, you already know all of this, but I want to explain to J.P. and Alex. Ten different authors, each assigned to write one sixty-five-hundred-word chapter of a single book. It was doomed before we started. Ten short stories, maybe, even connected novellas. But a chapter each, all for the same book? Anyway, we each got a bible—that's like a set of rules for what we have to write, J.P., in case you think we were on some holy mission, because we sure weren't. We all met a few times to talk about the work, the authors who lived in New York, but trust me, we were no Algonquin Round Table. All in all, an experience I obviously tried to forget, although I got twenty-five thousand, which was great, and a cheesy one percent of the royalties. But we never saw any royalties."

"I got forty-five thousand, and one and one-half percent," Bruce interrupted.

"And a larger font on the cover—bully for you," Maggie said, glaring at him for a moment. "If I might continue? Jonathan wrote the bible because the whole thing was his idea in the first place, and he was the biggest draw. With Jonathan's name to carry us, and help from the next couple of authors down the line, like Bernie said, the idea was that the book would hit the *Times* and Kirk could then technically put *New York Times Best-selling Author* on all our book covers. He'd have seven new *NYT* mystery writers in one shot."

"Only it didn't work," Bernie added. "Jonathan wasn't easy to work with, was he, Maggie?"

"Easy? I wanted to kill him. We *all* wanted to kill him, didn't we, Bruce? He kept changing the bible, demanding a million rewrites from all of us. I worked with it because I had to—the advance money kept me in peanut butter for a long time after Kirk dropped me and I could come up with Cleo Dooley and Saint Just. But Faith nearly had a breakdown. She'd call me, screaming, ranting, begging me to help her because—ohmigod, Faith! Do you think she got a rat? She'd never tell, you know. Not Faith. Everybody has to love her. She'd never tell anybody she ever got hate mail."

"Yes, we'll consider that in a moment, shall we?" Alex said, leading Maggie over to the couches so she could sit down. "Bernie, as publisher of Toland Books, you probably have the most information on everyone involved. Can you possibly give us a . . . is the word *rundown?*"

"I can do that, Alex," McCrae said. "Unlike Maggie, I've kept in touch with most everybody who stayed local. Jonathan still lives in New York, but Maggie's right, *No Secret Anymore* really did him in and he's not writing anymore. I think he gave everything he had to those first few books, and then the well went dry for him, poor bastard. I don't think I've seen him in months. Frankly, he'd started getting a little bit weird."

"He's not *selling* anymore, you mean," Bernie put in with a small sniff. "But you're right on the other thing. Whatever Jonathan had, boy, did he lose it. His last three books—ever since *No Secret Anymore*—they all bombed. Kirk offered him another contract two years ago, but he wasn't real happy about the terms, and he turned us down. He can still live pretty well on his royalties, I suppose. *My Only Friend* is in its twenty-sixth printing. Oh, sorry, Bruce. Go on. No—wait. You do know that Lucius Santana died a few years ago? Skydiving, if you can believe that one. Okay, I'm done. Now you can go on," she ended, popping another cherry into her mouth.

Maggie grabbed a tablet and pen from her desk and

began making a list as Bruce told them that Jonathan West had become a semi-recluse. Rather the way Francis Oakes had done. Rather the way she herself had sort of begun doing, until Alex had come into her life . . . but she refused to think about that. Writers, lots of them, were pretty much stay-at-home people, that's all. Not everybody is a party animal. . . .

Bruce kept on talking and Maggie kept scribbling:

Jonathan West. New York. Rat??????

Sylvia Piedmonte. Massapequa Park, Long Island. Rat. Left town.

Garth Ransom (Buzz Noonan). New Jersey. Currently in Africa. Possible rat.

Kimberly Lowell D'Amico. Missouri. Rat??????

Lucius Santana. New Mexico. Deceased.

Frederick Brandyce. New York. Rat. Left town.

Bruce McCrae. New York. Rat.

Felicity Boothe Simmons. New York. Rat??????

Moi. New York. Rat.

Francis Oakes. New York. Rat. <u>DEAD</u>!!!

She looked up from the page. "I think we can safely say we've figured out at least part of this whole thing, at least enough to show a definite pattern. Do we really still need to know if Jonathan, Faith, and—" she took a peek at her notes; God, she really was bad at names, wasn't she "—and Kimberly also got rats? Yeah, I guess we do, just to nail down our theory."

"I've got Jonathan's phone number," Bruce said now, reaching into his pocket and pulling out a small electronic organizer. "Shall I give him a call? Ask him if he got a rat in the mail?"

"Good idea, since you know him. And then we have to call Kimberly D'Amico, too," Maggie said. "And Faith, I guess. Hey, wait a minute, Bruce, don't call him yet, not until we think about this a while. Maybe Jonathan is the one who sent the rats. I mean, think about it. Maybe he blames us for his career going into the toilet and he's finally popped his cork, or something. You said he'd been acting strangely lately, right? We could be calling a murderer. Damn, why did Steve have to leave so soon? Alex, what do you think?"

Alex paused in the middle of shining his quizzing glass against the front of his sweater. "Oh, you've remembered that I'm still here? How gratifying. I was about to go into a sad decline."

"Knock it off," Maggie told him. "Come on, we're all a part of the same team, right? Do we call these people or not?"

"I think if we're careful not to alarm them that, yes, Mr. West, Miss D'Amico, and your friend Felicity should be notified as soon as possible. It will also be interesting to see how our Mr. West reacts, won't it? But I would not stop there, as we are not at a point where we can rest on our laurels. It may come to nothing, but we were led in the direction we now agree upon only after reading the letters from Mr. Bryon and Mr. Gates, wasn't it? Mr. Valentino Gates? I would suggest we pay morning calls on both gentlemen. I would further suggest that we offer to include Wendell on those calls, if he's so inclined."

"Which he doesn't seem to be," Maggie pointed out. "Bruce, you're calling Jonathan now?"

Bruce held up one finger as he held his cell phone to his ear, then shook his head. "He's not answering— wait, his machine picked up. Jonathan? Jonathan, hi, Bruce McCrae here and I'm calling at . . ." he looked at Maggie, who mouthed the word *seven*, ". . . around seven o'clock on Tuesday evening. I don't want to alarm you, Jonathan, but we may have a small problem." He looked up at Alex. "I have an appointment tomorrow morning, but two friends of mine would like to stop by and talk to you. You remember one of them—Alicia Tate Evans? I know what you're thinking, but it's important, Jonathan, honest, so be nice and let them in, okay?"

He sighed, closed the phone. "I hope I got through to him. I'm betting he was standing right beside the machine the whole time, listening to me. Maybe I should cancel my appointment and—"

"A generous offer, but I believe we'll manage, thank you. Three morning calls then, Messrs. West, Bryon, and Gates," Alex said, looking at Maggie, who nodded her agreement.

"I've still got Kimberly's number on file back at the office, I'm sure, if you think it's really necessary to call out to Missouri."

"I think not, Bernice," Alex told her. "Depending on what we are able to discover tomorrow morning, Steve would be best equipped to notify the police in Missouri. Maggie? Do you wish to call Felicity, or shall I?"

"Can't we just stop by and see her tomorrow morning? Add her to the list? To the *end* of the list? I'm telling you, if she got a rat in the mail she'll lie and say she didn't. Everybody's got to—"

"Love her, yes, I heard that," Alex said as Bernie and J.P. gathered up the piles of letters and stuck them back into their folders, then into the briefcases. "Are we all leaving so soon?"

"Don't try to stop them," Maggie whispered, trying not to move her lips, then said, "Oh, gosh, do you have to? It's still early. We could . . . we could play charades?"

Two short minutes later, Maggie clapped her hands together as she grinned at Alex and said, "All right! Nothing like the suggestion of charades to clear a room. I thought Bernie was going to fall over herself, trying to get out of here. So? What do we do now?"

"You're such a gracious hostess," Alex told her, slipping his arms around her shoulders and pulling her closer to him. "But you'll notice that I'm still here."

Maggie ducked out from beneath his arms, putting some space between them. "Yeah . . . about that. This." She fluttered her hands helplessly. "You know. We probably should talk about it . . . consider the consequences if we . . . well, just because we . . . nobody says we're going to . . . at least not so that anybody else knows, because—will you please stop grinning and help here?"

"Certainly," he said picking up his glass of wine. "An isolated incident. Succumbing to temptation. A pleasurable but perhaps fleeting infatuation that should not weigh too heavily on either of us. Mutually satisfying—possibly even transcendental in nature—but by no means including a serious commitment by either party. Is there anything else you might have had me say to the many light-o-loves you've paired me with over the years? Ah, I know. Shall I buy you a diamond necklace, or some other such trifle, *sweetings*?"

"Bite me," Maggie said, storming past him and into the kitchen to wrap up the meat and salads. Nobody had eaten much, and now she had to figure out what to do with three pounds of macaroni salad, starting with what the heck she was going to put it in. "Oh, wait," she said, stopping before she got out of the living room. "Do you think Sterling is hungry? I could make a sandwich and take it over to him? And macaroni salad. He likes that, right?"

"Actually, Sterling had a request before I joined you this evening," Alex told her. "He would like to go ice-skating if our meeting adjourned early."

"Ice-skating? He just got beat up, for crying out loud. Are you sure?"

"I'm merely repeating the request as it was told to

me. But, if you would rather not, I'm sure Sterling will understand."

"No, don't do that. The way I'm figuring it, you're not going to let me out of your sight anyway, not until we find the killer, so we might as well do something fun. I'll go change, and grab my ice skates. Fifteen minutes? Then we can walk over to Rockefeller Center. I've . . . I've got all this *energy* I don't know what to do with."

Alex tipped up her chin, smiling down at her. "Energy. Is that what it is we're feeling? Shall we explore that notion?"

"Alex, don't—"

But he did. He did, and she was glad.

Chapter Fifteen

"You seem rather well pleased with yourself this evening, Saint Just," Sterling remarked as they waited in the foyer for both Socks and Maggie. "Almost inordinately so, actually."

Saint Just realized he had been smiling for what would appear to be no good reason, and took a moment to lightly scratch at his cheek while he composed his features into one of only gentle amusement rather than lingering . . . was the word *joy?* Odd. He was accustomed to his life being neatly divided, each area separate from the other. But now thoughts of Maggie seemed to have infiltrated all those neat little boxes, scrambling them inside his head. Pleasurably. "The meeting with Bernice and the others was fairly fruitful, Sterling, as a matter of fact. How long did Socks say he would be?"

"Well, he didn't, actually. He just made me promise not to leave before he got back. He loves skating, he told me. And Maggie?"

When he'd left her, Saint Just knew, she was still lying in bed, her chin in her hand as she watched him dress as she apologized for writing him with a dueling scar on his shoulder—the scar she'd earlier kissed, as he recalled the thing. Then, being Maggie, she'd asked if it bothered him during damp weather, and he'd remembered how living inside her mind had often entailed being very light on his feet, in order to avoid the tumbling mass of her constant and diverse thoughts. "I'm sure she'll be down shortly, Sterling. Are you quite positive you know how to skate?"

"Maggie said so in *The Case Of The Overdue Duke*, Saint Just, if you'll recall, on page two hundred and twelve, to be exact—something about me enjoying skating in my youth—so I imagine I'm fairly proficient. It's so nice that we can do anything that she wrote we can do, although I still wish she'd deigned to gift me with more hair and less belly." Sterling frowned. "I don't recall that she ever wrote that you skate, Saint Just. Perhaps it's a talent you don't possess?"

Saint Just smiled, not worried, as he had never questioned his own abilities. He was, after all, Saint Just. "I imagine I'll pick it up fairly quickly, my friend, don't fret about me. I am evolving, if you'll recall. We both are. I can remember a time you would have taken to your bed for days, after the sort of adventure you had this morning."

"That? It was nothing, Saint Just. Having so successfully foiled the robbers, I do believe I'm almost invigorated by the experience. And my eye is only red and Socks doesn't think it will turn psychedelic, whatever that means. Ah, and here he is now. Oh my, doesn't he look . . . natty?"

"He most certainly does look . . . something," Saint Just said, watching as Socks hurried into the foyer. He was dressed all in black from head to foot in what appeared to be dancer's leggings and a form-fitting, long-sleeved pullover, a long white silk scarf wound around his neck, his hair covered in a skull-hugging black cap, a pair of black skates bound together by the laces and positioned over his left shoulder. "Is this then the traditional skating wear, my friend?"

"Who says I'm going to skate, Alex?" Socks said, winking at him. "The object of this game is to *look* like you belong while everyone else is looking at you."

"Ah, what you would call a dating opportunity, yes? I think I understand. Although don't you think that outfit might be a trifle . . . blatant?"

"If *blatant* means what I think it does, Alex, then damn right it is. That's the whole point. Or don't you believe in truth in advertising? Hi, Maggie."

"Socks," Maggie said, slipping her arm through Sterling's, which put Sterling directly between herself and Saint Just. So much for any fears that she might become a clinging vine—not that he could remember having any objection to that possibility. "Sorry I'm late. Are we all set to go?"

"I would suppose so," Saint Just told her, deftly removing her knotted-together skates from her shoulder and placing them over his own. "And you're sure skates are sold at the skating rink?"

"Pretty sure. I know there are rentals. Oh, it's colder out here than I thought. Socks, are you warm enough?"

"I think he believes he's *hot*, actually," Saint Just whispered in her ear as she passed by him and onto the street while he held open the door.

Maggie grinned at him. "You're so sexy when you're modern. Oh, and let's take a cab, all right? It seems we're getting a later start than I'd imagined."

"And you can't imagine why," Saint Just said before asking Socks if he might attempt to hail a cab for them.

"Yeah, Socks," Maggie called out gleefully. "Do a couple of high kicks—that ought to stop traffic."

"Everybody's a comedian," Socks grumbled as he

headed for the curb, then put two fingers into the corners of his mouth and let go with a shrill, piercing whistle as he held his right hand high in the air.

Ten seconds later, they were in a nice warm cab and heading for Rockefeller Center.

As was, or so it appeared, the rest of the civilized world.

"We'll have to stand on line if we want to skate," Maggie told them as they piled out of the cab. Then she frowned. "For about a week. Jeez."

"It moves fast, Maggie. The tourists never last long. They just want to be able to tell their lodge buddies back home that they ice-skated at Rockefeller Center. We'll hold a place for you while you find skates for Alex. Sterling can rent a pair when we pay for the rink time—you're paying that, right?" Socks suggested, and then he grabbed Sterling's arm and led him to the end of the long, snaking line.

"Are you sure you want to do this?" Maggie asked as Saint Just, his hand at the small of her back, steered them through the crowds of tourists who stopped without notice or a thought to where they were standing when they spotted anything that took their interest. "Buying skates, I mean."

"To be truthful, I believe I'd rather steel myself to the idea of renting a pair, as the thought of locating an establishment where I can purchase a pair without having to queue up for the privilege is rather off-putting." He smiled down into her face. "Does that make me a snob with questionable standards in hygiene?"

"No," Maggie said, grinning at him. "They use sprays—disinfectants—in the skates after each wearing. I doubt your feet will turn black and fall off. Besides, we may never get on the ice. You did see that line, right? Let's just go up top and watch for now, okay? Count noses, maybe? If I remember it right, only a hundred and fifty skaters are allowed on the ice at one time."

Saint Just took one last look at the line, to see that at least ten more people had joined it, standing behind Socks and Sterling. "The queue is approximately fifty people. Very well, let's take a small tour."

"Would you like me to tell you about Rockefeller Center? I can do that, you know. Most tourists don't really understand all of it. For instance, my mother insists on calling it *Rocker-feller* Center, not that I correct her—I don't have a death wish. Anyway, John D. Rockefeller sponsored the whole thing, and it is a big thing. It's not just the area where the rink is, where the tree is—it's actually an entire complex, stretching between Forty-eighth and Fifty-first Streets. There are fourteen or more buildings, including Radio City, of course. But it's mostly offices. It's the center of broadcasting, stuff like that. And . . . well, that's it, that's all I've got."

"Then, please, allow me to expound a bit more, all right? You neglected to mention the art, both that of the buildings themselves, which are mostly in the Art Deco style, as well as the statue of Atlas, and Prometheus here, of course," he said, gesturing toward the large, recumbent statue that was one of the main focal points of the area.

"You already know all of this? You know about golden boy? I never knew who he was supposed to be, other than a huge golden man smack in the middle of the central fountain. Prometheus, you said? Man, and I live here."

"I live here now, Maggie. It is a man's responsibility to know his surroundings. And Prometheus is arguably the most tragic of the ancient Greek gods. You are aware that he angered Zeus by sneaking gifts to the mere mortals Zeus disdained? Fire, woodworking, numbers, the alphabet, healing drugs—on and on and on."

"Zeus didn't want us to have that stuff?"

She was such an attentive pupil . . . he'd simply ignore her way of lumping many things together as *stuff*. Thankfully, when she wrote, she was much more articulate. "Indeed no, Maggie. And, when he found out what Prometheus had done, he ordered the god shackled to the side of a crag high in, I believe, the Caucasus mountains. Every day Zeus's own eagle would tear at Prometheus's flesh—paying particular attention to the poor fellow's liver, for reasons I don't know—and every night that flesh would heal so that it could all begin again the next morning. This went on for centuries, I understand."

"Well, aren't you fun? You know, Alex, in your spare time, you ought to think about being a tour guide here. Just a great big barrel of laughs for the good folk visiting here from Des Moines." Maggie made a face. "Poor guy. He looks a lot better here. Imagine being in torment for centuries."

Saint Just merely nodded, for now was not the time to bring up the possibilities for his own future. He was, after all, as Maggie had made him. He and Sterling had already realized that Sterling would not gain or lose weight, no matter how he tried. A small thing, perhaps, but even small things can prove a point.

He and Sterling would not age unless Maggie wrote them as aging. They would not die, unless Maggie killed them. They were her creation.

Saint Just did not, however, believe he would be like Prometheus, living forever in agony—and life would be agony once Maggie was not here with him. No, Maggie would age, eventually fly free of this mortal coil, and Sterling and Saint Just would depart along with her.

Unless they evolved, which was Saint Just's all-consuming project, each of them becoming more his own man, his own creation—thus more in control of their own destiny. Neither would be immortal, of course, but, Saint Just often wondered, how much would he change, would his thinking change, if he were to know that he was suddenly vulnerable to all the various vagaries of mortal life as was his dearest Maggie. Would he so easily thrust himself into dangerous situations, if he were no longer assured of a happy outcome?

When he'd discussed the entire thing with Sterling, his friend had made allusions to a puppet named Pinocchio becoming a real boy, a happy ending that seemed to satisfy Sterling but did little to ease Saint Just's mind on the subject.

"Alex? You look a million miles away all of a sudden. What's wrong?"

Saint Just smiled at her. "Nothing, my dear. It would appear the shops are open this evening."

"Oh, goody. First stop, the truffle shop over there, where the trumpeting angels are—see them? I *love* the truffle shop. Wait until you see it. It's small, but always decorated so nicely—for the tourists, I suppose. But at Christmas it's spectacular. We'll have to stand in line there, too, but that's all right, because you always have to wait in line for chocolate this good. It's a rule of chocolate, I think. But don't tell Steve, because when I took him in there and there was a crowd, he flashed his gold shield to get waited on right away. Imagine that one, Alex. Steve, being pushy. Anyway, now he stops there all the time—well, on payday."

"You're rambling, Maggie. May I say perhaps even babbling," Saint Just told her as they sidestepped a frazzled-looking couple, each carrying a screaming toddler. "We're having an enjoyable evening, remember?"

"Yeah. Right. Maybe that's because I'm nervous. Or maybe it's because I'm definitely nervous." She looked up at him again, sighed in a rather theatrical way. "I can't help myself. I have to say it. We can't keep doing this, Alex."

"Doing? Doing what?"

Maggie rolled her eyes. "Oh, cute. You know darn well what we're doing. Did. We can't keep doing it, okay?"

"Because . . . ?"

She stopped to wait while he opened the door to the crowded shop. "Because we don't know what we're doing, that's because."

"I beg your pardon, madam," Saint Just told her, finding himself rather willing to amuse himself at her expense. "I've been laboring under a misapprehension? I'm *not* an exemplary lover? Perhaps if you were to be more . . . specific with your complaints?"

Maggie winced. "Would you, for crying out loud, keep your voice down?" she muttered from between clenched teeth.

But he kept on, enjoying her embarrassment, his mind happily away from Prometheus . . . and Pinocchio. "But I'm serious, my dear. Perhaps if you were to tell me precisely where I've failed? Is it something with the technique? My kisses, perhaps? Are they lacking?"

"I'm going to *kill* you," Maggie said, grabbing his arm and all but dragging him back to the narrow pedestrian plaza. "And I really wanted a truffle. Look, here's the thing. You're a romantic hero, the kind where the Doubleday Book Club puts an *explicit sex* warning at the end of the book blurb in the catalog. Yet you've been here for a while now, and nothing's been happening for you, right? We won't get into my lack of love life because it's embarrassing."

"I'll assume you're trying to make a point here?"

"Yes, I am. We're both . . . available to each other. Proximity, you know? It was only natural that at some point we'd . . . get together. But it doesn't mean anything."

"There you go again," Saint Just said, shaking his head in mock despair. "If you'll excuse me, I believe I feel a need to go find a woods somewhere and tiptoe inside to fall on my sword."

Maggie rubbed her mittened fingers against her temples. "I should write you a note. I do much better writing this stuff down. And it's not that you aren't good. I mean, hell, you're perfect. I wrote you, remember? I sort of have an *in* on what women want, what they like . . . what I like. So you're a great lover. I just don't know that this is going anywhere, if it even *can* go anywhere— you know, that whole *poof* thing—so maybe we just oughta slow things down for a while, that's all I'm saying."

Saint Just stepped closer and ran the backs of his fingers down her cheek. "Is that what you want, Maggie? What you really want?"

She looked up at him at last, her eyes wide. "Are you nuts? No, of course that's not what I want. You're the freaking perfect hero, remember? What kind of masochist do you think I am? I'm pointing out possible reasons for what happened earlier . . . and the first time. I'm just . . . I'm simply trying to be adult here."

Saint Just smiled. "And you're being very, very adult, my dear. I commend you. And you've had your say, so that I am forewarned and will protect my heart, I promise." Then he leaned closer, whispered in her ear. "Of course, it's also only fair to say that it already may be too late for that last small bit."

Maggie stepped back, her mouth opening and closing rather like a fish—but he adored her, so he believed she looked quite delightful. "I . . . you . . . we're slowing down, Alex. You evolve, and I'll go on a hunt for my brain, and we'll . . . well, we'll just . . . you know. Let's go watch the ice-skaters for a while."

Believing they had taken this particular conversation as far as it could go without possibly sending Maggie into spasms, Saint Just agreed. They found a place at the railing and looked down at the rink and the people crowding the surface. He tried to understand the concept, but it was proving difficult.

"Everyone is going in the same direction. Round, and round, with nothing to look at but the back of the person in front of you. They look rather like lemmings heading for the sea, except there's nothing but that endless oval, is there? Who's leading?"

"Nobody's leading, silly. Everyone's just skating, that's all. If they don't all go in the same direction there'll be pileups, and it won't be pretty. Oh, wait, look at that guy."

Saint Just looked where Maggie was pointing, to see a young man in suit and topcoat, skating backward. Unnecessarily, he said, "He's going backward."

"He's plowed, that's what he is. Drunk as a skunk," Maggie said as the businessman bucked traffic in a rather wobbly reverse. "Oh! Down he goes. One . . . two . . . three . . . four—and he's up. And he's . . . skating backward! He's too drunk to go forward. That's hysterical—oh, he knocked into somebody. That poor girl, he really knocked her down hard, didn't he? Uh-oh, the boyfriend approaches. This should be interesting. . . ."

Saint Just watched and waited. He didn't have to wait very long.

"That's . . . that's *Steve*. Alex? That's Steve. Steve and a . . . Steve and a blonde." Maggie blinked furiously, leaned over the railing. "Velcro blonde. Look at her— she's all over him. He . . . didn't he say he had to work tonight?"

"I believe he said he had something to do," Saint Just said, watching Maggie's face for her reaction.

"A date. He had a date. He's probably had a bunch of dates, unless the blonde gets that chummy right out of the gate. Well, huh." Maggie looked up at Saint Just. "Why don't you look as surprised as I feel?"

Saint Just put his palm to his chest. "Shall I say that I am aghast, agog?" He tipped his head slightly. "Would you wish me to call him out? I would, of course, as your every wish is my command. Although perhaps I should first point out that you and I have been more than . . . dating."

Maggie made a face. "Good point, damn it. And you know what? I'm relieved. Really. I mean, I love Steve, he's a doll. But . . . but it wasn't going anywhere, was it? Not with you around. The first time in my life I meet a guy I could really like, and my imaginary hero shows up to mess with my mind. I mean, what are the odds?"

"Probably not quite as high as the good *left*-tenant would have liked to believe," Saint Just said as he waved to the man, then gestured toward the side of the rink. "I think he's seen us. Ah, yes, he has, and now he's pointing to a spot over there and leaving the ice. Shall we join him?"

"Yeah, why not," Maggie said, doing a pretty good imitation of dragging her feet as they made their way to the edge of the crowd. "Am I smiling? I suppose I should be smiling. Smiling, and cheerful, and delighted to meet the blonde and—this is ridiculous. He's the one who should feel embarrassed, not me. Right?"

"Feel free to cling to me like a limpet if it will help your disposition at all. Oh, and you have my permission to address me as *darling*. Or, if you wish, we could change our minds and give him the cut direct, depressing his intentions quite effectively, or at least it would with someone more sensitive—which the good *left*-tenant is not. He confided in me, only a few short weeks ago, that he enjoys professional wrestling exhibitions on television. Imagine that? I would have told you sooner, but I wanted you to see the light, as it were, on your own."

"Bite me . . . *darling*," Maggie said, but allowed Saint Just to put his hand on her lower back as Wendell and his female companion, the former nearly tripping over his untied shoelaces, approached them.

"Maggie . . . Alex—hi!" Wendell said, much too cheerfully, Saint Just would have told him. "How about that—meeting you guys here, huh? I mean, who would have thought that—"

"Not you, obviously," Saint Just drawled, turning his attention to the young lady. "*Left*-tenant, if you would be so kind as to introduce us to your friend?"

"What? Oh, right, right. Christine Munch—Maggie Kelly and Alex Blakely."

Realizing that this would be the extent of Wendell's introduction, Saint Just took it upon himself to take Miss Munch's extended hand and bow over it, saying, "Charmed, I'm sure."

Christine Munch giggled and then pressed her cheek against Wendell's sleeve.

Just the sort of female the good *left*-tenant needed. Saint Just felt *much* better. "Ah, Miss Munch, what a delightful laugh. A whisper of springtime on this chilly December evening. Oh, I just realized that Wendell here has been a bit remiss—haven't you, *Left*-tenant? Miss Munch, this dear woman is indeed Maggie Kelly, but she is also Cleo Dooley, a very famous author."

"Alex, for cripes sakes . . ."

"An author? Wow, no, Steve didn't tell me." Christine's smile faded and she shrugged. "I'm afraid I don't read. Well, I know *how*—I just don't do it. Sorry. Does anyone really have time for that anymore? Oh, but I'm sure you're very good."

"Oh, yes, I'm excellent." Maggie gave Saint Just a closed-mouth smile accompanied by raised eyebrows, all combining to form a silent *I told you not to do this stuff because it always comes back to bite you*.

"Um . . . Maggie?"

She looked at Wendell. "Yes, Steve?"

"About . . . this," he began, and Saint Just longed to box the lummox's ears, for it was clear that the good *left*-tenant was about to open his mouth and insert *both* of his feet. He wasn't certain, but he believed the modern-day parlance was that, when it came to the ways of women, Steve Wendell was a *schmuck*.

"Wendell," Saint Just broke in quickly because he was, at the bottom of it, a good-hearted man. "Maggie and I are so delighted to meet Miss Munch. We've been fretting about you, you know, leading a lonely bachelor life. Have you two been seeing each other long?"

"Since just before Thanksgiving," Christine Munch said happily. "He rescued me in the subway when some kid tried to grab my purse." She looked up at Steve, her huge blue eyes innocent and uncomprehending of any tension. "My knight in shining armor."

"Gag me . . ." Maggie whispered out of the corner of her mouth, then said brightly, "Well, then, that explains it, doesn't it? Alex and I left town on Thanksgiving, didn't we, darling?"

Years of training, most probably employed to keep an unmoved, steely expression when dealing with felons, stood Wendell in good stead, except for a momentary flaring of his nostrils as he looked at Saint Just before the virtual penny, as it were, dropped, and he seemed to realize that he'd just had a very lucky escape.

"Does anyone want to go get some coffee?" he asked in a tone that seemed hopeful that no one would. "If not, I just want to tell you that Bernie called me on my cell earlier to tell me about this Scott Imhoff fellow. The celebrity stalker? I checked him out, and it's not him. He's been in lockup for a month now." He grinned. "You'll never guess who he was after this time—our mutual friend, Holly Spivak."

"Holly *Spivak*," Christine gushed, nearly going to her knees in delighted shock. "You *know* Holly Spivak? From Fox News? Ohmigod, Steve, why didn't you tell me you know someone *famous*!"

Maggie leaned close to Saint Just. "Hear that faint chopping noise, Alex? That's me, under the knife. Chopped liver. I love people. Really. I can't imagine why I don't try to get out more, don't you?"

Saint Just manfully repressed a smile. Maggie was such a—writer. Longing for anonymity, upset when no one knew who she was. "Then that's one suspect eliminated, *left*-tenant, good. However, Maggie and I intend to visit Valentino Gates and George Bryon tomorrow, simply to satisfy our own curiosity, if you were about to ask. Oh yes, and one thing more. After you left our small party earlier, we all realized that we might have found a connection between the rats and our killer."

Maggie stepped slightly in front of Saint Just. "My story, Alex. It's true, Steve. You see, all the people who

got rats also had all contributed to this one book together and—"

"All the people who got rats are connected through a
book? Bernie didn't tell me that. Well, I sort of cut her
off, I guess, because I was running late, picking up
Christine here. Sorry. So you found a connection. Let's
hear it."

"We don't really know much more, Wendell. There
are still a few names to check on, two here in the city,
and one out west."

"Then you've got a hunch, a lead, but nothing definite
yet. All right, good work, but we'll still need to concentrate on the CUNY area, if that's all right with you
junior detectives—at least until we have something more
definite to go on. I'll call you tomorrow morning sometime, Blakely, and get the names from you. You two
want to check on Gates and Bryon, be my guest, but
I'm betting they're harmless. Just run-of-the-mill flakes.
But that's it, then you're out of it, agreed?"

"Out of it?" Maggie jammed her hands on her hips.
"You had spit before we figured out the connection,
Steve, and don't hand me that CUNY connection again,
because I'm not buying it—that's politicians thinking
CYA and public relations. So don't tell us we're *out of
it*. If Alex and I are right, I could be a *target*, you know.
I got a rat, remember. Two of the authors left town—
Alex, do you remember their names? Never mind, it's
not important. What's important is that someone sent
rats and now one of the someones who got one is dead
and some of the someones who got rats took a hike,
cutting down on the number of local targets still available to Rat Boy—and I'm one of those targets. So don't
you tell me to—"

"Maggie?" Saint Just inquired gently as she stopped
talking, her finger still in the air, her mouth still open.

"You've harangued yourself into an unhappy conclusion, haven't you, my dear?"

"I'm a target," she said quietly. "Me. A target. Somebody could be wanting to *kill* me. Be watching me, right now. Waiting for his big chance. I don't feel so good. Alex? Let's go get Sterling and Socks and go home. And lock the doors. . . ."

"If you'll excuse us?" Saint Just said, inclining his head to Wendell and Christine. "Miss Munch, it truly has been a delight. And don't worry, Wendell. I won't leave her for a moment."

"Yeah, I already had that one figured out," Wendell said flatly. "Like I said, I'll get those names from you in the morning, of the local authors. Pay them a visit. Just keep her safe. House arrest until this is over."

At that Maggie rallied. "House arrest? Hey, I'm not the bad guy here, damn it! It's Christmas. I've got shopping to do, a life to lead. Don't you say *house arrest* to me, Steven Wendell."

Saint Just sighed. "You never knew her very well, did you, Steve?" he said kindly. "But it's not to worry. I've long since known that my mission in life is to be at Maggie's side," Saint Just said. "Miss Munch, please forgive our interruption and enjoy the remainder of your evening."

Within five minutes Saint Just had rounded up Sterling and Socks, who had gotten to precisely the head of the line and were next up to pay for rink time. Sterling protested for a moment, but then looked at Maggie, who was still rather pale. "Has something gone amiss, Saint Just?"

"Nothing more than earlier, no, Sterling," Saint Just told his friend as they all four climbed into the cab Socks had hailed with his usual expertise. "Maggie has just belatedly realized that she may have somehow become the target of a killer. Happily, we are here to protect her."

"Protect me, yes. But don't smother me, okay? I mean, I'm not one of those stupid women who say, oh no, I refuse to stop living my life, change my routine, when they know damn full well some depraved stalker with a machete and a hockey mask is out to kill her. I mean, I'm not *stupid*. But I've got Christmas staring me in the face in a couple of weeks. I've got things to do."

"So, first on the list, my dear, would be to solve the crime, yes?"

Maggie blinked several times, and then a slow smile lit her face. "Exactly! And did you see Steve back there? Tomorrow is soon enough for him to hear the other authors' names and just how we put it all together? Oh yeah, he's all hot to solve the case. Not! He's playing pattycake with Christine Mun-something, that's what he's doing. Well, you know what? We're going to solve it *for* him."

"Because you need something to do, because having something to do—anything to do—is better than locking yourself in your condo until the miscreant is locked in a cell."

"You betchum, Tonto!"

"She is woman, hear her roar," Socks piped up from the front seat. "Have I ever told you guys how much I like being a part of the gang?"

"We have a gang?" Sterling asked, concerned. "A coterie, perhaps, but a gang? Isn't that above all things wonderful! Should we have a name? Gangs have names. I know this because Vernon and George used to belong to a group called the One-hundred-and-thirty-fifth Street Hell Warriors. Although Mary Louise told me it was purely a social club. Still, I think we should have a name."

"Maggie's Menagerie," Maggie suggested drily, sliding across the cracked leather seat and into Saint Just as the cabbie took the turn too fast.

"Alex's Allies," Saint Just teased, if only to see some color coming back into her pale cheeks. "Blakely's Boys—oh, wait, that rather leaves you out, doesn't it, my dear? Shame on me. Very well, we'll be all-inclusive, shall we? A bit you, a bit me? We'll call ourselves Saint Just's—"

"We're here," Maggie said, cutting him off. "And it's Maggie's Menagerie, end of discussion. At least give me the illusion that I'm in charge of *something* in my own life."

Chapter Sixteen

Maggie barreled into the foyer of the building ahead of everyone else, still trying to come to grips with the obvious. The obvious that should have been obvious from the beginning. And not one obvious, but two.

Obvious One: She never should have gone to bed with Alex. Twice. She most definitely shouldn't have taken up his invitation to call him *darling* in front of Steve. But that was just all too, too bad. Mistake or not, and even though he drove her crazy half the time, she was keeping him.

Obvious Two: She was walking around with a target on her back. The object of a deranged killer, because underanged killers don't send rats to people. A nut job was after her, and he'd already killed poor Francis Oakes. Knocked him senseless and then strung him up like a chicken in one of those grocery store windows down in—"Daddy?"

Evan Kelly stood up slowly from the lobby couch, his smile bordering on sickly. "Hello, pumpkin," he said quietly, then sort of held out his arms, sort of didn't . . . leaving the option of hugging him or just standing there gawking at him up to Maggie.

Who stood there and gawked at him.

"Is something wrong? Mom? Is something wrong with Mom?"

The graying, slightly built man held out his hands—to ward off Maggie's fears, she supposed. "No, no, pumpkin, your mother is fine, just fine. Well, as fine as a woman can be when she's just discarded her husband of nearly forty years."

"She did *what*? She threw you *out*? Ohmigod. How . . . how long have you been here?"

"I . . . I'm not sure," her father answered, looking both frazzled and distracted. "A little over an hour? I told that fellow over there I was here to see you, but he didn't know where you were. Why?"

Maggie needed a target, that's why. It was stupid, but either she exploded over something or she'd start thinking about how she'd suddenly become a sort of pseudo-orphan, a child of divorce . . . and, not unimportant to consider, a woman who was soon going to have her father bedding down in her guest room and her lover sleeping across the hall. The whole thing stank from any angle she wanted to see it from.

"Paul!"

The part-time doorman looked up from his copy of *Guns And Ammo* and blinked at her. "Huh?"

"You left my father sitting down here for over an hour? He told you who he is, I know he did. Why didn't you let him into my condo?"

Paul, who was a manly man, an imposing, dangerous figure, but only in his dreams, got off his stool behind the podium and hitched up his uniform pants. "Couldn't do it, miss. Against the rules. Can't be too careful who you let upstairs, you know."

"Was it against the rules a couple of weeks ago when

you let those robbers into—hell, I don't remember his name. You helped the crooks carry out a wide-screen TV, for cripes sakes! But my father? Oh, no, not my father. What? He's got the look of a criminal? He's got a dangerous glint in his eyes behind those bifocals? Maybe he's carrying concealed Metamucil? You have got to be the *worst*—"

"Mr. Kelly, what an unexpected pleasure," Alex said, deliberately walking between the cringing, clearly terrified doorman and Maggie the Terrible. "Maggie neglected to tell me you'd be visiting the metropolis."

Maggie deflated. What was the point, anyway, except to delay the inevitable. "Mom threw him out," she told Alex, then headed for the elevator. "Come on, let's all just go upstairs and figure this out, all right?"

"Hello, Mr. Kelly," Sterling chirped, just entering the lobby in his usual happily oblivious way, Socks right behind him. "Do you remember me? Sterling. Sterling Balder. You and I had the drumsticks on Thanksgiving. Oh, and this is my friend, Argyle Jackson. Socks, say hello to Maggie's father."

Socks stepped forward, extending his hand. "We've met once before, I think, sir, when Maggie first bought the condo. Good to see you again, sir."

"Yes, thank you." Evan Kelly smiled weakly, and then turned to Alex, who had already secured the man's one small piece of luggage. "What is he wearing? Is he in a Broadway show of some sort? He walks the street like that?" He shook his head. "I don't understand New York."

Maggie grinned at Socks, who for the first time that evening seemed to believe he might want to cover his crotch with his hands. "Come on, Dad. I'll make you something to eat—I've got lots. Oh," she said rather inanely, she knew, as everyone piled into the elevator and the door slid closed on Socks, who waved goodbye with only one hand, "But I don't have any puffed rice. . . ."

Fifteen minutes later, with everyone settled in Maggie's living room, all of them watching Evan Kelly spoon potato salad into his mouth, she finally asked for details, even though she didn't want to hear them.

"You know your mother can be . . . well, difficult," Evan told her with a weak smile. "And determined. Most certainly determined. When she gets an idea into her head, there's no getting it out again."

"I've wondered where you acquired that particular trait, my dear," Alex said from his perch on the back of the couch as he lifted a glass of wine to his lips.

"Right," Maggie shot back at him, but quietly. "She's down, very nearly out, so hey, here's an idea—why not stomp on her? Thanks, Alex—just what I needed, to be compared to my mother."

Sterling was clearly upset over the entire matter. "You allowed her to banish the master from his own hearth? Oh, sir, excuse me for being so blunt, but you really shouldn't have countenanced that. I am a bachelor, I admit, and probably designed to remain so, but my own father gave me copious advice on the rights and privileges of a gentleman. One of those rights, sir, is the assurance of his own chair by his own fireside. Oh, and a female as companion and helpmate. But, sir, not in charge. Never in charge. I think you should be best served to return home right now and assert your rights."

Maggie had joined Alex behind the couch. "Part of me agrees with Sterling," she told him, "while the modern woman in me wants to tell him he's a chauvinist pig who ought to remember he's now in the twenty-first century. The last part of me, of course, is laughing its butt off at the idea that Dad would ever stand up to Mom."

But, it would seem that Evan Kelly agreed with Sterling. "It's as much my house as it is hers, isn't it? Not that it belongs to either of us," he added, the spine he'd momentarily straightened somewhat collapsing again against the soft cushions. "She's probably already called Tate, and told him all about his horrible father, and demanded that Tate call me and tell me never to darken his door again."

"Tate really owns the house, remember? Scoring points with Mom and Dad for being the good son, while at the same time using the house as a great investment that's going to make him big bucks someday," Maggie reminded Alex. "And, since my big brother has made an art out of playing one parent off the other for as long as I can remember, Dad probably has it right. Which leaves Dad to—"

"Move in with his favorite daughter?"

"Oh, Alex," Maggie said, sagging against him. "We've got to do something to get those two lovebirds back together."

"Because you are a possible target for a killer and your father could somehow become an innocent victim?"

Maggie frowned, suddenly remembering what, only an hour earlier, had been the biggest problem in her life. "Oh, right, that, too. I was thinking more of the idea that Dad would be here all the time . . . and Sterling's across the hall with you all the time . . . and I know I said we shouldn't do what we did, but let's get real here, Alex, okay? Nobody only takes two bites of an apple."

"I adore it when you try to avoid speaking frankly on what should be a simple subject for two people who have so recently been intimate."

Maggie winced, barely holding back from clamping a hand over his big mouth. "Would you shut up?" she growled at him. "I *write* that stuff—I don't *say* that stuff. I most especially don't say that stuff with my own *father* sitting on the other side of the room. Cripes, Alex . . ."

Evan Kelly swallowed down another mouthful of potato salad, having already explained that his wife had shown him the door before dinner, and looked at Maggie. "I don't know how she knew."

Maggie's eyes nearly popped out of her head—they actually *hurt* as she looked at her father. "She *knew*? She knew what, Dad?"

"About Carol, of course," Evan said, leaning forward to put down his empty bowl. "I was listening on the extension when she called you to tell you about Carol. That's why I knew I could come here. I knew you'd understand."

"Well . . . well, you guessed wrong, Dad," Maggie heard herself say, then winced, because she certainly wasn't helping her dad here, was she. "I mean, I understand that Mom can be . . . difficult. But to have an affair? After forty years? That is what we're talking about here, right? An affair? With . . . with a little chippie named Christine—I mean, Carol."

"Feeling a tad confused, my dear? Allow me to clarify for you. Christine would be the *left*-tenant's little chippie."

"Shut up. That was *not* a Freudian slip," Maggie told him, then left him and returned to the couch, to sit down facing her father. "Are you going to divorce Mom and marry this Carol person? Because, hey, I'm fine with that. I mean, I'm grown, I'm gone—I have nothing to say about what you guys do. Although Maureen's probably going to figure out that that leaves her to take care of Mom, and she's either going to run away to join the circus or double up on her happy pills." She raised her hands. "But, hey, that doesn't matter, either. Your life, your decision. Tate will have a cow—that could be fun—and Erin? Hell, talk about ducks and backs."

"Excuse me? Maggie, you're really upset, aren't you?" her father said, clasping his hands together on his knees. "You left us, all of you, except Maureen, who probably should have. What does it matter what your mother and I do? I love Carol, Maggie, and your mother knows it."

"Oh, God, you weren't supposed to say that," Maggie told him, rubbing at her stinging eyes. "You were supposed to ask me to help you get back with Mom. You've been married forever. You've got four kids. You . . . you have a *history*. You can't be in love—you're *married*. This is just a . . . an infatuation. Some midlife crisis thing. Why can't you just go home, buy a silk shirt and a gold neck chain, maybe a red sports car, and forget about this Carol woman?"

"Pardon me for interrupting your litany of suggestions, but Maggie? Your message light is blinking," Alex told her. "Perhaps messages from your mother? She may be worried about your father?"

Maggie jumped to her feet and leveled an accusing finger at her father. "Yes! Yes, that's what it is! You left her all alone, and she doesn't know where you went, what you're doing, how you are—all that stuff. She wants you home, Dad. You two can work this out, you'll see. Counseling! Yes, that's what you need—counseling." She looked at Alex. "Hit the button, okay, and turn up the volume."

Alex inclined his head in agreement and pushed the appropriate button on the answering machine a second before Maggie's brain kicked into Slightly More Rational Mode and she realized that her mother hadn't left a "nice" message since answering machines had been invented.

There were three messages. All from Alicia Kelly.

Message One: "Tell that no-good philandering tomcat that his clothes are on the back porch where the neighbors won't see them."

Message Two: "Evan? I've closed all our joint accounts. You're now as fiscally bankrupt as you are morally depraved."

Message Three: "Margaret, inform your father that he has a dentist appointment tomorrow at two."

Well, at least the woman had been succinct.

Maggie, in a move born of desperation, latched on to that third message. "Aha! You hear that? She's worried you'll miss your dental appointment. She *cares*."

"Maggie, sweetings, let it go," Alex told her, putting his hands on her shoulders and gently guiding her toward the hallway. "Your father looks tired. I suggest you let me help you prepare the guest room for him, and we'll all revisit the situation in the morning."

She dug in her heels. "We can't do that, Alex. I'm a target, remember? You're the one who reminded me. I can't take the chance of exposing my dad to danger. I'll get him a room somewhere." Ducking out from under Alex's hands, she returned to the living room. "Dad, I'm going to get you a hotel room, all right? Just until we see how things go once Mom calms down."

Evan Kelly got to his feet, which wasn't that imposing a sight, as he and Maggie might both be slightly built, but they were the Lilliputians in a family of near giants, his own wife topping him by a good three inches, as a matter of fact. "Margaret, I don't think you heard me. I love Carol. I am not going back to your mother. Not unless she apologizes."

Maggie shook her head, just to make sure her brains hadn't come loose and might rattle around inside her skull. She didn't usually take her mother's side in anything—she'd *never* taken her mother's side in anything—

but this one hit her somewhere in the "we're fellow fe-males" place where she lived. "You *love* this Carol per-son, but you want Mom to apologize? For what?"

"I'm not very good at this, am I? I don't really love Carol. I just said that. I lied. I'm sorry."

"Okay . . . I think. And you just said that to Mom, too, right, lied to her, too? But why should Mom be the one apologizing?"

Evan lowered his head, fairly whispering his next words. "She had an affair with Walt Hagenbush. Ten years ago. She told me all about it on our wedding an-niversary, three months ago. She told me she needed to confess what she'd done because—well, I'm not quite sure why. I think it's her menopause, truthfully. She hasn't been handling it well. But that doesn't matter. What matters is that nothing has been the same for us since she told me."

Maggie sucked in three breaths before ever breath-ing out again. "Mom—*my mother*—had an affair? Oh, that's just ridiculous. Who'd ever—no, scratch that, that isn't nice. But, seriously—who'd be that brave? Walter who? With *Mom*? Alex, I think I need a—"

"A brandy, I agree," Alex said, already heading for the drinks table. "Sterling, for reasons I don't care to delve into too deeply at the moment, you also would seem to be in need of a small restorative."

"Yes, thank you so much, Saint Just," Sterling said, taking a large white linen handkerchief from his pocket and dabbing it at his forehead. "Our poor Maggie. We've never had a divorce in the family, have we? It's all so . . . so sordid."

Actually, as far as Maggie was concerned, it all was beginning to seem pretty stupid. Her mother had com-mitted the worst sin in marriage. Not having an affair, although that was pretty bad, but telling her husband about it ten years later. Ten years! Who the hell cared, ten years later?

Well, her father, obviously. He'd stewed, he'd simmered, and then he'd gone out and found Carol, the chippie. She said as much. "So you went out and found Carol to get some of your own back on Mom, right?"

"Just so I could say that I'd had an affair, too, yes," Evan agreed as Maggie dedicatedly nursed the snifter of brandy, hoping for numbness to set in somewhere besides her lips and molars.

"So did you? Or did you just tell Mom that you did?" Maggie grimaced as she looked at Alex. "And do I really want to know the answer to that question?"

"No, my dear, I don't think you do. I also believe that you do not want to insinuate yourself between your mother and father in this matter, also a point toward keeping your knowledge as minimal as possible."

"Too late, Alex—I'm already going to go to my grave thinking about my mother and some . . . some Walter. Alicia Kelly, checking into a by-the-hour motel. God."

"I should be going," Evan said, getting to his feet. "I called ahead and have a room at the Marriott waiting for me, but I felt sure your mother would try to contact me here. And don't worry about money, Maggie. I've maintained a MasterCard account in my own name for several months now. I do watch Dr. Phil now and then, you know. Cheaters have to be up to all the tricks. But your mother must know more of those tricks than I do, because she found me out, didn't she? Perhaps I wanted her to?"

"Oh, God," Maggie said a few minutes later, once Alex had put her father into a cab and come back upstairs. "I knew we were dysfunctional—but who could have imagined any of this? And you want to know the worst? It's Christmas. Who do I go to for Christmas? Mom or Dad? Hey, do you think I can just send them both cheese trays and stay home? I mean, there's got to be a pony hiding somewhere in this pile of—oh, never mind."

"Maggie, shame on you," Alex said, heading for the door once more. "As I recall the thing, you have an appointment with Dr. Bob in the morning. What do you say I meet you at his office at ten, at which time we'll be off to Greenwich Village. Oh, and then a visit to your friend, Felicity, to learn if she, too, received a rat in the mail."

"I suppose we have to do that, huh? Tell Faith, that is. And Jonathan West, too. I don't trust Lover Boy to take us seriously on any of this. Jeez, love makes people weird, doesn't it? Steve used to be a good cop who never thought about the political end of a case, even broke rules when he felt the need. He's probably thinking about his future now, with Christine in the picture. And Dad used to be a good—never mind. Go home, Alex. I think I'm going to have a pity party, and I don't want you to see it."

"I could stay," he said quietly.

She blinked back tears, nodded. "I know. But not tonight, Alex. You know," she added, trying to smile, "you can make a perfect hero, but you can't make a perfect life. Only in fiction, you know? It's why I write happy endings. I like happy endings . . . but I don't see one here. Not right now."

He'd barely closed the door when Maggie was wishing him back, but she didn't go after him. She was too used to being on her own, working things out for herself.

Except she hadn't really been alone. Not since puberty, according to Sterling. Alex had been . . . had been her imaginary friend.

Now he was her for-real lover.

Speaking of lovers . . . both her parents had taken lovers.

And Rat Boy was still out there.

What a mess.

"Time to play Snood," Maggie said out loud, heading for her computer and what she knew would be at least two hours of mindless Snood shooting.

When she woke up the next morning she was on the couch, the almost empty brandy snifter still balanced on her stomach, and she could hear her alarm clock buzzing down the hall in her bedroom.

"Dr. Bob!" she said out loud, and ran to take her shower, grab an iced cinnamon-and-sugar Pop-Tart, and head for the psychiatrist's office.

Five minutes into the hour-long session, she was wishing she'd overslept and missed the appointment.

"Well, now, Margaret, this is an upsetting situation your parents have put you in, isn't it? How do you propose to deal with it, hmm?"

Maggie reached for her second tissue of the session. "Isn't that what you're supposed to tell me? Isn't that why I pay you the big bucks?"

"I'm not here to solve your problems for you, Margaret."

"Yeah, you got that in one," Maggie muttered into the tissue, then blew her nose. "But I don't know what to do. He's on one side, she's on the other—and I'm smack in the middle. I'm taffy, that's what I am, being stretched in two directions at once."

"Oh, that reminds me," Dr. Bob said, reaching down on the side of his desk and coming up with a small blue box tied with a silver ribbon. "Here you are, Margaret.

I'm giving out sugarless fudge this year, except to my bulimics and anorexics, of course. They'll receive autographed first editions of my new book—well, the one that's just come out in paperback, that is. Oh, would you like one, Maggie? Instead of the fudge, you understand. Although I did tell you it's sugarless, correct? I know you're on a diet."

Maggie just let that one roll over her, one more problem in her life, and one she didn't have time for right now, thank you. Good old cheerful Dr. Bob should just be happy she hadn't as yet reached for a cigarette. *Yet* being the operative word, because she was teetering on the brink.

"Can we get back to my mom and dad? I'd call the sibs—my siblings, that is—except I already know how each of them will react, and it won't be good. I want to help Mom and Dad, I really do. I just . . . I just don't want to get involved, you know? That's selfish, isn't it?"

"Self-preservation, Margaret. It's in our nature, and perfectly understandable. But let me help direct you, as you're clearly conflicted. For the moment, your parents are finding their own way, reacting in their own way, and they both deserve the time and space to do just that, without interference. Your job, if you'll think of it that way, is to be supportive but nonjudgmental."

"Kind of hard to do that with Mom on the phone every three seconds and Dad living here in New York."

"True," Dr. Bob said, leaning back in his oversize leather chair. "You are on the horns of a dilemma, aren't you, my dear?"

Maggie held up one finger as she chuckled in what she hoped was a rueful way. "Oh no, that one doesn't work for me anymore. You pity me, I do a knee-jerk stand-up riff for me and say it's not all that bad. I have a great career, lots of friends, a nifty condo, cup more than half full, yadda-yadda. The old self-esteem bit. But it won't work this time, Dr. Bob. And you know why? Because my life is a mess on so many levels, that's why. Someone's out to kill me. Did I mention that?"

Dr. Bob, who had been scribbling something on a yellow legal pad, slowly turned his head to look at her from beneath his thick eyebrows. "Really," he said in that hugely irritating neutral voice of his. "And how long have you thought someone was out to get you, Margaret?"

Maggie actually picked up her purse and opened it, began to search inside for a nonexistent pack of cigarettes, before she stopped herself. "Not out to *get* me. Out to *kill* me. Oh, cripes, never mind. It's nothing for you to worry about."

"Because Saint Just will protect you, hmm?"

Okay, now she *really* wanted a cigarette. "You know what, Dr. Bob? One of us needs a shrink. What do you mean, *Saint Just* will protect me?"

"There's an ethical question here, I believe. But as I never registered him as a patient, and he most certainly didn't pay for my time . . . yes, I think I'm safe in telling you this, Margaret. Your Saint Just was here the other day."

"My Saint Just," Maggie repeated, getting that Alice-down-the-rabbit-hole feeling again. "Here. As in *here* here? To see you? You've got to be kidding. Why?"

Dr. Bob shook his head. "No, I'm afraid I can't allow myself to go that far. But he was here, and he does seem to enjoy being referred to as Saint Just. And he is most definitely quite protective of you. And, while he seems rational, I must tell you, Margaret, the man appears to be laboring under an illusion. One of . . . well, very nearly omnipotence, I'd say. Very self-assured, extremely confident. Bordering on arrogant, I'd have to say, although totally charming."

Maggie grinned. She couldn't help herself. "Yup, that sounds like Alex."

"And you see nothing odd in that, Margaret? That your cousin should have cast himself in the role of your imaginary character, your fictional hero? And, as we both know from recent events that have reached the media as well as been discussed between us in this office, the man seems to have a penchant for embroiling himself in . . . adventures."

"He's not the Lone Ranger on that one, Dr. Bob. I'm in those adventures, too, remember?" Maggie said, beginning to bristle a bit. "And none of them were our fault. Things just . . . they just seem to happen to us, that's all. Kirk, for one, was certainly not my fault. Like helping Bernie when she found her first husband had come back from the dead to die in her bed. And don't tell me it was our fault that someone went apeshit at that romance convention. Oh, and England? We just happened to be there, that's all. I mean, come on, like it was *my* idea to discover that guy swinging from his neck outside my window? And look at Rat Boy, for crying out loud. I sure didn't ask him to send me a dead rat, or that stupid poem threatening to kill me—or at least hinting at it. Who would *ask* for that sort of—"

Dr. Bob held up his hand, stopping Maggie in midrant. "You're serious, aren't you, Margaret? Saint Just—that is, your cousin Alex—was serious? There's someone possibly out to kill you?"

"Finally! *Yes*, someone may be out to kill me. One guy is already dead—Francis Oakes. The police are on it—well, sort of—and I'm being very careful, but yes, I'm feeling like I have a target painted on my back, and it's not a nice feeling to think that someone could actually wish you dead."

"And how *do* you feel about that?"

"How do I feel?" Maggie searched for words. "Angry.

Confused. Vulnerable." She took a deep breath and then let it out slowly. "Mortal."

"Ah, yes, I understand," Dr. Bob said, carefully placing his pen on the yellow pad and giving Maggie his full attention. "We are all mortal, aren't we?"

"Most of us," Maggie mumbled under her breath, then nodded. "I don't like to think about that. More than anything, that's what's got me going, I think. Thinking about that, that is. I . . . I don't think about that. Dying."

"But when you do?"

Maggie looked up at the psychiatrist. This wasn't why she'd come here this morning. She'd come for some magic answer about her parents. "I don't know. I think . . . when I think about dying I think that's okay, because it would be the end of the world and everyone else would go out with me. That's not too crazy, because when I . . . die, *my* world would end, so that would mean the world is sort of over, right? For me, at least, even if it does go on somewhere else. I mean, think about it. They killed JFK, for one, and the world didn't stop. We'd just like to think it couldn't go on without us."

"So, in your mind, you're making a fiction of fact, a fiction that makes you comfortable with the idea that, just maybe, you're indispensable to the world?"

Maggie considered this for a moment. "Yeah, okay. Hey, like they said, whatever floats your boat." Then, growing more and more uncomfortable, she went on, stealing from something Bernie had once said to her, "Besides, I figure I'm going to go in my sleep at one hundred and three, with a young stud sleeping beside me." Then honesty won out. "No, that's not true. I'd be too self-conscious about my wrinkles to let a young stud near me. I think I'd rather have my M&M's and a cigarette, to tell you the truth. The one hundred and three, however, still stands."

"You're avoiding facing what you feel and fear, Margaret, and in your usual way, with an attempt at humor."

"I wasn't funny? I thought the M&M's and cigarettes were kind of funny," Maggie said, then gave it all up as a bad job. "Why are we talking about dying? I sure don't want to talk about dying."

"You know, Margaret, it is often a comfort to know that one will be leaving something behind when he or she dies. Something of themselves. Some mark that proves that, yes, they were here."

"Well, I do have my books. I'll be leaving my work behind." Maggie had a quick thought about Francis Oakes, the recently deceased Francis Oakes. That had been his legacy, a few books. A few very forgettable, probably out-of-print books. And wasn't that a cheery thought?

"Yes, of course, your marvelous books. Is that it, Margaret? Perhaps you'd want more. Something more personal? Children, perhaps?"

Maggie blinked. "Children?" She thought about Alex and his, their, special circumstances. *Here's your daddy, sweetheart—he's not really real, I made him up, but we're just going to run with that, okay?* Wasn't that just swell. Man, talk about a way to screw up the next generation! "Children . . ."

Dr. Bob pushed back his French cuff and looked at his watch. "Well, that's it for this week. Same time next week, or would you rather go back to our usual Monday morning sessions?"

"Wait a minute," Maggie said as the good doctor pushed on the arms of his chair as if to stand up. "That's it? I'm to be sympathetic but neutral with my parents, someone might be out to get—*kill* me, so I should think about what I might leave behind if he does? That's it? Oh, and the sugarless fudge," she said, getting to her feet. "Can't forget the fudge, can I? No, Dr. Bob, I will not see you next week. I think we need a break. Maybe even a clean break. Children? Yeah, just what I wanted to think about. Merry Christmas!"

Chapter Seventeen

"Here you go, sport. Merry Christmas."

Saint Just neatly snagged the gaily wrapped box before it could do serious damage to his solar plexus and fell into step beside Maggie, who seemed hell-bent on going somewhere, somewhere far away from him.

"Allow me to hazard a guess. Your session with Dr. Bob was not all you'd hoped?"

Maggie sliced him a look that chilled the air between them below that of the actually rather fine, sunny December morning. "I'm not speaking to you."

"Actually, my dear, you are. You just did."

"Don't split hairs with me you, you *traitor*. And get us a cab."

"Oh, dear," Saint Just remarked with a sigh. "Obviously your Dr. Bob is not a man of his word."

"Oh, he's a man of a *lot* of words," Maggie said, climbing into the backseat of the cab Saint Just had neatly summoned to the curb. Once they were both settled in the backseat and Saint Just had given directions, she asked, "What were you thinking? Why did you go see him? To rat on me?"

"An interesting choice of words," Saint Just said as he reached across Maggie to take hold of the seat belt strap, as she seemed rather preoccupied at the moment with subjects other than her safety. "In truth, my dear, I had two reasons for dropping in on the good doctor. One, I wished to see this man who has been a part of your life for so many years—"

"And what did you think of him?"

"I found him to be an interesting mix of intelligence, avarice, and, perhaps, an inflated sense of self-consequence."

"That's nice. He thinks you're a nutcase," Maggie told him, not without a hint of satisfaction in her voice. "Possibly certifiable."

"Indeed."

"And arrogant."

Saint Just merely smiled. "My second reason for visiting the gentleman had to do with our . . . Rat Boy. I wished Dr. Bob's educated opinion on the potential seriousness of the threat. That, of course, was before we'd been informed of the unfortunate demise of Francis Oakes."

"Well, there's a first—you, asking for help. And what did he say?"

"He said I should tell my hypothetical friend that, yes, there could exist reason for real concern."

"Your hypothetical friend. Hoo-boy. That's how you presented everything? Hey, well, that wasn't transparent, was it? But, if Dr. Bob knew I was your hypothetical friend, why didn't he let me know he knew? I *told* him someone might be trying to kill me and all he wanted to know was how that made me *feel*."

"Perhaps there are limits to the man's unprofessionalism?"

Maggie nodded. "Yeah, that's probably it. Or he thinks we're both past saving and headed for padded rooms."

"There is always that," Saint Just agreed as the cab slid to the curb and he handed the man a ten-dollar bill, refusing change. "And here we are, the domicile of one Valentino Gates. Shall we? Oh, and forgive me for not mentioning this sooner, but I was a bit distracted. *Left*-tenant Wendell phoned this morning to report in. I believe he's feeling somewhat guilty for not taking our theory more seriously last night."

"That's an understatement. He barely listened to us."

"He did, however, listen to Bernice this morning. She gave him the list of authors for *No Secret Anymore*, as well as their whereabouts, as best we know them, and he was kind enough to contact Kimberly Lowell D'Amico in Missouri—who did not, it would seem, receive her own dead rat and poem. Which, I'm afraid, has put the good *left*-tenant back into the ranks of the unimpressed as regards our theory."

"Oh, great," Maggie said as Saint Just held open a thick wooden door that probably owed half that thickness to several generations of paint. "Though that doesn't really prove anything. All the rats were sent to authors in and around the city. All that could mean is that Rat Boy didn't trust dry ice to get one of his macabre little presents all the way to Missouri without being discovered along the way. Then again, considering the state of the New York post office, the damn rat could still be there."

"That's true enough," Saint Just agreed, having located Gates's apartment number on one of a row of mailboxes in the narrow foyer. "Third floor. Shall we climb?"

"Like we have a choice in this dump? Back to the packages. Those packages had to cost a lot. The dry ice. The postage. Rat Boy could have run out of postage."

"Or rats," Saint Just supplied helpfully, earning himself a speaking glance from his beloved as they paused at the second-floor landing.

"Funny. So do you agree with Steve now?"

"Unfortunately, no. I would rather believe that geography played a part in our unsub's plans."

"Unsub. Unknown subject. Next you'll say Feebies for F.B.I., and then I'll have to hit you," Maggie said, still leading the way up the stairs. But once at the third-floor landing she turned back to him, her expression troubled. "What are we going to say to this Valentino Gates guy, anyway? Hi, did you send me a dead rat?"

"A rather direct approach, but I doubt the man will then immediately fall on our necks to confess to murder. To be truthful, I haven't thought much beyond meeting the man, sizing him up as it were, taking his measure."

"Oh, well, that's fine then, as long as you have a *plan*, bright eyes," Maggie said, her sarcasm marred only by the fact that she was slightly out of breath from the climb.

Saint Just raised her hand to his lips. "Being romantically involved with a gentleman supposedly makes women soft and malleable. May I say how delighted I am, sweetings, that you are proving the exception."

"Hey, take it somewhere else you two, you're blocking the landing."

Saint Just looked behind him to see a rather large man standing two steps below them on the stairs. A rather large, angry man with forearms like hams and apparently the disposition of a warthog, with the manners to match. It was as if he and Maggie somehow had been transported to the Regency-era dregs of Piccadilly. Fairly certain the answer to his question would be in the negative, he nevertheless inquired: "Valentino Gates?"

"Think you're funny, don't you? Do I look like that pansy?"

The growled reference rather baffled Saint Just, but

he decided to assume the question had been rhetorical and did not require an answer. "Well, then, sir, please don't allow us to detain you any longer from what I am convinced is your very important business." He stepped back slightly, allowing the man to step onto the landing. "Ah, obedient as well. There's a good fellow. Be on your way now."

"Oh, jeez, how did I know this was going to happen?" he heard Maggie half groan from behind him. "Hold onto your knickers—here we go."

"Think you're smart, don't you?" the large man said, looking down at Saint Just, who had slightly mistaken the man's height if not his breadth. "How'd you like a quick trip down to the second floor, pansy boy? I can arrange that, you know."

"Excuse me, but you really don't want to try that," Maggie warned, pushing herself back into the corner. "Trust me in this one, Popeye."

"Popeye? And aren't you the funny bitch," the man said, distracted by the sight, Saint Just believed, of a woman clad in clean clothes and possessing all her teeth. "Whaddya say you and me get rid of this clown and have us some fun?"

"Hey, that's original. I never heard that line before. Alexander? Stop playing with the nice gentleman and let him go away."

He'd brought this on himself, Saint Just knew that the moment he'd first opened his mouth and heard himself spouting those lines from one of his books—words Maggie originally had put in his mouth. Only one more example of his knowledge that he was, thanks to Maggie, invincible. Which did not mean that Maggie was, or that he himself couldn't end up rather *creased* at the conclusion of this encounter.

Which did not, as it happened, keep him from neatly inserting his cane between the buffoon's legs as the fellow stupidly attempted to advance on Maggie, and then bringing it up with a considerable amount of force. After all, even a gentleman should be allowed a little fun from time to time.

The thud of the man's body hitting the landing, to be followed by his rather high-pitched whimpers, served as their introduction to Valentino Gates, who opened his door to check on the commotion.

"Mr. Gates?" Saint Just asked, raising his voice above the whimpers, inclining his head to the slightly-built man with the look of a poet whose greatest wish would be the opportunity to starve in a garret. "Mr. Valentino Gates?"

"Ah . . . er . . . yes, I suppose so." Gates looked down at the man who was now rather inelegantly grasping his most private parts as, bent double, he did his best to climb to the next landing. "What did you do to Quentin?"

"Quentin?" Maggie deserted her corner. "You'd think he would have gotten himself a nickname. Butch, Spike—something. No wonder he's so angry. I'll bet he had the snot beaten out of him on the playground every day before he grew that big. By the way, nice job, Alex."

"Thank you, my dear, I do my best."

Valentino Gates looked ready to bolt. "Who *are* you people? And . . . and what do you want from me?"

Saint Just was fairly certain Quentin wouldn't be back for an encore any time soon, but he'd already made up his mind about Valentino Gates. The man had all the spunk as well as native intelligence of a sea sponge, and couldn't possibly have killed anyone. It was best to simply make up some farradiddle out of whole cloth and then take their exit as quickly as possible.

With a wink to Maggie, who he knew could be trusted to follow where he led—not happily, but she would follow, and only afterward verbally tear a strip off his hide—he said brightly, "Mr. Gates, a fair question. Yes, most definitely. Allow me to explain, my good sir. We are members of the Francis Oakes fan club, Manhattan division. Ah, poor Francis. I am Blakely, Alexander Blakely, acting president, and my companion here is our recording secretary, Miss Kelly, Miss Ma—"

"Velma Kelly," Maggie interrupted, sticking out her hand to the astonished-looking man. "We inquired at Toland Books as to who, locally, had written fan letters to Mr. Oakes in the past, and your name was among those given to us. We're taking up a collection to help with the . . . um . . . the arrangements, and wondered if—"

"Velma Kelly? Isn't that the name of one of the characters from that movie, *Chicago*?"

"Broadway musical. It was a Broadway musical before it was a movie."

"Who cares? You're no Catherine Zeta-Jones, I know that. What's the other one's name? You know, the blonde with the chubby cheeks? She was really cute."

"Mr. Gates," Saint Just said quickly, because Maggie had opened her mouth again and he was fairly certain Valentino Gates would not be happy with whatever she chose to say. "The donation?"

"Yes, you said that. A donation for arrangements. What arrangements? And, for the record, I never wrote a fan letter to that pitiful hack. He couldn't write his way out of a paper bag. And they turn *me* down?"

Saint Just and Maggie exchanged looks, Saint Just's one of wry amusement, Maggie's one that very clearly telegraphed her feeling that they'd been wasting their time.

"Mr. Oakes was killed a few days go, Mr. Gates," Saint Just said, then watched for the man's reaction. "Murdered. Murder most vile, one might say."

Valentino Gates staggered backward, but then seemed to collect himself, although he had gone quite pale. "I . . . I didn't know. Murdered? Gee, that stinks, doesn't it?"

"Yes, indeed. It's not for public knowledge, you understand, but we've been led to understand that the sad event took place very shortly after Mr. Oakes received a rather disturbing package."

"Package," Gates repeated.

"A rather disturbing package."

"Disturbing," Gates repeated.

"A rather disturbing package containing a dead rat and a threat."

"Threat? You mean . . . you mean a threat to *kill* him?"

"No, a threat to *not* kill him," Maggie said, her sarcasm level rising once more. "Of course a threat to kill him."

"I . . . I don't know anything about that. I . . . I've got to go now." Gates dug into his pocket and came out with a ten-dollar bill. "Here—for Oakes."

Once the door had closed, Saint Just held up the bill. "Lunch is on Valentino, if your appetite doesn't extend beyond hot dogs on the street."

"You're impossible," Maggie told him as they headed back down the stairs. "But did you see the look on the guy's face when you started talking about the package and the threat? I thought he was going to pass out. Oh, no, he knows nothing about any package, does he? Oh, and he didn't even know Francis is dead. You caught that, right? That's the one part I believe. Nobody's that good an actor."

"I agree," Saint Just said, holding open the door to the street, then enjoying his first breath of air in some ten minutes that did not contain the pungent aroma of incontinent cats and, he believed, week-old cabbage. "Mr. Gates is officially removed from our list of suspects in the death of Mr. Oakes. He is not, however, removed from the list of those who might have had something to do with the package and threat. In fact, I believe he has just leapt to the top of the latter list. Or do you disagree?"

"No, I'm right there with you. He knows something about the packages. It's possible we've got two things going on here—my Rat Boy *and* your unsub, to borrow your description of the killer. After all, Francis is the only one who's dead, not that I'm wishing anyone else dead, you understand. Most especially me. I've got . . . I've got unfinished business, and I'm not ready to go yet."

"Ah, a topic for an interesting late-night conversation one day soon, I do believe," Saint Just told her as he guided her along the street, turning at the corner to approach Bryon's bookstore, as he had planned out his route earlier, using a city map. "Are you ready for suspect number two?"

"Not really, no, considering how suspect number one really shot a hole in our theory. But let's get it over with and then go see Faith, God help me. Just in case Valentino back there *is* the best actor in the world. Oh, and what was all that with Quentin? I should be mad, but it was kind of fun, actually. Were you showing off for me, big boy?" she asked, grinning at him.

"Truthfully, I don't know why I behaved as I did, other than to say that I've noticed that, sometimes, when thrown into certain situations, I open my mouth and your version of me comes spilling out."

"So it's my fault Quentin will be walking funny for a week. Is that what you're saying?"

Saint Just smiled at her. "Yes, let's, as you say, run with that one."

"Bite me. Where's this bookstore?"

Bryon's Book Nook was located in the middle of the next block, a rather narrow store wedged between a Thai restaurant and a print shop. There was a single show window that hadn't seen a cleaning rag in possibly decades, and the interior was musty-smelling, with towering, odd-shaped bookcases jammed in cheek by jowl, leaving little room for Saint Just and Maggie to walk without turning sideways.

"Rather a charming hodgepodge, don't you think?"

"I think I've just discovered that I'm claustrophobic," Maggie told him, whispering, as if perhaps they were in a library, or a church. "I want to check out his mystery section, see if I'm there."

"Naturally," Saint Just said, following where she led. "Ah, there we are."

"Yeah. *We*," Maggie muttered as she went down on her haunches, as the *D*'s were shelved on the bottom shelf. "One, two—he's got five of the latest hardback, so that's good, considering the size of this place. And one each of my backlist." She got to her feet. "I think I'm going to like this Bryon guy. Be nice to him, okay?"

"Me? I am nothing if not congenial."

"Yeah, tell that to Quentin, now that's he's going to have to sing soprano in the church choir."

"Your attempts at bawdiness are delicious," he told her, which earned him another of her very *speaking* looks just before a middle-aged gentleman approached dressed in baggy corduroy trousers and a dandruff-dusted black turtleneck sweater that seemed to serve to keep his chin raised, it was that tight and that high.

"May I be of some assistance? You appreciate a good mystery novel?"

"Actually," Saint Just said, knowing Maggie would never do so, "my friend here is an author, and has learned, to her delight, that you have deigned to shelve her books in this very prestigious establishment. Is the owner in? I'm sure Miss Dooley would like to convey her thanks to the gentleman and then perhaps autograph the copies on the shelves."

"Dooley? Oh, yes, you mean Cleo Dooley. My assistant, Bruce, insists I carry her, and I must say, she sells very well to a . . . certain element. I'm George Bryon, the owner. And you'd be Ms. Dooley?"

"Yeah, good guess. What certain element?"

George Bryon lifted his hands in a slightly fluttering movement. "Oh, you know. The *popular fiction* crowd."

"Ah, yes, I understand what you mean now. The hoi polloi, the great unwashed—that crowd?" Maggie countered, stepping closer to Saint Just. "I take it all back— be as snarky as you want to be."

Saint Just trotted out the same story he'd used to such interesting effect on Valentino Gates, and was not disappointed in Bryon's reaction, for the man's already pale complexion colored hotly at the mention of the dead rats, even before Saint Just had gotten to the part about Oakes's murder.

"I don't know anything about Francis Oakes or any dead animals or threats, and I resent the implication that I should or do. As for a contribution? Don't be ridiculous."

But Maggie, at least, wasn't done, and gave the man another verbal push. "Gee, that's too bad. The last place we stopped? The guy there gave us fifty bucks. Valentino Gates. He seemed real broken up about Francis. Do you know him? Gates, I mean?"

"I most certainly do not." And with that Mr. George Gordon Bryon turned on his heel and made a rather dramatic exit past a heavy green velvet curtain that led—Saint Just peeked—to a small room holding several rows of folding chairs and a small podium.

Maggie pushed him aside and took a look for herself. "Oh, he probably holds readings back there. I hate that. Bernie tried to send me out on a tour where I'd do readings from my books, but I shot her down. Somebody wants to read my books, let them read them. I'm not going read them *to* them."

"Because you loathe being the center of attention," Saint Just said as once more they found themselves standing on the sidewalks of New York.

"Yes, thank you, you finally figured that out. So you're not going to do what you did back in there ever again, right? Not in bookstores, not in public, not ever. I'm Maggie Kelly. If I wanted to blow my horn, I'm damn well capable of doing it myself. But I don't. I just want to write my books and be left alone. It's easier. And not half so insulting. At least I can pretend I'm famous—until somebody like Steve's Christine, or Bryon in there shoots me down. Which *always* happens. One time, just one time, I'd like somebody to gush—and I don't mean just about the love scenes, but the book, the *writing*. Is that too much to ask, huh, is it?"

"This leads back to your family, doesn't it?" Saint Just asked, slipping his arm around her waist. "Your family and their lack of appreciation for your talents. People like that insipid boor back there only serve to reinforce that lack of the parental praise you still crave. Poor Maggie."

"You ever visit Dr. Bob again, Alex, and I'll have to write a wart on the end of your nose," she said and stepped to the curb, hailing a passing cab. "You coming?"

"And how could I turn down such a gracious invitation?" Saint Just purred, holding open the door of the cab for her, then giving the driver an address on the Upper East Side, just out of the fashionable area.

"Faith is just off Park. Where are we going?"

"Ah, I forgot to tell you, didn't I? The good *left*-tenant has agreed to meet us at Jonathan West's apartment. We'll just be on time, as it works out."

"Steve? No, I don't want to see him." She tapped on the plastic divider and gave the driver her own address, then sat back and folded her arms beneath her breasts. "And don't tell me I'm being chicken."

"I most certainly will not, considering that I haven't the vaguest idea what that means. I do think you're only avoiding the inevitable, however, and can only wonder why."

"I don't know," Maggie said, looking at him with those innocent green eyes. "I'm happy for him. I'm happy for us—for as far as it goes. But I think we all need a little . . . *space*. Or weren't you as uncomfortable last night as I was? No, never mind, you don't have to answer that. You're never uncomfortable, are you? Besides, if Valentino and good old George put their pointy heads together and sent the rats—which may or may not be a viable theory, based on their reactions—then we're wrong and the rats and Francis's murder have nothing to do with each other except a coincidence in timing. Right?"

"Correct. Lowering, but correct. And, if correct, all we've learned is that two dedicated fans of Jonathan West may have taken it upon themselves to send empty threats to several of the authors who collaborated on *No Secret Anymore*, even as one of our conspirators has just soundly denied knowing the other. Except, as the author in Missouri is, shall we say, sans rat, we may not even be correct in that assumption. It would go a long way toward proving at least that part of our theory if Mr. West and your friend Felicity did receive missives from, as you call him, Rat Boy. Not to Wendell, of course, who puts little stock in things like our *feelings* about those we believe to be suspects, but it would help satisfy my curiosity, which is why I do not as yet intend to inform the good *left*-tenant of what we've just discovered about our new friends, Gates and Bryon. "

"Yeah, well, then you just keep your secrets while

you go along and use poor Steve to help you satisfy your curiosity. As of now, I'm out of it. I've got shopping to do, remember? I guess the idea of getting Mom and Dad a flat-screen TV for their family room is sort of shot, huh?"

"I'd rather you didn't leave the apartment for the nonce," Saint Just told her, putting his hand on her arm as the cab pulled up in front of their condo building. "I wasn't worried this morning, as you traveled in a cab directly from the condo to Dr. Bob, but I don't much care for the idea of you roaming about willy-nilly."

"Look, Alex, it's over. Steve was right to shoot us down, and right to concentrate on the CUNY area. We gave it our best high school try as mystery writer and her hero, and we fell short, our theory doesn't hold water, or at least not enough of it. End of story."

"Maggie?"

"Oh, all right, all right, I'll fool around on the Internet, see if I can get some of my shopping out of the way. Except I hate that. I like to see things, touch them. You can't do that on the Internet."

"Yes, you're a very tactile person, aren't you, in your own delightfully suppressed way? Thank you, my dear," Saint Just told her, not really knowing why he was still concerned, but confident enough in his feelings of disquiet that he was relieved to know that Maggie would behave while he was gone. "However, that still leaves us with Felicity and Mr. West, I'm afraid, before we can put a firm period to the end of this adventure."

"You're going to talk to Jonathan, so that's one down. I'll go upstairs and call Faith, Scout's honor, ask her if she got a rat so that she can lie to me if she did," Maggie said, rolling her eyes. "Now let me out."

"Certainly," he said, lifting the wrapped box. "Your fudge?"

"Give it to the driver. Just don't tell him it's sugarless, or he won't take it. I mean, who would?"

Five minutes later, the ten-dollar bill Valentino Gates had given him now, along with the box of fudge, residing with the cabdriver, Saint Just joined Steve Wendell on yet another sidewalk, this one in a decidedly more upscale neighborhood than were the locations of his first two morning calls.

"Wendell, so good to see you. My apologies for my tardiness," he said as the lieutenant pulled open the door to the vestibule and fairly leaned on the buzzer button above the mailbox marked *West*.

"Right. Let's cut to the chase here. You and Maggie—you're together now? I always thought there was something there." He depressed the button four more times in quick succession.

"My, that was direct, wasn't it? I will gladly accept your felicitations, *left*-tenant, should you wish to offer them, but I have no intention of applying to you for permission."

"But you're cousins."

"Very distant cousins, as you already know. And now, for the comfort of both of us, we'll leave the subject. Mr. West is a bit of a recluse, according to Bruce McCrae, and may not answer his buzzer. I suggest we find another way to gain admittance."

"Do you now," Wendell said, looking as rumpled as usual, but more distracted than usual. "We're coming up empty at CUNY, you know. Overtime for a dozen cops, and all we've gotten out of it so far is a minor-league peeper and a pizza delivery guy looking for an address two of the idiots rolled on. Guy was so scared he dropped forty-seven bucks' worth of double cheese the department now has to pay for, hoping we don't get sued. We're back to square one, Alex, unless this hunch of yours and Maggie's plays out, and my captain is not a happy man, which means I'm not a happy man."

"I understand completely. In the main, I am not the sort to do this sort of thing, you understand, but when needs must, and to assist a friend? Yes, I think I can make an exception here," Saint Just said, depressing the button above the name *Myers*. When a woman's voice came through the speaker, he leaned closer and said crisply, in his best American accent, "Police, ma'am. Patrolman Swidecky, badge number two-four-six-seven-nine-oh. We've got word of a possible intruder in the building. Can you buzz us in? We'd appreciate it, ma'am. And then please remain in your apartment until we give the all clear. You are in no danger, ma'am."

"I could have done that, *Officer* Swidecky," Wendell groused as another buzzer sounded, followed by the opening click of the inner door lock.

"Yes, *left*-tenant, but you wouldn't have, at least not without first putting us both to the trouble of a tedious argument about right and wrong and other trifles we really don't have time for, do we? Remind me to stop by and thank Miss Myers when we're finished." Saint Just bowed and gave a graceful sweep of his arm. "After you?"

"You're a real piece of work, Blakely. I don't know what in hell Maggie sees in you. For that matter, I don't know why I'm here with you, watching as you break every rule in the book."

"It's my engaging personality, plus, perhaps of more importance to you, the liberating feeling derived from working *outside* some of those pesky rules every now and again," Saint Just said, swinging up his cane and resting it jauntily against his shoulder. "All in all, you really can't help yourself. Besides, thus far, we've made a fairly successful pair of crime solvers, don't you think?"

"Yeah, I do. But I'll deny it if you ever repeat that to anybody."

Perhaps because of the way Saint Just had taken charge downstairs, once they'd reached the sixth floor, Wendell was quick to step in front of Jonathan West's door and pound on it three times with the side of his fist. "Jonathan West! Police! Open up, Mr. West!"

"Ah, your usual subtle self. I believe I would have declared myself to be the plumber, warning Mr. West of a broken water pipe in the apartment above his. But, to each his own," Saint Just said as they waited for Jonathan West to open the door.

And waited.

"He's not in there," Wendell said. "It figures. My day's been going just great so far—why would anything change now?"

"Now, now, let's not go into a sad decline, *left*-tenant. The man is a recluse, and possibly quite shy. You may have frightened him with your so-gentle approach. Then again, all things considered, we could be standing out here while Jonathan West's body molders on the other side of this door."

"Molders? Oh, right. You're thinking I can justify breaking down this door, aren't you? You know, you watch too much television, Blakely, you really do. Especially the Patrolman Swidecky bit. But I'll tell you what—I'll go find the super, flash my shield, and have him let us in. You stay here. *And don't do anything.*"

"Certainly not, and may I say, I do not appreciate the insult," Saint Just said, and then waited until the elevator doors had closed behind Wendell before he reached into the inside pocket of his sports coat and took out the lovely new set of lock picks Mary Louise had gifted him with as thanks for arranging her modeling job with *Fragrances By Pierre*. The picks were in a velvet-lined case. Very attractive, in a larcenous sort of way.

It was a matter of less than two minutes before Saint Just was rewarded with the sound of the last tumbler turning over, and just in time, as the elevator doors opened once more and Wendell stepped out. Alone.

"The super wasn't there," he said, standing half in and half out of the elevator, holding open the door. "Let's go, come back later for another shot at finding him. Ms. Myers is on three, you can stop there on our way down, Patrolman Swidecky."

"Very well," Saint Just said, "although I'm becoming more and more concerned. This reclusive business, you understand. Jeremy informed me that Francis Oakes hadn't left his apartment in over two years. Can we but wonder if Jonathan West is cut from the same sort of cloth? Both writers, you understand. Perhaps I could just try the door?"

"You think it's open? That never happens."

"Oh, *left*-tenant, everything happens, sooner or later, if we're only patient. Ah, and it has happened now," he said, pushing open the door. "Mr. West, are you in there? New York City police department, Mr. West. Don't be alarmed."

"Will you freaking cut that out?" Wendell complained, pushing past Saint Just and into the apartment. "Jonathan West! Police! Show yourself!"

"As subtle as a red brick to the brain box," Saint Just said, shaking his head as he followed after the lieutenant, only to be brought up short directly behind him as the air inside the apartment all but slammed into his nostrils. Reaching into his pocket after using his elbow to nudge shut the door behind them, he withdrew his handkerchief and put it to his nose. "*Left*-tenant?"

"Over there," Wendell said, pointing to what at first glance appeared to be a large gray lump on the carpet. He had already taken out his revolver and held it straight out in front of him with both hands as he visually swept the large room. "And he's pretty ripe. Don't touch anything, I've got to call this in."

"I wouldn't dream of it," Saint Just said as he measured the apartment with his eyes. "He lived rather simply, didn't he? Is this what is called a studio apartment?"

Wendell slipped his cell phone back into his pocket but kept the revolver unholstered. "Yeah, that's what it's called. Everything in one room, except the bathroom, which I have to check out now. Stay here. And don't—"

"Touch anything. Yes, *left*-tenant, I believe I understand crime-scene protocol. However, we could do with a little light, couldn't we?"

"Better than tripping over evidence, I suppose, and I've got to check that bathroom. All right, a light," Wendell said, pulling on thin latex gloves he'd gotten out of his pocket and reaching past Saint Just to turn on the overhead light. "Damn, another body."

"Four-legged, happily," Saint Just said, also seeing the open shoe box on a low table in front of a rather flamboyantly carved lime green on green satin couch. "I suppose, as you would say, Maggie's and my theory is back in the game?"

"Yeah, it sure looks that way. Where's Maggie?"

"Safely ensconced in her condo with Socks on guard duty downstairs, thankfully," Saint Just told him, keeping his sword cane balanced lightly in his right hand, although he believed there was no one hiding in Jonathan West's bathroom. At least no one with a working sense of smell.

While Wendell went off to do his pull open the door, point the pistol, check out the area routine on the bathroom and closets, Saint Just did his own visual inspection of the apartment from where he stood. It was all rather pathetic, actually. The furnishings were extraordinarily good, if showing signs of wear, as if West had purchased them years earlier with a much larger living space in mind, so that the pieces were out of scale for this smaller room.

What was it called? The polite term? Oh yes, downsizing. Mr. Jonathan West had downsized, most probably because finances had forced such an economy on him. A sad man, living in a sad little apartment, living a sad little life. It was Francis Oakes's life all over again— merely with a better address and more comfortable furniture.

Saint Just was happy that Maggie had chosen not to come with him. Not only did he not wish her to see yet another dead body, but a room such as this would only reinforce her belief that wealth and fame could be fleeting, affirm her lack of confidence in herself and her abilities—not to mention how much tighter she would begin to squeeze every penny.

With Wendell once more back in the main living area, his weapon now holstered, Saint Just approached the body with him. "That's quite a copious amount of blood around the body, isn't it? And arterial spray, I believe is the term," he added, pointing his cane in the direction of the bizarre stripes of dried blood on the nearest wall.

"That's what happens when somebody slices open his wrists. Hey, stay back over next to the—oh, never mind. I don't know if it's the blood smell or the decomp, but I've got to open a window."

Saint Just was more than happy to shift his gaze from Jonathan West's bloated, eyes-open body and move away from that body—and the flies that appeared to be feasting on it and the blood that had soaked into the carpet. The sound of those flies, the buzzing, was most unnerving, not that Saint Just would allow himself to react in any way.

He stepped carefully to the coffee table, where the rat, similarly decomposing, could be seen inside the shoe box, although he could not see any evidence of the poem that had been included in with Maggie's rat, and the others.

"I don't see a poem," he told Wendell, who had opened not one, but two windows, allowing some much needed cool, fresh air into the apartment.

"And I suppose you want me to look for it?"

"The thought had occurred, yes," Saint Just said, refolding his handkerchief and replacing it in his pocket. "Ah, wait, I think that could be it—I see a corner of rather stained paper sticking out from beneath the animal's body. Strange. West never read the note? It's as if he merely opened the box, then abandoned it here on the table. One would think if one were to commit suicide out of fright after receiving a threat, one would first have had to *read* that threat. Although," he continued, thinking out loud, "West could have *lifted* the rat out of the box, read the poem, and then replaced the— no, nobody would do anything like that. I know I most certainly wouldn't."

"You enjoy talking to yourself, Blakely? And we both know this wasn't a suicide. The rats are just a prop the killer understands and we don't. Not when we've already got one body that looked like a suicide," Wendell said as he stepped carefully around the room. He opened the cabinet under the sink with his gloved hand. "Wow, look at this. Good old Jonathan liked his Jim Beam, didn't he?"

Not understanding the reference, Saint Just approached the small kitchen area that at least boasted a breakfast bar to somewhat separate it from the living area, and looked into the plastic trash bin. "Oh," he said, seeing the empty bottles. "Mr. West enjoyed his liquor. Open that cabinet, if you will, *left*-tenant."

"More bottles, about ten of them," Wendell said, closing the cabinet door once more and opening another.

"More bottles. That's some serious drinking he had going on. All right, no more of this, okay? The crime-scene guys will be here any minute now, and I want to make some notes."

"Certainly, *left*-tenant," Saint Just said, his attention now on the length of counter that was crowded with several small kitchen appliances. Saint Just had quite an appreciation for small kitchen appliances, an interest he would rather not dissect as to exactly *why* he liked them so much.

The appliances put him in mind of something that appeared to be missing from the room. A computer. Surely a writer, even one who had, as Bernie had told them, not written in years, would have a computer. A writer would sell his couch, his television machine, his soul, before he would sell his computer. There was a rather lovely kidney-shaped cherrywood desk in the room, positioned in front of the bank of three tall windows. But no computer. In fact, the desktop was completely clear save for a photograph of—well, goodness. Bernice Toland-James certainly was a popular lady, with a romantic past probably best left unexamined.

Still, no computer? Odd. Very odd.

As was one of those small kitchen appliances behind him, now that he thought about the thing. Careful to keep his hands locked behind his back, Saint Just turned back to the long counter to lean over and peer at the out-of-place appliance, noting the cobwebs that had been woven just inside its openings, which were odd in themselves, for Jonathan West may have been reduced to the Manhattan idea of genteel poverty—and most anyone's idea of devoted tippler—but he seemed to have taken great care in keeping his surroundings neat and clean.

But this appliance wasn't even plugged into the outlet. It was just there, complete with cobwebs, one appliance out of many—while all the others were plugged into a plainly visible six-outlet power cord.

And then he saw it—something where it should not be. He then glanced over his shoulder at Wendell, who was busily writing in his spiral notepad—most probably detailing how he had found the door to West's apartment slightly ajar and had entered only because he'd believed he'd had reason to suspect imminent danger to the occupant.

With the man fairly well occupied with his inventive fiction, Saint Just began speaking out loud, because he needed a bit of noise, didn't he? The sort of noise the lieutenant would dismiss as inane background chatter as he continued to scribble on his notepad. It wasn't the best of plans, but he was laboring under the knowledge that they would soon not be alone in the apartment, and really didn't have time to formulate a better one.

"Quite a devotee of small kitchen appliances, wasn't he, Wendell? Perhaps the late Mr. West was an Internet shopper? This Foreman grill is very much like mine, only a smaller size—the two-hamburger, chicken breast, or chop size, I'd say. An interesting can opener—I believe it also might serve as a knife sharpener, which is quite handy. Microwave, toaster oven—ah, and that's a rotisserie turkey cooker, unless I miss my guess. Food processor, a very simple toaster. Now, I cannot help but wonder, why would a man with limited space feel the need for both a toaster oven *and* a toaster? The toast from toaster ovens is far superior to that of simple toasters, don't you think? I do. Do you suppose one of them is broken? Maybe this one?"

As he said the last words, holding his handkerchief to cover his fingers, Saint Just nudged the control lever on the toaster, at which time the mechanical workings inside were released to spring upward with a short, metal-on-metal grating sound.

"Hey, what was that? Damn it, Blakely, I told you not to touch anything!"

"My most profound apologies, *left*-tenant. I have such an insatiable curiosity about kitchen appliances. It's a failing, I know," Saint Just said, the computer disk that had been inside one of the toaster slots already neatly secured in his sports coat pocket. He left the kitchen area and then suggested that it might be best for the good lieutenant if he was not on the premises with him when the crime-scene investigators arrived.

"You're right. I'm getting a little tired of explaining you, to tell you the truth—especially if any of the network newshounds picked up anything on a scanner and show up. The department doesn't need another exclusive Holly Spivak-Alexander Blakely television circus," Wendell said, flipping his notebook closed. "Besides, I don't want Maggie to be alone, even if it's you I'm sending to her. Who else should we be watching? I left Bernie's list back at the homicide table."

Saint Just mentally ran down the list, picking and choosing. "There's Bruce McCrae. J.P. is babysitting him, I believe is the term. Maggie, of course. And Felicity Boothe Simmons. The rest have all either fled the metropolitan area or are, alas, recently deceased."

"Felicity Boothe Simmons? Oh, God, not that space cadet. She'll demand protection. *Loudly*. Count on it."

"A problem easily solved," Saint Just said helpfully. "I'm sure Maggie would be more than willing to open her home to Miss Simmons for the duration. You do plan on solving these murders sooner rather than later, don't you, *left*-tenant, I would most sincerely hope? I said Maggie would be *willing* to house Miss Simmons. I am not saying that she will be particularly overjoyed to do so. Therefore, it goes without saying that we will look forward to frequent updates from you."

"I'll be sure to keep you in the loop," Wendell said

with what actually looked to be a bit of a sneer. He moved to stab his hand through his shaggy hair, but then stopped as he noticed he was still wearing the latex gloves. "Go away now, Blakely. Just go away. You've got to have something else to do besides driving me nuts."

Saint Just thought of the computer disk in his pocket. "As a matter of fact, I do. I most certainly do. But may I first say how very gratifying it is to be working with you again, *left*-tenant."

"Yeah. It's freaking terrific. We're a hell of a team. *Go!*"

Chapter Eighteen

A S they rode the elevator to the thirty-seventh floor of Felicity Boothe Simmons's building, Maggie leaned against the wall of the car, still trying to come to grips with the idea that Jonathan West was dead. Murdered.

"Poor guy," she said, sighing. "His last book? It was named to, I think, four different worst books of the year, most disappointing books of the year—that sort of thing—lists. You know, media critics' polite way of saying *loser*. I can't imagine what that feels like—to see your book on a list like that. I just know I don't ever want to know how it feels."

"And you won't, my dear," Alex assured her. "I won't allow it."

"*You* won't allow it? God, Alex, I should start following you around with a pen and notepad. I mean, that was a funny line—not. Now, quick, tell me again why I had to come here with you. I'd almost figured out which iPod I'm going to order for Sterling. All I have to do now is compare prices."

"You know why you're here. You're a woman, Maggie. Felicity is a woman. I think she'll handle the news better, coming from you."

"Me? Me who can't stand Faith—*that* me? You're such a cockeyed optimist, Alex."

"Yes, thank you. Now isn't this odd. Gates lives on the third floor, West resided on the sixth, and here is Felicity, on the thirty-seventh. In New York, it would appear that the higher up you live, the more affluent the building."

"And I'm on the ninth floor. I remember. Hey, did you get a look at that foyer downstairs? It's furnished better than my condo." As the elevator slid soundlessly to a halt and the doors opened, she added, "And no wisecracks. My condo is furnished just fine, thank you."

"You have a three-foot-high pink plastic flamingo in the corner of your bedroom."

"Yeah? So? Kirk gave it to me last year as some kind of joke, I guess. I may have gotten rid of him, but I sort of like the flamingo. Does it bother you? That Kirk gave it to me, I mean?"

Alex used his cane to hold open the elevator doors until Maggie belatedly realized she hadn't moved, and stepped out onto the plush carpeting. "No, my dear. It offends me aesthetically. Ah, this is Felicity's door. I neglected to ask. Does she live alone?"

"I'll just pretend you meant that as a serious question. Get real, Alex, who'd live with her?" Maggie looked at the door. Damn. Felicity's building foyer was better than hers. This door was better than hers. Higher, wider— and there were two of them; actual double doors, sort of carved, sort of antiqued. "She's got Christmas wreaths hanging on her doors?" she said. "Okay, they look good. I could do that, you know. A nice live wreath, with pinecones, a pretty red ribbon. Then I could post a twenty-four-hour guard so that somebody doesn't rip me off. Of course, if I wired it just right—"

"Maggie, dear heart, would you care to ring the bell?"

"—maybe with a live grenade," she told him, completing the thought as she shot him a dirty look, because he knew what she knew—that she was only delaying the inevitable. "Her assistant told me she'd be home by one. I told you that. I could have just phoned her and told her about Francis and Jonathan. I still don't see why we had to—oh, all right, all right, I'm ringing. Look, see me ringing the bell." She frowned. "I don't have a bell. Why does she have a bell? The concierge already called her. Why don't I have a concierge? Why do I have Paul the putz?"

"Maggie, hello! Oh, and Alex, too. I could barely believe it when Pierre called up to say I had company. Come in, come in—I've been just *dying* to show you my new place. I only moved in a month ago, you know. No, of course you don't. I didn't get my housewarming present yet, did I? Naughty, naughty."

Maggie glared at Alex, who had the decency to shrug his shoulders in an apologetic way before she followed Felicity *Boobs* Simmons into the large, marble-tiled foyer with at least a fifteen-foot ceiling and a crystal chandelier that could have played the stunt double in *Phantom of the Opera*. A huge round table sat in the middle of the foyer, a two-foot-high vase on top of it, loaded with a fresh flower arrangement that had to stand another three feet high. "Wow, Faith, this is really . . . something."

The foyer opened into an enormous living room, salon, saloon—whatever it was, it was freaking *big*, and decked out in gold and white and—good God—*pink*, and in the style of Louis XIV or XVI, or one of those Louis. Heavy silk draperies slathered all over twenty-foot-high windows, puddling on plush white carpeted floors. A white fake Christmas tree decorated all in pink and silver that nearly reached that ceiling was backed by the wide, curving marble staircase that led to an exposed balcony and the second floor of the unit (she had a second floor!). The tree was lit with a million small fairy lights. Revolving. It probably even snowed on itself.

"Check around, Alex," Maggie said as Faith made herself comfortable on a white-on-white silk brocade couch that could probably comfortably seat thirty-two people. "She may have stashed Marie Antoinette here somewhere."

"Maggie? Are you just going to stand there? You've seen fine furnishings before, surely?"

"You can take the snark out of Brooklyn Heights, but you can't take the snark out of the woman, or something like that. You know what I mean," Maggie said to Alex out of the corner of her mouth as she smiled at Faith, then spread her arms as if to encompass the entire room. "Why do I feel this sudden hunger for cotton candy?"

Felicity's tinkling laugh affected Maggie like knuckles on a cheese grater—meaning the sound wasn't so bad, but it was still damn painful. "I'll take that as a compliment, Maggie. It is delicious here, isn't it?"

"Oh, yeah. Delicious. Who's that over the fireplace?" Maggie asked, gawking at the life-size painting. "The guy leering over the nursing-mother redhead."

"Derek Whitehead, of course, modeling for my latest cover. I don't know the female model's name—they're so interchangeable, aren't they. That's the original art. I have all my covers in oils—the rest are back there, in my suite of offices; I'll show them to you later. I plan to always have the current cover above the fireplace. So you like it? Oh, I know you're positively salivating, aren't you! I won't tell you what I paid for the place, but if you thought five million you'd be thinking *much* too small. But what do I labor so hard for, if not to allow myself a few creature comforts?"

"A warm bath and fuzzy slippers are creature comforts, Faith. Chicken noodle soup and bread and butter with sugar on it are creature comforts. Just call this place what it is, okay? You, showing off."

"Yes, I am, aren't I?" Faith said, giggling again. "I can afford to."

"Three weeks, wasn't it?"

Maggie's allusion to the staying power of Felicity's latest hardback on the *NYT* finally took the smile from the woman's face.

"You were mean, Maggie. Suggesting that Bernie has found someone to replace me. Oh, yes, I knew what you were doing. You know, you may have saved my life at the last We Are Romance convention, and I'm grateful, but there is a limit to what I should be forced to endure from you. I was never anything but a loyal friend."

"Yeah, sure you were. Right up until the minute you forgot to invite me to your cocktail party at *WAR* because you wanted it limited only to your fellow *NYT* authors. The year before that conference, Faith, you and I roomed together and shared doggie bags we'd brought back from the Toland Books dinner, because we were so short of cash. Remember those days, Faith?"

Felicity waved away the question as she smiled over at Alex, who had been admiring a bust of some Greek goddess and doing the typical man thing of ignoring two women who were obviously indulging in a distasteful catfight. "I'm dying to hear your opinion of my new home, Alex. You English have such exemplary taste."

"It's quite *you*, Felicity," Alex said, and Maggie bit back a giggle of her own, because she knew a dig when she heard one—which Felicity did not.

"Oh, thank you, Alex," Felicity trilled. "Ah, and here

comes Trixie, my assistant. Honestly, I don't know how I'd exist without her. You understand, don't you, Maggie? I mean, how does one possibly answer all one's fan mail without an assistant? All those requests for bookmarks, autographed photographs. Oh, and Trixie arranges my speaking schedule, of course—just a million things I couldn't possibly have time for if I wanted to continue writing my books, pleasing my fans. Trixie, come here, dear. I want to introduce you to my good friends and you can then get them whatever they want to drink." She eyed Maggie up and down. "Diet soda, Maggie?"

Fun was fun, and all of that, but it was time to shut Faith up, damn it. "Francis Oakes is dead and so is Jonathan West and they both got dead rats in the mail and threatening poems and we've figured out that somebody is after all the authors who contributed to *No Secret Anymore*—some weird serial killer with his own reasons that nobody understands because we were figuring someone was out to avenge Jonathan, not kill him—so we know you got a dead rat, too, and your life could be in danger and . . . well, and Alex here figured you should know and take precautions."

Felicity's carefully painted mouth had dropped open somewhere around *some weird serial killer*. "What are you talking about? That's the most ridiculous thing I've ever heard, Maggie Kelly, and you just said it to frighten me. Shame on you!"

"I did not!"

"Oh yes you did. I know you, Maggie. You're mean. And to say that I received a dead rat in the mail? That's ludicrous. *You* might get one, I can see that. But my fans would never do such a thing. None of my readers would ever send me a dead rat."

"No, only your friends," Maggie said with a grin.

"That's it, Maggie, mock me. But I know my fans.

They *love* me. They send me afghans they've knitted for me. They send me homemade cookies, needlepoint bookmarks—Fruit of the Month!"

Maggie snapped her fingers as she turned to point a finger at Alex. "That's it. I can get Tate a year's worth of Fruit of the Month Club stuff. Smother him in grapefruit. Barrage him with Bartlett pears. Drive him crazy with boxes of . . . of kumquats."

"Maggie, dear, your mind is wandering," Alex pointed out as he polished his quizzing glass with a fine linen square of cloth.

"Oh yeah, right," she said, turning back to Felicity once more. "You had to have gotten a dead rat, Faith, everybody else did. Okay, not Kimberly D'Amico, but she lives in Missouri and we think they ran out of postage—"

"Or rats," Alex supplied helpfully, holding up his quizzing glass now as he examined a bit of jade in the form of a butterfly.

"Right, or rats. Something. But everyone else got dead rats and poems. Everyone who lives in this area got a dead rat, and now two of those people are dead. Murdered. You got one, Faith, so don't lie and say you didn't and try to blow our theory."

"The hell with your theory. I did not get a dead rat, Maggie Kelly."

"You did so."

"Did not!

"Did too!"

"*Did not*!"

"*Did* —"

"Ladies, ladies, please. Miss—Trixie, is it? Pardon me for saying so, but you seem a bit uncomfortable. Is there by any chance something you'd like to say?"

Maggie turned her attention to the rather mousy young woman who was one of those people who seemed capable of becoming invisible. "Yeah, she doesn't open her own mail, does she? Trixie? Did Faith get a rat?"

"Uh. Um. Ms. Felicity? I'm afraid you did, ma'am. One day last week, I really don't remember the exact day. It was disgusting, ma'am, and I threw it down the chute the moment I saw what it was. If there was a poem, I didn't see it. I only saw the rat. I . . . I'm sorry."

When Felicity just sat there on her lovely white brocade couch, both manicured hands to her silicone-enhanced breasts, her BOTOX-plumped lips moving soundlessly, Maggie looked at Alex and asked, "Okay, now what?"

"In a moment, Maggie. There are those who were not born with your admirable resilience," Alex said, walking unerringly to a large armoire that, when he opened the upper doors, revealed a mirrored bar. He poured both Felicity and the assistant glasses of wine and pressed them into their hands before asking of Trixie: "What do you remember of the package, my dear? Most, I'm afraid, have been destroyed, and although we doubt the perpertrator was kind enough to include a return address, I would like to hear just what you remember about what you saw. Do you think you can do that?"

"Thank you." Trixie drank down half of the wine, then nodded furiously. "It was . . . it was just one of those bags, you know? From the post office? I'm sorry, but I don't remember a return address. I could feel that there was a box or something inside the package, something the size of a shoe box, I thought, and when I pulled it out, it was gift-wrapped, so I opened it and—"

"It was *gift-wrapped*? Alex, you didn't mention that before. Was my rat gift-wrapped?" Maggie asked.

Alex shook his head. "No, my dear, it was not."

"Ha!" Felicity exclaimed in triumph, lifting her glass in a salute, as if she'd just won some sort of contest.

"You're pathetic," Maggie told her, shaking her head. "And so am I. We've got two murdered writers, Faith, and you or I could be the next target."

"Maggie's correct, Felicity, and charming as I believe Trixie here to be, I would not feel comfortable allowing you two ladies to remain here, or for Trixie to remain here with you gone. She could become an accidental victim of the person or persons looking for you."

Trixie finished off her wine in one long gulp, some color finally in her pale cheeks. "Okay, folks! That's it, that's all I've been waiting for—a good excuse. Felicity? You are the *worst* boss in the history of lousy bosses, the pay stinks, and you can consider this my two weeks' notice in full. Oh, and the next time you want someone to paint your toenails, *pinkie*, spring for a fucking pedicure. I'm out of here!"

"I . . . well . . ." Felicity smiled weakly up at Alex. "Not to sound trite, but good help is so hard to find, isn't it?"

"How many *assistants* does that make, Faith? You probably go through at least two a month. You know, just in case the concierge and doormen are running a pool I might want to get into."

Felicity got to her feet. "That's none of your business. And now that you've lost me an assistant and frightened me half out of my mind, why don't you just leave. And don't worry about the housewarming gift. I'd just throw that down the chute, too!" She collapsed back onto the couch, her chin quivering. "If I knew where it was."

Maggie looked at Alex, who was returning her look levelly. "What? You're blaming *me* for this? I wasn't the one who wanted to come here, remember? She makes my teeth hurt, Alex, and you know that. Ever since she dropped me—"

"Like a hot rock after she'd found success and you

were still struggling to survive and, so that you don't feel the need to remind me, after the two of you had made a pact that whichever of you became successful first would help the other one. Yes, I remember. But that does not negate the fact that she, too, is a potential victim."

"Yes, I know that. I'm not stupid. She has to get out of here, go somewhere until the killer is caught."

"Did you hear that, Felicity?" Alex said, sitting down beside the woman and taking one of her hands in his. "You can't stay here, my dear."

"Yeah. Right. You can't stay here, Faith."

"Which is why you'll be moving in with Maggie for the duration."

"Yeah, which is why you'll—*what*! Oh no. No, no, no, *no*!"

"Maggie, it's only common sense. It will be much easier to protect you ladies if you're both in the same place. Unless you'd want to move in here?"

Maggie looked around at Faith's palace, which more and more reminded her of a cross between Barbie's Dream House and Madonna's Material Girl phase. "Nope, not happening, Alex. She gets to go slumming in my guest bedroom. I'll move the flamingo in there so she feels more at home, but I'm not coming here. So that's it, Faith. Get up, get moving. Pack your toothbrush and let's go before I change my mind and leave you here."

Felicity was dabbing at her eyes—very carefully—with Alex's handkerchief. "Thank . . . thank you, Maggie. I . . . I could go to a hotel, I suppose?"

Maggie was beginning to feel guilty, damn it. "You can't just stay locked up in a hotel room. No, it's better if you move in with me. Alex and Sterling will be right across the hall, and Steve might want to talk to you. It's just better this way. Not great, but better."

Felicity got to her feet. "All right. But I have to pack. Oh, and see if you can find Brock."

"Brock? What's a Brock?"

"My dog, Maggie. I named him after the hero in my last book. He's very shy, and is always hiding somewhere when he hears voices other than mine. Check in the kitchen, will you? He likes to hide behind the bottled-water holder. You do have one, don't you? A bottled-water holder? I only drink bottled water. Toxins, you understand—hell on the complexion. Well, never mind, I'll have Trixie—that is, I'll order some delivered. Oh, and don't forget to pack Brock's food and his dishes. And his toys. And his eyedrops—I think Trixie keeps them in the cabinet beside the Sub-Zero. And his bed—how could I forget his little bed? You should see it, Maggie. It looks like real zebra fur. That's upstairs, in my suite. I'll take care of that."

As Felicity spoke, she was climbing the staircase to the upper floor, her last words issued as she leaned over the balcony, then turned, opened a pair of gold-trimmed double doors, and disappeared.

"One day, Alex Blakely, you will pay for this," Maggie told him as she stomped in the direction, hopefully, of the kitchen. "You won't know when, you won't know how—but you *will* pay for this. Brock. Who names a dog Brock? And what are Wellington and Napoleon going to say, huh? A dog, Alex. Poor babies, they'll be frightened out of their minds. Wow, granite counter-tops, cool. And an island. I've always wanted an island. Brock? Here, Brock. Where are you, Brock? Wanna go bye-bye, Brock? Oh, my God, *that's* Brock?"

It was small, smaller than Napper. Tan. With eyes so big they looked as if they might pop out onto the floor if someone touched them. With ears bigger than its entire head.

"I think it's a Chihuahua," Maggie said, inching closer,

bent nearly in half, her hands on her knees. "Hello, Brock. Aren't you a sweetie, huh?"

The dog immediately piddled on the tumbled sandstone tile floor, and then sat in his mess.

"Oh, this is going to be fun," Maggie said as Alex chuckled behind her.

"With luck, my dear, it will only be for a few days."

"I'll hold you to that, Alex. Now let's find all Brock's stuff and get out of here."

Except that, thirty minutes later, Felicity had still not reappeared downstairs, so that Maggie had to go on the hunt for her while Brock and Alex waited.

Maggie poked her head into the *suite*, as Felicity had called it, trying hard not to notice the king-size bed, with its canopy, the whole thing propped on a dais, no less. "Faith? Come on, what's keeping you, I want to get—what in hell are you doing? We're not going to Europe for a month, you don't need all of this."

"Yes, Maggie, I do. I've got a television interview tomorrow afternoon—you'll arrange transport for me, won't you? I need to take at least two outfits, just in case the interviewer wears something the same color, or in a similar style. But you know that, don't you? No, of course you don't. I saw you on the *Today* show, you know. You and Katie both wearing red? Good planning would have avoided that."

Maggie was biting on the inside of her cheeks now, as Felicity ducked back into the bathroom—Maggie could see part of it, and she was pretty sure the ladies' room at Grand Central Station was smaller.

Felicity reappeared again, this time carrying two toiletry bags, and with a large canvas bag with the words *Gold's Gym* printed on the side slung over her shoulder. "My workout necessities. You have a treadmill, of course. I'll miss my elliptical, but I understand we have to make some small sacrifices at a time like this."

"I don't have a treadmill, Faith."

"Don't be silly, of course you do. Everyone owns a treadmill. Look around, you've probably piled it high with dirty clothes and just can't find it. Then again, that probably explains why you look a little . . . chubby?"

"I am not chubby," Maggie gritted out from between painfully clenched teeth. "I quit smoking, and my metabolism is adjusting, that's all."

Felicity smiled. "My mistake. All right, I think that's it. Ready?"

Maggie looked at the five suitcases on the floor. "Sure. And, hey, just to show I'm not a poor sport about this, I'll help carry this stuff for you. I'll take some, and you and our helpful Alex can carry the rest, okay?"

She picked up one of the small toiletry bags and left the room, swinging it in her hand like Little Red Riding Hood on her way to Grandma's house, and smiling for the first time since Alex had come home with the news about Jonathan West.

Chapter Nineteen

Saint Just had been pleased to receive the call from Salvatore Campiano and the excuse to distance himself from females for a space, as dangling constantly at women's shoe tops was proving tedious. Even Maggie was proving tedious, in her own inimitably adorable way, and it was time for the company of men.

He had not as yet had time to examine the contents of the computer disk he'd found in Jonathan West's apartment, but that could wait until later. With Maggie's desk and computer situated in her living room, it would be better if Felicity had retired for the evening before he showed his small prize to Maggie.

He was also delaying the inevitable argument he would get from her about tiresome things like tampering with a crime scene, absconding with evidence, and being a general trial to her. That would take at least twenty minutes, but then she would agree that it might be interesting to see what the disk contained. In other words, she was just as bad as he was—only she felt this need to at least pretend to feel guilty about it all, while he labored under no such sensibilities.

He had made his excuses as Maggie and Felicity were still arguing over the animal situation, which had proved problematic for some time, as the cats had cornered Brock beneath Maggie's desk and were refusing to let him out again. With Wellington on one side, Napoleon on the other, Brock had been industriously demonstrating the surprisingly copious capacity of his bladder by releasing some of its contents in occasional frightened spurts, all over Maggie's carpet.

Yes, it would be good to be out and about, doing more manly things. Gentlemen had needs. Gentlemen needed space, for one thing. Gentlemen needed to show that they were men, first and foremost, enjoying the company and manly pursuits of others of their gender. That's why gentlemen's clubs had been in vogue nearly since the beginning of time. He himself belonged to Whites, Brooks, and his own very exclusive club, the one he'd founded two years after coming into his majority—the club so exclusive it did not even deign to bother with a name.

Perhaps that's what was lacking in his life now that he was residing in twenty-first-century Manhattan. A club of his own. A dark and comfortable space filled with the smells of aged brandy, good cigars, fine leathers. A place where devoted servants pressed the morning papers with a warm iron before delivering them to the members, and even washed the coins a gentleman must by necessity carry in his pockets. A place where a wagering book was always available, and a gentleman could rely on the daily boiled dinner to be a reminder of his childhood if he deigned to partake of it. Boon companions with whom he could debate the politics of the day, discuss sporting events, play a few hands at whist or perhaps set up a faro bank—even brag just a bit about their accomplishments at turf and table. And all without the worry of women in their midst.

Who would he ask to join him? That was a bit of a dilemma, wasn't it? By rights, only those of the peerage, or with families that could be traced back to the time of William the Conquerer would be even considered for membership.

Then again, these were, for the most part, often dull-as-ditchwater gentlemen whose blood had been combined one too many times, leading to a propensity for weak chins, knobby knees, dreadful overbites, and the occasional peer who seemed happiest when dribbling into his soup.

Thank goodness for Sterling. Saint Just enjoyed Steve Wendell, and Socks was a near constant surprise to him. Then there were George and Vernon but, no, they wouldn't do. They were simply too young. He remembered the story—Maggie had recounted it in one of their books—of the disaster caused when a London gentlemen's club catering to younger members had been shut down for renovations and the members of one of the more prestigious clubs had offered to share their own space with them for the duration.

Rolls had been tossed, not passed, from one end of the dining table to the other. Noise and drunkenness had been a major problem. And then there was the young gentleman who had poked his nose against that of a slumbering member in the smoking room and then loudly inquired, "I say, is this old codger sleeping or dead? I want to sit down."

Saint Just stepped out onto the sidewalk, still pulling on his black kid gloves, for the day was turning to early December night and the temperature had dropped considerably. He'd have to discuss the idea of their own club with Sterling when next he saw him. Sterling understood the need for some sort of decorum, after all. Not too high in the instep, but an establishment required a certain level of dignity in order for it to be a comfortable haven.

"Sterling?" he said a moment later as his dignified and decorous friend approached along the sidewalk, all but skipping, still clad in his bright red Father Christmas costume, and flanked by his Merry Men, who seemed to be flagging slightly in their green elf suits. Ah, well, perhaps the idea of a gentlemen's club could wait for another day. "Vernon. George. Have you had a productive afternoon?"

"It was above all things marvelous, Saint Just," Sterling told him, giving his bell a hearty ring, at which time George, not looking all that merry, reached over and snatched the thing out of his hand.

"I hear that frigging bell ring one more time, Sterlman, I'm going postal all over your pudgy little body," George warned tersely. "I warned you, remember? Dingding, ding-ding! Hour after hour! I can't stand it any more!"

"There, there, George." Saint Just lifted a hand to his mouth to hide his smile. "Don't you all look—festive."

"Vernon was a huge success, Saint Just," Sterling told him happily. "He brought that small folding table with him, and he put these three walnut-shell halves on top of it, with a dried pea—that's what it was, wasn't it, Vernon, a dried pea? At any rate, he encouraged everyone to watch him place the pea beneath one of the walnut shells and then he mixed them round and round on the tabletop and people gave him money to guess where the pea had gone. They hardly ever guessed correctly. Wasn't that a brilliant idea?"

"I think I'd call it *inventive*," Saint Just said, looking at the youth lately known as Snake, the one whose mother, a recent resident of the state's penal system, had given her son an engraved switchblade for his birthday. "And how much money did you earn this way for Santas for Silver, hmmm?"

"Uh . . . well, I . . . I don't know, Alex. I put it all in the chimney. Didn't I, George?"

"Yeah, that's right. That's what he did. In the chimney. All of it."

"Of course he did. Unless he forgot some of it? Perhaps slipped a few bills into his pockets for safekeeping and then simply forgot about them? All that money for the needy children—we wouldn't wish to overlook a penny of it, would we? I have a thought—why don't you just check your pockets, my friend. Now."

"Yeah, sure, Alex," Vernon said, digging in the pockets of his elf costume and coming out with a wad of crumpled bills in both hands. "Wow, look at that. I must have forgotten to put some of it in the chimney, huh?"

"A forgivable offense, as your heart was in the right place, wasn't it, Vernon. Now, if you'll simply hand the money over to Sterling?"

"It's all right, Vernon," Sterling said, stuffing the bills into the chimney. "Oh, this is so exciting. I'll wager Mr. Goodfellow will be handing out gold stars to the three of us tomorrow for collecting more money than any of the other Santas. Won't that be nice?"

The boys grumbled, their faintly sickly smiles failing to register as anything less than delight to the innocent, trusting Sterling.

"And there was no trouble?" Saint Just asked George, who shook his head.

"A couple of guys looked like they wanted to try something, but that's all. You need us again tomorrow? Please say no."

Saint Just reached into his pocket and took out his money clip, counting out two hundred dollars and handing the money to Vernon and George. "For your trouble, you understand, and you will still be paid your usual rate for the Street Corner Orators and Players. Now, I'm sure you'd like to be on your way and out of those charming outfits. I'll phone you in the morning if I need you. Thank you again."

"Yes, thank you, you're both splendid, *splendid* gentlemen. And didn't we have *fun*!" Sterling said, shaking their hands as they both looked at him as if he was a sweet, slightly slow fellow they would kill for if such a thing became necessary.

Once the boys were in a cab and on their way—even a Snake and a Killer, Saint Just supposed, would not readily wish to ride the subway in green elf suits—Saint Just told Sterling about the demise of Jonathan West and the new living arrangements he would find upstairs, including the resolution he had reached concerning Brock.

"Miss Simmons refused to be parted from her animal, so Napoleon and Wellington will for the nonce be residing with us. I've moved Henry's cage to the top of your wardrobe chest, where I'm sure he'll be safe. I'm sorry, Sterling, but it was the only solution I could think of at the time, as Brock seemed near to suffering an apoplexy."

"That's all right, Saint Just. I'm sure you'll discover the identity of the murderer soon enough, and we'll all be able to return to our usual routines. Is that where you're going now? To solve the murders?"

"I am nearly unmanned by your faith in my abilities, my friend. Actually, I'm off on a small errand on an entirely other matter," Saint Just said, motioning to Paul, who had just come on duty.

The idiot boy waved at him.

"Allow me to clarify my gesture, Paul. Gratified as I am to see you, I was indicating that you should attempt to secure a cab for me."

"A cab? You want a cab? Jeez. All you had to do was ask. You didn't have to go all fancy talk on me."

"Remind me, Sterling, if you will, that I have decided to gift Paul with a lovely assortment of sugarless fudge for the holidays."

"How kind of you to remember him at all. Do you want me to come with you, Saint Just?" Sterling asked, hefting his Santas for Silver chimney. "I could just go upstairs and change. It would only take a minute."

"No, Sterling, thank you. You go see to the animals if you would, and then visit with Maggie and Miss Simmons until I return. Do try to keep them from clawing at each other, all right?"

Sterling frowned. "But you said you put the cats in our condo."

"Maggie and Miss Simmons, Sterling. I was referring to the ladies."

"Oh," Sterling said, looking confused as Saint Just inclined his head toward his friend before passing a bill to Paul and entering the cab that would take him to Long Island.

The restaurant he entered forty–five minutes later could not have been more than twenty feet wide, but it was at least three times as long as it was wide, and the air smelled delicious; a mix of oils and sauces and, most definitely, garlic.

He saw Salvatore Campiano almost immediately, as the man, a large white square tucked into his collar, stood up and waved a spoon in his direction, summoning him to the table the man occupied alone, although the pair of pilot fish stood slightly behind him, one to each side of their employer.

"I'm fascinated by the *Godfather* movies," Saint Just said as he took his seat to the left of Campiano. "Do you mind that I am loathe to sit with my back to the door? Oh, and if you'd be so kind as to answer a question for me, as you told me earlier on the telephone that you own this restaurant."

Campiano spoke around a mouthful of linguine. "Anything. Anything you want to know. Of course, then I should have to kill you," he ended, laughing so hard at his own joke that he began to choke on his food and one of the man-mountains quickly stepped forward to slap him on the back as he glared at Saint Just. "*Basta*! Enough, Tony! What—I'm a baby here? You going to burp me? The man is asking me a question."

"Sorry, boss," Tony said, stepping back once more, his large hands folded in front of him as he stood, legs slightly apart, a near twin to the other bodyguard. Rather like Gog and Magog, the pair of straw giants that once stood sentinel outside the London Guildhall.

Gentleman that he was, Saint Just went on as if nothing had happened, and asked his question. "It is a matter of logistics, sir. As the history of your . . . of your profession, shall I say for lack of a more fitting descriptive word . . . is numbered by several occasions upon which a gentleman, such as yourself, is shot down by his enemies in an establishment such as this—why do you persist in taking your meals in such an establishment? That is, defensively, you're fairly without options here, aren't you? Only one way to go if under attack, and sitting here rather like a duck on a pond. What is it I'm not seeing, Mr. Campiano?"

Campiano shrugged. "My boys here, they're armed. Show him, boys."

Before Tony or his companion could pull their large personal cannons from their waistbands, Saint Just had captured Tony in a headlock, while the point of his unsheathed sword stick caressed the Adam's apple of the second bodyguard. The patrons at a table near them all hit the floor with an alacrity that brought a small smile to Saint Just's lips.

"Tell them I mean no harm, Mr. Campiano," Saint Just said, tightening his grip on Tony's thick neck as the man struggled to shake him loose. "Tell them I'm merely attempting to demonstrate my point, that point being that, were I serious, Tony here would already be shaking hands with his maker, this other gentleman would be skewered, and you, sir, would have swallowed your last bite of linguine."

Campiano sat back and applauded Saint Just's efforts, motioning for him to release his men. "Ah, my friend, but you would never have gotten so close if I had believed you dangerous."

"And that, sir, if you don't mind my saying so, along with the physical limitations of this narrow restaurant, is the problem. It is not enough to appear dangerous, as do these two fine gentlemen here. One must *be* dangerous, so that no one with assassination on his mind even dares to approach so closely."

"Like you, pretty boy, huh?" Campiano said, holding out his hands to take the sword cane, which Saint Just handed over without a qualm. "An unusual toy. I like it. I like you. But we're at peace now, and have been for years—just businessmen, you understand. All legit, *capisca?* Still, I'm curious. What do you suggest I do, besides training these two to be faster on their feet?"

For the space of two hours, as Saint Just discovered what he believed would be a lifelong passion for something called meatballs, the men discussed strategy, from Caesar's brilliance on the continent to Napoleon's tactical blunders at Waterloo. It wasn't quite his gentlemen's club, but he was enjoying himself to the top of his bent, a gentleman, in the company of another gentleman.

Using condiments and broken bread sticks as props, Saint Just then demonstrated a reconfiguration of the restaurant, making the path from door to main table one of staggered dining tables—a maze to be navigated rather than the current large center aisle, with all the tables against the two walls.

"Now, after removing that large front window and replacing it with something solid so that it isn't obvious from the street that you are at dinner, I would then place half-wall dividers here, and here—decorative, but of bulletproof glass, of course—I've seen something very close to what I'm thinking of on the Internet. The seconds gained by the maze, combined with the quick access to protection that still allows you to see your attacker should even the playing field, don't you think? Oh, and the ceiling is high enough for you to build a catwalk, as I believe is the term, from one side to the other, so that two men can be stationed up there, able to see everything that is going on below them. Well-dressed so as to not alarm your patrons, well-mannered, but discreetly armed, of course."

"O'course," Campiano said, poking Tony's gut with one of the bread sticks. "Why you didn't think of this, huh? A catwalk? I like that." He peered at Saint Just as a waiter took their empty plates. "All this from watching *Godfather*? You're more than a pretty boy, aren't you? I should have known that. And you say what you think."

"I'm sorry," Saint Just said. "I fear it's a failing of mine. But, Mr. Campiano, in order for a gentleman to enjoy his leisure, it is, I believe, imperative for him to at all times be prepared for any . . . contingency." He smiled. "*È questa verità?*"

"It is truth, yes," Campiano said, returning that smile. "But enough of this. You want to know about this Goodfellow? Not a nice man, not a gentleman of good heart, like us—you and me. I sent one of my boys by, just for a quick look-see, and he recognized him right away.

Same cell block up at Attica a few years ago, *capisca*? Gino, tell the man what your cousin Johnny told you."

Gino looked at Saint Just as if he wanted to break his sword cane over his head, but then he just shrugged, for his master had spoken. "The guy's real name is Donny Dill—they called him Pickles. He was on the tail side of a nickel when my cousin knew him. Fraud."

"A nickel?"

"A five-year sentence," Campiano supplied helpfully. "Now he's out, and back to his old tricks. You want me to take care of this for you, my friend? I cannot let this stand, now that I know."

Saint Just shook his head. "No, thank you very much, but I believe I should attempt to handle the matter on my own."

"You sure? I'm no angel myself. But to steal from the poor at Christmas?" He shook his fist in the air. "*Vorrei per alimentare a questo uomo il suo proprio naso. Capisca?*"

"My Italian has its limits, but I believe you said you'd enjoy feeding the man his own nose. I applaud the sentiment," Saint Just said evenly, reaching for a small bunch of grapes from the fruit plate just deposited on the table. "My plan is to pay our friend a small visit tomorrow morning, to see if I can point out the error of his way, persuade him to terminate this operation he is pursuing. . . ."

"Scam. He's working a scam—that's how we say in American. You foreigners maybe don't know that," Campiano said helpfully, then took a large bite from a ripe apple. "And the money?"

"It's my hope he will turn that over to my associate—a very kind, trusting man—who will see that it is all delivered to a legitimate charity. That is a large part of my plan, Mr. Campiano—that my friend not realize he has inadvertently become part of a, as you said, *scam*. I wish to protect his innocence, and, yes, his almost childlike belief in the inherent goodness of his fellow man. This is important to me."

"And if this Pickles dweeb says no?"

Saint Just tugged a single juicy purple grape free and held it in front of him, looking at it. "Yes, I've considered that possibility. It's a ticklish thing, sir. You see, I have this other friend who does not understand that there may be times when one feels the need to *handle* things outside the boundaries of established law."

"A woman, yes? It's always a woman. And you listen to this woman?"

"When possible, yes."

"And when this is not possible?"

Saint Just merely smiled—a smile other men understood. "I'd appreciate being able to borrow these two fine gentlemen from you for a short space tomorrow morning—them or someone with their same rather intimidating physical appearance."

Campiano moved his chair closer, hunched his shoulders. "You're thinking muscle? In the morning, you say. Gino's taking his grandmother to the podiatrist over in Hempstead at nine—she's got the hammertoes very bad. But he'll be back by ten. Come on, tell me more of what you want."

"I'm thinking, sir, that a show of strength is rarely a bad thing. All I would need is for them to stand just inside the door, mute, while I negotiate with our Mr. Dill, feeling free to look as menacing as they wish. They could crack their knuckles a time or two, if you don't think that's too dramatic."

"No, no, they're good at that. Aren't you, boys? And if this doesn't work? If this Pickles prick says no?"

"Well, then, sir, I will have tried, won't I? My conscience—thinking again of my friends—would thus be clear as I hand Mr. Dill over to you with my compliments. I would not so insult you as to add that the money Mr. Dill has fraudulently collected would still be redirected to a suitable charity."

Campiano gave Saint Just a shove that nearly sent him sprawling onto the floor. "Why can't my niece Nikki meet a man like you? No, she goes for idiots, and surfboards. I like you, boy! I send you more fruit!"

"That would be very nice, sir. But, if I am not being too forward, I would prefer the possibility of a container of meatballs. I fear I am in love. . . ."

Chapter Twenty

Maggie went from asleep to awake in the space of a single heartbeat, her arms and legs thrashing as she tried to get away from the hand covering her mouth.

"Shhh, sweetings, it's only me. I didn't wish to wake Felicity. Can I safely take my hand away now? You won't cry out?"

She nodded furiously.

Alex lifted his hand.

Maggie punched him, hard, in the chest.

"Well, that was only to be expected," he said, rubbing at his chest as she kicked back the covers and swung her legs over the side of the bed—then hauled back to hit him again. "And even condoned," he added, neatly sidestepping the intended blow so that a still groggy Maggie sort of pinwheeled back down onto the mattress. "Once, that is. I didn't expect you to retire so early, my dear."

Maggie pushed her fingers through her hair, then rubbed at her eyes. "Faith thought we were going to have a pajama party—talk about boys and braid each other's hair, so I told her I had a headache and came in here. And it wasn't a lie, either. Still isn't, as a matter of fact. What time is it?"

"Nearly midnight," Alex told her, holding out her slippers, the white ones embroidered on the front with the words *left* and *other left*. "Please forgive me. There's something I feel I should show you, but I was detained on my errand quite a bit longer than I'd intended."

"Detained, huh? That's pretty Englishman's code for you ran out like a coward and left me here with Faith." Maggie pushed away the slippers and headed for the bathroom, wishing she could accomplish that feat in one straight line, but she couldn't. Sleep always turned her sense of direction and her balance temporarily stupid, and she half staggered toward the door, scratching at an itch on her left side. "Don't say anything else until I get back. I've got to brush my teeth and—I've got to brush my teeth. I'll meet you in the living room, okay?"

"Only if I can control my passion, my dear," Alex called after her quietly.

"Bite me. . . ."

Once blinking at the bright light in the bathroom, Maggie tried to focus on her reflection in the mirror above the sink. How many times had she written that her heroines woke wonderfully sleep-tousled? How many times had she continued at dawn a love scene that had begun the evening before and ended with the lovers sleeping in each other's arms?

Good thing she wrote fiction, because reality was a whole other bag of worms. Imagine how her readers would like it if she wrote a morning love scene filled with spiky, ratted hair, sleep-creased cheeks, a mouth that tasted like something had died in it—oh, and a crushing need to use the facilities?

Yeah, that'd sell a lot of copies. Critics complained that romance novels gave an unrealistic vision of life.

That wasn't true. Happily ever after—or at least lifelong commitment to each other—wasn't a fantasy. Heroines that didn't rumple, who were always freshly combed and dewy-eyed? Now *that* was a fantasy someone really should address. Just not her.

Still widely opening and closing her eyes in her attempt to shift her brain into gear, Maggie entered the living room to see Alex standing at her desk, holding a floppy disk by its edges.

"What's that?"

"Something I happened to discover this afternoon at Jonathan West's apartment, actually."

Okay, she was awake now. "You *what*?" She turned to look down the hallway, then repeated in a near whisper. "You *what*? That's . . . that's *evidence*, Alex. For crying out loud, you took *evidence*? Where was Steve? He doesn't know you have this, does he? No, no, of course he doesn't. Cripes, Alex, how many times are we going to have to go through this, huh? There are *rules*. *Laws*. *Consequences*. You can't just—where exactly did you find it? What makes you think it's special?"

"Fifteen seconds," Alex said, replacing the large gold watch he carried on a chair and tucked into his pocket. "I believe we're making progress."

"If I were more awake, I'd have a snappy comeback for that," Maggie said, carefully taking the disk out of his hand before sitting down at her desk and waking her computer. "Now tell me all about this thing before we look at it."

Alex's recounting of what had transpired at Jonathan West's apartment took only a few minutes, and by the time he was finished Maggie's curiosity had completely overcome any thoughts about the legality of what they were about to do. She slipped the disk into the machine and double clicked on the icon to open it.

"You know, I couldn't do this if I hadn't bought that

new program—Microsoft Office for Macs—because this is a Word program. I use AppleWorks because it comes free with my Mac, but I bought the Microsoft stuff because I'm always getting files in Word and then I have to tell the person I can't open them. Well, maybe I could, but I don't read manuals because I don't understand them. Click here, stupid—that I understand. Ah, here we go."

She slipped on her computer glasses and leaned closer to the monitor as Alex read over her shoulder, turning her new wide-screen monitor slightly in his direction. "'There exists in this world a fine line between love and hate. Lovers do not believe this, of course, until the moment . . .' It's a manuscript?"

"Yeah, sure looks like it. Well, that's okay then, except if you'd copped a copy of Jonathan's favorite solitaire program you wouldn't be going to jail," Maggie said, using the mouse to roll through the first pages. "No title page, no header, no pagination—nothing. And see all those squiggly red underlines, those squiggly green underlines? Red's for misspelled words, green is for bad spacing, incorrect phrasing, stuff like that."

She swiveled around to look at Alex. "This is Jonathan's all right. Bernie told me this is how he used to send his stuff in to her. It drove her nuts, but Jonathan said he was an *artiste*, and couldn't interrupt his muse for mundane things like headers, and punctuation. He didn't run the spell-checker, that's for sure. But the program keeps a page total at the bottom and there are over four hundred pages here, Alex. This is probably a complete manuscript. Wow, an undiscovered West. How about that. Bernie will go nuts. It'll sell, even if it stinks, just because Jonathan was murdered."

"Is there a way for you to know when he wrote this?"

"Sure," Maggie said, swiveling back to the desk once

more. "I just need to hit info and—there it is. Created, January second of this year, and modified—meaning the last time he changed anything on it—November nineteenth. He'd just finished it a couple of weeks ago. And you found this in the *toaster*?"

"Unusual, I grant you, although we should admit that anyone looking for the computer disk would hardly look there, so it was quite safe—although why he would feel the necessity for safety is troublesome. Then again, the man did drink a bit, and what seems strange to us may have appeared quite logical to him. But more unusual is that I did not see a computer on the man's desk."

"Maybe he had a laptop and kept it in a closet, or something?"

"Perhaps. We'll have to inquire of the *left*-tenant, as I'm confident he conducted a thorough search of the premises. However, not being bound by rules of evidence and all that sort of drivel, why don't we suppose, just for the moment, that someone—our murderer—removed Jonathan's computer."

"Because they wanted something that was on that computer," Maggie said, fully alert now and happy to take this ball and run with it. "And maybe that's why you found the disk in the toaster. Because Jonathan was afraid someone was trying to steal his work and wanted to hide a copy? But why would anyone want to steal Jonathan's manuscript? His last books were lousy."

"May he rest in peace," Alex said with a wink, then poured them each a glass of wine and they moved to the couch, Maggie curling up in one corner. "Plus, as long as we're considering things—if we're to connect the dead rats with the murders, and those rats were sent by devotees of Mr. West's books, why is the man dead at all?"

"Right. That doesn't make sense, does it? I was so caught up with Faith and that urine machine that I hadn't really thought about that too much yet. Why kill Jonathan? Unless we're wrong, and some fan—fans—of his aren't behind the rats, and someone just wants everyone who contributed to *No Secret Anymore* dead. We took a giant leap of logic there, Alex, assuming it was someone who felt we'd destroyed Jonathan's career. Maybe there's something in the plot of *No Secret Anymore* that pulled some nutcase's chain."

"Can you summarize the plot for me?"

"Sure. Crime in the past uncovered in the present. Ten chapters, ten suspects, then Jonathan wrapped it all up in this *ridiculous* epilogue that made about as much sense as one of those ING commercials. Do you think we have to go back to Valentino Gates and Lord Bryon? That one or both of them is Nevus—Rat Boy? Because I still say they couldn't kill anybody. Oh, that's right! That's where we got the idea about someone wanting to avenge Jonathan—from the fan letters. But with Jonathan dead?" She shook her head. "Man, I don't know what's going on, but I have the feeling you're going to tell me that Faith has to stay here, right?"

"I'm sorry, my dear."

"Not half as much as I am. She got all nuts about someone trying to kill her and refused to take Brock out for his evening walk, and Paul wouldn't do it and Sterling was sleeping on the couch when I went looking for him, so I had to walk the damn dog. And she dressed him up first in his own coat and booties—booties, Alex!—even a stupid matching plaid tam hat with a pom-pom on it. So there I am, walking this damn dog, carrying a plastic bag with me for his—well, you know what for. I'm not doing it again, Alex. Let her toilet train the mutt, or something."

"You went out on your own?" Alex asked, getting to his feet. "I thought we understood—"

"No, *you* understood. *I* had a whiny little dog crossing his back legs and looking like his eyeballs were starting to float. Besides, nobody could have done anything to me out there—they'd be too busy laughing their butts off at Brock. Now go away and let me read more of Jonathan's opus, because we're going to have to figure out some way to give it to Steve tomorrow without having him slap us in handcuffs. Well, you. I'm just the accessory after the fact. Go away now—I can't read anything with someone hanging over my back."

Maggie would have kept reading all night, until she'd finished the manuscript, except that reading Jonathan's jumble of mistakes along with his words had her eyes crossing by page two hundred and she gave it up and went to bed, only to wake up to the sound of someone chanting . . . *and two, and three, and four, and rest. And one, and two, and three . . .*

She slammed her way down the hall to see Faith dressed in skintight Day-Glo pink workout leggings and a matching sleeveless top that definitely strained around the boobs. She had a small step thingamabob in the center of the room and was hopping up and down on it as some ditz with an annoyingly nasal voice counted out cadence from the TV.

"*What* are you doing?" she asked, stepping between the television and Faith. "Are you nuts? It's seven o'clock in the morning."

"It's eight-thirty, and I'm exercising, which would be obvious to you if you ever did it," Felicity told her, not missing a beat as she hopped up, hopped down, hopped up again. "Oh, Sterling came by earlier and took Brock out for me—wasn't that nice, isn't he a dear? Brock wasn't feeling cooperative, though, so Sterling will have to do it again. Come on, Maggie, have a nice big glass of OJ and join me."

"I'd rather eat glass," Maggie said, heading for the kitchen and the orange juice part of Felicity's recommendation. Sipping from a large tumbler, she made her way back to the living room, swinging her right hand in time with the television workout Nazi as Felicity laid on the floor, her hands under her lower back, bicycling her legs in the air. "Feel the burn, oh yeah, baby, feel the burn!" she instructed, undoing the dead bolts on the front door and hoping no one had walked off with her newspaper.

"Bernie? J.P? What are you two doing here so—"

"We met up in the lobby," J.P. told her. "It's eight-thirty, why aren't you dressed yet?"

"Why do you think I'm a writer—so I don't *have* to get dressed."

The two women slipped past Maggie into the living room, Bernie waving a copy of the *Post* above her head. "You've done it again, Maggie. Made the front page this time, too. Look!"

Maggie tried to reach the newspaper. "I would, if you'd stop waving it like a flag. And what do you mean I—oh, *God*!"

Bernie gave her a kiss on the cheek. "I couldn't be prouder of you if you were my own daughter—which you're not, because I'm not that old. Isn't it terrific! You can't *buy* this kind of publicity."

"'Life Imitates Art—When it comes to death, is best-selling novelist Cleo Dooley a carrier?' Oh, yeah, Bernie, that's just terrific. Just peachy," Maggie said, opening the newspaper. "Oh, look at this—a sidebar listing all the murders I've been involved in—even England. They've got a freaking timeline! Who *told* them?"

Bernie peered over her shoulder. "That's the only thing I don't like. If they were going to put up a sidebar, why couldn't it have been a listing of your titles. I should messenger one over. You know, in case they do a follow-up story tomorrow."

"You're a sick woman, Bernie. Damn, there it is,

second paragraph. My real name," Maggie said, reading the article as she sat down in her desk chair, trying not to think about how all of these murders had only begun happening since Alex had shown up in her life. "Look at this—they've got Francis. They've got Jonathan. They've got the rats? Bernie, they've got the *rats*! I thought Steve said they were going to withhold that information from the press. Somebody talked. Somebody *leaked* this to the press, somebody who knows what we know. Is it only the *Post*? Because if it's only the *Post*, maybe that's not too bad and—oh, shit."

Three women looked at the ringing telephone while the fourth sat on the floor, legs spread, trying to touch her nose to her knee.

Ri-i-ng . . . Ri-i-n-g . . . Ri-i-ng . . . Ri-i-ng . . . My Doberman pinscher, Satan, is home but I'm not, please leave a message at the beep . . . BEEP . . ." You ungrateful child! I opened the paper this morning and what do I see but—"

"Okay, question answered. The story hit more than the *Post*," Maggie said, diving across the room to turn down the volume on the machine. "Love you, too, Mom," she said, grimacing at the machine before heading back to her glass of orange juice. There were already a bunch of messages, but she'd turned off the ringer on her phone in the bedroom, so she'd missed them. Thank God. "Faith, will you cut that out!"

"Four more, Maggie," Felicity said, bending her head once more, this time grasping her ankles with both hands.

"Yeah? Well, you'll have to do your own counting," Maggie said, picking up the remote and switching off the television.

"What's she doing down there anyway?" J.P. asked, coming back into the room carrying a glass of orange juice. "Is that Pilates? I don't know about Pilates. Pontius Pilate, I know about him, but that's not it, right? I put the kettle on. You don't have anything but instant coffee?"

"Sorry," Maggie said, reading the article once more. "If I had known you were coming I'd have hired Juan Valdez and a damn donkey."

"Um, testy this morning, isn't she?" J.P. said, lowering herself onto one of the couches. "Silly me, I figured you might want to cash in on that offer of free legal advice for life. My advice, by the way, is to hop the first Disney cruise and get the hell out of Dodge. Lose yourself in with the other cartoon characters."

"Funny," Maggie said, tossing the newspaper at her and then looking down at Felicity, who was now lying prone on the floor, her arms and legs splayed out as her silcone rapidly rose and fell as she breathed through her mouth. "All done? Good. You look terrible, Faith, by the way. Anything I can get you? You just have to ask, being my guest and all. So, what do you need? Pillow? Blanket? A chalk outline?"

"I like this girl, I really do," J.P. said, chuckling. "Hey, there goes your phone again, sunshine."

"I know that, J.P. I'm ignoring it. If I ignore it long enough, it might even go away."

"Yeah, I keep thinking that about the Bush administration. . . ."

"Good morning, ladies," Alex said from the doorway, and Maggie grabbed the *Post* and went at him with full intentions of beating him about the head and shoulders with it.

Naturally, he snatched it away from her first. "Yes, I've seen it, thank you. Socks brought a copy up to me earlier. I don't think they got your best side, unfortunately," he told her, and Maggie knew he was right, even as she wondered where the hell the *Post* had gotten her photograph.

"Oh, wait, I remember that photo," she said as Sterling struggled to slip a nervously yapping Brock into his little plaid coat yet again. "That's the one someone got as we were leaving Bernie's condo that one time, I think. I was the unknown female companion, right?"

"Yes, I believe you're correct," Alex told her, depositing the newspaper in the large trash can beneath Maggie's desk. "Ah, and before I forget, surrounded as I am by all you lovely ladies, Maggie, your father phoned me this morning when he couldn't reach you."

"Dad? Damn, I forgot all about him. Do you see what's happening to me here, Alex? *Everything*, damn it, that's what's happening to me. I forgot my own *father*. What did he say? Is he all right?"

"He's fine," Alex assured her. "But he's also on his way back to Ocean City, feeling that you have enough on your plate right now without having him underfoot."

"He saw the *Post*."

"Oh, sweetings, the story is not limited to the *Post*. I was first alerted to the fact that the media had picked up on the story as I watched the early morning news."

"Television, too? Why? Why me? I mean, seriously, folks. This story is about Francis, and Jonathan, not me. So why do I get singled out? What did I ever do to anybody? I mind my own business. I don't cause trouble. No, I don't *do* anything, I don't *go* anywhere—"

Sterling looked up from his task of maneuvering Brock's legs into the plaid coat. "We just got back from England, Maggie."

"Shh, Sterling," Alex told him. "Don't interrupt her. I think she's almost done. Are you almost done, Maggie? We do need to move on now. First, would you like to hear the message your father left for you?"

"If it was the only message on there, sure," Maggie said, looking at the rapidly blinking red message alert light. "Oh, okay, I'll do it."

"Fine," Alex told her, heading for the door once more. "But I'm afraid you'll have to excuse me. Sterling? Please remember that you and George and Vernon are to meet me just outside the Santas for Silver headquarters at ten-thirty."

Maggie wanted to ask Alex what was going on at ten-thirty, but he was gone before she could open her mouth, leaving her with nothing much else to do but listen to the messages. There were six:

"Miss Kelly, this is Roseanne Miller calling, from the staff of Fox news? If you'd be so kind as to return this call, Miss Spivak would like to arrange an interview at your earliest convenience. Our number here at the studio is—"

Maggie hit the *skip* button. "I don't think so, Ms. Spivak," she said, hunting for her nicotine inhaler on her desktop as Bernie woke her computer.

"Margaret? This is your mother . . ."

"Yeah, wouldn't have known that one on my own," Maggie said, hitting *skip* again.

"Margaret, Dr. Bob Chalfont here. I just saw the morning news, and I'm very concerned about you, my dear. If you feel the need to talk about this, arrange an emergency appointment, please don't hesitate to—"

Another hit to the *skip* button.

"Margaret, it's Dad. I was hoping to talk to you, pumpkin. I saw the newspapers. Are you all right? Why didn't you tell me about this? Look, I'm going to go home this morning. Well, not home, not really. But I have a friend who has a summer place on Eleventh Street he rents out and he said I could crash there— that's the term, isn't it, *crash?* Isn't that what bachelors do? So, don't you worry about me, I'll be fine. I'll even try to . . . try to talk to your mother, see if we can't work something out. Just as soon as she apologizes. All right, I'll call Alex—he gave me his cell phone number in case I needed it. A good man, Alex. I like him, and I know he'll take care of you. And I'll call you tonight."

"As soon as she apologizes? He's still on that? They're both nuts," Maggie said, shaking her head. "Maybe I can just send them each a nice poinsettia. . . ."

"You ungrate—" Maggie hit the *skip* button with the speed of a frog snagging a fly in midair.

And the last message: "Maggie, it's Bruce McCrae. Sorry to bother you. Is J.P. there with you? We had a . . . we had a small disagreement this morning and I wanted to apologize, so if she shows up, will you have her call me, please? Thanks. Maggie, I saw the news, read the paper. How did they get that stuff about the dead rats? What's the matter with these cops, giving out inside information like that? Unnamed source, it says. What a crock. I can't believe Jonathan's dead, can you? And it blows our theory all to hell, too, doesn't it? Well, anyway, you're not there, obviously, so I'll hang up now. But if J.P. stops by, have her give me a call, okay? Thanks again. Stay safe."

"Trouble in paradise?" Maggie asked J.P., who had commandeered Maggie's plastic container of M&M's from the desk. "And here I thought yours was a match made in heaven."

"Zipper it, sunshine," J.P. said, picking through the container and taking out three blue M&M's, Maggie's favorites. "So I'm not the sweet, gullible little girl everyone thinks I am. I'm a criminal attorney, remember, and I don't take anyone at face value. I was checking up on him and, big deal, he caught me. That's all. But, hey, a girl can't be too careful these days."

"Checking up on him? How? And don't eat the blue ones. I always save those for last."

J.P. shrugged and picked up one more blue M&M, popped them all in her mouth. "You wouldn't want them back anyway, I already touched them. And nothing too terrible. Remember how we talked about getting people's cell phone records online? For a fee? I tried it with Bruce's number that first night. I don't know why, I just did. And Bruce came in and saw the printout I got back this morning before I could hide the damn thing. He'll get over it. He *is* over it—he just said so in that message."

"Maggie?"

"Not now, Faith," Maggie said, trying to ignore the fact that Felicity had come into the room wearing one towel on her head, one wrapped around her body from breast to thigh, and that's all. "And get dressed. Sterling will be back soon and you'll give the poor guy a heart attack."

"Maggie," Felicity went on as if Maggie hadn't spoken, "I can't stay here. You don't have bottled water, you don't have a treadmill. You don't have a steam shower— Maggie, *everyone* has a steam shower. There isn't a single green leafy vegetable in your entire refrigerator. I can't live like this, I really can't."

"Tough," Maggie said, turning her back on the woman. "Believe me, I don't want you here any more than you want to be here, but we're just going to have to make the best of it, that's all. Now go get some clothes on. Please."

"Well, *fine*. But I'm ordering a treadmill, Maggie. And a bottled-water dispenser. And some *broccoli*! You can consider them all a present once I'm gone—oh, and then we're even-Steven for everything."

"Wait—no, you can't—I don't want—oh, God. Anybody—is there a *Welcome* sign on my back that I can't see? And why do I let her think I'm a doormat?" Maggie said as she made her way to her desk and began hunting through the top drawer for a nicotine cartridge to slip into her holder. "If anyone knew just how *bad* I want a cigarette right now. . . ."

"Not my drug of choice, but I know how you feel, hon," Bernie told her sympathetically. "Hey, how are you liking this, anyway?"

"Hmm? How am I liking what?" Maggie asked, ashamed to realize how good it felt to feel the nicotine cylinder pop open inside the inhaler. She lifted it to her mouth, ready to take a long, smokeless drag of air and chemicals.

"Bruce's book, of course," Bernie said, pointing to the computer screen. "He only gave you a draft, I see, not the finished product, but it's wonderful, isn't it? Maggie? Are you choking?"

Maggie's attempt to hold back a startled exclamation after her initial inhale had only made things worse, and now she'd swallowed down the wrong throat, as she used to call it when she was a kid, and her eyes were tearing as she ran into the kitchen for a glass of water. A minute later she was back, wiping at her eyes with a dish towel she'd grabbed from the counter. "Did you say what I thought you said?"

Bernie shrugged. "What did I say? You're reading Bruce's new book. I haven't read all of it yet, but if it holds up, I'd have to say it's the best thing he's ever done. He was a good six months past his deadline, you know, and I was beginning to worry. Especially since his last book didn't exactly burn up the lists. Maggie, are you sure you're all right?"

"No, I'm *not* all right. I've got to think, okay? Just everybody be real quiet, and let me think. Damn it, where's Alex?"

"The phone's ringing, sunshine," J.P. said as Maggie paced the carpet, sucking on the nicotine inhaler.

Maggie just waved in the machine's general direction and kept walking as Steve Wendell's voice came over the speaker.

"Maggie? I wanted you and Alex to know, I guess. We did a rush on the post, and West's wounds were not self-inflicted. The ME could tell from calluses on his hands or something that he was right-handed, and the cuts were definitely made by a left-handed person. We already knew some of that, considering there was no bloody knife or razor on the scene. Plus, he had a hell of a knot on his head. So it looks like the same MO as Oakes—knock the guy out, then hang him up or slit his wrists, make it look like suicide, but not so much so that we wouldn't be able to figure out it was murder. Really stupid. Anyway, it sure looks like we've got a very specialized serial killer here, so stay home, okay, and don't let anyone up to the condo, even if you know them. There was no forced entry, so we're thinking West and Oakes might have known their killer. West and Oakes? Hey, sounds like a singing group, doesn't it? Okay, gotta go. You'd damn well better be in the shower, and not out running around."

"Ah, he cares—isn't that sweet," Maggie groused, "and it's Hall and Oates that's the singing group. Duo. Whatever."

"Bruce is left-handed. . . ."

Maggie stopped in her tracks to turn and look at J.P. "What did you say? Why would you say that? You think *Bruce* killed them?"

"No, of course not," J.P. said, grabbing more blue M&M's. "It was just a comment, that's all. Bruce is left-handed. Big deal. My cousin Chaz is left-handed. It doesn't mean anything."

"But you checked on his cell phone records," Maggie prodded. Her mind was going in several different directions . . . but every different thing she thought about kept coming back to Bruce McCrae.

"I told you. A woman can't be too careful these days."

"You went to *bed* with the man, Jemima!"

"Don't call me Jemima—and I went to bed with that *body*. Big difference, sunshine."

"I'll agree with that," Bernie said, having left the desk, and dipping a hand into the M&M's container on her way over to the couches. "There was this pool boy in Miami about five years ago who'd oil me every day beside the pool—and in my suite. *Hmm*. You want to talk about *bodies*—"

"Bernie," Maggie said flatly, "don't help."

"Okay, here I am—where's Sterling?"

Maggie turned to look at Felicity, who was dressed now, war paint in place, and carrying a garment bag over one arm. "Sterling? He's walking your dumb mutt, who's probably constipated from all the treats you gave him last night. And then he's meeting Alex at ten-thirty. Why? And what are you all dolled-up for?"

"My in-ter-view, Maggie, remember?" she said in a singsong voice, the kind where the *you're so stupid* is not actually heard but definitely implied. "A new cable show, *Noreen At Noon*, except we're taping at two for tomorrow's show. Still, I need to be there early, to make sure everything is running smoothly. Well, if Sterling can't take me, how will I be able to go? Everybody says I can't be alone. Maggie, you'll have to go with me."

"And you'll want me to carry your garment bag and open doors for you, right? Maybe run off and get you a sparkling water to ease your parched throat? Sure, like that's going to happen."

Bernie stood up, raising her hand. "Your intrepid publisher to the rescue, Felicity. I've got my driver waiting downstairs. You'll be safe with him."

Felicity pouted. "You won't go with me?"

"We're a little busy here, Felicity," Bernie told her as, behind Felicity's back, Maggie frantically mouthed the word *no* over and over again as she shook her head. "Just go down there and tell Clyde where you need to go."

"Your chauffeur's name is Clyde?" Maggie said after Felicity wafted out of the condo on a nearly visible flying carpet of expensive scent.

"No, but I can't remember it, so now he's Clyde. Since they come and go so fast, I figure, from now on, they're all going to be Clyde. Hey, I tip well. Oh, and José quit to take a job as a roadie for some rock group, because I know you're going to ask—he said the fringe benefits were better. Now, why couldn't I go with Felicity? Not that I wanted to, you understand."

"I'm not sure. I'm not through thinking yet."

"Well, could you give us a clue about what it is you're not through thinking about yet?"

Maggie narrowed her eyes at J.P., considering the question. "No, I don't think I should. I think I should wait for Alex. Not Steve, not until I talk to Alex because then Steve would know that Alex had—well, I can't think about that part yet." She wheeled about to look at Bernie. "The manuscript, when did Bruce give it to you?"

Bernie frowned. "Why?"

"Bernie, work with me here—*please*," Maggie said, putting her hands together in a begging gesture.

Bernie looked at J.P. and said, "Oh boy, I haven't heard her sound this desperate since the night she wanted me to include her on my invitation to go backstage at *Spamalot*. Okay, Maggie, okay, I'm thinking—ten days ago? Two weeks? My assistant had to have logged it in, if you really need to know exactly. I was busy on something else—like getting ready to go to England with you to pick up a little bubonic plague—and let it sit until the other day. But that's probably close to the timeline. I know you authors think we're

supposed to read something the moment it comes in—
even if it comes in eight months late—but that's not
how it works, and you know that, too. But Bruce has
been bugging me by e-mail every damn day, so I started
it and called him just before we left for England and
told him that at least for the first fifty pages it was
pretty damn good, and I'd get back to him when I was
finished reading. Which I haven't done yet. Now tell
me why you need to know this."

Well, that wasn't making any sense. "So the manuscript was in your office before even Francis was murdered, let alone Jonathan? And you told him you liked
it so far, also before Francis and Jonathan were killed."

"Yes, I think I already heard something like that
somewhere. And you need to know this *why*?"

Maggie put out her hands, waved off the question.
"God, I wish Alex was here—not that I'd ever tell him
that, because he'd never let me forget it. But I think—
yes, I'm pretty sure I'm heading in the right direction.
You have to do me a favor, Bernie. No, *two* favors,
okay? One, do what I'm going to ask you to do—and
two, don't ask me why I'm asking you to do it." She
took a deep breath and said the words quickly as she
exhaled: "I need you to call Bruce and tell him his
manuscript stinks. And that's just for starters. . . ."

Chapter Twenty-One

"I'm so sorry, Saint Just," Sterling said, breathlessly skidding to a halt on the sidewalk near the headquarters of Santas for Silver. "Brock was proving most uncooperative and all of that, and I barely had time to leave him with Socks before I donned my Father Christmas suit and met George and Vernon at the corner. I believe Socks requires a bit of remuneration, by the way. At least he was holding his hand out to me, palm up, as I raced by him."

"Not a problem, Sterling," Saint Just told him, nodding greetings to the Merry Men. "George, how nice of you to carry Sterling's chimney for him."

"Uh-huh. You said you wouldn't need us for very long today, Alex. Is that true? These costumes rent by the day, you know, so if we can get them back before one o'clock that would be solid."

"Right," Vernon echoed, looking past Saint Just to the two very large gentlemen standing about ten feet behind him. "Hey, I think I know one of those guys. Wow, that's Tony Three Cases. Geo, you know who I mean. Tony Three Cases. Right over there—look. No, don't look! Oh, okay, look, but don't make it obvious. He walked away with three whole big cases of cigarette cartons from that trailer a bunch of guys boosted in Queens a few years back. Wouldn't drop the cases and run, even when he heard the sirens. Just kept his cool, kept on moving down the sidewalk carrying these three big cases, and the dumb cops figured he had to be legit and just drove right past him." Vernon reverently lowered his voice. "Tony Three Cases. He's a legend, Georgie-boy. We're in the presence of a freaking *legend*."

Saint Just smiled in genuine amusement. "You are such an endless fountain of delightful information, Vernon," he said. "However, for today, I'm afraid you must also reconcile yourself to forgetting that you've seen the gentleman and his friend."

Vernon looked ready to weep. "But . . . but I was going to ask for his autograph."

"Saint Just? You look quite serious. Is something amiss? Why did you want to meet with us here? And who *are* those two men?"

"No one for you to concern yourself about, Sterling. You do trust me, don't you?"

Sterling drew himself up very straight. "I'm insulted that you would even broach such a question to me, Saint Just. Of course I trust you."

"Ah, splendid. In that case, what I need you to do is to come inside Santas for Silver headquarters with me— you, too, boys—and stand flanking Sterling a few feet inside the front door while I conduct some business with Mr. Goodfellow."

"Business? I don't—"

"Shhh, Sterling, I'm not quite finished. While you three are standing there, looking just as splendidly festive as you do now, my other friends will stand behind you looking, er, looking as festive as they know how to look, I suppose. Mr. Goodfellow and I will adjourn to his office for a few minutes, no longer than a few minutes, I'm sure, and then we will be on our way again, everyone back to their own individual pursuits. Is that clear?"

"No, Saint Just, it most certainly is not. But I've learned not to question you. There's something unpleasant afoot, though, isn't there? Something with Mr. Goodfellow . . . something with Santas for Silver. Oh, Saint Just, please don't tell me he's decided to terminate my association with Santas for Silver because of that ruined costume! I've offered to pay for it, I really did, and—"

"This has nothing to do with your costume, Sterling," Saint Just told him, and then shook his head. He was so new at this—this thinking more of others than he did of himself, the investigation of the moment, the pleasures of the moment. All this evolving, this business of becoming more real, more attuned to the emotions of others? Being mortal wasn't easy. Worth every problem, absolutely—but never easy. "Must I tell you the truth, my friend? I will, if you insist."

"No, of course not, Saint Just. I've never questioned you before, have I?"

"We're both expanding our horizons, the parameters Maggie set for us, aren't we? Yes, well, another discussion for another time. Are you ready?"

"At all times, Saint Just," Sterling said, adjusting his beard, which had begun to sag slightly. "Lead on, MacDuff!"

Saint Just longed to grab his friend's head, remove the red velvet cap and wig, and plant a kiss on the fellow's balding pate. "The entire quote, Sterling, is 'Lay on, MacDuff, and damn'd be him that first cries, Hold, enough!' and has to do with Macbeth's last words, shouted out as he challenged MacDuff to a fight to the death. I hardly think the quote fits the occasion, but I know the sentiment is there."

Sterling frowned. "It's not *lead* on, MacDuff? Well, now, why did I think it was, I wonder."

"I believe, Sterling, that is because Maggie says *lead*. It is my conclusion that it's an American corruption of the immortal bard's words. This is, after all, a country that spells *light* 'l-i-t-e.' " Saint Just halted just at the edge of the large window that made up the front of Santas for Silver, and peeked inside. "Ah, and here we are, and there is Mr. Goodfellow, not in his office, but being extremely friendly with Miss McDermont. How convenient. Come along now please, gentlemen—you all know what you are to do."

"Not really, Saint Just," Sterling pointed out as Tony held open the door for them and Gino remained on the sidewalk, glaring at passersby until everyone was safely inside the building, before joining them. They were, as Saint Just felt sure Maggie would term them, *goons*, but they were very well-trained goons.

He and Tony did have a small conversation before Sterling had arrived, one that had to do with the way Saint Just had "made us look bad to Mr. Campiano," and Saint Just had offered his profound apologies before inviting both men to "take another turn at him" if they so desired—get some of their own back, as it were. "I had the element of surprise riding with me, gentlemen, but I am convinced I could not be so successful again."

Tony had declined Saint Just's invitation, if Saint Just would only tell him where he had procured the sword cane, because he was fairly certain he'd look good carrying one himself, to which Saint Just had agreed that the bodyguard would look *fine as ninepence* . . . to which

Tony had said, looking at Gino, "Hear that? Ninepence? Didn't I tell you he's one of them aliens?"

Smiling at the recent memory, and still faintly puzzled as to why he'd offered to teach Tony how to use the sword stick to its best advantage, Saint Just assured himself that his cast of characters was in place behind him before he lightly tapped his cane on the floor and politely cleared his throat.

Marjorie McDermont reacted first, pushing away from Goodfellow with some alacrity and pulling down her tight black sweater. "Thank . . . um . . . thank you, sir. I believe the eyelash is out of my eye now," she said, and then, her eyes wide as she looked at Tony and Gino, she bent down to pick up her purse. "I think I'll go down to the corner to get some coffee."

She brushed past Saint Just, turning only in time for him to see that her mascaraed eyes were not only wide with fright but also wise in the ways of the denizens of the street. "I didn't see *nothin'*," she whispered to him as she went. Ah, yes, Tony and Gino had been a masterstroke of inspiration, at least now that Maggie had impressed upon him the need for him to avoid violence whenever possible. Violence nosed out most everything else in many cases, but a bit of carefully constructed deviousness ran a close second.

"What's going on here?" Goodfellow asked, his gaze also concentrated on the inestimable Tony and Gino as he slowly backed toward the door to his office. "I don't want any trouble here."

"Trouble? Indeed, no, who would, Mr. Goodfellow? Although I will say that you are in a bit of a *pickle*," Saint Just said blandly as he advanced on the man, watching Goodfellow's hands that, happily, remained at his sides. "A word or two, that is all I require. Shall we retire to your inner sanctum?"

"Huh? I remember you now. I'm not going anywhere with you. Nowhere I can't see *them*, anyway. What do you want?"

"Saint Just?"

"Not now, Sterling, if you please," Saint Just said, stepping closer to Goodfellow and keeping his voice low. He would have enjoyed playing with the fellow, but Sterling appeared to be getting restless. "Let's endeavor to do this as quickly and as painlessly as possible, Mr. Goodfellow. It has come to my attention, sadly, that you are not a nice man, sir. Nor are you honest, or concerned about the plight of widows, orphans, and the like. My friend Sterling Balder, however, *is* concerned. A good heart, that's what Mr. Sterling Balder possesses. A good and a pure heart."

Goodfellow sneered, at least until he remembered who else was in the room. "Yeah? So?"

Saint Just smiled. "Ah, you're listening. Good. But do lower your voice, we're having an intimate conversation here, remember? As to your question, I will say— *so*, my good man, in order not to disillusion my friend, rob him of his enjoyment of the generous, giving spirit of the season, I have decided two things. Would you like to know what those two things might be, Mr. Goodfellow? Or should I say Mr. Dill?"

"Yeah, yeah, I figured that one out. You know who I am. You're here to rob me, aren't you? You don't just want protection money—you want it all."

"Protection money? I'm afraid I'm unfamiliar with the term. I was just saying something on this head to my companions, as a matter of fact. You Americans certainly do put your own delightful spins on the King's English, don't you? None of which really matters, my good sir, as you were correct with your second assumption. Yes, Mr. Dill, I want *all* of your money. After some consideration, I've decided that felons of your ilk would disdain banks, wishing to keep your ill-gotten gains close to you. I want you to go into your office now, gather it all up, every last bent penny you've accumulated in your nefarious and dishonorable scheme, and I want you to hand it all over to Mr. Balder and his four friends here, who will then donate it all to the charity of Mr. Balder's choice. I believe he holds a particular affection to something called Toys for Tots. And then, Mr. Dill, I want one more thing. I would appreciate it very much if both you and Santas for Silver were to disappear."

"Or?" Dill asked, looking very much as if he might soon become quite sick to his stomach. "Those are Campiano's guys standing over there, aren't they?"

"In point of fact, at the moment, sir, they are *mine*, on loan from their employer, you might say, so I suggest you give a valiant attempt to tear your pitifully terrified gaze away from them and lend me all of your attention."

"I heard you. You want me to believe that you want the money for that nimrod over there."

"Another word with which I am not familiar, but I do believe you've just insulted my good friend. You do this, I imagine, Mr. Dill, as you believe I possess no limits to my patience. I feel it only fair to inform you that you'd be incorrect in that assumption."

"Okay, okay, I've got it. I know when I'm screwed. A . . . a lot of it is still in coin . . . everything comes here every night, and I've just been sorting it and keeping it all piled up back there. But there's a lot, and it's pretty heavy."

"Really? Never fear, Mr. Dill, although your concern is gratifying. I have it on good authority that one of my associates, Anthony by name, is quite capable of carrying bulky, ungainly weights."

Donny Dill took one last peek over Saint Just's shoulder, then seemed to attempt to hide himself behind Saint

Just. "I was right. Tony Three Cases. Christ. Look, how about I cut you guys in. Fifty-fifty. No—sixty-forty. I'm not a greedy man. Come on, what do you say? Seventy-thirty?"

"I suggest you sit down, Mr. Dill. Use Miss McDermont's chair, why don't you. I don't believe that astute lady will be returning any time soon."

"Sit . . . sit down?"

Saint Just sighed. "You are a rather tedious fellow, aren't you? Yes, sit down. Smile. And then inform Mr. Balder that you have been called to the national headquarters of Santas for Silver—shall we say in Seattle?— and therefore you sadly must of necessity immediately cease operations here in New York."

"That's where you're sending me? Seattle?"

"No, Mr. Dill. Where you go when you leave here is of extreme unimportance to me. I simply desire you gone, although I do dare to suggest that a warmer climate may put some color back in your cheeks. Now, to continue if I might? As you must by necessity depart in an hour, you are turning all responsibility for the collected funds over to the eminently trustworthy Mr. Balder, with the impassioned hope that he deliver those funds to his favorite charity, as Santas for Silver may be disbanding. Are we clear, Mr. Dill?"

Dill, who was now sitting behind the desk—Saint Just could not help but smile as he heard the man's shaking knees making repeated contact with the wood— merely nodded before saying out of the corner of his mouth, "You really won't kill me?"

"And ruin such a lovely day? Certainly not. It is, after all, the Christmas season. Now, are we agreed?"

Donny Dill, at last seeming to believe that he had made a lucky escape, nodded furiously.

"I had so hoped you'd understand. And I also hope

you will take some time, Mr. Dill, to consider what has transpired here and perhaps mend your ways, redirect your feet onto the straight and narrow."

"Uh-huh, yeah. Sure. Can we hurry this up? I . . . I gotta go to the bathroom. . . ."

It was with a smile on his face and a spring to his step that Saint Just returned to the condo an hour later, lightly tipping his hat to Socks as he approached the door the man held open for him. "Ah, Socks, what a splendid day. Maggie's upstairs?"

"Yup, and all by herself, too, now that the delivery guys left."

"You're going to explain that statement, correct?"

"Sure. Ms. Simmons had a treadmill sent over, and one of those bottled-water dispensers. Maggie tried to tell the guys no, but the stuff's up there now. Money sure gets you service faster than no money does, huh? Maggie's not too happy, so I wouldn't go up there now, if I were you. Oh, and Ms. Simmons is still out, Ms. Toland-James has taken a cab to her offices because Ms. Simmons has the limo, and the damn dog is right inside here, tied to my stool. Sterling told me not to take him back to Maggie until he'd done his business, which he did about ten minutes ago, on my shoe. You'll take him back upstairs for me?"

Saint Just considered this for the space of two seconds. "No." He then handed Socks a twenty-dollar bill, promised him another if Brock was still in one piece when Miss Simmons returned to collect him, and headed upstairs to Maggie's condo . . . to come face-to-face with an agitated Maggie.

"Look at this. *Look* at this. I've got a damn hulking, ugly treadmill in my living room."

Saint Just walked across the room to inspect the machine. "Yes, I see that. Well, my dear, you were just speaking of this corner recently, as I recall it, saying you still had done nothing about finding something to fill it."

"Oh yeah, right. And that's just the perfect thing, too. Much classier than a lighted curio cabinet, or that painted chest we saw a couple of weeks ago. But it's missing something, don't you think? Maybe I should toss a sweaty, smelly towel over it. The perfect accessory." Maggie flopped down on the couch. "I still don't believe it. She says something not two hours ago, and *bam*, here come these guys with that . . . that *thing*. Unpacked it, set it up, took everything away with them—I ended up tipping them fifty bucks, which shows you how stupid *I* am. Ten minutes later, here comes this guy with the bottled-water dispenser. It's in the kitchen, if you want to look at it. Actually, that was a pretty good idea. I signed a two-year contract. Not that I'll be here to drink the water—not once Faith comes back and I strangle her."

"You didn't have to accept either delivery, you know," Saint Just pointed out, pouring himself a glass of wine. For a man of his era, water had never been a viable option, most especially in London, but he would have to try this bottled water at some point. Just not right now.

"I know I didn't have to take the stuff, Alex," Maggie said, leaning back against the couch cushions, to run her hands down her belly. "But Faith looks pretty good, you know, and I really probably should exercise, especially now that I'm not smoking anymore. I mean, can you see me at some gym? The only people you see at gyms are those people who don't need gyms, and I'm a good ten—eight pounds from going to a gym. So I guess I'll keep it—but not in here. Oh, and it folds up, so that's good. You and Sterling can help me move it to the guest bedroom once Faith is gone, okay?"

Saint Just nodded, then asked, "Certainly, but why

didn't you simply have the deliverymen assemble it there?"

Maggie rolled her eyes. "Are you kidding? Faith has five suitcases open in that room. Clothes everywhere. *Stuff*, everywhere. She was always like that. We'd go to conferences together and she'd sprawl out all over the room. Her shoes, her clothes, her toiletries. I had about enough space for my toothbrush and a lipstick in the bathroom. Oh, and she used *all* the towels. And then there was the bath powder. *Everywhere. Clouds* of bath powder."

"Correct me if I'm wrong, but it would seem that you should have been relieved when you two no longer shared your accommodations."

"I know," Maggie said, her head down. "But we had fun, Alex, we really did. There's a lot to be said for being poor together, struggling together. Then she hit the lists and got all weird." She looked up at him. "I'm not all weird, am I? I love being on the lists, but I don't ever want to get all weird."

Saint Just patted her head as he walked behind the couch, then sat down on the facing couch. "Confident. I would be gratified if you could believe more in yourself and your talent, my dear. Other than that, I wouldn't change a hair on your head."

Maggie smiled sheepishly. "Thanks, Alex," she said, sitting up straighter. "So you like me, right?"

"Correct," he said slowly.

"And you respect my opinion."

"Certainly. In all things." He took another sip of wine, wondering when she'd get to the point.

"So if I told you I did something, you'd be all right with that? Even if I didn't run it by you first?"

He thought of his earlier interlude with Mr. Donny Dill. "You are under no obligation to consult with me on every small thing, my dear."

"Right. But this isn't a small thing. I think Bruce McCrae killed Francis and Jonathan."

Saint Just did his best to not react. "Really. And may I ask how you came to hold this opinion?"

"Well, I don't really *hold* it. I'm thinking it. Except when I'm thinking I'm completely off-base. We need everything to fit, right, and not everything fits. I mean, some does, but some doesn't. Still . . . I did something. Had Bernie do something. Not that I told Steve what I did, because you'd just end up in jail, and that can't be a good thing, right? So we have to find another way to prove what I think I know . . . if I'm right."

Perhaps he'd like more wine. Yes, probably so. Saint Just got to his feet and made his way across the room to the drinks table. "Would you care to elaborate on what you've just said? Or, even better, start at the beginning and tell me exactly what you've thought . . . and what you've done?"

"Okay, sure. Here's how it went down. Bernie was sitting at the computer, touching things the way she does, and she saw Jonathan's manuscript up on the screen. Only she thought it was *Bruce's* manuscript. Bruce's manuscript, Alex, not Jonathan's. Even though you found it hidden in Jonathan's apartment."

"Yes, my dear, I believe I'm following you," Saint Just said, retaking his seat. "But while I'm still digesting this, do go on."

Maggie stood up, sat down again with one leg tucked up under her, obviously near to bursting with what she had to tell him and unable to sit still. "Here's where it gets really interesting. I didn't tell Bernie what I thought, of course—oh, or J.P., because she was here, too—I'll get to that part. And I forgot to tell you what Steve said when he called, didn't I? Damn, Alex. I've got so much going on. Dad—oh, he called, he's back safe and settling into his friend's apartment. And the phone finally stopped ringing, so that's good. Well, not *all* good, because I'm hoping Bruce calls—except I wanted you to be here when he did. So I was almost glad to have all those delivery guys coming in and out—so I wasn't alone, you know?—because you weren't around and I really, *really* needed to talk to you—"

"Maggie, dearest, take a deep breath. I don't think I've ever seen you this agitated."

"Well, I am. If I'm right, I've had a killer right here, in my own home. If I'm not, I could have broken up J.P. and a wonderful guy. If I'm right, we won't have to worry anymore and Faith and Brock the Wonder Kidneys can go home—that's big on the I-hope-I'm-right side, let me tell you! But if I'm wrong, then I may have sullied someone's character, not to mention his career. But if I'm right—"

"Maggie. This is so unlike you."

"No kidding. But it's not every day I try to unmask a murderer who may or may not have considered me for his next victim. Well, maybe not, not lately—but you know what I mean. I *know* Bruce. This is just so much more *personal*. You know?"

"I do, indeed. Now, from the beginning?"

It took some time, but he finally understood what she'd done. Without telling Bernice why, she'd asked her to phone Bruce McCrae and tell him his manuscript was not up to his usual standards and would need tremendous amounts of rewriting, reworking, if it could even be salvaged.

"I know how I felt when Bernie said that about that dumb exorcism drivel I wrote about you, so I figured it was the best way to get a rise out of him," Maggie told him.

But her ploy had not elicited the reaction she'd hoped

for. McCrae had taken the news rather well, which, Bernice had told her, was completely unexpected, as McCrae was always very vocally defensive of his work.

"Then I had her ask him to come over here tonight, around eight, to talk to him about the book, because Bernie is bunking in with me now, too, as you thought that, as publisher of Toland Books, she, too, could be in danger."

"I said that? Really?"

"I had to think of something," Maggie told him, "and that was all I could come up with. I figured we should confront him, you know?"

"We. How gratifying. I can remember a time—most probably because it was only days ago—when you wouldn't have been as willing to consider us, well, a team."

"Yeah, yeah, yeah—'ray, team," Maggie said, actually blushing. "Back to confronting Bruce. *After* we figure out what he did, how he did it. I've been making notes—they're on the table in front of you. But then I realized that, unless he confesses—and he won't unless he's an idiot, which he isn't—we have no way of proving anything. No way to prove he was Rat Boy—nothing."

"I don't think he is—Rat Boy, that is," Saint Just told her, scanning Maggie's scribbled list of questions and thoughts concerning Bruce McCrae. He looked up at her, for she was on her feet now, pacing. So much was going on in her life right now, changing in her life right now. Was it any wonder she was nervous, poor thing? "Do you?"

"No, unfortunately. Something as gross as dead rats just isn't his style—Bruce's, that is—except that, of course, would be the beauty of the thing, wouldn't it? Remember, he writes mysteries, makes up plots for a living. He isn't going to think like your usual murderer. He'd plan a murder like someone else would plan chess moves, always working three moves ahead. It's like—it's like we have to try to outplot him, or something, and I don't know who's better at plotting, him, or us—who's got the better endgame."

"We do, my dear, without question." Saint Just deposited his wineglass on the table and got to his feet. "Go fetch your coat."

"What? Why?" Maggie asked, although, to his delight, she was already on the way to collect her coat, gloves, and scarf. "Where are we going?"

"First, to luncheon, as I haven't broken my fast all day and it's already well past one o'clock. After that, I would suggest the shop of your choice and the purchase of a new winter coat."

Maggie slid her arms into the coat and looked down at the front of it. "Oh, come on, it's not that—okay. Then what? Because you'd better have more than that."

"Oh, I do. Then, my dear, we will travel again to Greenwich Village, where we will visit once more with both Mr. Gates and Mr. Bryon, and this time we will not be quite as conciliatory as we were on our initial visits."

Maggie exited the condo ahead of Saint Just as he held the door open for her. "Oh, goodie. Do I get to be the one who's snarky to Lord Bryon?"

After a leisurely lunch at Bellini's where they discussed strategy, and a delightful interlude at a small, exclusive boutique Saint Just had chosen weeks earlier as the perfect establishment for Maggie, they were in another cab and on their way to Greenwich Village. Maggie looked splendid in a new, thigh-length camel wool coat and soft rust and loden green cashmere scarf that flattered her coloring. Her old coat, along with a long black cashmere dress coat even Maggie had to agree was worth the hefty price, would be delivered to her condo.

Saint Just adored it when the world worked to his order.

"So, who do we tackle first?" Maggie asked, rubbing her gloved hands together in the sort of gleeful anticipation best suited to young tots confronted with their first amusement fair—or perhaps an evil inventor admiring his first successful monster.

Saint Just looked out the window of the cab as it slowed in traffic. "I had thought we would confront Valentino Gates at his apartment, but it would appear he's on the move." He leaned forward and knocked on the partition. "You can let us out here, thank you."

"He looks like he's going to a funeral in that black suit," Maggie said as they followed after Gates, staying on the other side of the narrow street. "And doesn't he own a coat? It's freezing today."

"It would be my opinion that Mr. Gates is on his way to something both important and local, something for which he felt he needed to dress appropriately, if not warmly. Ah, and there he goes, around the corner. You remember what's located halfway down that street, don't you, Maggie?"

"Bryon's Book Nook, check," she said, nodding. "Maybe we'll be lucky, and get ourselves a twofer. You be good cop—I want to be bad cop."

Saint Just looked at her curiously. "It's gratifying to see you so enthusiastically into the game, my dear."

"Yeah, well, people have been playing with my head long enough. I've got a checklist. Mom, Dad, Rat Boy, Boobs, Bruce, Dr. Bob, Christmas. And, lest we forget—*Brock*, the incontinent canine. I need to check something off, and we may as well start here. I mean, maybe it's selfish, but I want my life back—and my condo. I had no idea it was so small until Faith moved in. You and Sterling together didn't crowd me as much as she does. Unless I just started thinking bigger, now that I've seen Faith's place. An office suite? I've got a desk in the corner of my living room. And everybody eats my M&M's. I want a separate office, Alex, I really do."

"And no one could blame you," Saint Just assured her as they cut across the street and watched Valentino Gates disappear into Bryon's Book Nook. "We'll give them a moment, and then join them."

"Right. Hey, look at this," she said, pointing to a black-edged notice taped to the dirty window of the bookstore. "'To commemorate the life and career of Jonathan West. A gathering of his friends and admirers, with remarks, readings, and refreshments.' Oh, wow, the regulation bookstore three R's. And it's today, Alex. In an hour. Bryon really was a fan."

"As was Mr. Gates, who is perhaps even our chief mourner? Shall we join them now, my dear, and avoid the crowds?"

Maggie grinned at him. "I love it when you're snarky."

They entered the store, Saint Just performing a quick inventory of patrons that did not take long, as there were only two, and then they headed for the curtain and the room they'd seen previously. "As I recall, there is this entry, and a marked and lighted exit to the right and rear, most probably leading to the street. We'll need to position ourselves so that those portals are at least partially blocked, agreed?"

"Agreed. So, do we say we're here for the three R's, fans of Jonathan's?"

Saint Just considered this. "No, I believe we ran out that string announcing ourselves as Mr. Oakes's fan club—and by introducing you to Mr. Bryon. Let's just join them, then simply see what develops."

He held back the curtain to allow Maggie to precede

him into the small, poorly lit room, where they quickly moved into the shadows and visually inspected George Gordon Bryon as he stood behind the podium, unaware that he had company, fussing with various papers. Gates, Saint Just noticed, was nowhere in sight. Perhaps they'd overlooked him among the towering shelves in the book-store proper? He repositioned Maggie so that their backs were against the wall.

"Holy cow," Maggie whispered, staring wide-eyed at George Gordon Bryon. "Would you look at that? The balloon pants and slippers. The red and gold silk robe. The pin at his throat. The *turban*. I know that out-fit—I've got a copy of the portrait in one of my re-search books. The sixth Baron Byron himself, painted as a corsair. All that's missing is the mustache." She cocked her head and looked again. "The mustache . . . and the soulful eyes, the rounded chin, the intense ex-pression, the proud carriage. Okay, let's face it—Bryon looks like he's decked out for Halloween."

"A sad man, one who lives, soars, only in his dreams. Byron wrote his dream, lived his fantasies and, as I've now been able to read a biography detailing what hap-pened to him after he was drummed out of England by his enemies, most unfortunately died in Missolonghi, fighting the good fight. But this man? Ah, Maggie, this man only dreams of the daring, the adventure, the right-eous crusade."

"But maybe he found a crusade," Maggie whispered as Bryon sorted through a small stack of file cards he'd picked up from the podium. "Maybe he found Jonathan West, and took up his cause? Maybe he even knew Jonathan personally—should we go see if his books on the shelves here are autographed? No, scratch that, let's just run with this before he sees us. Let's say he did know Jonathan, and got to hear Jonathan curse us all out for having ruined his career. And let's suppose Bryon finally decided to *do* something about it."

"Bryon and Gates. But where, I wonder, did they find the rats?"

"Are you kidding? In this dump? All he'd have to do would be set some traps at night. But now we have to ask ourselves the biggie, Alex. Two biggies. Did they send the rats? And, if they did, why in hell did they send one to Jonathan? I have a theory about that second part, but only if the answer is yes to the first part."

"Shh, sweetings, I believe the man is about to rehearse his prepared speech."

George Gordon Bryon, a pair of horn-rimmed reading glasses now perched on his nose, cleared his throat as he held up one of the file cards. "And so, in closing, allow me to most humbly and heartfeltedly proclaim— old Jonathan West was the very, *very* best. And the very, *very* best was he. Lesser talents betrayed him, they *mocked* and *dismayed* him, but never a better will we ever know."

Maggie spoke before Saint Just could warn her to silence. "*Ever know?* Alex, did you hear that? That should be *ever see. See* rhymes with *he*. Bryon wrote those poems. He *is* Rat Boy. And *heartfeltedly* isn't even a word, for crying out loud. Oops. Alex, stop him!"

Saint Just was already on the move, however, as Maggie's voice had risen in tandem with her joy of discovery and Bryon had heard her, seen them, and taken off at a full run for the door below the *Exit* sign.

Chapter Twenty-Two

"I know you. George and I talked about you and your friend—and your lies. You shouldn't be here," Valentino Gates told Maggie as he grabbed her by one shoulder and whirled her around to face him.

"Oh, yeah, right, I'm scared," Maggie said, shrugging out of the man's grip. She'd really had a long week, and she wasn't in the mood for dramatics unless they were her own. "You send dead rats and lousy poetry to people, trying to frighten them. But that doesn't exactly make you and Bryon frightening. It makes you pathetic."

"You ruined Jonathan West's life," Gates shot back at her, although he didn't try to touch her again.

"Wrong, buster. *Jonathan* ruined Jonathan's life. He wrote a couple of pretty great books, and then he went wacko with his own importance. The plot, the premise, the gang of contributing authors—everything about that stupid book was his idea. The characters were his idea. He wouldn't let anyone else edit anything. He rewrote all of our chapters until we didn't even recognize them anymore. That was Jonathan's book—our names were just on it with him. He dug his own hole, Valentino, with his own inflated ego."

Then she stopped, ran the lines of what she'd said past her mental eyesight one more time. "Wow, that was almost profound, wasn't it?" She shook her head. "Look, Valentino, I'm sorry, but if Jonathan lost his edge—whatever—after the book tanked, it wasn't because of anything the rest of us did. Nobody likes to blame themselves, so Jonathan blamed us. Hey, and don't look now, but none of us exactly got a big career boost from that bomb. I had to change my name and start over from scratch. But that's the thing, Valentino—I started over. Jonathan quit."

"He published more books. But the critics were against him."

"Wrong again, Valentino. He dusted off two old manuscripts that should have stayed in the drawer and made Toland Books publish them. It was the only way they could get him to fulfill his contract and hope to get back any of the advance money they'd poured all over him. They shouldn't have done it, but they did—well, Kirk did, Bernie tried to talk him out of it. But no matter what, Valentino, Jonathan West never wrote another word after *No Secret Anymore*. Not until he—never mind."

"Having a pleasant coze with Mr. Gates, my dear?"

Maggie turned to smile at Alex, who was urging Bryon ahead of him at the point of his sword cane. "Put that thing away. Remember, Alex, you promised to use your powers only for good. Hey, Lord Bryon, you lost one of your magic slippers."

"I want you people to leave. Coming in here uninvited, accosting me in my place of business," Bryon said, dusting off his costume. "I'm going to go call the police."

"Saving us the trouble, thank you," Alex said, sheathing his sword stick. "Or would you rather simply tell us why you sent dead rats and atrocious rhyme to Miss Dooley here and others?"

"It was his idea."

Unfortunately, both Gates and Bryon uttered the same accusation at the same time, and it was some moments before Alex could physically separate the two men.

"It's never pretty when thieves fall out," Alex said once everyone was seated on four of the folding chairs in the room. "Now, gentlemen, decide between you which of you is going to tell us what we want to know."

It was Bryon who spoke, recounting his and Valentino's admiration for Jonathan West. When West happened into Bryon's Book Nook one fine day, they'd all three of them formed a friendship that had, over the ensuing years, gone all the way to the point where Jonathan was mentoring Valentino, inviting the two of them to his apartment for drinks and conversation—all that good stuff meant to have the two fans all but worshipping at West's shrine.

As Jonathan fell deeper into the bottle, many of his conversations with the men had to do with Toland Books and, most especially, the ungrateful authors who had ruined his career.

"We begged him to forget all of that and write another book," Valentino told Maggie. "He didn't want to do it, but then, about a year ago, he outlined a plot idea to us. Just last month he even read us bits and pieces of what he'd written—didn't he, George? And it was brilliant! We were so honored!"

"He talked about a plot with you? He read you something?" Maggie grinned at Alex in triumph and not a little relief. It would be tricky to maneuver the timeline, but at least now there was a way to prove what she and Alex believed, without landing Alex in the slammer for absconding with evidence—Steve would go along with them; he always did. "So, if you were asked, you'd be able to say that Jonathan West read you a portion of his new novel? You'd recognize those portions if someone read them to you again. Do I have that right?"

Both men nodded furiously.

"But he said he'd never publish it. He'd never open himself up to such vitriolic criticism and humiliation again. We begged, and we begged, but he wouldn't do it. And we knew why," Valentino said. "It was because of you—you and the others who ruined him. A bright light, gone from the literary world because of hacks, no-talents."

"Literary world? Oh, come on. He wrote mystery novels. *I* write mystery novels. See? That was Jonathan's problem. He wanted to be the critics' darling. I hate when a writer becomes ashamed of what he or she does well, just because it isn't *literary*."

Bryon's upper lip curled rather effectively. "We decided that Jonathan would never agree to be published again until the greedy vermin that had eaten away at his *literary* soul were punished, were given a good scare, even." He subsided against the back of his chair. "So we sent you all the rats. We thought that would make Jonathan feel better, maybe even make him want to publish again."

"You forgot Kimberly Lowell D'Amico," Maggie told him.

"No, Valentino couldn't find an address on her," Bryon explained. "He sent half, I sent half, but he couldn't find her address."

"Let me take a wild stab at something here, just for my own satisfaction," Maggie interrupted. "One of you gift-wrapped your share of the dead rats, yes?"

"Valentino did, for some ridiculous reason, yes. But

it was all for naught, because when we told Jonathan what we'd done—sure he'd be pleased to have had some revenge—he told us we were incompetents, idiots, and banned us from his apartment. He even threatened to call the police to tell them what we'd done." He then angrily whirled on Valentino Gates. "But that was no reason for you to kill him, you fool!"

"*Me?*" Valentino looked, as Maggie might write in one of her Saint Just mysteries, suddenly pale to the marrow. "I didn't kill him. *You* killed him. Didn't you?"

Alex got to his feet, holding out a hand to Maggie. "I think we're done here, sweetings. Neither of them killed Jonathan West or, as would naturally follow, Francis Oakes. To question them further would only muddy the waters for *Left*-tenant Wendell, who most certainly will be interviewing them shortly."

"Agreed. Just one more question, Alex." Maggie looked at Bryon who, ridiculously, seemed the more intelligent of the two men. "Why did you send Jonathan a dead rat?"

Gates and Bryon exchanged looks, and then answered in unison, "We didn't send Jonathan a rat."

"No, I thought not. Thank you, gentlemen," Alex said as he tucked his cane under his arm. "And remember, gentlemen, when the constable arrives, that the truth shall set you free. Or some such drivel. Maggie? Shall we be on our way?"

Maggie was still feeling pretty darn good when she and Alex got back to her condo. In fact, she was almost giddy—right up until the moment she walked in to see all the suitcases piled in the living room.

At that point, her mood rose to the nearly euphoric.

"Going somewhere, Faith?" she asked as she saw— mercy of mercies—Brock's small traveling cage.

Faith laid her full-length pink faux fur coat over the control panel of the treadmill. "Oh, Maggie, you're back. Good. Yes, I'm going somewhere. Noreen invited me to hide out with her at her lodge up in Stowe until the murderer is caught. I think she said Stowe. Somewhere up there, anyway. Oh, and she wants to interview you for her show. You know, the murder mystery author turned potential victim? You need to do it, Maggie, it would be great PR."

"Not happening, Faith, thanks anyway," Maggie said, grabbing the container of M&M's and frowning at how few of the colorful candies remained, none of them blue. "Is that what you talked about in today's interview, Faith? The fact that you're also a potential victim? You cried, didn't you. You always cry."

"Noreen's hoping for a daytime Emmy," Faith said, ignoring the insult, probably because she thought it was a compliment. "I hope so—for her sake. She's a lovely woman."

"So you two struck up a friendship this afternoon? You and Noreen."

"Oh, yes, definitely. You can't know how *overcome* I was by her show of friendship—offering to harbor me in my hour of need. She even escorted me back to my apartment. She was absolutely *mad* about the decor—we'll be taping a video tour for her audience, to air before Christmas, naturally. I picked up a few more things, my boots, my ski togs, and she'll be sending a car for me in—oh, twenty minutes. I just have time to redo my makeup. Excuse me."

Maggie, tongue literally stuck in cheek, watched as Felicity toddled back down the hallway on her four-inch heels. "You're welcome, Faith, I was happy to have you," she muttered, then gave in to impulse and tried on the faux fur. She had to admit it really did feel good, even if she was pretty sure she looked like cotton candy on a stick.

"It's not your color, my dear," Alex said, walking in

unannounced, as usual. "And not nearly elegant enough for you."

"Saved by the belated sucking up," Maggie told him as she slipped out of the fur and draped it back over the treadmill. "Faith's flying the coop, she got a better offer."

Alex smiled. "You are having an enjoyable day, aren't you?"

"It's definitely better now than it was when it started out this morning, I'll say that. What time is it?"

"Mr. McCrae should be arriving in approximately ninety minutes, if that's what you mean."

"It is. That gives us time to eat something, and I want to shower and change. There are still leftover lunch meats and salad from last night. Do you think Sterling wants some?"

"Sterling, as a matter of fact, is out celebrating with George and Vernon and two new friends, having spent an enjoyable afternoon of their own performing good deeds."

"Oh. So the Santas for Silver thing is going all right for him? I told you I checked it out on the Internet. And you were worried. Sometimes, Alex, you're like a mother hen with one chick when it comes to Sterling. Not that I don't think it's sweet."

"Well, actually—ah, Felicity. I hear you're leaving us. Maggie and I are, of course, devastated."

"Yeah, right. I may cry myself to sleep tonight," Maggie grumbled.

"You think you're being sarcastic, Maggie, but you really do love me," Felicity said, kissing Maggie's cheek. "I know what you did, honey, opening your home to me out of your concern for me, and I mean it when I say thank you. Friends forever, remember? We made that vow."

Maggie felt her spine melting, as usual. They had

been really good friends, once. "Yeah, okay, Faith. Friends forever."

"Good," Felicity said, slipping into her fur. "In that case, let me remind you that you still owe me a house-warming present—a big one, because that's a top-of-the-line treadmill over there. Now, gather up Brock for me and call for the doorman to help with these bags. I don't want to keep Noreen waiting."

"Sucker," Maggie groused under her breath as she went hunting for the mutt. "I never learn. I've got a great big *S* frigging tattooed on my forehead."

But ninety minutes later Felicity was already well on her way to Stowe, Maggie had had that shower and a huge rare roast beef sandwich on rye, and she was more than ready for Bruce to show up and watch Alex—*help* Alex—with one of his famous Viscount Saint Just denouement scenes.

"Good cop or bad cop?" Alex asked her as Socks, who'd remained on duty just for this purpose, buzzed twice, then twice again, signaling that both Bruce Mc-Crae and J.P. Boxer were on their way upstairs.

"I'll follow your lead," she told him. "But I do need to get a couple of licks in, if you don't mind. If we're right about all of this, it could have been me, you know, and not poor Francis. All set, Steve?"

"Here they go, Dumb and Dumber ride again. I should have my head examined—except that you guys always seem to make it work. Get him talking, get him to say something incriminating. But make it fast, okay?" Lieutenant Steve Wendell, who really did owe Maggie one, picked up his can of soda and retired to the kitchen, out of sight but not out of earshot while Alex opened the door for their *company*.

"Where's Bernie?" Bruce asked as he shrugged out of his coat—one of those ridiculous khaki raincoat things with epaulettes on the shoulders, flaps and pockets everywhere, and cinched by a wide belt. Talk about looking like Secret Squirrel. Jeez.

"She was unavoidably detained at the office," Alex said smoothly, then offered their guests drinks.

Okay, Maggie was nervous now. She'd been excited, but now Bruce was here, sitting directly across from her. The killer.

"Um, Bruce? Bernie told me. You know, about your manuscript? Gosh, I'm sorry. She rained all over my last manuscript, too. I don't know what's wrong with her. She used to be more understanding."

Bruce sat forward on the couch, his fingers laced together, as J.P. began rubbing his back. "I know. That call I got this morning? It was like a slam to the solar plexus, you know? I worked so *hard* on that book. I *love* that book—sweated blood over it. I just don't understand her problem. That's why I was glad she invited me over here tonight." He accepted a glass of wine from Alex, looking up at him. "Bernie said it was your idea that she move in here with Maggie and Felicity. So you really think this Nevus guy could be after Bernie, too?"

"In point of fact, no," Alex said, and then inclined his head to Maggie, who took it from there. How nice for Bruce to provide their segue for them. And how smart of Alex to have gone back to Valentino and Bryon with just one more question.

"Not Nevus, Bruce. *Nexus.* You know—to bind, to connect. A connected group—like all of the authors connected to *No Secret Anymore.* Rat Boy, well, Rat *Boys*, they said they'd run a spell-checker before printing out all those copies of the poem for everyone, but since *nevus* is a word, the spell-checker didn't pick up the typo. Neither, obviously, did our Rat Boys. Isn't that something? We were never going to *connect* anything that way, huh?"

Now J.P. sat up straighter. "You found him—them? You found out who sent the rats?"

Maggie nodded. "Tell them, Alex."

Alex stood at the end of the couch where Maggie sat, looking at Bruce as he spoke. "Certainly, Maggie. Yes, J.P., we unearthed them, and they didn't kill Francis or Jonathan. They're merely fairly harmless idiots who, unfortunately, innocently provided the real killer with a most timely bit of assistance as well as helping to muddy the waters so that the killer could not only kill but perpetrate a fraud."

"That's a lot of big words and bigger accusations you're tossing around, English," J.P. said, figuratively donning her criminal defense attorney hat. "You have a suspect for all this murder and fraud business?"

"As a matter of fact, yes, we do, and thank you, J.P., for so quickly bringing us to the nub of the matter. Mr. McCrae, would you care to confess, or shall we have to deal with a tedious point-by-point breakdown of your motive and opportunity?"

"Me?" Bruce smiled as he looked at each one of them in turn. The kind of smile, Maggie thought, that you could see on football players, basketball players, anyone who knew damn full well they'd committed a foul, but were trying to act as if the referee had just made a big joke at their expense. The kind of smile that was just a little too wide, while the eyes remained a little too nervous, even cagey. "You're accusing *me*? Are you nuts?"

"Yes, Maggie, are you nuts?" J.P. seconded the question. "Bruce never killed anyone. We had a long talk this afternoon, because I was pretty sure you were thinking that way this morning. Don't ever play poker, Maggie—when I dropped that left-handed bomb, you jumped on it way too fast, then backed off even faster. Jonathan West and Francis Oakes were Bruce's friends. Look— I'd given him this, to protect himself when I wasn't around, and he gave it back to me this afternoon. See?" she concluded, unzipping her large pocketbook and holding up the Glock as evidence.

"Cripes, J.P., put that away before you drop it and it goes off. Besides, I have an idea," Maggie said, now that the idea had surfaced with Bruce's fake smile. "Let's do a play-by-play, J.P., a sort of non-video review, shall we, and then you decide? I'll start."

She got to her feet and began pacing behind the couch. "To begin, let's all remember that Bruce, like me, is a mystery writer. I know something about mystery writers, about the process. We set up a situation, we put in a bunch of what-ifs and suspects, we toss in a couple of red herrings to put the reader off the scent, and then we sit back and look for holes in our plot. Question ourselves, question each point, address that plot from every angle so that there are no more holes except the sneaky ones we want there so the reader can look back later and say, wow, there it was, but I missed it. That's how it works—hopefully. In other words, we think in terms of what can go wrong with our premise, how our killer can screw up."

"Marvelous," Bruce said, sitting back and crossing his arms over his broad chest. "Maggie's giving us a workshop for beginners."

"Shut up, Bruce," J.P. said, moving slightly away from him. "I know her longer than I know you, remember? Let her have her say, then you can try to tear apart her testimony on cross."

"Ouuu, the lawyer speaks. Fine, but I want a drink first—or don't you think I know you're trying to set me up for a fall here," Bruce said sarcastically, getting to his feet. "Go on, Maggie. I can wait to sue you until to-morrow."

Maggie looked at Alex, who nodded his head once more, encouraging her to continue laying out her reasons for believing Bruce guilty.

But she didn't know where to start, which was still the problem.

Okay . . . she'd lay it out the way she did a synopsis. She'd tell Bernie a story—except Bernie wasn't here, this wasn't really a synopsis, and she really wished Bruce and his muscles would sit down again.

"Bruce, let's do the crimes first, all right? We'll get into the particulars of how you screwed up later, if you still insist in saying you're not guilty."

"Fine. Maybe I should take notes? I mean, a Cleo Dooley plot? That has to be worth something. Maybe we could collaborate on a book? No, never mind. That didn't work all that well the first time, did it?"

"Gratified as you must be, McCrae, listening to the drone of your own voice," Alex said tightly, "we'd like you to sit down now and allow Maggie to speak. If you can prove her wrong—prove *us* wrong—it will save you an interview with *Left*-tenant Wendell, as he will be our next audience."

Maggie swallowed down hard on her nervousness. She knew that Bruce could leave at any time, just walk away, and there'd be no way to stop him, not unless Alex was in the mood to play hero, and she hoped he'd remember that Steve was in the kitchen, listening, and that unsheathing his sword stick probably wouldn't be a good idea.

So it was definitely time to cut to the chase, hit Bruce in a way that would force him to stay, and mentioning Steve seemed to do the trick. In fact, Bruce suddenly looked eager to match wits with them. Yeah, well, she'd soon put an end to that!

"You ripped off Jonathan's new manuscript and passed it off as your own," Maggie said, and then waited, letting out her breath slowly as Bruce looked at her for a long moment, and then sat down.

"A masterstroke, my dear," Alex said, leaning down to speak into her ear. "As good as an anchor strapped to his ankle. Now move quickly."

Maggie nodded, cleared her throat. She had it together now, she knew where to start, where to go with this synopsis.

"You stayed friends with Francis and Jonathan after *No Secret Anymore*. You said so. You visited them, the whole nine yards. And while Francis sort of faded away, and Jonathan had all but dropped off the map, your career kept growing very nicely. Except, wow, now you were having trouble, too. Like Francis, like Jonathan, something had gone wrong. You'd lost something, some edge, and you couldn't write. You'd hit a wall, you were already past your deadline, and you were desperate. We all get blocked once in a while, we all get desperate. But you were scared, and getting more frightened every day you sat at that computer and looked at that blank screen, that blinking cursor."

Oh, yeah, she was getting into it now. Bruce was her character now, and she was telling his story, laying out his fears, his motivations.

"Maybe you weren't really a writer. Maybe you'd been faking it all these years, and now you just couldn't fake it anymore. The world would realize you couldn't write, not really. We all think that, every time we sit down to start another book. First book, twentieth book, hundredth book. It doesn't matter. The same fears come back. But it was worse for you this time. You saw Francis, his despair, his small apartment, the way he'd hidden himself away, frightened of the world that had disregarded his books. And you saw Jonathan West.

Who'd been bigger than Jonathan West? Man, if he could fall, how could you not fall? You could be him, you could be Francis. We all could be them, we're all just one book away from being them, aren't we?"

"You always did have a flair for the melodramatic, Maggie," Bruce told her, lifting a tumbler of scotch to his mouth. "I'm talented. I don't have crises of confidence and I never have. That's for lesser talents. Like you. You even failed at romance, and that's formulaic drivel anyone can write."

The urge to say *bite me* rose and was quickly batted down again, along with her ready defense of the romance genre, as Maggie pushed on, doing her best to stay on point as Bruce tried to steer her away from it, and into personal attack. Hey, she'd spent five years listening to Dr. Bob's advice on how to argue effectively with her family—she recognized that sort of underhanded tactic now.

"Then, one fine day, you stopped in to visit Jonathan and learned that he was writing again. Not only was he writing, but he was willing to show you, his good friend, what he'd written. And you were blown away. It was good. It was very good. And you couldn't write a coherent grocery list, could you? You went home, and stewed, and then an idea hit you. The sort of idea a good mystery writer jumps on immediately. And you are a good mystery writer, Bruce, you really are. You just didn't want to wait out the dry spell, or work your way through it. You visited Jonathan again, and you somehow made a copy of his manuscript on a blank disk while he was in the bathroom or passed out drunk, and took it home with you, put your name on it, and sent it off to Bernie. After all, Jonathan had said he'd never publish it, and he was a drunk, a recluse. He'd never even know you'd ripped him off."

J.P. raised her hand as if she was in class. "You're

saying Bruce thought he could get away with something like that?"

"No, not really. I think he was desperate, and he didn't think the whole thing completely through before he acted," Maggie told her honestly, because this part was still a little murky to her. "What I think was that he needed *something* to give to Bernie because he was so overdue on his deadline and, even though Bernie is a terrific woman, she's also a tough businesswoman, a lot tougher than Kirk used to be. Now that Kirk's dead and she's in charge, she's going pretty heavy with the hammer, even demanding that some authors hand back their advance money if they're too far over deadline. Bruce just wanted to shut her up, that's all—at least at first. But, once he'd done it, sent in Jonathan's manuscript as his own, he had to know—quickly—if she liked it, if she'd publish it, or if he'd just bought himself a little more time to write his own book. Because, wow, he had a problem, didn't he? He'd acted, and then realized he'd taken a pretty big risk in doing what he did, if the manuscript was as good as he thought it was."

"This is ridiculous. You're saying Bruce was that desperate—desperate enough to steal another writer's work?"

"Oh, J.P., it's not like he'd be the first person to do it. Or the first to get away with it. Plagiarism happens all the time, and always because the thieves—and they are thieves, damn it, raping our brains—think they'll never be caught. Bruce just took it a step further and stole from Jonathan's imagination *before* the book was in print. Anyway, when Bernie called him, told him she loved the manuscript so far—that's when he realized he'd have to get rid of Jonathan before the book came out. It was too dangerous to just believe that Jonathan would never know. And, hey, who knew if Jonathan might someday decide he did want to see if he could be published again with this new manuscript. Any way you looked at it, Bruce, Jonathan had to go. You had months to plan the how of it before the book came out, work up a foolproof plan, but then Jonathan offered you a gift, didn't he, Bruce?"

"Me? You're asking me? Please, this is your pipe dream. I'm just sitting here, wondering how much I can sue you for. That last contract Bernie handed you, Maggie? Didn't *PW* report that as a four-book, mid–seven-figure deal? I always forget—one's libel, one's defamation. J.P., honey, you'll have to help me sort that part out, okay?"

Alex sat down beside Maggie and patted her hand reassuringly. "He's only blustering, but I'll take over now, I believe. Where were we? Oh, yes, Jonathan West offered you a gift, McCrae, unwittingly of course. He told you about these two overly zealous fans of his who had just sent out dead rats and threatening poems to the authors who'd worked with him on *No Secret Anymore*. He was upset, had banished these fans from his sight, but wanted you to be aware—you, his dear friend—of what they'd done. And that day or the next, a dead rat did in fact appear in your mailbox. And, with that rat, an idea. A way to salvation, a plan meant to solve all your problems."

"Exactly," Maggie said, happy to see that Bruce's smile might still be there, but it was still as false as the guy who'd just clotheslined an opposing player and then turned to protest to the ref, "Who? Me? You're blaming me?"

"It was a very good plan," Alex went on, swinging his quizzing glass from its black riband as he spoke. "Jonathan, odd character that he was, would receive this horrendous threat and commit suicide. Of course, these zealous fans would not have sent a rat to Jonathan, but that was no matter. After all, you already had one in your possession, didn't you? All you had to do was remove the outer packaging and replace it, with Jonathan's address on the new envelope. That business of having taken the box to the police and then throwing it in the trash was merely a hum meant to establish you as a potential victim. A clever ruse, actually."

"Right," Maggie broke in eagerly. "But there were still plot holes. One murder tricked out as a suicide? No, that was a little chancy. Because Jonathan was famous once, even if he wasn't now. The police would make a very thorough investigation. Much better to have Jonathan be just one of several murders with pretty much the same MO, right? You called Sylvia Piedmonte and . . . oh yeah, and Freddie Brandyce, but they both took off, so you couldn't use them as part of your plan. Oh, and Garth Ransom—Buzz—he was off shooting rhinos or something."

"I don't believe hunters are allowed to shoot rhinos anymore, my dear. Let's just say he was in Africa, for clarity, you understand."

"Picky, picky, Alex. And don't interrupt, I'm really moving now. So, Bruce, who else was out there? Oh, wait, how about good old reclusive Francis Oakes? Little guy, he wouldn't put up much of a struggle. Nobody'd miss him, and he'd have his own dead rat there, you wouldn't even have to go find one of your own. So, first Francis, and then Jonathan—the police said Jonathan had been dead for a while, so you probably made the murders a real one-two punch, huh? Except nobody was looking for Jonathan, nobody knew he was dead, so you came knocking on my door. Maggie Kelly, the woman who's already known for . . . well, for stumbling over bodies. And now, wow, we've got a serial killer here, and Jonathan is just one of two victims so far— just tossed into the mix with the other victims. Who was next, Bruce? Me, right? I was here, local, couldn't really put up much of a fight against a great big guy like you. I was going to be number three, wasn't I? I knew you. I'd let you in the door. And you'd kill me. Bastard!"

"Sunshine, calm down," J.P. said, moving over to the other couch, to sit beside her. "I can see where you'd be upset, but you haven't really proved anything, except the stealing the manuscript part. But that's a far cry from murder. You've said nothing that would indicate that the fans who sent the rats in the first place aren't the killers. Bruce was a potential victim here, too."

"Oh, sure, that's what he'd like us all to think. The very *helpful* potential victim, by the way. Remember how he offered to call Jonathan, even left a message on his machine? And by then, Jonathan had already been dead a while. And you must have been thrilled when J.P. checked your cell calls, because there was the record of your concern for Jonathan, all down in black and white. I'll bet it's the same with Francis—calling his apartment long after he was dead, leaving messages. Talk about sick! But it's so much what a smart mystery writer would do to cover his tracks, setting up the misdirection, the red herrings, the whole bit. Man, Bruce, you left tracks all over the place, once I took a good look at your mistakes. Mostly, you were just too darn helpful. And you just couldn't help showing off, watching everyone stumble with the investigation, leading us all along where you wanted us to go, watching as your perfect crime played out. Ego, it gets them every time. But you tried too hard, Bruce. I always can tell your killer in your books—you use too heavy a hand, just the way you did here."

"That and the fact that we've seen Jonathan West's manuscript," Alex inserted helpfully, just as Maggie was on a roll. "That did assist us somewhat in our conclusions, didn't it? But you're right, my dear, he did wish to puff himself up. Did I mention that I spoke with Miss Holly Spivak earlier and she was kind enough to tell me that, yes, she knew Bruce McCrae personally. Not that the woman would ever betray a source, but I believe we now know how the media became informed of the details of the case."

Maggie pointed a finger at Alex. "And that's another thing. The manuscript. Bruce has a Mac, like me. Bernie checked for me, and Bruce sent his version of the manuscript in on a Mac formatted disk, using AppleWorks. The disk we have is PC, with Microsoft Word. Jonathan's disk. I'm not sure what that means, but I'm pretty sure it means something a computer nerd could prove. You know—dates created, dates modified. Oh, yeah, he's screwed. Really screwed."

"Okay, we're done here. Looks like the serial killer's going to strike again. *Three* times in one night."

Maggie turned to look back at Bruce, to see that he'd grabbed J.P.'s Glock out of her purse. "Right, just my luck," she said, shrinking back against the cushions. "But it isn't going to work, Bruce. *Steve!* He's got a gun."

"Steve?" Bruce shook his head. "You try to pull an old stunt like that, and talk about me being heavy-handed? Like, sure, I believe the lieutenant is going to pop out now from behind a potted plant. Give me a break."

"I think you'll be getting more like thirty-five to life," Steve said from the hallway, and Maggie turned to see him in a two-handed stance and looking—well, she wouldn't want to cross him at the moment.

Bruce McCrae, however, didn't seem to hold the same opinion. Then again, Maggie wasn't facing thirty-five to life, was she? As Maggie watched, she heard the explosion of the Glock, saw the flash, and turned just in time to see Alex hit the floor hard after the force of his body had, hopefully, redirected Bruce's aim away from Steve.

"Alex!" Maggie yelled, already on her feet before she realized what she'd done. *Stupid, stupid move*! That was all she could think as Bruce grabbed her and pulled her in front of his body as a human shield.

"Halt! Hold it right there, McCrae, and let her go," Steve commanded, still with his weapon aimed at Bruce . . . okay, it really was sort of aimed at her, Maggie thought, trying hard to swallow as Bruce's forearm threatened to cut off her breathing, as he dug the muzzle of the Glock into her waist. God, how she hated being Penelope Tied to the Railroad Tracks. It was getting so *old*.

"I don't believe the gentleman is willing to do that, *left*-tenant," Alex said, getting to his feet, picking up his cane and using it for leverage. "And, although it may mean little to the point, the gentleman is also in extraordinary physical condition. Perhaps we can come to a solution satisfactory to all of us?"

Steve kept his weapon trained on Bruce. "Blakely, not now. Why in *hell* do I ever listen to either of you? You know the paperwork this is going to cost me—if I don't end up walking a beat on Coney Island."

Bruce tightened his grip, probably so that Maggie would make a sound and redirect everyone's attention to them. It worked. "Aaargh! Hey, guys, I have an idea. How about we just let him go? He's not going to kill a cop—nobody's that stupid. Right, Bruce? How about you just leave, hmmm? You know, we'll walk to the elevator and you can use me as a shield until the doors open, then toss me straight into their arms, ruining Steve's aim until the doors close again with you inside. Come on, Bruce, you've seen it work a hundred times in the movies. It's a good scenario. Isn't it, Alex?"

"Good idea, sunshine," J.P. said, holding a couch pillow in front of her as if it might protect her from a bullet. "And the sooner the better. There's a full clip in that thing. Enough for everybody."

"The idea does sound workable," Alex said with maddening calm. It must be nice to know you can't die. Maggie only hoped he'd remember that *she* could. "What say you, *left*-tenant? Are you thoroughly opposed to McCrae here taking his exit?"

"She goes with me, all the way to the street."

"Oh, I don't think so," Alex drawled, the cane now in both hands. "There are limits to my magnanimity, even if you, for the moment, have the upper hand."

Maggie knew he was planning something, something heroic. She just wasn't sure if her heart was up to those heroics. "No, no, it's okay, I don't mind," she said quickly. "Come on, Bruce, let's go. Just back up to the door and I'll reach behind you and open it. Really. Anything I can do to help."

"Maggie—"

"Please, Steve," she said, cutting him off. "I'm almost more afraid of your gun than I am his, because I can see yours. We'll be fine. Won't we, Bruce? You don't want to shoot me, or anybody. You just want to get away. Hop a bus, hail a cab. Get yourself lost in the city until you can think of some nifty way to disappear. You're smart, you can do this. So—let's get you started, okay?"

Maggie closed her eyes in relief as Bruce's grip tightened slightly as he began moving backward, toward the door.

One step. Two. Seven?

Maggie reached back a hand and located the doorknob on the second try.

She pulled it open.

"Oh, thank you, I wondered how I'd do that with a cat in each hand," Sterling said behind her . . . just before Napoleon, who was just the sort of animal to carry a grudge after being banished in favor of a dog, leapt free of Sterling's grasp to land, all claws out, on Bruce's back.

This time when Alex grabbed her and pushed her away there was no snow-covered evergreen to break her fall, and she landed with a thud on the hard floor, all the air knocked from her lungs, pretty little silver stars dancing in front of her as she tried to both breathe and admire Alex and Steve subduing Bruce, slapping on the cuffs.

Sterling, still holding Wellington, could only stand there, a puzzled look on his face, poor thing. Once again he'd been the hero, after assuring everyone weeks ago, after the first time, that he would rather not do anything even vaguely heroic ever again.

"Be—beautiful," Maggie managed as J.P. pulled her unceremoniously to her feet. "Not . . . not exactly as we'd planned . . . but any landing you can walk away from, right?"

"I'm so sorry, sunshine," J.P. said as she led Maggie to one of the couches. "I should have realized he'd go for my gun."

"We all should have realized that," Alex said as he closed the door, Steve and Bruce already headed downstairs. "Truthfully, I didn't think we could make him confess, at least not tonight. I should know that all murderers are, at the heart of it, cowards. You were splendid, Maggie, by the way. All things considered, another rather grand adventure. J.P., did you happen to notice where that shot impacted? I'm afraid I was too busy coming to grips with the notion that I'd attempted to tackle a brick wall."

"No, I didn't. You saved Steve's life, you know. Cops don't fire unless fired upon—not the good ones, like Steve. Maybe in the ceiling?"

Maggie got up and began looking for a bullet hole. Not that she really cared, but it beat a bout of hysterics any day.

"Nope, not the ceiling," she said, wandering closer to the place where Steve had been standing. "Not the wall, not the—oh, cripes," she said, burying her head against Alex's shoulder as he slipped a comforting arm around her. "He killed my treadmill. . . ."

Epilogue

Dear Fred,
Okay, Fred, here's the scoop—I can't write to you anymore. It was a good idea at the time, it really was, but now things are getting just a little personal between Alex and me, you know? Well, of course you don't know, because I didn't tell you, did I? Trust me—we got personal. Three times so far.

All right, so maybe I'll tell you something. Sex, after thinking you might be dead at any moment, is interesting. *Very*. All that reaffirming life stuff, I guess, something like that. In any case, it's really none of posterity's business, right?

And Alex and I have come to a few conclusions in the last week or so. Conclusions and maybe even compromises. For one, I'm going to allow him to protect me. I used to see that as him interfering with my life, but a couple of hard jolts that knock the wind out of you, a Glock stuck in your ribs—stuff like that?—can really change a woman's perceptions, you know? In other words, if Alex wants to believe he's a hero, I guess I'm just going to have to let him believe that. So we're good there.

What I'm having trouble with is this new idea he has that he has something to say about the development of his character as he appears in my books—operative words here, Fred, *my books*. He's talking about getting married and setting up his nursery, continuing the family name. Can you believe that, Fred? I can't do that. Once he stops being the greatest lover in England, the series is over.

Nobody wants to read about the Viscount Saint Just in love. Not unless . . . hmm. Not unless he gets married and she's really a Cartwright bride. You know what a Cartwright bride is, Fred? I'll tell you. There was this television show a long time ago—*Bonanza*. There were three sons, regulars on the show. Once in a while the writers would give one of them a love interest, because otherwise they'd be worried they had the sixties version of *Brokeback Mountain*, I guess (and as they said on *Seinfeld*: not that there's anything wrong with that), and because female viewers like some romance in their Westerns.

Anyway, the writers were also smart enough to know that none of these guys could live happily ever after or the show would go down the tubes—ergo the curse of the Cartwright bride. Ah, Hoss fell in love. Ah, Hoss is going to get hitched. Ah, Hoss's fiancée just got run over by a stagecoach—*splat*! Those Cartwright brides never lasted more than three episodes, tops.

It was kind of like being the only guy in a *Star Trek* episode wearing a different colored shirt than everyone else.

So I can't do it, Fred. A Cartwright bride would be a cop-out. Saint Just has to be who he is, and the heck with this evolving stuff Alex keeps talking about.

Which is all a roundabout way of saying that Alex

and I are fine, we're actually doing pretty well . . . but I don't think we're going to be evolving too much any time soon. To tell you the truth—since I'm going to delete this the moment I'm done here—I don't know if I'd be as attracted to a domesticated Alex. How's that for honesty?

Which takes me to what I *am* going to be doing.

A funny thing happened on the way to Christmas at my parents, Fred—they got separated. Oh yes. One is living in the house, and one is batching it in an apartment on the other side of town. I am now the product of a broken home. I'm also—along with Alex and Sterling—due in Ocean City in two weeks, to *celebrate* the holidays. Yeah, Fred—ho, ho, hoo-boy!

Yeah, well, I don't want to think about that right now, or the fact that all three of the sibs will be there, choosing sides, making everything worse.

So maybe I'll think some more about what Alex wants?

I could give him a loveless marriage, right? You know, a marriage of convenience, only because it is time he set up his nursery—Alex is right about that one. It would be historically accurate.

Okay.

So I give him this independent woman, see. They battle—right off the bat. Two strong personalities, going at it . . . . but slowly, against their will, they're drawn to each other. Big-time. Physically. They keep dancing around each other; advancing, retreating, keeping the readers happy. And all the while she helps him solve crimes. It could work.

Maybe it could work.

I don't know if it could work for Alex and me—I mean, Saint Just and the female character. I did mean that, Fred. That was *not* a Freudian slip!

Tell you what, Fred. I'm going to put this in a folder

with the first time I wrote to you, just in case I need to talk to you again. You don't mind being *Untitled Folder*, do you, Fred? Just in case Alex goes snooping on my Mac again?

And you are cheaper than Dr. Bob.

That's a joke, Fred—a joke!

See you after Christmas!

Maggie Kelly